Man o' War

"Man o' War was the mightiest Thoroughbred the American turf has ever known. His career came to a roaring stop in 1920, after he had won 20 races in 21 starts.

"This book, although partly fictionalized, is a vivid, moving 'word picture' of Man o' War—from the night he was foaled through all his racing triumphs. It will hold your attention from start to finish."

—Louis Feustel, *trainer of Man o' War*

"The Black Stallion is about the most famous fictional horse of the century."
—*New York Times*

The Black Stallion
The Black Stallion and Flame
The Black Stallion and Satan
The Black Stallion and the Girl
The Black Stallion Legend
The Black Stallion Mystery
The Black Stallion Returns
The Black Stallion's Blood Bay Colt
The Black Stallion's Courage
Son of the Black Stallion
The Young Black Stallion

Man o' War

by WALTER FARLEY

BULLSEYE BOOKS

Random House 🏠 New York

For Rosemary

A BULLSEYE BOOK PUBLISHED BY RANDOM HOUSE, INC.
Copyright ©1962 by Walter Farley
Copyright renewed 1990 by Rosemary Farley, Alice Farley, Steve Farley,
Tim Farley, and Random House, Inc.
All rights reserved under International and Pan-American Copyright Conventions.
Published in the United States by Random House, Inc., New York, and
simultaneously in Canada by Random House of Canada Limited, Toronto.

This book was originally cataloged by the Library of Congress as follows:
    Farley, Walter
        Man o' War
        New York, Random House [1962]
        SUMMARY: "A Fictional biography of Man o' War."
        I. Man o' War (Racehorse)   SF355.M3F3 636.12   62-9000
        ISBN: 0-394-86015-2 (trade paperback)

Manufactured in the United States of America

21 20 19 18 17 16 15 14 13

Contents

Author's Foreword

What you are about to read is a *fictional* biography of Man o' War, in that there was no stableboy named Danny Ryan. His actions and conversations with others are purely imaginary on my part and used to tell the story of Man o' War as I know it. That such a person as Danny may have existed (comparable, if not as I have drawn him) among the large entourage following the champion, I have little doubt. Such love and devotion as Danny had for Man o' War are not uncommon among those tending a racehorse, or any horse, be he a champion or not.

I saw Man o' War before his death in 1947. Like many boys and girls, I wanted to visit the well-known horse farms in Kentucky, and one summer my father took me there. I saw many fine stallions, for all horse lovers are welcome in that country and no one who behaves himself is ever turned away. When we reached Faraway Farm, there were many visitors swarming through the gates. For my father this was the highlight of our tour, since he had seen Man o' War race and "the flame-col-

ored stallion was the greatest horse that ever lived." To someone like myself, who had not been around long enough to see
Man o' War race, he was a legendary horse, a monument, a
part of the history I had read on American racing. I was excited, too, but not prepared at all for the moment to come.

I recall adding my name to a guest book, which according to
my father already totaled over half a million visitors. I followed
the large group into the stallion barn, thinking that if Man o'
War had belonged to the public in his racing days, things
hadn't changed much for him.

We approached his big stall, and Will Harbut, the black
groom who took care of him, looked us over, rather critically, I
thought, as if deciding for himself how much we knew about
horses and Man o' War in particular. Like others in the
throng, I had read many stories in magazines about Will
Harbut's love and care for Man o' War in these—his later
years—at Faraway Farm. I was prepared to listen to his well-
publicized and very complete monologue on Man o' War's
record and the accomplishments of his foals. But at that moment my father's hand tightened on my arm, directing my attention to the stall itself.

The door had been swung open and Man o' War stood
there. I was prepared to see a great champion and sire. But
suddenly I knew that while I had never seen him race, it made
no difference at all. I felt as my father did. I was lucky to be
there, close enough to touch him if that had been allowed.

Man o' War stood in the doorway, statuesque and magnificent. There was a lordly lift to his head and his sharp eyes were
bright. He didn't look *at* us, but far out over our heads. If his
red coat and mane and tail had faded with time, as my father
said later, I was not aware of it. Nor did I notice the dip of his
back, deepening too with age. I could not even have said

whether his massive body was red or gold or yellow. I was aware only of one thing—that for the first and perhaps the only time in my life I was standing in the presence of a horse that was *truly* great, and it would be a moment always to be remembered.

What accounted for this stirring of the heart? For that is what it was. If one attributes it to the emotions of youth, what about my father's adulation of Man o' War? And all the others of his generation who had seen this horse and felt no differently? Was the look in Man o' War's eyes responsible for it? His gaze, I recall, shifted occasionally to look at us. They were deep, intelligent eyes and very bright. More often than not, however, he seemed not to know we were there at all, his gaze fixed and far away, so intent that I could have sworn he was watching something far beyond our vision.

Or was it the regal lift of his head, the giant sweep of his body, or the dignity with which he held himself up for our inspection? Or, perhaps, a combination of everything, for there was nothing about him that did not seem right to me. Whatever accounted for it, I stood in his presence in quiet reverence, unmindful of anything but Man o' War. I heard only snatches of the eloquent recital that rolled from Will Harbut's tongue. *"He's got everything a hoss ought to have and he's got it where a hoss ought to have it. He is de mostest hoss. Stand still, Red."*

It has also been said of Man o' War that *"he touched the imagination of men and they saw different things in him. But one they all remember was that he brought exaltation into their hearts."* Whatever else may be written or said of Man o' War, I know this to be true from my one visit to an aged but majestic stallion. It was with the hope that I could impart something of what I felt to you that I wrote this book.

Many years have passed since Man o' War raced. The few who remember him on the track will tell you that all the great champions that have raced since—Equipoise, War Admiral, Whirlaway, Assault, Citation, Native Dancer, Nashua, Secretariat, Seattle Slew, to name a few—were only "the best since Man o' War." To them Man o' War is *the* one to be remembered. He alone is their yardstick of time.

There are fewer people still who remember Man o' War as a yearling. If you believe them, most all saw in him the spark of greatness at the time. But the facts usually indicate otherwise. And there is only a mere handful of people who recall Man o' War as a suckling colt at the side of his dam, Mahubah, at Nursery Stud.

To reconstruct this story of Man o' War, I have used to best advantage the city newspapers and national magazines published at the time, as well as the many excellent publications devoted especially to Thoroughbred racing and breeding— among them, *Daily Racing Form, The Morning Telegraph, The Blood Horse, The Thoroughbred Record,* and *American Racing Manual.*

I have used also the facilities of many fine libraries and referred often to John Hervey's *Turf Career of Man o' War,* which would have been published in book form had it not been for the noted track historian's untimely death before the manuscript was completed; the rough manuscript is part of the Harry Worcester Smith Collection at the National Sporting Library, Middleburg, Virginia, and has also appeared serially in *Horse Magazine.* Without the use of all these sources to supplement my own file, this story of Man o' War could not have been written.

WALTER FARLEY

Racetrack Special

1

It was hardly the time or the place to be thinking about a horse, *any* horse, the man decided, even Man o' War. He pulled up the collar of his overcoat and pushed his head against the drizzling, chilling dampness that penetrated everything he wore right down to the flannel undershirt beneath his heavy gray suit. It was unusually cold for only the 22nd of October. But one couldn't count on anything in New York. Full of surprises, always.

He glanced up at the buildings rising like giant pyramids above him. Even Times Square wasn't square. It was a triangle, noisy and garish. And now that the morning was just about over, Broadway was coming to life, with theater and store managers trying to pierce the milkiness with pale, flickering lights. It was a losing battle. The fog wasn't going to lift for a while. Maybe he wouldn't even be able to see the backstretch of the big track at Aqueduct.

As he turned west on 42nd Street his way became more crowded and noisier than ever. Yet as he pushed his way

through the surging throng he allowed his large head to emerge
a bit more from his overcoat, much like a giant sea turtle peek-
ing out from its heavy shell. He watched the marquee lights
flashing on and off and, somehow, they seemed to warm him.
He became less uncomfortable, less dissatisfied with the
weather. He didn't try to understand his love for the hum and
roar of the city, not just *any* city, just New York. He was a
country boy and he should be thinking more about the warm
October days of his youth in Kentucky. Now those were the
good years of quiet and peace and horses. But he wouldn't
trade one inch of this paved street for all of Kentucky's green
acres, not anymore! The way he'd felt as a kid was long since
over.

Reaching the subway entrance, he turned into it and left
42nd Street's lights and hubbub behind. He stopped at a
newsstand, picked up several papers, then hurried down a
flight of steep steps as if diving into a cellar.

The smell of the subway grew stronger in his nostrils and he
could see the long line forming before the change booth. Over
the booth a sign read:

SPECIAL

AQUEDUCT RACETRACK

SPECIAL

He pulled out a dollar bill from his pocket and glanced at his
watch. Only 11:45, so there was plenty of time to make the
racetrack train. The line waiting to get to the change booth
was fully two blocks long, and he realized Aqueduct would
have a full house today despite the weather. Slowly he moved
forward with the others.

At the change booth he got two halves for his dollar, put one in the turnstile, and took the escalator to the lowest platform in the station. There he leaned against one of the pillars with the big "42" painted on it and waited for the train. He didn't read his newspapers. It was far more interesting to watch the others and catch snatches of their conversation.

"Wonderboy should take the third race," a man said. "He likes distance and he's been working good." The speaker was leaning against the same pillar, almost rubbing shoulders with the big man but talking to no one in particular, just mumbling his thoughts.

Somebody in back answered, "No, that one will drop dead at the half-mile pole. He ain't got a chance."

But the big man listening knew that the fellow could have meant, *"You're dead right. That's the bravest, fastest horse in the race but let's not spread it around, Mac. Let's keep him to ourselves."*

The big man nodded to let everyone know he was glad to be included in the discussion. He felt completely happy and at peace with himself and the world. Taking a stub pencil from his pocket, he wetted the end and made a note on the margin of his paper regarding the third race. Everyone was a giant going to Aqueduct and a dwarf coming home. On the way out all horses sounded good, all had a chance.

Suddenly the train came roaring into the station and stopped with one of the car doors opening directly in front of him. It was a good omen. *Open Sesame*, he thought to himself, and smiled. He had no trouble getting a good seat and soon would be on his way to what he called his very own "Arabian Nights."

The train remained in the station, its doors open. After a few minutes the first signs of impatience became noticeable as passengers put down newspapers to glance at their watches.

The big man shifted uneasily with the others. He, too, had reasons for wanting to get to the track ahead of time, and he couldn't understand the delay. He became grumpy, suddenly hating the hollow-eyed, unshaven man standing in front of him.

The train finally started and the tension cleared. Once again the passengers pored over their newspapers, ignoring each other and rocking to the train's motion. The stations began flashing by with no slowing of the Special . . . first 34th Street, then Washington Square, then Canal Street. Faster and faster the train traveled, now into a turn with screeching wheels, now downgrade into the tunnel beneath the East River.

The big man felt better. It was his job to go to the track. He had to be there whether he liked it or not. Looking across the aisle, he found a young man staring at him curiously. When their gazes met, the youth looked away with a shrug.

For some reason he, too, turned away quickly. Once more his mood became surly. He even found himself raising a mental barrier between himself and the young fellow across the aisle . . . as if it had suddenly become very necessary for him to protect himself. He took out his pipe and refilled it slowly, taking all the time in the world, studying it.

The train slowed and finally came to a screeching halt in what must have been the very middle of the tunnel beneath the river. He looked up at the roof of the car, wondering how many gallons of water lay above. He glanced around at one passenger after another, ignoring only the youth across the aisle. Everybody else was reading, seemingly unaware of the sudden stop, the deathly quiet. New Yorkers were used to traveling the perilous, rickety lanes beneath sand and concrete and water. They had learned to wait patiently for the tracks to be cleared and the power to come on again.

He found the young man's eyes upon him again. This time

their gazes held. "Do you smell something?" he asked finally, grimacing and sniffing.

"Only the brakes, Pops. Don't worry about it." *Pops? Pops?* Once again the big man raised the mental barrier between the youth and himself. The young squirt. What right had he to be calling him *Pops*, a man only in his fifties? Why did this kid annoy him so much, even before the *Pops?* Was it the hat pushed back so cockily on his head? Was it the smile on his face, that one-sided, familiar, maybe even mocking smile?

"The subway route isn't all it's supposed to be," he said, not knowing why he kept the conversation going.

"But look at the bright side of it," the young man countered. "We're dropped off right at the track door. What other track in the country has the luxury of a subway entrance?"

"Yes, New Aqueduct is a fine track," the big man admitted. "They did a good job of renovating it." Again he studied the other, noting the torn trench coat that did not speak well for the youth's prosperity. Yet there was that smile again, revealing his fine, white teeth.

"Aw, it's just a big supermarket," the youth went on. "A fellow could bring his girl to Aqueduct now and lose her for a week. Too big, too much comfort, too much courtesy. You know what I think? It's too good for us now. Take all those plush restaurants and escalators—"

"It also has the best horses," the big man interrupted, hoping to put this flashy boy with the flashy dark eyes in his place.

"Yeah, a Taj Mahal with horses, that's what it is. You can have the New Aqueduct an' I'll take the old, inadequate Aqueduct. It's too heady for me. I like to be able to find people . . . maybe even get pushed around a little and kid about 'Footsore Downs' like we did before. Now we got seats to park in. It's all too lush, too lavish."

The big man put his pipe in his mouth without lighting it.

His eyes didn't leave the youth's. Was it the uncommon energy evident in every movement that bothered him so much? Was he truly getting old and resenting youth? No, it couldn't be. He knew too many other young people whose company he enjoyed. Then what was it?

"If it'll make you any happier," he said not without irony, "the new steam room isn't hot enough. The jocks are still doing road work just like back in 1919." Now whatever made him think of that? he wondered.

The youth laughed. "You oughta know, Pops. But I ain't surprised that they ain't got the steam hot enough for the jocks. Imagine that, over $30,000,000 for the plushiest racing plant in the country an' they can't get up enough steam!" He dug an elbow into the ribs of the fellow sitting beside him. "Hear that, Bill? The jocks ain't got any steam at Big 'A.'"

"Get lost," his companion said. "So my jock still dropped his stick leaving the gate yesterday in the last race. Racing is racing, here or anywhere else, steam or no steam."

The big man smiled. "That's exactly what I meant," he said hurriedly to prove his point. "Old tracks vanish and new ones rise in their stead. Yet in many respects it's the same now as it was in the beginning."

The youth shrugged his thin shoulders. "Well, it's round and it's a racetrack if that's what you mean."

"No, it's oval-shaped, not round," the big man corrected. "And it has a three-inch cushion of dirt and sand on top of clay, the same clay base pounded upon by Domino, Exterminator, and the greatest of all, Man o' War. It's the best there is, but good for nothing except racing horses."

The youth was watching him with those mocking eyes again. "You're just a bunch of blueprints, aren't you, Pops?"

The train started forward with a lurch, giving the big man

the opportunity of turning away without admitting defeat. He watched the tunnel lights stream by, thinking that he could have told the youth lots more if he'd wanted to. Oh, the jockeys were well taken care of at New Aqueduct, despite the fact that the steam boxes weren't yet what they should be. In the huge room that was the jockeys' quarters, the washbasins were three inches lower than normal. No washing tippy-toe for the little men at Aqueduct, no sir! And the fellow across the way would have fitted in nicely there. He was the size of a good jock.

The big man's eyes returned to the youth. Was that it? he wondered. Was he actually resentful of the fellow's size? Was he envious of his short, less-than-average height? He studied him again, so small and slight and brown from the sun. He wondered if the youth had ever had a desire to ride a fast horse. Probably not or he would have been doing so long ago.

It hadn't been that way with himself. He would have given anything to have been born small, light-boned, easy on a race-horse's back and mouth. But why think of that now? Imagine going back so many years! *Come off it!* he told himself bitterly. *You're an old man, like the kid says. It's all over.*

The train pulled up the steep grade, passed a local, and the lights of Borough Hall station flashed by. On and on it thundered under the teeming streets of Brooklyn, passing the Hoyt, Lafayette, and Franklin Avenue stations. Blue flashes from switches splattered the darkness and more platforms came and went, a stream of lights and benches, posters and people. All was blurred and meant nothing to the passengers aboard the Racetrack Special.

At exactly 12:25 the train came up from below, bursting into the daylight. It continued to climb, riding high on elevated tracks above an ugly neighborhood of crowded houses.

The fog had lifted but it was still raining, making the houses below look more gloomy than ever. A yellow taxi went by, the only colorful thing around.

The big man turned toward the east. Soon they'd be at New Aqueduct. Soon there'd be all the color anyone could want. The sky was lighter over that way too. Despite the fact that the rain was now falling in sheets, he suspected that it would be clear by the time they reached the track.

The young voice boomed at him from across the aisle again. "There's something else I don't like about New Aqueduct, Pops. I don't like the band playing all the time. It makes it hard for a guy to think, that's what it does. I'm for no music at all at a racetrack. Silence. Silence except for runnin' horses."

"George Seuffert wouldn't like to hear you say that."

"What's he do?"

"He's the bandleader."

The youth laughed. "That's great, just great," he said. "I guess he figures they built him a $33,000,000 band shell, heh, Pops? Ain't that what New Aqueduct cost the state?"

"I suppose so," the big man said, "about that." He got to his feet along with the others, for the track station was the next stop. Purposely he stood beside the youth, his great height and breadth making him look gargantuan alongside the slight young man.

"Have a good day, Pops."

"Same to you. The Man o' War Handicap should be a great race. I'm looking forward to it."

"Anything with a $100,000 added purse should be great, Pops, anything at all."

"But *this* race is very important. It's the first race named in Man o' War's honor. It's been long overdue."

"Tell me, Pops," the youth asked, the one-sided smile on his face again, "was this Man o' War really any good? You know what I mean . . . like Hillsdale?"

The big man's face flushed and there was sheer pity in his eyes when he said, "You never saw Man o' War. You never did or you wouldn't mention him and Hillsdale in the same breath."

"Of course I never saw him, Pops. He was before my time, way before it."

"Only 1920. That's really not so long ago."

"*1920*," the youth repeated, puzzled. "Not so long ago? Is that what you said, Pops? Maybe to you it isn't. But I wasn't even born until twenty years *after* 1920."

"I guess not," the big man said, shaking his head. "I guess you weren't at that." The doors were opening and he moved toward them, his legs suddenly old again. "It's too bad you never saw him. He was the greatest horse that ever lived."

"Sure, Pops. Sure. Have yourself a time, now, a ball."

He walked down the ramp from the subway station. How could you explain to someone so young that there hadn't been a horse like Man o' War since the golden chestnut had roared to a stop at Kenilworth Park back in 1920? He was truly the mightiest Thoroughbred the turf world had ever known!

The wind had driven off the rain, and now it was blowing in such gusts that the big man had to bend over as he moved along. Some men were already chasing their hats, and women were holding down their skirts with both hands. The huge ramp shook a little beneath the blasts and signs swung crazily, threatening to rip loose. The big man pushed his head forward, plowing through the wind and keeping his eyes fastened on the towering glass-fronted stands a short distance away.

Yes, how could he explain to anyone born after 1920 how brilliant Man o' War had been? He broke all the records and he broke down all the horses. He was everything said of him and more, lots more. For it wasn't only what he did on the racetrack. When you stood outside his stall, just looking at him, you'd get a feeling of awe and humility. Man o' War had known he was the king and he had left no successor. His like would never be seen again.

The big man shoved his way past men hawking their papers and programs in gravelly voices. "*Morning Telegraph* and scratch sheets. *Telly* and scratch. *Telly*-scratch. Here y'are, every one a winner." The big man smiled and shook his head, at the same time shifting his feet to avoid colliding with the little men. The quickening pace helped get rid of his train legs, working up the circulation and carrying him along with the steady stream of people.

The wind felt colder but he didn't mind it, for the sky was clearing fast. There was a good chance it would clear and the sun would come out brilliant and warm, maybe even drying the track. Weather clear, track fast . . . that was the way it should be on Man o' War's day, with every hole filled in, and every clod of dirt flattened, curried, and manicured. A perfect day for the first Man o' War Handicap! Suddenly the cold air felt good and the big man's legs felt young and strong again. He held his head up against the wind.

Maybe the old days were gone, as people said, and most of the old champions forgotten. But today they would be remembering the big one again, Man o' War. No longer would he be just a legend swirling across a distant sky. No, starting today a great race would honor him at the track where he had run his toughest race against John P. Grier. Today the track world would pay homage to the memory of the king of the American turf, the most famous, the swiftest, the greatest of them all . . . Man o' War!

He began to feel like a schoolboy in love for the first time. He straightened his tie and pushed back his hat, not too jauntily the way the kid on the subway had worn his but not conservatively either. There was no other place in the world he'd rather be on this day. Here he belonged with others like himself, paying respect to Man o' War.

But how many of all the thousands in the stands had known the king? Few, at best. To most of them, Man o' War was just another name to remember along with Equipoise and Twenty Grand, Zev and Gallant Fox, War Admiral and Whirlaway.

"Was he really any good, Pops?" the kid had asked. *"You know what I mean . . . like Hillsdale?"* Or he might have said, "like Native Dancer, like Citation, like Nashua?" Horses that could not have nibbled Man o' War's saddlecloth!

Careful now, he cautioned himself. *You're treading on dangerous ground. There are some who think that maybe Citation* . . . But no! None like Man o' War had ever paraded to the post again in all the years that had gone by. Like so many others he had watched and waited and hoped, his eyes growing dim, waiting for *his* return.

After reaching the end of the ramp the big man walked briskly to a side gate, showed his pass, and squeezed through the turnstile. Once inside he put his head down again, jostling those who walked beside him. He mumbled his apologies without bothering to look up and heard only return grunts in answer. For a reason he could not explain he felt suddenly alone again, unattached and anonymous.

He was making for an official door beneath the grandstand when suddenly he stopped. For a moment he stood still as though undecided. Then he moved again, changing direction and taking the clubhouse escalator. He was one of a steady stream of people riding skyward, but he did not feel the electric air of the racetrack that flowed from one person to another. Instead he felt subdued and humble, almost as he had the last time he'd seen Man o' War standing in his stall, his head held high but his eyes liquid-soft and gentle.

What he wanted to do would not take long and he had plenty of time before going to work. He got off the escalator at the third floor and entered the clubhouse restaurant. He did not join the crowd standing at the velvet ropes waiting to be seated, but turned to the large portrait of Man o' War that hung over the center doors.

This was the Man o' War Room . . . a room named in the great horse's honor. The heavyset man stood before the portrait, the expression on his face becoming soft, almost shy. No longer did he feel alone. He sat down on a couch where he could gaze at the picture without being in anyone's way. He wanted to look at him again, to remember the way it was.

He'd been the luckiest of all. He'd been there that first night, the night a chestnut colt with a star on his forehead had been foaled. In a way it had been his own beginning as well as Man o' War's. He had no trouble at all remembering everything that had happened. It was near midnight and very quiet when he had walked down the dirt road in Kentucky. . . .

March 29, 1917

2

Miles of board fence ran along both sides of the road, white against the darkness of the fields beyond. But the boy's gaze never left the road in front of him and his long, thin face was heavy with concern. He walked fast, his arms swinging loosely against his big-boned but gaunt frame. He had made an important decision. He had come to a turning point in his life. He was going to quit school and go to work at Nursery Stud.

Like a gangling Great Dane he moved through the night mist, his nostrils sniffing the scent of new grass in the meadows. Soon he'd smell the warm bodies of horses, but he'd have to wait until he got closer to the barns.

It wouldn't be many days before the familiar scent, stronger than anything else, would pervade the night air all around. But now, at just the beginning of spring, the nights were still too chilly for the horses to be turned out. In another few minutes it would be midnight and the beginning of the 29th day of March, 1917. He'd better get moving faster. He might be late as it was!

15

Turning off the road, he went over and climbed the fence and set out across the fields at a run. It was nothing new to him, this getting excited about being around when a racer was born . . . a horse who wouldn't set foot on a track for two years. It was part of his life not to miss the foaling of a Thoroughbred, a part of living in Kentucky. If he'd been living anywhere else it would have been different. But here in Lexington, horses were everything and there was nothing strange in thinking that the most wonderful sight in the world was the earliest hours in the life of a racehorse!

With knowing eyes he looked over the big breeding farm, loving the cleanliness of its fences and fields and barns. There were hundreds of acres, all for the use of horses alone, with dozens of fenced paddocks, each serving a specific purpose in the raising of Thoroughbreds. It was a costly business, far more expensive than he could ever guess. It was a good thing Mr. Belmont was rich for otherwise there would have been no Nursery Stud. To a man like Mr. Belmont the sport lay not so much in the winning of races as it did in *breeding* the best horses. That's what made foaling time so interesting around here . . . one never knew when one might be looking at the baby horse who would turn out to be the greatest of them all!

Mahubah was the broodmare closest to foaling time, he knew. They'd been expecting her to foal for three days now but she'd kept putting them off. What was she waiting for anyway? Didn't she know her time had come? Or maybe she just liked being treated like a queen, being bathed and brushed and pampered all the time. Maybe she knew what she was doing, at that.

He liked Mahubah, even her name, which in Arabic meant "good greetings, good fortune." She was well bred, rangy, and young. She should foal a good one. He hoped it would turn out to be a colt. A colt could beat a filly any day.

The boy ran faster, his long legs moving with surprising grace. A big grin suddenly drove the seriousness from his face, a face already brown from the sun and clean and seasoned as if it were washed regularly with saddle soap. He grinned because he had just remembered that more foals were due in April than any other month that year. During the next few weeks there would be a parade of baby horses for him to watch entering the world!

He sure wouldn't want to live anywhere else. Where but here could one find such an interest in horses? No other business could compete with the breeding and raising of Thoroughbreds. And where else was the grass so blue, so rich in calcium and vitamins? Of course you had to have special Kentucky eyes to see its bluish tinge, otherwise it was green like any other grass, except in the fall and winter months when it turned real brown. What would people from anywhere else think if they saw him get down and start nibbling away at it, as he did once in a while just for kicks? They'd think he was crazy, that's what! And where else could people talk to horses the way they could here? No, there was no other place he wanted to live but in the heart of the Bluegrass Region— Lexington, Kentucky.

He looked ahead at the foaling barn. There were no bright lights burning, so nothing had happened yet. If the foal had come, the place would have been lit up like a Christmas tree. Who knew but the barn might stay dark all night, like last night and the one before? Then he'd be up all night again for nothing. And he knew only too well what would happen to him at school for being so sleepy. Well, all that would end pretty soon. Pretty soon he'd be working here and spending every minute of his time with the horses. So even if he was tired tomorrow, it would be worth it. Mahubah was a fine mare. Her colt could be the one. He just might be.

Since he knew he had time, he went first to the stallions, as
he did every night. Opening the barn door quietly, he peered
into the dimly lit interior. He could just make out Fair Play's
lofty head outlined against the stall window.

"Hello, big horse," he called softly.

Fair Play moved to the door of his stall, his golden coat
picking up what light there was in the barn. He stood before
the iron bars, his eyes searching and eager for attention.

The boy touched him gently, rubbing the white, diamond-
shaped star in the center of his forehead. "Your wife's going to
have your son tonight," he said. "She's not going to put us off
any longer. I'm sure of it. He'll be a good one. You'll be
proud."

Suddenly the stallion moved away, going to his water
bucket. The great crest on his neck was arched like a drawn
bow as he bent down to the water. He didn't drink but played,
blowing into the water and splattering the spray about the
stall. He shook himself and remained where he was, ignoring
his visitor's pleas to move forward.

"Moody, that's what you are," the boy said finally. "One
moment you want attention and the next you want to be left
alone. That was your trouble on the track, too. Maybe you
didn't have your daddy's bad temper but you had a mind of
your own all the same. You could run away with a race when
you were in the mood, but when you weren't you just wouldn't
run for anyone. Worse still, you wouldn't even train. You just
didn't think it worth your while. Now what kind of colts are
you going to sire with that kind of temperament?"

The boy shrugged his shoulders and turned away. Maybe
Fair Play would get *great* colts, who knew? Mr. Belmont believed so, that was for sure. He believed Fair Play would turn
out to be the best sire he had ever owned.

The golden stallion had won ten of his thirty-two starts as a racehorse. Not the best record in the world but certainly not the worst. And Fair Play had proved he could carry weight and go a distance. He wasn't a big, strong horse, either. He wasn't quite sixteen hands but he was beautifully proportioned. You couldn't fault him anywhere. Even if you picked him apart he'd come out perfectly made. Well, maybe Fair Play would turn out to be a top sire and maybe he wouldn't . . . only one out of ten thousand stallions ever did.

Going on to another big stall, the boy peered between its iron bars with the utmost care and reverence. For here was the *king*. Here was Hastings, sire of Fair Play and for many years America's leading stallion. And now at the age of twenty-four he was still siring winners!

The boy kept his hands away from the bars, for the aged stallion was as mean and vicious as he'd been as a colt. Had it not been for his evil temper, Hastings would have been a great racehorse. Even the stories one heard about him were enough to stand a fellow's hair on end.

Hastings had been so fired-up on the track that nobody could handle him. He wanted action and competition, all right, but instead of racing he'd try to run down all the other horses, his mouth open and teeth bared, ready to tear the others apart. He sure was brave; there was no doubt about that. He recognized no barrier, no master. He was a devil, a hellion, fighting bridle and saddle and his rider and trainer right up to the very end of his track career. He didn't want anyone to tell him what to do. He just wanted to run *his* way, and when people tried to control him he exploded into ten thousand demons!

His owners had quit with him when he was only four years old. He'd won a few races, most of them famous stakes, but it was too exhausting to prepare him for further campaigns. So he had been put to stud and, miracle of miracles, he'd turned out to be a top sire!

But Hastings *still* didn't trust anybody. Everybody was his enemy, even now. So the boy stayed well away from the stall while the aged stallion remained in a far corner, fire in his eyes and with his lips drawn back. In the dim light his brown coat looked black, and the white, diamond-shaped star he had passed on to his son Fair Play stood out in the darkness.

What would his gift be to Mahubah's colt? the boy wondered. Would he give his grandson simply the white star or something far more important? Maybe some of that competitive fire that burned so strongly in his black heart . . . *but some sense along with it,* enough to make the colt manageable? Boy, what a gift that would be! What a colt they would have, if that ever happened!

After a few minutes the boy turned away and walked quickly to the foaling barn. He entered the barn almost on tiptoe and stole quietly down the corridor. When he came to Mahubah's stall, he looked inside and knew for sure she was going to have her foal that night.

She was restless, moving about in the dim light without noticing him at all. And that was very unusual for Mahubah. But anyone could have seen that she had other things on her mind. She rustled her straw bedding and pawed the clay beneath, her warm smell enveloping the stall.

Watching her wasn't like watching the stallions. Here there was peace and quiet . . . but there was even more than that, the boy decided. It was hard for him to explain how he felt. It was as if Mahubah seemed to know she was playing a part in something very big, and she got that feeling over to him. Or perhaps it was the knowledge that soon he would be witnessing some-

thing that was as old as time—the giving birth to a new crea-
ture—that filled him with awe. Anyway, he knew that whatever it was, Mahubah aroused a special feeling in him and the
stallions didn't, impressive as they were.

She was gentle, like her father, Rock Sand, and his father
before him. Might not her gentleness and willingness to please
help control the hot, surging blood of Hastings and Fair Play?
Mr. Belmont thought so. But "nicks," as they were called—
the breeding of one illustrious line to another to produce a still
finer line—were common breeding procedures in that part of
the country. Everybody had something to say about them.
Sometimes they worked. More often they didn't. But nobody
was going to quarrel with Mr. Belmont. His thinking behind
the mating of Fair Play and Mahubah was pretty sound. Besides, it was his own money he was spending.

All that wasn't too important just now. What mattered was
that Mahubah should have a sound, healthy foal and stay well
herself. It didn't matter what "nicks" figured in it. Except, of
course, when one remembered that all this planning had
started more than three hundred years ago, when horse owners
first began trying to breed faster and hardier horses.

No, the boy decided, it wasn't going to be easy, this final
waiting for Mahubah to have her foal and wondering if he
might not be the fastest, the strongest, the bravest of them all.
Maybe, after more than three hundred years, the perfect horse
would be foaled tonight. . . .

Mahubah's Foal

3

The boy shifted uneasily from one foot to the other, more restless than Mahubah. How much longer would he have to wait for her to foal? Minutes? Hours? There was one way of finding out. There was one man who would know, almost to the very second.

Turning away from the stall, the boy went to the small room at the end of the corridor. He found the old black groom sitting in his rocker as patient as could be, rocking back and forth and reading a magazine. A good foaling man, the boy knew, should take everything very calmly, almost like a doctor, but still . . .

"How's Mahubah?" he asked, trying to keep the uneasiness from his voice. "How is she?"

"She's fine, Danny, jus' fine." The man put down his magazine but didn't stop rocking. "You been climbin' down your mom's rose trellis 'most every night now, ain't you?"

"It's the only way I can get out," Danny answered, meeting his friend's watchful, kindly eyes. "They don't like my prowling around nights."

"This ain't prowlin', boy. No, I wouldn't call it that."

"I know, but you tell them that." He found himself swaying back and forth to the slow rhythm of the rocking chair. "Why do most mares have to foal so late at night? Why do they have to make it so tough on everybody?"

"To make it easier on themselves, I guess," the man said softly. "They prefer the dark hours, Danny, an' I reckon it goes back a long time, maybe even to the first horse. It's always safest to have babies when no enemies are pokin' themselves around. Foaling's a bad time for a mare to be caught, so the darker it is the better."

"Mahubah's about ready to have her foal, isn't she?" Danny knew his voice sounded anxious, but there wasn't any reason for covering up his uneasiness any longer.

"About ready . . . but not just yet." Like his eyes, the man's voice was patient and kind. "We got time, Danny, plenty of time. Don't you worry none now." He took a big gold watch out of his baggy coveralls, glanced at it, and added, "Besides, she hardly needs me none. Mahubah ain't goin' to have no trouble, no trouble at all."

The boy felt the anger begin to rise within him. How could the man be so sure she didn't need help now? What did he have anyway, X-ray eyes?

"Maybe we ought to get out there," he suggested, ". . . just in case something's happened."

His gaze shifted to the foaling equipment in the room . . . to the clean pails and hot water, to the antiseptic and bandages and scissors and soap and towels and jars and hose. All was in readiness for Mahubah and the colt to come. He turned anxious eyes on the foaling man again.

"Don't you go worryin' so," the man repeated. "I got everything I need to know right down here." He took a small notebook from his pocket and waved it in the boy's face.

"Here's the real work, Danny, done another time, some of it years ago. This tells me what I need to know about Mahubah and all the other mares havin' colts this season. Some mares will foal early, some late. Some will walk an' kick the sides of their stalls just before havin' their colts; others will jus' lie down and foal quiet as can be. Some will have plenty of milk an' some won't have nary enough. Some will hate their foals; others will be pow'ful jealous, not even lettin' me get close to them." He shut the book, grinning as if he'd explained everything. "So I jus' sit around and wait for things I know are goin' to happen. That's all I have to do."

But the boy wasn't satisfied. His voice, like his eyes, became fierce. "What notes do you have on Mahubah? What makes you think you can sit 'round here reading when she might be having her foal even now? How do you know she's not going to have trouble? How do you know?"

There were only patience and understanding in the man's voice when he answered, "I know how you feel, Danny. And I know, too, a little about how Mahubah feels. She'd like to be left alone right now." Again he glanced at his gold watch. "In a little while she'll break out in a sweat an' pin her ears back. Then we'll go to her."

The boy knew that when he had left Mahubah, her dark coat had been dry and slick and polished. "You mean she'll break out in a sweat just before her time comes?"

The man nodded. "An' she'll have her foal quickly. She won't be mean, no suh, an' she'll have plenty of milk."

"But how will you know when it's time to go to her?"

"She'll neigh when her times comes," the man said. "That's here in the book, too. She sort of trumpets her foal's coming. Until then we best leave her be."

The boy sat down in an empty chair. What he'd been told sort of finished things. They'd just have to wait for Mahubah's trumpeting. That's all he could do, wait . . . no matter how hard it was.

"I've decided to quit school," he said finally.

"You're what?" For the first time the man stopped rocking. "Why would you do anything crazy like that, Danny?"

"I made up my mind tonight." The boy looked up and had trouble meeting his friend's gaze. "I want to work around horses all the time. I'm sick of books." His voice wavered, not sounding nearly as fierce as he had meant it to be. "I want to be like you."

"A foalin' man? Sure, Danny." The man's voice was soft and kind. "Not many of us left around, that's for sure. Good ones, I mean. Maybe only five in the whole county. It takes time, an' a foalin' man's judgment has got to be as good as his experience is long. You got to be a born animal man to begin with. You got to have patience an' gentleness an' good sense or all the technical things you learn about foaling mares don't do you no good, nohow."

The boy's eyes held the man's. "Do I have it? Can I learn to be a good one?"

"You're a fine boy, Danny, an' you're smart. It's in you to want to be a lot of things just now. It takes a little more time to find out for sure jus' what it is you want most an' what you're best at. Remember last year how you were goin' to be a jockey? Remember?"

"I remember," the boy said dismally. "But I grew too much. I got too big. Look at me."

The man stood up, only a little taller than the boy. "It would take a big horse, Danny . . . a big one for you to ride, all right. You ain't even stopped growin' yet."

"That's what I mean. That's why I'm going to be a foaling man!"

The old man smiled. "Like I said, Danny, it's got to be more than that. Why don't you jus' look around a little more before you decide for sure? You got plenty of time yet. Maybe you'll find something you want to be even more than a foalin' man."

"But I want to work with horses."

"I didn't mean for you not to, Danny. But there's no good reason for you to go quittin' school. It won't take you much longer to finish than it will for one of this season's colts to get to the racetrack. You jus' keep comin' 'round here like you been doin'. I was lucky to get my start with good people. You be lucky too. Folks 'round here can teach you a lot. You jus' watch 'em and listen . . . that's all you got to do."

"Just keep coming around," the boy repeated, puzzled, ". . . like I been doing?" He shook his head vigorously. "But don't you see, I want more than that! I want something I can hold on to. I want to *do* something."

He stopped abruptly. How could he expect anyone to understand what he meant when he wasn't even sure himself? Maybe it was something a lot of fellows his age went through. He wanted to be something but he wasn't sure what it was. And yet he was anxious to be on his way.

". . . somethin' you kin hold on to," the man repeated slowly. "Is that what you said, Danny?"

The boy nodded and for a moment he felt lower than he ever had in his life. And that, too, he couldn't understand or explain. He felt the man's hand on his shoulder and then heard the soft voice, almost as if the words were meant for a young, frightened colt.

"Danny, I got myself an idea. You take one of these new foals an' you hold on to *him*. Go along with him, learning with him. Maybe by the time he's ready for the racetrack, you'll be ready too. At least, maybe you'll know better what you want to do."

Mahubah's neigh reached the small room, shrill and high pitched, as if echoing the old groom's words. They ran for the door together, the boy reaching for the knob ahead of the foaling man.

"I'm going to take Mahubah's colt," he said eagerly. "That's what I'm going to do. I'll go along with him, learn with him . . . like you said."

This was the way he had heard that it happened sometimes. As if everything was being arranged by Fate. As if this was the way it was supposed to be.

"I'm going to stick with Mahubah's colt from the very beginning," he went on. "I'm going the same places he is and hold on to him tight!"

The man's eyes twinkled. "Sure, Danny, but you'd better not get your heart set on a colt. This one jus' might be a filly."

"No, it'll be a colt, all right," the boy said. He couldn't have been more sure of anything in his life. He wasn't going to spend his time hanging around with any girl!

The lights were turned on, and the barn came alive with a festive brilliance. When they reached Mahubah's stall, they found her moving restlessly about, her ears pinned back and her body flecked with sweat.

"You'd better go right in," the boy said anxiously.

"Nope. Never hurry a foalin' mare, Danny. Learn that the first thing. Stay outside unless she's carrying the foal in a bad position for delivery. Mahubah ain't. Hers is fine, jus' fine. She won't have no trouble, no trouble at all."

But in spite of the man's reassuring words, the boy began to perspire even more than Mahubah. And his eyes never left her even for a second.

"Don't you go frettin' because you're anxious about her," the man went on. "I got forty-one years behind me an' you

ain't. I've seen every problem that can come up. I've turned
foals so they can be born right. I've brought 'em back to life
even when you'd swear they were dead. An' I've quieted mares
who wanted to kill their colts after havin' em. No, Danny,
don't go frettin' none. You jus' watch, that's all I want you to
do. Jus' watch and learn."

The boy said, "But aren't you going to tell them at the
house?"

The big gold watch came out of the coverall pocket again,
and the man glanced at it. "I told them she'd have her colt
'bout now. Besides, they'll see the lights."

Mahubah kept walking around her stall, flicking her ears in
their direction every once in a while as if she were listening to
them.

"Won't be long now, Danny. All we got to do is make sure
she lays down near the center of her stall an' not up against the
wall where it would be hard to help her if she does need a
hand. But she probably won't be gettin' herself into any trouble. Nature will take care of everything."

The boy tried to stop worrying about Mahubah but it wasn't
easy. Then she finally went down very carefully, right in the
center of her stall. This was it. This was the beginning of life
for Mahubah's colt.

From the far end of the barn there was a scurrying of feet as
several men ran down the corridor and came to a stop before
the stall. "Any trouble?" one asked urgently.

"None at all," the foaling man answered without taking his
eyes off Mahubah. He watched every movement to make sure.
He watched one tiny foot protrude from Mahubah and waited
anxiously for the other to appear. Becoming a little worried, he
opened the stall door and went quietly inside. Making out the
tip of the second small hoof, he took hold of it and pulled

gently until it, too, was free. The knees of the foal followed next and then came the tiny muzzle against the forearm.

"Jus' look at those big nostrils!" Danny wanted to shout but didn't. It was best to remain quiet, very quiet.

The old groom waited, holding his breath as he always did for the foal's head to appear and the eyes to look into his for the very first time.

Mahubah moved hard and then he was staring at the foal's small, wedge-shaped head. Just look at that star! It's diamond-shaped like his daddy's and granddaddy's. They've marked him, all right . . . or is it a filly? Hold on! Here come the shoulders. They're big shoulders. This is no small foal but one that's big-boned and heavy. Easy, Mahubah. Easy, girl. It won't be much longer now. There, there come the hips and the rest of him, right down to that little tuft of tail.

The navel cord broke and the foal lay still beside his mother. It was a colt, all right, just as the boy had wanted. The old man rubbed the foal gently with a soft rag, moving him a little so Mahubah could nuzzle or lick him without getting up. He wanted her to stay down and rest as long as possible.

Turning back to the foal, he wiped the big nostrils clean of fluid and membrane. He watched the colt breathe deeply and found himself breathing in slow rhythm with him. He painted the navel cord with an antiseptic, for there must be no infection. And all the while the colt's eyes were open, watching him. They were big, wonderful, inquisitive eyes, not at all timid like most foals'. This one was born unafraid.

Finally the foaling man stepped back, cleaning the straw and taking his pails with him. He stopped outside the stall door and watched with the others. There was little more that he could do. The rest was pretty much up to the colt, and that was the way it would be for the rest of his life. Mahubah's

newly born son either had greatness in him or he didn't have it
. . . only time would tell.

The colt got to his feet while his mother was still lying
down. He stood on awkward, disobedient legs, wavering trium-
phantly. He fell down but tried again immediately, placing two
perfectly formed front hoofs in the straw and then quickly getting his hind hoofs upright. This time he stayed up on his
overlong legs, his bright eyes turned on his mother as if he were
impatiently waiting for her to appease his hunger.

The nursing instinct was his strongest basic impulse, and he
needed no urging, no help from outsiders. As soon as Mahubah got to her feet he went to her, walking on legs that were
braced at unbelievable angles . . . and yet to everybody who
was watching they were the straightest legs in the world.

"Why, he hardly wobbles," one man said. "Just look at
him."

"Bigger than most," the foaling man said. "Stronger than
most. Straighter than most."

"And with his grandpappy's star," another man said.
"Y'know, he just might be the one, at that."

"Might be," still another onlooker commented cautiously.

"He's got the body and the breeding," the man who had
first spoken said now. "Time will tell."

"Only one way we'll ever know," one of the more cautious
men pronounced dramatically. "And that is to see what he
does on a racetrack. He must prove himself to packed and
shouting stands. He must come out to the roll of drums. He
must carry glistening silks. He must level away at the head of
that long testing stretch and prove himself in battle with the
fleetest of his contemporaries. Yes, the test of the racecourse is
the only one that counts."

"That's a long way off yet," another said, smiling.

"Not so long."

Only the boy Danny remained quiet. He was much too busy watching this wonderful tableau. Was there anything to compare with the first few minutes in the life of a foal?

The colt was nursing. Big and strong as he was, he needed his mother very much, not only for her life-giving milk but also for the warmth of her breath, her caresses, and her constant reassurance. And, tired and weak as Mahubah was, she gave him everything he asked for, licking his tousled coat while he nursed.

The boy wondered if she had known what it was all about or whether her foal had come as a very pleasant surprise to her. And did she care what all these men had to say about her colt and about the great things they expected him to do? To her, he must appear strikingly beautiful, with no gauntness of body or awkward, stiltlike legs. To her, every movement he made must be a picture of flowing grace. And he would grow handsomer as he moved around where she could see him better.

"And you, Danny, what do you think of him?" the foaling man asked finally.

"I only know I wouldn't want to be anywhere else," the boy said quietly. "That's all I know."

Man o' War

4

Danny didn't find school easy that day, knowing that Mahubah's colt was waiting for him back at Nursery Stud. He told himself over and over again to take it easy, that the colt wasn't going anywhere. The night before should have taught him the rewards of patience. It was the mark of a good horseman. Still, he wanted to learn it *fast*.

Thirteen hours after the colt had been born, Danny was back at the farm. He leaned on a paddock fence watching Mahubah being followed obediently by her son, who never let her get more than three or four feet away from him. The colt nuzzled her constantly to get something to eat, and when he wasn't nursing he was rubbing his downy nose against her muzzle.

"It won't be long before those funny legs of yours straighten out," the boy called. "Then you'll get a chance to see how fast you can move them."

The day was warm and Mahubah remained in the sun, avoiding the shadows at the edge of the paddock. Early spring rains had brought the grass to a lush green and the ground was spongy beneath her hoofs. Her nameless colt darted around her, the blood dancing in his veins. His was a brand-new world and there was much to be discovered!

The boy followed every movement of the colt. One of these days he would get this colt to come to him, enticing him with a carrot or an apple. But now he was best left alone with his mother. What a leggy, large-framed colt he was! And how much he looked like his father! But he'd be redder than Fair Play, much redder. Anyone could tell that even through the baby hair. And, man, look at that stride for a new foal! Big he was. Big and red. Big Red.

It wouldn't be long before they'd fit a halter to his head and start leading him around. But today, his first day, he was left free to feel the wind and sun for the first time and to smell, too, the redbuds and the dogwood blooming beside the paddock fence. It would be a good life for him, a really good life, with everything a horse could want. He would have the best of everything, because that's the way it was at Nursery Stud.

"Hello, Danny."

He turned quickly at the sound of the woman's voice, recognizing it. "Hello, Mrs. Kane," he answered.

Together they watched Mahubah's colt, Danny waiting for the woman to pass judgment on him. There weren't many women who could have taken over a man's job as Mrs. Kane had done since her husband's death. She ran things now. She was the superintendent of the big farm and it was no easy job.

So keep your eyes and ears open, he cautioned himself. *You can learn a lot from her. As you were told last night, you're lucky to get your start with good people. So listen to everything Mrs. Kane has to say.*

"He could be the best of this year's crop, Danny," she said, her keen eyes following Mahubah's colt.

"He's got the size for it," the boy answered.

"And the breeding," she added. "In fact, Mr. Belmont has such high hopes for this colt that I just sent him a telegram at his New York office."

"You don't usually?"

"No, not usually. I knew he'd be specially interested in this one's arrival," she said.

"And you?"

She smiled. "I have high hopes for him, too."

"You've bred other Rock Sand mares to Fair Play," he said. "Have any of the colts shown anything?"

"There's just one of racing age," she answered. "His name is Sands of Pleasure, and he's been winning. There'll be other winners of this cross. Mr. Belmont is sure of it."

Her gaze left the boy for Mahubah. "She is a fine mare," Mrs. Kane went on. "She is not loaded with fat and she has produced a strong and vigorous colt who will require little attention. He looks as if he has the resistance to withstand infection from most any quarter."

"Is he her first colt?"

"No, her second. Her first is a full sister to this colt, and we named her Masda. She is now in training and showing good speed."

"Then Masda should give you an idea what to expect from *him*," he said.

"Perhaps . . . and perhaps not. One never knows what to expect even with the same mother and father, Danny. Like children, they can be very different."

A cloud passed over the sun and suddenly the weather turned cold and gloomy. The boy felt a chill pass over him, and he turned to Mrs. Kane to find her, too, shivering a little.

"I must go now, Danny," she said quickly. "Watch him for us. Don't let him get into any trouble."

His gaze followed her. Everybody was busy here at the farm. They went from one foal to another, from one horse to another. He was the only one satisfied with watching just one colt.

The chill swept over him again. His eyes turned skyward. There were ominous clouds, running before a high wind and almost certain to bring rain. But it was far more than the threatening storm that bothered him, if only momentarily.

The world he lived in was not so different from the world of a foal. When everything went well, as it had gone last night, it was thrilling and exciting. When it did not, it was terrifying.

At home and school the talk was that soon the United States would be at war with Germany, entering the terrible conflict that was already being waged in Europe. If that happened, this colt might never know the career for which he was born.

Suddenly the sun broke through the clouds. Danny smiled again. It was wrong to have such gloomy thoughts on the colt's birthday. This was *his* day and they should make the most of it!

The colt was trying to imitate his mother, spreading his awkward legs and bending them, trying to reach the grass. Soon he toppled over and for a moment lay still, rubbing the grass with his nose and working his lips. He pulled a few blades free and held them in his mouth without eating them. He had no taste for grass yet. He rolled over, kicking his long, unmanageable legs in the air and seeming to revel in his newly found strength. But a moment later he'd had enough, for he stretched out on his side and closed his eyes, letting the sun warm his furry body while he slept.

The next few weeks slipped by and life for Mahubah's colt

changed rapidly. Danny watched him run faster around the paddock, happy that his legs were more apt to go where he wanted them. He fell less often. He could reach the grass with his nose simply by bending his knees a little, but he still didn't care for the taste of grass. He much preferred his mother's milk, and his appetite was great and continuous. His large frame began filling out; his strength grew. He drank in the wind and it intoxicated him. He raced in the sun, but never too far away from Mahubah. And Danny was certain that the colt was beginning to wonder when he would be allowed to play with others his age, those he saw with their mothers in the big field beyond. He would show his heels to all of them! But most of the time Mahubah's colt just slept in the sun, so for him April 6, 1917, was no different from any other day.

For Danny, who joined him after school, it was a day of fear and uncertainty. The United States had declared war on Germany. A lot of people would go to the fighting front, maybe even his own father. Many would die for a cause they strongly believed in. Then of what importance was this red colt he watched so closely? Who cared if he could run fast or not? What did it matter, with the whole world up in arms?

Yet he stayed with the colt, knowing that to him it was still important. If he couldn't fight himself and had to remain at home, there were some things he had to hold on to, and Mahubah's colt was one of them.

The weeks swept by and he found himself holding tighter than ever to Mahubah's colt. Only the old men remained at Nursery Stud. All the others had gone to war.

He helped with the care of the young stock and was allowed to lead his colt behind Mahubah as they walked from barn to pasture. He was one of the first to know that the blood of the grandsire Hastings ran strong in this red colt.

"Easy, Red, easy," he whispered. But the stout colt pulled

furiously against the lead shank, not actually fighting but playing hard, and eager to be off with the other youngsters who
now shared his day.

"He's goin' to turn into a real warrior, that one," an old
groom warned. "You be strong, Danny-boy, an' push him
back. Don't you go lettin' him get away with anything now.
He's big and quick, that one, an' he ain't goin' to get no easier
as we go along."

"You're doin' good, Danny," another said. "You're doin'
jus' fine as you are. Don't you let anyone tell you to push that
colt. No, sir. Some you might be able to push, but not that
one. He'll push back, he will. Fightin's easy for him to learn,
an' he's quick as lightning. Hold him good and take all the
time you want. Don't you go losin' your temper with him
none. You be rough an' he'll jus' be rougher. He'll never
amount to anything then, he won't. Ask him nicely, boy.
Maybe he'll listen to you like a baby. Maybe he will."

What a baby! Danny decided. A young tiger was never so
quick . . . or smart . . . or strong. The colt flew at the end of the
lead shank, and Danny had to use all his strength and size to
control him.

"Easy, Red, easy," he called over and over again, thankful
that he wasn't as small as a jockey after all. And finally one day
he reached the point where the big colt obediently followed
Mahubah to the field without giving him a fight.

The grooms stood around watching him break away with
the other colts. When he played he was the first to whirl,
dancing on his long legs and avoiding the others with the grace
of a bird in flight.

"He's quicker than the rest," one groom said.

"An' brainier," another added. "He's the best of the year's
crop. He sure is."

"Yeah, but what he'll do on the track is somethin' else."

"*If* he ever gets there."

"Y'mean . . ."

"I mean what y'think I mean. They made Mr. Belmont a major and sent him off to Europe, didn't they? So there's no tellin' what'll happen to Nursery Stud. Heard some folks say, too, there won't be any more racin' until the war ends. Some say more'n that. Some say the Major's thinkin' of selling off all his young stock. So who knows what's goin' to happen to this colt or any colt or even us?"

Danny listened to this startling news. Regardless of what Major Belmont decided to do about Nursery Stud, he knew one thing for sure—he wasn't leaving Mahubah's colt. Wherever the colt went, he'd go too!

Later, he found he needn't have worried, for while the war raged overseas, life went on pretty much as usual at the farm. The days grew longer and the nights warmer, just as in any other year. Mares and colts lay down to sleep at night in dark pastures and spent their days in the cool, fly-protected barns. And Danny enjoyed his best summer vacation from school.

He never strayed too far from Mahubah's colt, and his tales of Red's speed and prowess were by far the most listened to of any on the farm.

"I've got him standing still even when I rub his shins," he said proudly. "Boy, he sure was ticklish there. And I don't think a faster colt's ever been foaled . . . at least, I've never seen one."

"You still got a lot to see yet, Danny," an old groom told him. "We've had colts here who got the best of everything and yet turned out pretty sour when they reached the track. They had the best breeding, the best handling, the best trainers 'n jockeys 'n everything else. Then they won nuthin', nuthin' at all."

"But every little thing we do is important," another said. "An' no one ever knows when he's got the best colt there is. Danny is doin' right well. He's got his colt used to bein' handled and actin' better than any of the rest of us could do."

The first groom shrugged and said, "Mebbe so. Anyway, it ain't goin' to be *Danny's colt* no longer. Not by name, it ain't. Nope, they gave him his real name this morning. They sho did."

"*They* nothin'," and the second groom grinned. "There's only *one* person who names horses here an' that's Mrs. Belmont. The Major wouldn't have anyone else doin' it, no suh."

"That's what I said. An' she got around to namin' Danny's colt."

"She give him a good one? Never was a good racehorse with a bad name."

"She chose a mighty pow'ful one, she did. 'Pears to me nuthin' could be more pow'ful than one of them big battleships I bin readin' about."

"Battleships? Is that what she went and named Danny's colt?"

"You makin' fun? You know well as I do she wouldn't go namin' any horse Battleships. No sir, she named him Man o' War, that's what she did. Ain't that what they call them battleships?"

"Man o' War," the old groom repeated, rolling the name around his tongue almost as if he were savoring it.

"Man o' War," repeated Danny, his eyes finding the big colt out in the pasture. "It's good, all right. But I think I'll still call him Red."

The Weanling

5

September came and Danny went back to school. But that didn't keep him away from Nursery Stud. Every afternoon he walked through the field full of suckling foals. He knew most of them by name, for, immature as they all were, their heads bore a close resemblance to their parents'. Most of them carried their parents' white markings, too—the splashes of body white, the stockings, the stars and blazes. Danny never had trouble spotting Man o' War's star and the narrow stripe running down the center of his nose.

He watched Man o' War grow taller than the others and become a bit arrogant in his newly found strength. So he worked all the harder with him, knowing that gentle treatment now would save a lot of trouble later on. He handled him daily, and it became as much a part of his routine as feeding, watering, and mucking out stalls.

The old grooms were happy to have his help.

"We sho got plenty to do around here, Danny-boy, we sho have," one said. "Jus' keepin' these stalls clean like they should be ain't easy. Broodmares are lots dirtier than horses in trainin'. They sho is."

So Danny worked hard around the farm, but hardest of all with his colt. Man o' War was as spirited as a young foal could be, and Danny had no intention of breaking that spirit. He used soft words, soft cloths, soft brushes and hands.

He studied Man o' War's appetite as closely as everything else. When the time came, he started feeding him whole oats rather than rolled oats. He watched him go eagerly beneath the field "creep" rail, a rail high enough for the youngsters to get under for their feed but too low for the mares. Gradually, Man o' War was developing an appetite for grown-up food and becoming less dependent on Mahubah for his nourishment.

Sometimes Mahubah, even though she was among the best of mothers, tried to get under the "creep" rail and into the field pen where her colt ate at will. She was getting oats and bran and cracked corn in the barn but her appetite was enormous, for she not only was supplying milk for her growing, demanding son but was again in foal to Fair Play. Danny always shooed her away from the feed pen gently for he was sympathetic to the demands of motherhood.

With the coming of early fall he watched Mahubah's dark body start to take on its winter coat, shading to a heavy seal-brown. She was a big, strong mare, standing just under sixteen hands, but the strain of nursing Man o' War while carrying her new foal was beginning to tell on her. Danny became very anxious for her to be relieved of this double duty.

Man o' War now weighed more than five hundred pounds and stood over thirteen hands. He was eating eight to ten quarts of feed daily and looking for more. He no longer needed his mother's milk. But despite this, he was almost certain not to take his weaning calmly. He was much too devoted to

Mahubah. He never allowed the other colts to jostle her in pasture, flaying them with his long legs when they crowded too close.

"When will you separate them?" Danny asked the old man in charge.

"Soon's Mrs. Kane tells me to go ahead."

"He's big enough to be weaned. What's Mrs. Kane waiting for?"

"She weans when the time's right, when it best suits our work schedule and when the colts are ready for it."

"Isn't that about now?"

"The time's all right, boy. But you notice Red's got the sniffles, don't you?"

"Just a little," Danny said. "It's not much of a cold."

"It's enough to keep us from weaning him yet," the old man said adamantly. "Weaning's a shock on any colt, no matter how big an' strong he is. He dries up a little, 'specially since he can't run up to his ma and nurse like he's bin used to. So that ain't good when the colt's got a cold to boot. You know as well as I do that you need a lot of liquids when you got a cold, an' colts ain't no different."

"You going to wean all the colts at the same time?" Danny asked.

"Most of 'em. A few of the smaller colts I'll save till later." His aged eyes followed Man o' War. "But you're right, the sooner we wean that fellow the better," he added. "He's as big an' pow'ful as they come."

Danny watched and nodded. "Yes," he agreed, "he's sure ready. An' he's a big strain on Mahubah."

"He sho is. He's a handful, all right."

Danny wondered if losing Mahubah would cause Man o' War to become even more aware of his own presence. After all,

he'd been close to the colt since birth, closer than anyone else.
And with the weaning their relationship might grow stronger
than ever.

His gaze followed Man o' War as the big colt raced to the
far end of the pasture, leading a group of youngsters. They
played for a long time, ignoring the mares' constant whinnies
for them to return. No longer were any of the colts dependent
upon their mothers.

Finally the day of weaning arrived and all available men
were summoned to the side of the broodmares and colts.

"You take Red," the old foreman told Danny. "Soon he'll
be a yearling, an' he's goin' to act like one now. You hold him
good. He thinks the world is his."

Slowly the long line of mares and foals moved along. In the
distance, more than a mile away, was the weanling barn. Along
with the other youngsters, it would be Man o' War's new
home. Danny kept him near a dark bay colt who had been his
most constant companion in pasture. Pairing up now would
make the weaning easier for each colt.

As they approached the weanling barn Man o' War became
more and more uneasy at the end of the lead rope. To Danny it
meant that his colt knew what was to come. He talked to him
softly, telling him that the separation would be hard to endure
only for a short while and that there were big plans for him.

They entered the new barn, and as soon as Man o' War set
foot inside the box stall that was not his own he became frantic. He whinnied for his mother but she was not at his side. She
stood outside the stall, frantic too, whinnying repeatedly as if
she knew she had lost her chestnut colt for all time.

It was no different in the other stalls. The chorus of shrill,
heartbreaking whinnies was the saddest sound Danny had ever
heard. He kept repeating, "It's all right. It's all right." But he

didn't believe his well-meant advice just then. Neither did Man o' War nor Mahubah.

The mares were quickly led away but Danny stayed behind, listening to Mahubah's shrill whinnies until they began to die in the distance. *She'll be out of earshot soon,* he told himself. *She won't be able to see him or hear him. She'll go back to her old familiar stall. She'll settle down fast, for they'll treat her like the expectant mother she is. They'll keep her in a couple of days, then turn her out, but far enough away from the weanlings so she'll never see him. Soon everything will be going smoothly for her again, like it did last year and the year before.*

Danny's thoughts turned back to the colt. Within twenty-four hours Man o' War would have forgotten all about Mahubah, but now he was in frenzied agony over her absence. To be left alone in his stall seemed more than he could bear. He ran from one side to the other, stopping only to rear and throw his flint-thin forelegs hard against the door.

Looking through the fine mesh screen at the top, Danny said, "Easy, Red. Easy. Don't hurt yourself now. You've got company. Lots of it. Just look around you."

There was no lessening of the barn's bedlam. None of the colts and fillies took the parting from their mothers calmly. If some cared less than others, they did not show it, being caught in the wailing uproar that swept the barn.

A few of the men stayed in the barn with Danny, walking up and down the corridors and making sure none of the youngsters hurt themselves. The stalls were free of feed buckets and water pails, which the colts might have run into in their frenzy. The stall windows were shut, for weanlings had been known to try to go through them.

One old man stopped beside Danny and said, "Don't let your colt get out of hand, Danny."

"Maybe we should put the bay colt in with him," Danny suggested, nodding to Man o' War's pasture companion who was in the adjacent stall. "He's not nearly as upset."

"If we have to, we will," the old man said. "But then we'll have to watch 'em to make sure they don't fight."

"I'll watch them," Danny offered eagerly.

"Let's hope we don't have to put them together," the old man said. "When the time comes for separating the two of 'em, it'll jus' be weaning all over again. Besides, Red's big enough to stand on his own feet. The quicker he gets used to it the better."

Danny's eyes passed over the big, muscular body of his colt. "Nothing's going to stop him ever," he said.

Several hours later Man o' War was the last colt to quiet down. All the others had become interested in each other, and memories of their mothers were growing short. What was most important to them was that their playmates were close by, and they spent most of their time looking at each other. Man o' War, too, finally moved to the side of his stall nearest his pasture friend. He lifted his head high, peering over the partition and pressing his muzzle hard against the screen the better to see the bay colt.

Danny remained in the corridor, watching but not bothering his colt. A long, hard night was ahead of Man o' War. The night would bring back memories of standing close to Mahubah's side, safe in the protection of her big body. He would not feel so arrogant then. He would take his first big step toward full maturity. And Danny would be there to watch him take it.

Darkness fell and the barn lights were turned on. They burned all night but the brightness did not trick the colts. Soon the heartbreaking whinnies began all over again, and hour after hour they continued as the colts called their mothers. Finally, sometime during the middle of the night, the barn grew quiet except for a lone call, Man o' War's whinny for Mahubah. His eyes alone were open. He alone remained on his feet. He wanted no part of the thick, comfortable straw bedding. He had no time for sleep.

"Easy, Red, easy," Danny repeated drowsily. He was determined not to sleep until his colt slept. And only when it was near morning did deep and total quiet settle over the weanling barn.

Flying Legs

6

The following day was easier for Man o' War and the other weanlings. When Danny reached the farm after school, he found them all quiet except for a few infrequent whinnies.

The old caretaker said, "They're fine now, Danny, an' it won't be long before every single one of 'em will pass right by his mother without so much as a glance. Their thoughts are of each other now and getting out to play."

"When will you turn them loose?" the boy asked.

"In another day or so. Don't want them so excited that they play too hard. They're big, strong animals now an' their play can be rough. A cut or bump could become a permanent injury. We got to be mighty careful."

"But their rough play gets them used to each other and not flinching in close quarters," Danny said. "That's important on a racetrack."

"It's still pretty hard to watch 'em go at it now. Their heels move pow'ful fast. No tellin' what they might do to each other. No tellin' at all."

Danny looked at Man o' War. He'd sure hate to see his colt put out of commission before he even grew up.

"You separating the colts and fillies?" he asked.

"We sure are. We don't want the girls getting mixed up with this bunch of roughnecks. That's what these colts are, Danny, each 'n every one of 'em."

Danny nodded in full agreement. There was no doubt about the colts being lots stronger than the fillies. You needn't be a horseman to see it, either. The fillies were far more slender, and when they moved it was with deerlike grace compared to the colts' powerful strides. And their eyes, too, were gentle and timid at times. They were shaping up.

Danny turned to the old man beside him. "But how come Fair Play's *daughters* are doing better than his sons? Isn't that what I heard Mrs. Kane say last week?"

The old man nodded. " 'Pears there's one racin' lots faster than the colts. That's Masda, a full sister to your colt, boy." His gaze swept to Man o' War. "That's what's causin' all the interest in Red. Masda's only a two-year-old an' she's got herself two wins, two seconds, and a third this summer. I heard tell she's got whistlin' speed."

"No wonder they're interested in him then," Danny said thoughtfully. "I mean more than just the way he looks and goes in the pasture."

"Sure, they're more than ever interested in crossin' Mahubah to Fair Play now." The old man paused to scratch his unshaven face. "Still, I heard Mrs. Kane say that Masda is pretty rough to handle. She don't take kindly to training any more than her grandpappy Hastings did. She turns all the fire burning inside her into a tantrum, so she don't have too much left to use in a race most times. So maybe the cross ain't what they think it is at all," he concluded soberly. "Might be that Mahubah's blood ain't strong enough to dominate all that hustlin', bustlin' blood of Fair Play and Hastings."

The following day the weanlings were turned out for the first time. But before the barn doors were opened, Danny and the other men walked around the large paddock picking up dead branches that had blown down from the trees and old sticks that had been forgotten. Anything that might cause injury to an excited youngster in an unfamiliar field was picked up. These men were taking no chances with their highly prized animals. During their long lives they had seen weanlings hurt themselves in very strange ways.

"I saw a colt run a little stick, just about so big," one said, spreading his hands no more than a foot apart, "smack into his stomach. How he ever did it no one knows. But he did. An' he died the same day despite everything we did for him. Can you imagine, a little stick costin' us a fine colt?"

So when the weanlings were turned loose, Danny was in the paddock to greet them. His station was at one of the corners, to prevent any piling up of excitable colts. He watched them come down the paddock in great leaps and bounds, overjoyed by their first taste of freedom in two days. A few were still looking for their mothers. Shrill whinnies pierced the air and there was a constant crash of bodies and legs.

Danny was tempted to close his eyes. A racehorse's whole career could end during these few minutes of exuberant play. He saw Man o' War's forelegs reach for the sky in the middle of a small, packed group of colts. Behind him a gray colt crashed against his hindquarters. Then the group broke up, scattering in all directions.

Man o' War came flying toward Danny and the boy raised his arms, trying to wave him down. "Easy, Red! Easy!" he called.

The big colt turned away, his long body leaning into the wind. He moved along the fence and then swept back up the field to join the others again.

As Danny watched him go, he knew Man o' War had forgotten Mahubah. The colt's only interest now was in playing with his companions. But soon the hard play quieted down and there was little running. The colts began to graze and then lay in the warm sun. Maybe they sensed that with fall at hand winter was not far off, Danny decided. Maybe they wanted to make the most of the sun and grass.

The following days passed quickly for Danny. He watched the colts' sunburned coats start to change. Baby hair was shed, revealing some colts to be of a different color from the one that had first appeared. Some brown colts became more black than brown. Some that had been black were now more brown. Others with a few gray hairs in their tails were becoming gray all over. But many colts stayed the same color, their long, matted coats unchanging. Man o' War was one of these. He was going to remain a chestnut red except for the star and irregular strip running down his nose. If anything, he would become more red with the coming months.

His training, along with that of the others, had already started. His hoofs were being inspected and trimmed once a month. He was taught to walk up and down ramps and in and out of strange stalls. Much of his racing life would be spent traveling, and all these things were better learned while he was still young. The aged, experienced men never used force in teaching him anything new. Patience and kindness was their method, luring him on when necessary with a container of oats or carrots, guiding him gradually until finally he went where they wanted him to go. Never once did Man o' War break out in open rebellion, and they had high hopes for him as he grew in weight and strength and became a yearling the first of January 1918.

"Maybe we got control of all that Hastings fire," one groom told Danny. "Maybe so."

Danny answered, "I hope so, but he's burning up inside. It could be a lot different when somebody gets up on his back."

"Mebbe so, but that ain't our problem, Danny-boy."

"We grow him big, that's all we got to do," another said.

"You sho talk like you were gettin' him ready for the sales ring," criticized the groom who had spoken first. "You sho do. Big and fat. Maybe you want to force him to grow fast? Maybe pour some skimmed cow milk into him?"

The other man grinned broadly. "Nope, Sam. Don't mean that at all. No sales ring for this here colt . . . never was for a Belmont yearling. Mr. Belmont ain't no market breeder. Nor his pappy before him. What's bred for us races for us."

"But times change," still another old man interjected quietly. "A war's goin' on. No tellin' what might happen. No tellin' at all."

"Not here . . . times don't change here," the first said angrily. "This farm ain't ever goin' to change. Nope, not ever."

All through the winter, with snow on the ground much of the time, Man o' War continued to grow as a colt should, evenly and naturally from proper feed and exercise. Nothing was done to force growth upon him and yet he was a hand taller than any of the other colts his age. He was growing up fast and he stood proudly in a stall that was sweet-smelling and newly clayed. It seemed to Danny that the colt knew he was destined for greatness.

The winter months gave way to spring and when the yearlings were turned loose to roam the soft fields, their exuberance knew no bounds. They ran hard, testing their speed against one another as if they knew that racing was their destiny. And Man o' War, even though he was always the slowest at the start, was always far ahead at the end of the pasture.

Danny watched him more closely than anybody else and was convinced that his colt would be one to reckon with on the racetrack. But would Man o' War, in spite of his great speed, turn out to be as temperamental as his full sister Masda, who raced only when she felt like it? Worse still, would he turn out to be uncontrollable like his grandsire, Hastings? Speed was useless without manners and the will to win. All three were necessary to make a champion.

Danny did all he could to pave the way to a successful career for his colt. Man o' War was close to a thousand pounds of hard flesh and muscle. He could explode any minute, and often did, rearing in the air to his full height with flying hoofs.

Danny spent hours with him in the pasture, leading him around to get him over his natural nervousness and excitement at being restricted in his movements. Seldom did Man o' War become fearful or disclose any violent action, for Danny went slowly and carefully. He did not want to introduce too many new things to his colt at the same time. He wanted no strain put on muscles and ligaments that were not yet fully toughened despite the colt's great size. He stopped often to adjust the halter so that the colt would become accustomed to having his head handled and would not balk when the time came to put on the bridle. But the bit? What would the big colt do when he felt the iron in his mouth for the first time? How much of Hastings would explode in him then?

And how would Man o' War take to a saddle on his broad back? Danny rested a little of his weight on him each day, just enough so that the weight of the saddle might not seem so strange to him. But the girth strap? What would happen when that tightened about the belly of this strapping colt with the hot blood of Hastings in him? Would he reach for the sky? And when he felt a man on his back, would a thousand pounds of living dynamite explode and rock the very earth?

"You're doin' real good, Danny," the head caretaker told Danny one day after watching them together.

"He's the best there is," the boy said proudly.

"Good for you to think so, Danny. Real good. A good groom's got to love his horse or he ain't a good groom. Maybe he can't rub speed into him but he can do plenty else. He even fights for his horse if he has to."

The old man's gaze turned to the other yearlings in pasture. "I'm mighty glad this crop is a large, strong bunch. They better be. Worst winter we ever had an' now it's the worst spring. I don't like this kind of weather. Maybe it's not so cold as other springs, but it's too cloudy and too rainy. They ain't gettin' as much sunshine as they need. Most of 'em still ain't got rid of their winter hair. I don't like it at all. Weather plays an important part in what to expect from yearlings. Wet and chilly weather ain't good for mares an' foals neither. It ain't even good for breeding. It ain't good for nothin'."

The foul weather that spring didn't let up. But in spite of it, life at Nursery Stud went on as usual. The yearlings were turned out every day it didn't rain, as were the broodmares with their young suckling foals in other pastures. Mahubah was one of these. She had long since forgotten her red colt, for now by her side ran his little brother and within her was still another foal by Fair Play. The cross that Major Belmont so strongly believed in was well on its way! But to what destiny? No one knew, and few actually cared. This experiment was the creation of a man far away from the scene, one who at the moment had little interest in horses and racing.

The First World War was at its height and horse racing in many states had been curtailed and even halted. Only a small field of eight Thoroughbreds went to the post in the forty-fourth running of the Kentucky Derby on May 11, 1918, at Churchill Downs, and the winner was Exterminator. The classic race was of little interest to the nation, for the end of the war seemed far away and there was terror in the air and under the sea.

Yet the days grew longer at Nursery Stud and warmer, too. The yearlings stayed out all night, as did the broodmares and their suckling foals, all grazing or sleeping beneath the moon and the rustling wind. It was peaceful and quiet at Nursery Stud, with only the inclement weather to fear.

"It's still too wet," the old foreman said. " 'Tain't no good for man or beast. No good will come of it."

But it was more than the weather that suddenly brought turmoil to Nursery Stud and saddened the hearts of all who were left.

"Mrs. Kane's heard news from the Major," one groom came running with the news. "He's quittin' racin'. He's sellin' everything but the breedin' stock. He's keepin' the broodmares and stallions but the rest are all goin', every last one of 'em!"

Danny listened to the startling news. *I'm still staying with my colt,* he promised himself. *I'm staying with him no matter what happens.*

Dark Days

7

Later that day Danny found Mrs. Kane watching the yearling fillies. "Is it true?" he asked. "Major Belmont is selling them?"

She nodded, the letter from Major Belmont still in her hand. "He feels the war may go on for years and years and that there is no hope of racing them under his own colors. He will keep five fillies for breeding and . . ." She paused, her eyes turning to the boy and offering a slight smile, "your colt, Danny," she added. "We told him Man o' War was the best yearling we had and he decided to keep him."

Danny managed to keep from shouting his joy. It wouldn't be right to show how happy he was, with Mrs. Kane and all the others so downcast over the prospective sale of so many fine horses.

"Will he send the others to the Yearling Sales?" he asked finally.

"No, he is reluctant to break them up and will sell them as a group for $60,000."

"Will he get such a price?"

"Even for these war years it is a bargain," she said quietly. "They are twenty of the finest-bred yearlings in the country. But if he doesn't get his price he will take less to keep them together."

"And the horses in training, will they be sold too?" Danny asked.

Mrs. Kane nodded.

"Then only Man o' War will be left to carry Major Belmont's colors," Danny said thoughtfully. "He'll win for him, Mrs. Kane."

"Perhaps," she said, smiling faintly. "I hope so, Danny. But very often what looks sensational on paper turns out to be mediocre."

"But he's not on paper anymore," Danny reminded her. "He's . . ."

". . . a fine colt," she finished for him. "That is all any of us think now. He should make a good racehorse and we have high hopes for him."

"No more than that?" Danny asked quietly.

"I would not be honest if I said yes," she answered.

Danny turned away. "I think he's going to be the greatest horse there is," he said. "Maybe even the greatest there ever was."

The days rolled by and the inclement weather continued. With it came a terror almost as bad as the war itself. An influenza epidemic swept the United States and it did not pass lightly over Nursery Stud. Nor did it restrict itself to people. One by one the horses came down with the dreaded disease. Most of them recovered but a few died. Fearfully, Danny watched his colt for any signs of illness.

During this time, too, many visitors came to Nursery Stud,

looking over the yearlings that were for sale. There were no buyers, and the price tag for the lot began to drop.

"They all missin' a chance of a lifetime, that's what they is," an old groom said.

"No one wants sick horses an' that's what they see," another added.

"Even if our colts weren't sick they wouldn't see them for nothin'," another remarked. "They too used to seein' big fat sales yearlings, they is. Ours might be thin but they be hard, too, an' strong . . . or else they be dead right now."

"You're right, man," the first agreed. "You sho can see what kind of bone skeleton our colts have. You sho can."

Then one summer morning the strongest colt of them all got sick. As Man o' War lay in his stall, the veterinarian said, "He's the last to get it, and the last to get over it, we hope."

"He'll get over it," Danny said. "I'll make sure he does."

From that morning on, night and day, Danny stayed with Man o' War, ministering to his colt and following the directions of the veterinarian as no other groom might have done. His main concern lay in taking every precaution to see that the influenza was not followed by bronchial pneumonia, for if that happened the chances of death were very great.

The big colt's fever lasted forty-eight hours, and his breathing was hard and irregular. Danny kept him covered with a light blanket and made sure the stall was dry and clean, well ventilated but free of drafts. The old men, watching outside the big stall, left the boy and colt alone most of the time, knowing that Danny was doing everything that could be done for Man o' War.

The veterinarian injected his vaccines but he knew, too, that the best of them were far from being one hundred percent effective. If complications followed, they were in for serious trouble. They could only stand by and wait, hoping Man o' War was strong enough to throw off the virus.

The high fever subsided on the third day and the colt's breathing became normal again. "I believe he's going to be all right, Danny," the veterinarian told the boy. "But keep your eye on him. Any disease of the lungs and respiratory system is most serious with a racehorse. All too often his wind is affected, and he's through racing."

Danny nodded and cared for his colt more diligently than ever. He didn't want Man o' War finished with racing before he had even set foot on a track! He fed him carefully when he showed an interest in food again, giving him small amounts of fresh green food and hot mashes. And when the weather was warm, he made sure the box stall had plenty of sunlight and fresh air. He groomed him thoroughly, hand-rubbing the underparts of his chest and abdomen. And he cleaned and disinfected the stall to make sure all germs were gone.

Finally the day came when Man o' War could be turned out to pasture again. He was kept in a separate field where he wouldn't be injured by the other colts. He raced along the fence, not as fast as before his illness, but with the same fire and determination.

"His wind is not broken," Danny told Mrs. Kane. "He'll be as strong as ever in a short while. You'll see."

Mrs. Kane watched the colt for a long time. "After all you've done for him, what I have to say comes hard, Danny," she said finally.

Danny looked at her but she averted her eyes.

"I've had another letter from Major Belmont," she went on. "He's decided not to keep this colt after all."

"Not keep him?" Danny repeated.

She nodded.

"But why, Mrs. Kane? Why'd he change his mind?"

Shrugging her shoulders, Mrs. Kane said, "It's not for me to question his decisions, Danny. Perhaps he didn't want others to think he was keeping the best for himself while selling the rest of his young stock. Or perhaps he's had a change of heart about this colt. It's the war, Danny, think of it that way. There will be other colts for you to care for, many others, when it ends."

"No," Danny said, "there's only one colt for me, ever." Sick at heart, he turned and walked away.

During the days that followed, it was with far different eyes that Danny watched the prospective buyers of yearlings come to Nursery Stud. He was fearful yet determined to prevent the sale of Man o' War in every way possible.

One morning he watched the yearling colts at play in pasture. Only Man o' War was being kept in a separate paddock, for the others were well recovered from their illness and were full of life. Danny knew how much the colt wanted to join the others, but Man o' War would have to wait until he was strong again and ready for hard play.

Down by the barns a car drew up and Mrs. Kane, accompanied by two men, got out. They came over to the fence near Danny and began discussing the yearlings.

Danny moved back into the shade cast by a big tree. He wanted to close his eyes and hold his breath until they'd gone. The group moved closer to him and he heard Mrs. Kane say, "Our price for these and the fillies I showed you is $42,000, Mr. Feustel. The Major is anxious to sell them as a group. You will find no better buy in the country."

The small, easygoing man beside her said, "After the epidemic it's remarkable that they look as well as they do."

Mrs. Kane nodded. "They may not be as fat as sales yearlings," she said quietly, "but they're strong. They had to be or they would not have survived."

Danny was glad to see that the man was showing no exceptional enthusiasm for the colts in the field. On the contrary, he seemed very cool and detached from the whole scene.

"They are a bargain," Mrs. Kane repeated. "If Mr. Riddle is anxious to organize a racing stable he can get no better start than by buying them."

The man glanced at his companion. "What do you think, Mike?" he asked.

The other shrugged his shoulders. "Who can say what is a bargain and what isn't?" he said. "Besides, Mr. Riddle isn't necessarily interested in bargains. He wants the choicest he can get."

The two men moved along the fence on the pretense of getting closer to the yearlings. They stopped near Danny and he heard the one named Feustel whisper, "Then we agree there's not $42,000 worth in the whole lot?"

The other nodded. "We'll tell Mr. Riddle that even at that price they're not a good buy. There are too many we'd have no use for."

Danny breathed easier and kept still as the men moved back and stopped beside Mrs. Kane.

"You worked with Fair Play when he was racing," Mrs. Kane said to Feustel. "You should be most interested in his colts, and there are several included in this group."

"Oh, I am," the man said. "In fact, that's one of the reasons I'm here. I liked Fair Play a lot."

A sharp neigh reached them and all eyes turned to the lone red colt watching the other yearlings. Danny felt his stomach drop. *If only Man o' War had kept still!*

Mrs. Kane said, "There's a fine Fair Play colt. The Major

had intended keeping him for himself but changed his mind. He's included in the group for sale."

Mr. Feustel nodded. "He's a big-boned colt, all right, but still not well. He's so thin he looks ridiculous for the size of him."

"He was the last to become sick," Mrs. Kane said. "He will recover rapidly. His dam is Mahubah."

The man nodded thoughtfully. "I saddled Mahubah for Major Belmont years ago. She was a pretty good racer." He paused before going on. "No, Mrs. Kane, I'm afraid I can't advise Mr. Riddle to buy the whole group. Sorry."

"He could get no better start in racing," Mrs. Kane said again. "I cannot stress that too strongly."

The man shrugged his shoulders, smiling to himself. "Perhaps so. Perhaps not. Only time will tell who is right."

During the weeks that followed, it seemed that Louis Feustel's opinion of the Nursery Stud yearlings was shared by other well-known horsemen throughout the country. The price for the entire group dropped to a reported $30,000 with no takers.

Danny's joy knew no bounds. Then, on the 24th of June, Major Belmont cabled instructions from France that all the yearlings, including Man o' War, were to be sent to the public sales at Saratoga, New York. There each horse would be sold *individually*, bringing what he could under the auction hammer. For Danny, too, it meant leaving Nursery Stud for good. He wasn't going to be left behind. Wherever Man o' War went, he would follow.

"Look Him Over"

8

During the second week of August the twenty-one yearlings from Nursery Stud were sent to Saratoga, New York, to be sold at auction. Along with them went their caretakers, and one of them was Danny. He had been given his first real job, if only a temporary one. He was to help with the care of Man o' War until the colt was sold to his new owner.

Danny said little during the long train ride from Kentucky, dreading the hour to come when Man o' War would be his no longer. Someway, somehow, he *must* find a way not to lose his colt . . . so he listened to the talk of the grooms, getting an inkling as to what to expect at Saratoga.

"I been here once before," the old groom in charge of Fair Gain said, "an' I saw a lady ridin' a gold bicycle with wheels jus' glowin' with diamonds. An' that same day I saw the biggest rug in the whole wide world. It was so big it came in on two flat cars an' they took it to this hotel where the finest, mos' elegant people in the world were stayin'."

Danny steadied Man o' War as the boxcar swayed over a rough stretch of track. Wealthy people would be bidding on the yearling colts, people who could afford to pay almost any price for a horse they wanted.

Turning to the old man, Danny said, "But maybe it won't be the same this year. There's a war going on."

"Maybe so, Danny. Saratoga won't be like it was, that's for sure. But you'll see some high-steppin' carriage horses on the streets. An' they'll be wearin' harness trimmed in gold an' silver with coachmen dressed in fancy clothes. You'll see."

"The big money is there, Danny," the caretaker in charge of the brown colt Richelieu said, "war or no war. Everybody goes to Saratoga this time of year for the races and the sales. They'll all be there, the biggest trainers, the biggest owners. An' their money will be spent buyin' colts, if for nothin' else."

Danny turned back to Man o' War and ran a soft rag over the rough, sunburned coat. Suddenly he stopped his grooming. Maybe it would be far better if he didn't have Man o' War sleek and polished and ready for the sales ring. Then maybe the prospective buyers would see only his faults—his lack of weight, his slight coarseness, his head a bit too high and forelegs forked a little too wide. Man o' War would look thin and hungry compared to the other sales yearlings at Saratoga. Maybe no one would buy him and they could go back home *together!*

Danny decided that from that moment on he would do as little currying, rubbing, and polishing as possible.

The weather was fine and warm when they arrived at Saratoga. It was midafternoon and the races were already under way. Danny caught a glimpse of the crowded stands, resplendent with military uniforms and women's silken gowns and

parasols. He could even smell the ladies' perfume mixed with
the scent of horses.

The men from Nursery Stud unloaded in the area reserved
for the sales yearlings. A news photographer was there to take
pictures; otherwise the area was quiet and empty of visitors.
Not until the following morning would the benches beneath
the trees be filled with people ready to pass judgment and ap-
praise the yearlings soon to go into the sales ring.

Danny put Man o' War into his assigned stall. The big colt
was quiet and unaware of all the excitement in store for him.
The boy ran a hand over him, roughing up the sunburned coat
still more. For a short while longer Man o' War would be completely his own. He didn't look forward to the next day at all.

Morning came sooner than Danny would have liked. It
began at five o'clock with the racehorses going to the track for
training. But the Nursery Stud area remained comparatively
quiet. Fair Gain was stabled next to Man o' War, and his old
groom told Danny, "The clock runs people here same as anyplace else. Maybe even more so. From now till eight o'clock
people jus' hang over the rail or sit in the clubhouse watchin'
horses work. When that's done, they come over here an' look
at yearlings. The afternoons they spend at the races, an' night
finds em buyin' yearlings they might have liked in the mornin'.
That's the way it'll go, Danny, right through Saturday. Then
we'll be free with no more colts to tend."

"Maybe," Danny said hopefully.

The old man raised his gray head to look at the boy. "No
maybes about it, Danny. That's the way it'll happen, 'xactly."

"But maybe they won't like our colts," Danny persisted.

The old man laughed. "They be a skinny bunch sho 'nough,
but they'll sell."

"But I heard that people buy only *fat* sales yearlings."

"Fat and sleek's the way they like 'em, boy. But ours are in good condition. They'll see that, too. An' they can see the bone structure of every las' one of them . . . that's important, too."

"That's for sure," Danny said. You could see their bones, all right.

"If they hadn't been sick an' we'd had more time, they'd be as sleek an' fat as the others," the old man said. "But with their breedin' they'll sell anyway."

Danny was silent and the old man studied him carefully. "Don't you go showin' this colt to anyone in his stall, Danny. When they come around an' want to look at him, you take him outside where he can be seen properly. A colt stands bad with his feet buried in straw an' up one place an' down another. Lead him out in the open where he can walk over a good, flat surface. An' you stand at his left shoulder. Don't you go walkin' 'way ahead of him, pullin' him along like. Hold the shank light but firm. Don't let him stretch his neck or turn his head. He'll look unbalanced if you do."

"I'll remember," Danny said quietly. And he made a mental note to do all the things he shouldn't so his colt wouldn't be seen to his best advantage.

"You ought to rub more gloss into his coat, too," the old man went on. "He don't look very polished this morning."

Danny nodded.

"Mos' people buy a yearling on bloodlines, but how he's made is important, too," the old man went on. "They'll study every part of him. That's why it's important you have him standin' right."

"He's made right," Danny said, turning to Man o' War. "They'd be blind if they didn't see it."

It was funny, he thought. Here he had planned not to show

Man o' War to his best advantage so that perhaps he wouldn't
be sold. And yet it would hurt him very much if people didn't
see the beauty and fine qualities of his colt. He was a mixed-up
kid.

"Red's a fine yearling, all right," the old man agreed.
"Maybe the best of the lot from the way he ran in pasture."

"But the buyers won't know how fast he can go."

"No, but they'll see he's bred right. An' they'll see how well
he fits together. They'll start with his head. It's not too big or
too small for the rest of him."

"And his eyes are large and clear with a strong look of bold-
ness," Danny said. "That's important."

The old man nodded. "Spaced wide apart, that means he's
smart," he said. "No bulges between 'em, either. Keen and
bold, that's Red."

"And his neck is right . . . the right length, the right proportion," Danny went on, proud of his colt.

"His shoulder is good, too. They'll look for that next."

Danny ran his hand over the angle of the shoulder blade. "It
slopes the way it should, from point of shoulder to middle of
withers. That's why he has that long, swinging stride in pasture."

"Maybe so, Danny. An' see how deep he is through the
chest. Plenty of room for lungs as well as heart."

Danny put his arms around his colt. "There's nothing small
about him. His heart is as big as the rest of him. He's going to
make a racehorse. I'm sure of it."

The old man shook his shaggy gray head. "Nothin's sure in
this business, Danny-boy," he said. "Some of the best runnin'
horses I've seen looked like nags. That's why a lot of folks here
will be buyin' colts on bloodlines only. They won't care what a
colt looks like jus' as long as he comes from a good family on
each side."

Danny shrugged his shoulders. "I guess they got to start somewhere," he said.

The old man glanced at his big gold watch. "It's near eight o'clock and jus' about time for them to look us over. Mind your business now, Danny. An' remember what I said. Don't you go showin' this colt in the stall to anyone. You take him out an' stand him right. That way you be as proud as he is."

The last racehorse had taken his morning exercise on the tobacco-brown racing strip at Saratoga, and the last breakfast had been served on the clubhouse veranda. It was the time between morning works and the first race on the afternoon program. It was the time for people to inspect the sales yearlings and make important decisions.

Danny had Man o' War ready for inspection. Oh, he didn't have his colt as groomed and polished as he could have done. But he had put the catalog hip number on Man o' War so people would know what yearling they were looking at. That was enough. He was going to display his colt just so he would be appreciated, not sold. There was a big difference between the two, he told himself.

Danny looked out of the stall and saw that the tree-shaded benches were already crowded with people who were paying little attention to one another. Their eyes were solely for the yearlings and the sales catalogs they held in their laps. Before long some of them would ask to see Man o' War; only then would he take the big colt from his stall.

Meanwhile, he studied these would-be purchasers of Man o' War, perhaps as closely as they examined the yearlings parading before them. He saw one old lady sitting by herself and reading her catalog intently through large horn-rimmed glasses. Her lips moved silently, and every now and then she looked up to study the yearlings passing before her. She would then turn back to her catalog and make a pencil mark on the page. Nearby others were doing the same thing, while still others ignored the benches and walked beneath the green shade trees examining yearlings at their leisure.

The crowd swelled with every passing moment, getting a little noisier but not pushier. Everything was being done in an easy manner. There was no hurry. This was Saratoga.

Danny, too, found himself caught in the slow, leisurely pace. He was reminded of the war going on by the number of uniforms in evidence, but some men were still dressed in dinner clothes from the night before and others, men and women alike, wore tweeds and silks. He knew that all these people were trying to forget, if only for a little while, the fighting being waged overseas. So, perhaps more than ever before, they were absorbed in the fascinating business of looking at young horses and trying to decide on their potential as racehorses. They were slow about it because they did not want this time to slip by too fast. For a few hours all could escape into the past and a world at peace. Here was quiet, good living, and easy-going charm. And there was no better way to start the day off than by looking at yearlings, with an afternoon of racing still to come.

Danny understood. And he watched many of the consignors of yearlings, too, go along with the carefree life instilled by Saratoga's natural charm. The sellers were doing everything possible to attract attention to their yearlings, some having large barbecues alongside their barns with grooms in white aprons cooking lamb and all the trimmings over small log fires.

Danny noted that the meat was disappearing faster than it took to cook it. There was no doubt that the barbecues were a success, but whether or not they would sell yearlings was something else again.

He turned back to Man o' War. "They're going after buyers

every way they can, Red," he said. "Everybody but us. We're sitting tight. Let them come to us."

Again he looked outside the stall. There was a crowd milling nearby and it was only a matter of moments before they would ask to see Man o' War. He studied these prospective buyers of his colt closely as they walked quietly around the yearlings in the adjacent stable.

Some of the men were squatting while inspecting the colts. Why? Danny wondered. Their reasons must be known only to themselves, for there was nothing they couldn't see from an upright position. The women in the crowd remained stately, erect, but their eyes were as knowing as the men's. Danny knew from what he had heard that this year the women were giving the men a lively tussle in the buying and selling of colts. Since he worked for Mrs. Kane, this had come as no great surprise to Danny. He had a lot of respect for women *who understood horses*. But at the same time he couldn't see Man o' War as anything but a man's horse.

It was a quiet crowd considering the large number of people, Danny decided. They exchanged greetings with one another but their eyes did not leave the yearlings for very long. It was all business, as if every single one of them was looking for the colt that would turn out to be the finest of the sale.

Not that the best horse would be bought for the highest dollar, Danny knew. Not by any means. Everybody realized that many a colt sold for some sensational price like fifty thousand dollars very often never reached the racetrack. No, the most successful colts sold in the middle range, around five to twenty thousand dollars.

People waited patiently for others ahead of them to finish examining a colt and then go on to the next one. They were all very polite, Danny noted, and very thorough, too. They

seemed to have a set pattern of inspection and it seldom
seemed to vary.

Those who were not afraid of horses—and this included the
women—stooped to pass their hands slowly and carefully over
the knees of each horse. Then they went to the off side of the
colt, stopped abruptly, and went back to check the forelegs
again before returning to where they had left off. Usually they
shook their heads on the chance of scaring off anyone else who
might be interested in a colt they liked. Finally they stood behind the horse to view his hindquarters. They would then ask
the groom to move the colt and very often would grunt as he
went forward. They would grunt again when the colt was
stopped in the same position as before. Their inspection would
end by their writing a short note in the margin of the catalog
opposite the colt's pedigree. Then they would pass on to the
next horse, their faces devoid of expression and without utter-
ing a word of comment, to begin all over again.

Danny waited for them to come to him. He could be as patient as anyone else. Besides, he was almost certain no one
would see the true greatness of his colt. Trainers and owners
might protest about fat yearlings, but they were not very apt to
buy skinny ones. And Red was certainly skinny compared to
the others. They'd be suspicious of such a thin yearling, sus-
pecting him of being a poor eater, which no one wanted in his
racing stable ... or of being sickly ... or neglected ... or
poorly raised and managed. There were lots of reasons they
might not like Man o' War.

His pedigree, too, could give cause for some concern, Danny
decided hopefully. Heredity was an all-important factor at the
sales, and if Man o' War had inherited his sire's and grandsire's temperament he would be almost useless on the racetrack. He must have not only their speed but a willingness to

use it, and Fair Play and Hastings had never possessed that necessary attribute.

Danny smiled to himself. He felt that he alone knew that Man o' War *did* have the competitive drive his sire and grandsire lacked. He had spent enough hours with Red in pasture to know. But the buyers wouldn't know. They had only bloodlines and conformation on which to judge Man o' War.

"Lead him out of the stall, please," someone said.

The first of the prospective buyers had reached them. Now it had begun and would continue until Man o' War entered the sales ring on Saturday night. "Let's go, fellow," he said quietly. Man o' War followed him. There was nothing impatient or unruly about him, Danny noted. He would take all this in his easy stride.

Danny led Man o' War out into the open where the people could get a good look at him. He brought him to a stop on hard, level ground where he could stand well balanced. He stood away from him, holding the shank lightly but firmly. He showed Man o' War to his best advantage because he was proud of his horse, not because he wanted him to be sold. He could have done it no other way despite the fact that he had not rubbed any gloss in the red, sunburned coat.

The inspection of Man o' War began, and during the hours that followed, Danny listened to the comments of some of the buyers, usually muttered to themselves or to a close companion. More often than not they were unfavorable. Not that such criticism was their true opinion of Man o' War, Danny knew, for they'd do anything to discourage others from bidding on a colt they liked.

"He's long in the middle, too long for the way I like them," one said.

"But he just *might* stay in spite of it," a companion mumbled in reply. "His quarters are good and muscular, right down through the thigh and gaskin. Some say the propelling power comes from there. I wouldn't know."

And later someone else said, "His cannons are too short. I like them long."

"But long cannons don't necessarily mean a long stride," another answered.

"Maybe not, but I'll still take them *long*."

"He has straight hind legs with height over the quarters same as at the withers. Might mean an extra long-striding horse in spite of what you say."

The other snorted. "I don't like them straight up front. I prefer them a little bent over at the knees. That way the horse is more likely to stay sound."

Danny listened, thinking, *You can't please them all*. No horse can.

"His pasterns aren't the right angle either. They won't support his weight the way they should."

Some people picked up the big colt's foot, and Danny watched them examine it closely. Man o' War had good feet and he knew how important it was, especially the frog. It was this spongelike rubber cushion that absorbed the first terrific shock of a thousand-pound horse galloping over a hard surface at high speed. To Danny the more frog, the more cushion. It was as simple as that.

But one man shook his head vigorously and said, "His feet are too narrow. They'll tend to go sore, spreading at the quarters. Might even result in a broken bone."

Danny had a hard time keeping still. Man o' War's feet weren't narrow at all!

"Watch out," he said as the man put down the colt's hind leg. "You're going to get kicked." He was glad when they went on to the next horse.

For a long while those who examined Man o' War kept their opinion of the colt to themselves. Then an old woman, who looked more like someone's grandmother than a buyer of yearlings, whispered to her male companion. "He has wide hips, which appeals to me. They're like a strong man with wide shoulders. They give a horse more power."

She glanced up to find Danny listening to her. "Move him, son," she said quietly. "On the dirt, not the grass."

Danny walked Man o' War down the row and back. He found the old lady examining the colt's hoofprints in the soft dirt.

"He overstrides a little," she whispered. "His hind feet extend beyond his front feet. I like to see a colt that reaches out with a good stride in his hind legs. And he has a swinging walk. He might be the one, Fred."

"I wouldn't know," the man said. "You're the expert."

Danny noted that when the old lady had finished her inspection of Man o' War, she was shaking her head in disapproval, just as almost everybody else had done. He wondered if she thought she was fooling anyone.

It went on like that for the rest of the morning.

"His neck is a little too short for me. He'll tire when he tries to go a distance," one man said.

"The neck doesn't affect a horse's running ability," another disagreed. "No more than a Roman nose does or even a swayback. And I don't like to see them any more than you do. Now the throat and jaw are something else again. There's got to be ample room for the windpipe or a horse chokes up while racing. The same goes for his nostrils. They must be large enough so he can inhale and exhale easily while running."

The other shrugged his shoulders. "You're not going to find the perfect horse anywhere, and some of the *almost* perfect ones can't run much."

"That's right. You have to give and take a little here and there."

They moved on to the next colt.

It was near noontime, and the sales area was thinning out, when a trainer Danny had seen at Nursery Stud came to inspect the stable's yearlings. It was Louis Feustel, and with him were a big elderly man and a woman. They approached Man o' War, Feustel nodding as he recognized Danny but giving all his attention to the colt.

The young trainer glanced around as if to make sure no one was within hearing distance and then said, "This is a good colt, Mr. Riddle."

The big man towering above him shrugged his shoulders. "I rather like the looks of him, too, Louis. He's big-boned, big-framed, everything necessary to make a good hunter, which I know something about. But a racehorse?"

Feustel nodded. "I think so, sir."

"But he's so tall and gangling, Louis," the lady said. "A little on the ungainly side."

"His condition isn't as fine as some of the others in the Belmont consignment," Feustel admitted. "But he's in much better shape than when I saw him at the farm."

"You rejected him then," Mr. Riddle recalled.

"Not actually," the trainer said. "It's true I liked some of the others better, and I certainly didn't recommend buying the whole lot, as I told you. But I'd still like to see you buy a Fair Play colt, and this one may be a good one."

"He's bred right," Mr. Riddle said. "No doubt about that. I suppose we could use him for a hunter if he didn't work out on the racecourse. As I said, he has the bone and frame for it."

"He's so thin I almost feel sorry for him," Mrs. Riddle said, fondly touching the big colt.

Louis Feustel smiled. "He's not hog-fat like most of these other yearlings, ma'am," he said. "But he's in sound physical shape and in medium flesh, the way I like them."

Mrs. Riddle nodded and turned to her husband. "I would go by Louis's decision," she said. "If he recommends that you buy him, do it. If he doesn't, don't. It's as simple as that, since he's the one who will be doing the training."

Mr. Riddle didn't take his eyes off Man o' War. "I still don't want to go too high just for a hunter prospect. What do you think he'll sell for, Louis?"

The trainer shrugged his thin shoulders. "It's hard to say, Mr. Riddle. No amount of experience makes anything certain in judging what a yearling will amount to or what he'll bring in the sales ring. But my guess is that this one won't go too high. He's pretty thin for most buyers, as Mrs. Riddle has pointed out, and he's got a full sister named Masda who's a fast racer but hard to handle. It's the Hastings coming out. That might scare off the buyers."

"And perhaps us, too," Mr. Riddle said, consulting his catalog. "Major Belmont is one of the best breeders in the country and I aim to get one of his colts anyway. There are a couple I like better than this one."

"I do, too," Feustel admitted. "And so do a lot of other people. They'll sell high."

"I like Fair Gain," Mr. Riddle said.

"And Richelieu and Rouleau," Feustel added. "All of them by foreign sires, and that's what buyers seem to like right now. You won't get any of them cheap, Mr. Riddle, even with a war going on."

They all stepped away from Man o' War, and Danny thought they were going on. Then Mr. Riddle turned back to the colt, his eyes moving over him again. Finally the big man

said, "Let's watch for this one, anyway. He's well worth considering on bloodlines alone, and I'll go a thousand or two for
him."

Louis Feustel patted the colt's neck. "I think we should go
higher than that, if we have to," he said quietly.

Mr. Riddle shrugged his shoulders, and it was his wife who
had the last word. "If Louis says buy, when the time comes, I'd
buy," she repeated her advice quietly.

Danny watched them as they went on to the next barn,
shaking their heads in disapproval of Man o' War. But he had
a gnawing feeling in his stomach that he had just seen the new
owners of his colt. He wouldn't have felt that way if it hadn't
been for Mrs. Riddle; when a woman entered a battle for anything, she usually didn't let go. And it seemed to him that
Mrs. Riddle wanted Man o' War. Maybe it was because she
felt sorry for him! That would be a laugh, a real laugh . . . on
himself.

Danny led the big colt back to his stall, and there he gently
ran a hand over the rough, sunburned coat. "Maybe I should
have spent more time rubbing you," he said, "and had you all
sleek and polished. But how was I to know she was coming
along?"

Sold!

9

Saturday, August 17, found the Nursery Stud yearlings ready to step into the sales ring. Danny watched the crowd gather beneath the ancient trees of the paddock, noting that the women, dressed in flowing silks and wide-brimmed hats, seemed as numerous as the men. He shook his head in dismay. There was no telling where their colts might end up, with so many women taking part in the bidding!

Danny stood at Man o' War's head, waiting for the Nursery Stud yearlings to be called into the ring. He held his colt close, scared but excited, too.

The people seemed nervous despite their gay chatter and laughter. They were out to buy colts that might win the great classic races to come. Famous trainers as well as famous jockeys were here, all enjoying their popularity, and ready to give new owners the benefit of their vast experience and knowledge of young horses.

The sale had already started, with the first consignment of yearlings entering the ring one at a time. Danny listened to the

chant of the auctioneer for a while and then turned to Fair
Gain's caretaker standing close by. "It won't be long," he said
quietly.

The old groom nodded his gray, cropped head. "Sure
'nough, Danny. That man's got rhythm, boy, real rhythm.
He'll sell our colts good."

Once more Danny listened to the musical singsong chant of
the auctioneer as he got a bid of nine thousand dollars on a
sleek bay colt.

"*Yeah!* I got nine, nine, nine. Who'll go ten, ten, ten? I
want ten, ten, ten. Give me ten, ten, ten."

Danny said, "They're bidding high prices after all, war or no
war."

"There's keen comp'tition out there, Danny-boy," the old
man said, his eyes never leaving the ring. "No one's goin' to
get colts cheap like maybe they thought."

The bay colt was bouncing around the ring on his toes. He
was a handsome, well-grown individual who wasn't going to
take anything quietly. He kicked out with his hind legs, almost
knocking the gavel out of the auctioneer's hand. Everyone
laughed, and the bidding jumped quickly to nine thousand five
hundred dollars.

"They sho like a colt with spunk," the old groom told
Danny, "an' this one's got plenty."

Danny watched the auctioneer as the man sought still
higher bids for the bay colt. It was no easy job selling yearlings,
he knew. The auctioneer had to please both the buyer and the
seller. He had to be nice to everybody, keep everything above-
board, and try to be fair. Such a job required the skill of a
horseman, the acumen of a businessman, the tact of a diplo-
mat, and the zeal of an evangelist. And this auctioneer, Danny
decided, was one of the best.

". . . I got five, five, five, ninety-five," the singsong chant went on. "Make it ten, ten. I want ten, ten, ten. Make it ten, ten, ten." Suddenly he stopped.

For a moment the area was quiet. Then the auctioneer said, "Now listen heah, folks. You all know that nine thousand five hundred dollars isn't much to bid for this heah colt." Although he spoke to more than five hundred people, his words were meant for the two lone bidders who remained in competition for the bay colt.

He singled out one of them, a man sitting in the back, and said, "Mr. Riddle, you're not going to let Mr. McClelland get this heah colt, are you? You went up to ninety-four. Will you make it an even ten thousand? That's not much money for this heah colt. You just look at him now."

Danny was standing a short distance away from the Riddle party. He saw Mr. Riddle, seated between Louis Feustel and Mrs. Riddle, shift uneasily in his seat. Then Mr. Riddle glanced at his trainer, faced front again, and raised six fingers.

Once again the auctioneer's chant claimed the area. "I got six, six, ninety-six. I want ten, ten . . ." He was looking at Mr. McClelland now. ". . . give me ten."

Mr. McClelland nodded.

"*Yeah!* I got ten thousand dollars. Make it five, ten-five. I want five, ten-five. Make it five, five, five . . ."

Once more the auctioneer's gaze swept to Mr. Riddle, who shook his head. He would go no higher.

The auctioneer's eyes traveled over the crowd, seeking a bidder who might keep this colt in the ring long enough to bring a still higher price. "All done?" he asked finally. "Are you all done at ten thousand?" He waited a moment more and then his gavel came down hard on the wooden platform.

"Sold to Mr. McClelland for ten thousand dollars."

Danny, along with everyone else, relaxed. But he kept his eyes on the bay colt, who was now refusing to leave the ring. He wouldn't be led out. He wouldn't back out. One of the ring attendants picked up a broom and whacked him over the rump. This unexpected tactic worked and the colt left the ring quickly.

Another yearling was being led into the ring, but for the moment Danny wasn't interested. So he moved Man o' War to a shady spot beneath the elm and maple trees, stopping just in back of the Riddle party. He didn't mean to listen to their conversation but snatches of it reached him.

"I'm sorry we lost that colt," Mr. Riddle said.

"Ten thousand was too much to pay for him," Louis Feustel replied.

"I think so, too. But I would like to buy about twelve colts here, and he was a good one."

"Better wait and see how they go," his trainer cautioned. "There will be other sales or we can buy privately."

Danny watched Mr. Riddle glance uneasily at his wife. There was no doubt that he was nervous, this being his first experience at the auction ring.

Louis Feustel said, "Remember to keep your eyes on the auctioneer and your face closed. Don't ever look at those bidding against you. Don't even look at me or Mrs. Riddle."

"I won't," Mr. Riddle promised.

The bidding began again with a black colt in the ring.

"I like this one," Feustel said without turning his head.

The bidding reached nine thousand dollars quickly, then seemed to stall for keeps. Danny watched Mr. Riddle try to conceal his anxiety, for he had made the last bid. But the auctioneer had no intention of letting the black colt go yet. He got busy and tugged the bidding, one hundred dollars at a time, to

SOLD! 81

fourteen thousand five hundred dollars. Mr. Riddle had long since dropped out when the auctioneer's gavel fell.

"Sold to Commander Ross for fourteen thousand five hundred dollars!"

"Too high," Feustel said again and Mr. Riddle nodded in agreement.

The bidding on the next five yearlings was slow and low, none selling for over three thousand dollars. Mr. Riddle didn't bid on any of them.

Danny was about to move away when he heard Louis Feustel say, "This next colt will get a good play from the buyers, but get him if you can. He's probably the best in the sale."

One of the handsomest colts Danny had ever seen entered the ring. He was a golden chestnut with brilliant white markings. His body was small compared to Man o' War's, but very compact and fully made.

There was a hushed silence over the area as the colt strode around the ring, every stride under marvelous control. There was no doubt that the buyers were very impressed with him.

"The stable talk is that he's as good as he looks," Feustel said. "He possesses immense speed. With that body and those legs he'll be able to whirl and get away, that's for sure."

"I took a great fancy to him earlier," Mr. Riddle said. "But I can't bid, Louis. Mrs. Jeffords told me she's going after him. I won't bid against her."

Danny saw Mrs. Riddle glance up from her catalog. "Just because she's my niece is no reason not to bid, Sam, if you like him that much," she told her husband.

Mr. Riddle shook his head adamantly. "No," he said. "She'll have a hard enough time getting him as is."

Danny turned his gaze back to the golden colt in the ring. He was close-coupled and short-legged. He'd leave the barrier fast, just as Feustel had said. But would he be able to stay? Did he have the substance to carry him over a distance race?

It was plain that the buyers thought so as soon as the bidding started. There was a clatter of bids from all sides of the area, and the flashy colt was up to ten thousand dollars in a twinkling. The tempo slowed after that figure was reached, but the auctioneer was not to be denied.

He stopped his singsong chant and looked over the large audience. The area was hushed and he had no intention of breaking the silence. It was the right moment to let them study this colt, perhaps to envision him in the winner's circle, a triumphant champion! There was no doubt that this colt was the darling of the sale, all right. He couldn't be prettier; that helped a lot in selling the ladies present. And he had the conformation to interest the professional horsemen as well. The combination was unbeatable, and the auctioneer had no intention of selling this colt yet.

His roving eyes found Mrs. Jeffords. She wanted that golden chestnut bad and so did a couple of other ladies in the audience, God bless them. He'd concentrate on this feminine rivalry a few moments. He smiled at Mrs. Jeffords, held her gaze a moment, and then, when she refused to increase the bid of ten thousand dollars, went on to Mrs. Riddle.

He would have liked to get her bidding on this colt, too. She and her husband were impressed with him, and they still hadn't bought a colt. But she shook her head, and he decided it was because she wouldn't bid against her niece, Mrs. Jeffords. He went on to the other ladies, his eyes asking for a bid over ten thousand, but none of them responded.

Finally he turned to the men without making any attempt to break the almost reverent silence. One ear was cocked for a sound from the rear of the platform. There was a bidder seated behind him, unseen by most of the audience, who had made the last bid. The man would go higher if necessary, and it was his job to see that he did.

The auctioneer decided it was time to say something. "Now, folks, you all listen to me," he told the crowd. "Heah we have what could be the very finest colt in this sale. He was bred in England. He's by Sweeper II out of Zuna by Hamburg. An' if those bloodlines aren't enough to make you all want him, just take a good look at him. You won't find a better-made colt in your lifetime! Yes, sir, *he could be the one,* folks. But I'll let you in on a little secret. No one's goin' to get this heah colt for no ten thousand dollars. He's too much colt for that price. Too many of you folks want him. So you're going to have to open up your wallets. But wait . . . wait now. Before you do, take another look at this heah colt. Study him; see for yourself there's not goin' to be another like him in this sale."

That was enough to say for now, the auctioneer decided. Let them look at this colt a few moments more. He had plenty of time and patience. He had said and heard all this before, many times. Maybe this Sweeper colt would prove to be worth ten thousand dollars and a lot more on the racetrack. But the chances were just as good that he wouldn't be worth a plugged nickel. No one could tell much about the racing prospects of a yearling.

The auctioneer watched the golden colt as it moved about the ring with all the fluid grace of a jungle cat. It wasn't up to him to judge if this colt would be the one or not. For all he knew he might have already sold next year's champion for a couple thousand dollars or even less. It had happened often enough before. His job was to get the highest bids he could on each and every yearling. And there was keen competition for this colt. He should be able to get more than ten thousand dollars for him.

"All right, folks," he said finally. "Heah we go again. We're goin' to sell this good colt right now an' you all better be on your toes or he'll get away from you. I got ten thousand dollars. I want eleven, eleven. Give me eleven. . . ." His eyes found Mrs. Jeffords, who was speaking to her husband without turning her head. Then he saw Mr. Jeffords raise five fingers.

"Yeah! I got ten thousand, five hundred dollars. Give me eleven. I want eleven. Give me eleven. . . ." His cocked ear caught the bid from the man seated behind him.

"Yeah! I got eleven thousand dollars. Give me twelve, twelve. I want twelve. . . ."

From far in the back, an old lady seated beneath an elm tree nodded her head.

"Yeah! I got twelve thousand dollars. I want thirteen. Give me thirteen, thirteen. . . ."

His eyes had shifted quickly to Mrs. Jeffords. Now they were on their way, a thousand at a time; with the sky the limit! "Give me thirteen, thirteen, thirteen. . . ." He waited for her or her husband to nod but he also listened for the voice from behind the platform.

Finally he got the higher bid from Mrs. Jeffords. "*Yeah!* I got thirteen thousand dollars. Give me fourteen, fourteen. . . ." He turned to the old lady again, but she was through. He listened for the voice behind him, and the bid came just as he'd known it would.

"Yeah! I got fourteen thousand dollars. I want fifteen, fifteen." He turned back to Mrs. Jeffords.

She was speaking to her husband again. Finally, almost reluctantly, Mr. Jeffords nodded.

"*Yeah!* I got fifteen thousand dollars." He knew Mr. and Mrs. Jeffords were almost through with the bidding. "I want sixteen, sixteen." He turned completely around to the man behind him, the only one left who could keep this colt in the ring. But all he got was a vigorous shake of the head. Still he waited, pleading for a higher bid. "Give me a raise of five hundred dollars then, just five hundred dollars. Don't let him get away from you."

It was obvious that the man wanted the colt but fifteen thousand dollars had been his limit. He shifted uneasily in his seat and wiped his face with a large handkerchief. When he took it away he nodded, then rose and left his seat. He had finished bidding.

"*Yeah!*" the auctioneer called. "I got fifteen thousand five hundred dollars. I want sixteen, sixteen. Give me sixteen. I want sixteen." He looked at Mrs. Jeffords to see if she would raise the bid one final time. She had no intention of losing this colt, he knew. She said something to her husband and the raise in bid came. It was only a hundred dollars but it was enough to buy the colt.

"*Yeah!* I got fifteen thousand, six hundred dollars! Are you all done?" His gaze swept around the area, missing no one. "Doesn't anybody else want this grand colt before I sell him?"

The bid was the highest he'd gotten for any colt in the sale, and he was satisfied. He banged his gavel. "Sold to Mr. Jeffords for fifteen thousand, six hundred dollars." But his eyes and smile were for Mrs. Jeffords, for he knew that the golden colt was really hers.

Danny listened to the auctioneer's gavel fall and he knew the time had come for the Nursery Stud yearlings to be sold. His stomach tightened. He watched Fair Gain being led into the ring. He listened to the rustle of catalog pages and the hum of voices. Fair Gain was considered by many to be the top colt in the Belmont consignment. He would not go cheap.

A few moments later Danny heard the opening bid of five thousand dollars and knew how right he was. Perhaps this colt would go for an even higher price than the one Mr. and Mrs. Jeffords had bought. His gaze shifted to Mr. Riddle, who was nodding his head at the auctioneer.

The bidding moved swiftly to ten thousand dollars, then Mr. Riddle raised it to eleven thousand.

Danny overheard Louis Feustel say, "Too high for this colt."

Mr. Riddle answered, "That's my limit. I won't go higher."

The bidding went on without Mr. Riddle, and finally the last bid was made. The auctioneer brought down the gavel. "Sold to Mr. Widener for fourteen thousand dollars," he announced.

It was the second highest price of the sale and a good start for the Nursery Stud yearlings. The auctioneer was satisfied with his work. He glanced at the Riddle party, knowing they had intended to buy quite a few yearlings for their new stable. But while Mr. Riddle had been an active bidder, he still hadn't taken a single one from the ring. Perhaps it would be the next colt.

"Mr. Riddle," he called, "are you sure you can see from way back there?"

"Yes, we can see all right," Mr. Riddle answered, "but we would like to get a little closer to the front if possible."

"Come along," the auctioneer said.

Danny moved forward at the same time, for his colt was next in the ring. He felt as if the ground were breaking away from him and he was falling into a great, black abyss.

The auctioneer watched the boy and the yearling colt step into the ring. For a few seconds he looked more at the boy than at the colt. That was a very strange thing for him to do, he decided. But he thought the boy was sick; his eyes were glazed and he moved as if his legs were made of wood. He hardly seemed to know where he was or what he was doing. And yet the colt was under control, moving lightly beside him.

The auctioneer shrugged his shoulders, glanced at the hip number on the colt, then at his catalog. "Heah's a good one, folks," he said, "a real good one by Fair Play out of Mahubah by Rock Sand."

He studied the colt for the first time, wondering why he seemed to be in such poor sales shape. It was not easy to sell a thin yearling, for bidders were far too suspicious of such a colt. But this one was proud and spirited despite his sales condition. He looked as if he thought he owned the world.

Man o' War. That was a powerful name for a colt. He liked yearlings with good names. There was something nondescript about referring to a yearling solely by its hip number, which was the usual case. He just might have something here to work on. He just might.

The auctioneer decided not to open the bidding right away. Give the buyers a chance to look at this colt a little longer. He was becoming a bit more impressive as he strode around the ring. If the buyers studied him closely, they might see more than his roughness.

The auctioneer also studied the big colt, looking for the best angle on which to sell this yearling. It appeared to him that Man o' War might well be a horseman's horse. Although he was not as sleek and shining as those that had preceded him, he was beautiful to see to those who knew horseflesh. His stride was free, rangy, and imperative. His head was high and his proportions magnificent.

The colt came to a sudden stop in the center of the ring but did not pull the shank away from the boy's hand. He was interested in the crowd and looked confident, too. His ears were set forward and his nostrils distended as if the better to sniff the scent of humans. In that moment he was a picture to behold, and it seemed to the auctioneer that every horseman in the crowd would want him. It was a good time to start the bidding.

"Listen heah, folks," he began, *"this could be the one.* You all know there's no finer breeder in the country than Major Belmont, and this heah colt represents his very best. This is Man o' War, a son of the great Fair Play by Hastings and out of the fine mare Mahubah by Rock Sand. You all know you just can't get better breeding than that."

He paused a moment, his eyes going over the crowd. Perhaps he shouldn't have opened that way, he decided quickly. Too many of the horsemen present knew that such a mating had already produced Masda, this colt's full sister, and that she was a flighty one for all her blazing speed. It was the Hastings in her. She was too nervous and excitable to make a racehorse, and Belmont had gotten rid of her.

It might be best to concentrate on what the buyers could see in the ring. "Take a good look at this heah colt, folks," he went on. "You won't find a better-boned individual than this one, no sir. He's strong. He's rugged. He'll take to training and hold his flesh under work. There's no extra fat to take off this heah colt, folks. He's ready to go! Now you all give me what he's worth, heah? Who'll open at five thousand dollars? I want five, five, give me five . . ."

The singsong chant swept through the area, but there was no response from the buyers. The auctioneer's eyes as well as his voice sought bids from the professional horsemen in the crowd. One by one they shook their heads. Perhaps they were recalling only too well the Hastings blood in this colt. Or perhaps it was his thinness and roughness. The auctioneer did not know.

Finally he found a trainer who held up one finger. Having no choice, he took the bid. "I got one thousand dollars," he said without enthusiasm. "Give me two, two, two. I want two. Give me two."

Again he pleaded with the professional horsemen to raise the bid. But he found only a few who showed any particular interest in this colt. The bidding went up a hundred dollars at a time and stopped completely at two thousand dollars. Should he let him go at that price? he wondered. He must have been wrong. Man o' War hadn't proved to be a horseman's horse after all.

He turned to those buyers in the crowd who still might be interested in the colt as a hunter. Sometimes people paid good prices for hunting prospects, and this might be such a case. Mr. Riddle was interested in the colt, and so was Mr. Gerry. He decided to concentrate on them, for he should get more than two thousand dollars for this big colt.

His searching gaze found Mr. Gerry, who raised five fingers.

"Yeah! I got two thousand five hundred. I want three thousand. Give me three." He got a nod from Mr. Riddle. "I got three, three. Give me four. I want four thousand." Back to Mr. Gerry and a nod. "*Yeah!* I got four thousand dollars. I want five. Give me five, five. . . ."

This was a little better, the auctioneer decided without stopping his chant. Whatever their reasons, these two gentlemen wanted the colt, and such rivalry was one way to get high bids for yearlings. The ladies in both parties were helping too, for they were talking to their husbands. God bless them again. If it hadn't been for Mrs. Jeffords, he'd never have gotten fifteen thousand six hundred for that Sweeper colt.

"I got four, four, four. Give me five. I want five." *Come on, Mr. Riddle,* he urged beneath his chant. *Give a little. Listen to your wife. She has your ear. And listen to Louis Feustel, too. It looks to me like he thinks you should go to five thousand dollars.*

Finally the bid came from Mr. Riddle but only for one hundred dollars more. The auctioneer was disappointed but he took it quickly to keep things going. "I got four thousand one hundred dollars." He turned back to Mr. Gerry. "Give me four thousand five hundred dollars, won't you?" he pleaded before swinging back into his chant. "I want five, forty-five. Give me five, five, five, forty-five."

Finally, after a long while, he got the nod. The tempo had slowed down and he was afraid Mr. Gerry had made his last bid. Only Mr. Riddle was left.

"I got four thousand five hundred dollars. I want five thousand. Give me five, I want five. Give me five . . ."

He caught Mr. Riddle glancing at *Mrs.* Gerry and scowling. His poise seemed to have left him for a moment, and he was apparently annoyed at the obvious part the women were playing in the bidding. His own wife, too, was talking to him again.

The auctioneer decided not to press matters for a little while. Give the women a chance to talk to their husbands, that was the order of the moment. He stopped his chant and turned to the big colt in the ring.

Man o' War was still striding about the circle, his shank held by the young boy. The boy seemed very attached to the colt, for he kept his free hand on him all the time, almost comforting him. It must be tough to become attached to a colt and then lose him in the sales ring, the auctioneer decided. Funny, he'd never thought of that until now. But this kid sort of brought it out of him. All the others handling the colts had been old men. They were hardened, used to it.

He sure was a handsome colt, all right. The more you looked

at him, the better you liked what you saw. Not often did one come along with bone structure like that. Maybe he should bring more than five thousand dollars. But even that wasn't a bad price. Only a few would sell higher, and as things were going, the average price per colt wouldn't be much over a thousand dollars.

This one might make everyone connected with him famous. And then again he might be a dud. No one knew. It was only human for people to see marks of greatness in a colt *after* he'd become great. But usually the facts didn't bear them out at the time of the sale. Take this colt. It was like pulling teeth to get the bid up to where it was.

"I got four thousand five hundred dollars," he began again, his eyes finding Mr. Riddle. "Won't you make it an even five thousand?"

He studied the gentleman's eyes. It was obvious that Mr. Riddle wanted this colt but was annoyed that the price had gone up as high as it had. The auctioneer waited a moment more, for he was almost certain he'd get a raise in bid from him. Hadn't Mr. Riddle gone up to over ten thousand dollars for several other colts, only to lose them? Therefore, if he *really* wanted this colt he shouldn't object to paying five thousand.

"I want five, five. Give me five," his chant started all over again. "Give me five. I want five."

Louis Feustel was prodding Mr. Riddle, too. Finally the bid came, but only for two hundred dollars more.

The auctioneer grunted beneath breaths. As he'd said, it was like pulling teeth. "I got four thousand seven hundred dollars. I want five thousand. Give me five. I want five, five. Give me five." Back to Mr. Gerry, and he got a raised bid of two hundred dollars more.

"*Yeah!* I got four thousand nine hundred dollars. *Now* give me five thousand. I want five, five. Give me five."

Quickly he turned back to Mr. Riddle. Could he get a raise from him? Mr. Riddle was very annoyed, no doubt about it. He seemed reluctant to go any higher despite Feustel's prodding that the colt was worth the price being asked. The auctioneer's gaze shifted to Mrs. Riddle. Only she might be able to convince her husband to go higher. There, she had his ear.

Without interrupting his chant, he waited for her to finish talking to Mr. Riddle. Then, finally, after what seemed a long while the bid came, reluctantly, almost resignedly.

"*Yeah!* I got five thousand dollars. I want five hundred more. Give me five thousand five hundred dollars. I want five. Give me five." He had turned back to Mr. Gerry, expecting and getting a vigorous shake of the gentleman's head. Mr. Gerry was done. But then he felt that way himself. He had spent enough time selling this colt with so many others still to come.

"All done?" he asked, his eyes sweeping the area. There was complete silence, and his gavel fell solidly against the wood of the platform. "Sold to Mr. Riddle for five thousand dollars."

He was turning back to his sales catalog when the boy led the big colt past him. *Was he mistaken or was the boy actually crying?*

Demon!

10

The race meeting at Saratoga ended but many of the yearlings purchased at the sales stayed on to be broken and prepared for their appearances as two-year-olds. Man o' War was among them.

No longer was the paddock an outdoor reading room with people occupying the benches and chairs beneath the elms and maples, silently studying their sales catalogs. Trainers and owners were still absorbed in the study of yearlings but in a different way. The paperwork had ended. No longer was there need for small neat figures and notes on catalog margins opposite a yearling's pedigree. Now the chips were down and the horsemen were girded for action, ready to find out the racing possibilities of the youngsters they had bought.

It was early in the morning and the sun filtered through the trees of the green and shaded acres. The sky was a shattering blue, festooned with big flat-bottomed puffs of white clouds. The tobacco-brown racing strip was empty, as were the stands. But the bright geraniums and petunias still nodded gently in the veranda window boxes, and the rosebushes about the course bloomed as full as ever. The grace and beauty that was Saratoga still remained even though the sprawling crowd had gone.

The old men employed by Nursery Stud gathered together their buckets and sponges and currycombs and prepared to depart for home. But Danny had no intention of leaving with them. He wasn't going to walk off as if Man o' War meant nothing to him.

So he stayed in the stall beside Man o' War, waiting for Louis Feustel to come and take him to the Riddle stable. Finally the trainer entered.

"Hello again," Feustel said, his eyes only for the Fair Play colt Mr. Riddle had bought.

"I'd like to stay with him," Danny said. It was now or never. "You got a job for me?"

"What's he like to be around?" Feustel never took his eyes from Man o' War as he left the boy's question unanswered.

"He's nice and he's smart," Danny said quietly. "But don't ever try to force him or you'll come out second best every time. Ask him and he'll do what you want. Push him and it's all off."

"You mean he's high-spirited without being quarrelsome?"

"That's what I mean."

"I guess you ought to know," Feustel said, turning to the boy for the first time and studying him as he had done the colt.

Danny ran his hand down one of Man o' War's legs and lifted his foot. "He's real easy to work around, Mr. Feustel," Danny went on eagerly, feeling that he might be getting somewhere with this man. "He's almost like an old cow in the stall, but outside it's a different story. Then he wants to go. He tries to be one step ahead of you every minute. You got to be on your toes."

The trainer smiled at Danny's outburst, then turned back to the red yearling. "He's no baby, that's for sure. Weighs about a thousand pounds, I imagine. Bigger than most of the others. That's one reason I liked him. And not a pound of sales fat on him, either. Nothing to stop us from breaking him right away."

Danny became more hopeful of getting a job. Feustel hadn't turned him down yet. True, he hadn't said *yes*. But he hadn't said *no* either. "I've handled him a lot," Danny went on eagerly, his eyes intent, his voice not as steady as he would have liked. "I don't mean that I've pampered him or spoiled him. But he's used to my hands running all over him and I've even rested my weight on his back. He shouldn't object too much to a saddle."

Louis Feustel nodded his head favorably. "There's no doubt all that will help us, Danny," he said. "If yearlings have been handled a lot they usually adapt themselves pretty well to the business of breaking. I've seen some accept bridle and rider in one session." He paused, turning to the boy again. "Can we do that with him?"

Danny met the man's gaze. "I don't think so," he said honestly. "It'll take more time than that. It's in him to put up some sort of a fight."

Louis Feustel nodded again. "I think so, too," he said. "And I'm glad you're not so carried away by your colt to tell me otherwise. It won't be easy breaking him, not with the blood of Hastings in him."

"But he's smart," Danny said quickly. He didn't want anyone to think his colt was as rebellious as his grandsire had been. "Once he learns what's expected of him—"

"I hope so," Feustel interrupted. "We'll find out soon enough."

"We," Danny repeated slowly. "You mean I get the job?"

"We need you more than you think we do, Danny," the trainer said. "It'll make it easier for us if the colt has someone he knows around. Stay with him for now, anyway. We'll see how things go. . . ."

Danny didn't hear anything more Louis Feustel may have said. He was going to stay with Man o' War, and nothing else mattered, nothing in this world.

Somehow the rest of the day passed quietly. Danny moved Man o' War to his new stall in the Riddle stable but that was all. It was a time for settling down and getting used to their new home. Danny was given one of the cots in the tack room near Man o' War and there was nothing for him to do but care for his colt twenty-four hours a day. Everything had worked out as he'd hoped it would. He could not have been happier.

That night he lay in his cot listening to the soft nickering of horses in adjacent stalls and the rustling of their feet in the straw bedding. He had no trouble telling which sounds were from Man o' War. His colt was making the most noise of all.

One of the grooms said, "That Fair Play colt won't settle down. He makes more racket than all the others put together."

"He'll be quiet in a few minutes," Danny said in the darkness. "It just takes him a little longer than the others."

"When they start breaking him, he'll sleep nights," the man said. "He'll be too tired to carry on like this."

"They won't tire him out," Danny said. "Not him."

The other groom laughed. "A bit in the mouth changes a lot of colts, kid. Yours won't be no different."

"Bits won't change him. He'll be up against it every minute. You'll see."

"We'll see, all right," the man said, laughing again. "But go ahead, kid. Brag about your colt, if you like. We all do it. We fight for our colts, too, if we have to. Even steal for them, if we must. I guess none of us would have it any other way."

"That's for sure," a third groom said in the darkness. "My colt is the best colt in the stable. Anybody who doubts it is a liar."

No one laughed or said anything. For a moment the tack room was quiet again except for the sounds of stabled horses.

"But don't think, kid, that you can rub speed in your colt if he doesn't have it," the first man said thoughtfully. "No groom can."

"Mine's got it already," Danny answered.

"Sure, so's mine. If we didn't love our horses we'd be pretty bad grooms. An' let me tell you, a bad groom can ruin a horse faster than a bad trainer. He can undo six months' work in a few minutes' time through bad handling or neglect."

"Go to sleep," the third groom said. "Save it until tomorrow."

"He's sore because I took a colt away from him last year," the second groom told Danny. "Proved to be too much horse for him to handle."

Danny was quiet. They all took pride in their charges, the same as he did. Only the final test upon the racetrack would tell whose colt was the fastest.

"Ever put a saddle on Mahubah's colt?" the first groom asked, as if wanting to continue the conversation far into the night.

"No," he answered. It annoyed him a little that everyone in the Riddle stable referred to Man o' War as *Mahubah's colt* or *that Fair Play colt*. "His name is Man o' War," he added.

"A pretty impressive name. But what do you call him?"

"I call him Red."

"*Every* chestnut horse in *every* stable is called Red," the man said.

"He's redder than most," Danny said, "and bigger than most."

"Big Red then," the man said quietly.

"Yes," Danny agreed. "*Big Red.*" He kept repeating the name over and over until finally he slept.

Early the next morning Louis Feustel showed up at Man o' War's stall with a short, heavyset man at his side.

"This is Harry Vititoe, Danny," the trainer said. "He's breaking our colts. Take Red out, please."

Danny snapped the lead shank to Man o' War's halter. He knew the time had come for some very important lessons in his colt's life. "Easy, Red. Easy," he said softly. "Show them how nicely you can act." But there was anxiety in his eyes as he met the gaze of the short man walking beside them.

"Don't worry," Harry Vititoe said quietly, as if he saw a need to soothe Danny as much as the colt. "I don't want a fight on my hands any more than you do. We'll go slowly and carefully. The less nervousness and excitement the better."

"Don't push him," Danny warned, "or he'll fight back."

"I won't," Vititoe said reassuringly. "Fighting puts too much strain on the muscles and ligaments of a young horse, aside from everything else."

Danny nodded. He liked this man, for, like his voice, his eyes were patient and understanding. And yet, just as important, his hands were strong and experienced. Whatever Vititoe did within the next few days would stay with Man o' War for the rest of his life.

A short distance away Mr. Riddle was standing beside Louis Feustel. There was a closed paddock nearby and the trainer told Danny to take the big colt to it.

For a while they only watched the colt, and Danny was very proud of Man o' War as he walked him around the paddock. His colt was eager and playful but tractable too. He was having no trouble with him.

"I hope he doesn't live up to his name," Danny heard Mr. Riddle say nervously.

"Notice how he's right up against the halter," Vititoe remarked. "I doubt that a bit will slow this one down any. We might have a fight on our hands before we're through."

"I hope not," Feustel said with concern. "He's got brains, this one has."

"He also has Hastings blood in him," Mr. Riddle said quietly. "He might fight like a tiger, as Harry says."

"But he's got Fair Play in him, too," Feustel answered. "I was with Fair Play a long time."

Harry Vititoe laughed. "Then you should know he wasn't much better than Hastings, Louis. Fair Play had only *disdain* for people."

"That's not the same as hating people," Feustel answered. "Hastings hated everybody, with no exception."

Danny brought Man o' War to a stop and straightened his long red mane. His colt was quiet and well mannered but alert and ready for anything. Who knew how much fire from his sire and grandsire burned within Man o' War, and whether or not it could be controlled?

"And don't forget, too," Louis Feustel was saying, "he's got Rock Sand in him. There never was a nicer, better mare." He waved Danny closer, and Harry Vititoe slipped through the rails of the paddock fence.

Danny waited for Vititoe to come to them. This man, weighing about one hundred and twenty pounds, had ridden with the best jockeys at one time. And soon, if all went well, he would be the first to ride Man o' War.

The ex-jockey smiled at Danny and put a gentle hand on the colt's withers. "There's no hurry," he told both Man o' War and Danny. "We've got all the time in the world. Maybe there won't be a battle at all."

The man's hand continued to move over the big yearling, over his neck and back, haunches and legs and feet. Man o' War scarcely moved. He had known such handling all his life and there was no reason for his becoming upset now. Danny was very proud of him.

It was only when the man ran his hand up toward the ears that the colt drew back.

"He doesn't like having his ears rubbed," Danny said quietly.

"Not many colts do. But he'll have to get used to it, if we're going to put a bridle on him."

Again the man's hands moved to the colt's ears. When he touched them, Man o' War went straight up in the air, almost tearing the lead shank from Danny's hands. Then the colt bolted, pulling the boy along the ground. Danny felt the dirt burn his legs as he was dragged helplessly across the paddock. He managed to hang on until Man o' War came to a stop.

Climbing to his feet, he went to Man o' War and placed a hand on the colt's quivering body. "It's all right," he said softly. "You didn't mean anything by it. You just didn't know." He led Man o' War back to the others.

"Do you want some help, Danny?" Feustel asked. "Or do you think you're better off alone?"

"Alone," Danny answered, "for now, anyway."

Vititoe was beside Man o' War again. "He moves awfully

fast for such a big, stout colt," he said.

"He doesn't want to be broken," Mr. Riddle said.

"What colt does?" Vititoe asked. "This one will learn. He's smart."

Danny saw the bridle that the ex-jockey now held in his hands. "You'll never get it over his ears," he said.

"I will if I take it apart," Vititoe answered. "I won't pinch his ears this time."

"Do you want his halter off?"

"No, keep it on him, and the shank too." Vititoe was taking the bridle apart. "I have to do this often. Most colts are a little head shy, and this way we don't have to force the headpiece over the ears. Nothing to it, Danny."

"I hope not."

The man looked up to meet the boy's anxious eyes. "Like I said before, we've got plenty of time. What we don't do today we'll do tomorrow. Brute force never works with this kind of colt; it would only ruin him here and now."

Danny nodded, his eyes on the bridle. "I thought Red was used to having his head handled, but I guess not."

"You did fine," the short man said. "Bridling a colt is always ticklish business. We just have to sort of kid him along, pet him, talk to him. Before he knows it he'll have the bit in his mouth." Vititoe had the headpiece unbuckled from the rubber bit. Carefully he slipped it over the colt's head without touching his ears. It was no different from having a halter put on, and Man o' War did not flinch or stir.

But the rubber bit still had to be put in the colt's mouth. Danny looked at it, wondering if Man o' War would take it quietly.

"Maybe the worst is over," Vititoe said hopefully. "Most

colts object more to the headpiece than the bit." He began slipping the bit into Man o' War's mouth, talking to him all the while.

Danny waited, his heart pounding. Suddenly the big colt jerked back from Vititoe's hands and reared to his full height again. Danny held on to the lead shank as once more Man o' War plunged across the paddock. This time Danny managed to stay on his feet, bringing the colt to a stop against the fence.

"It's only a piece of rubber," Danny told him, trying to keep his annoyance from his voice. "It won't hurt you. You're smart enough to know that." He led Man o' War back to the others, still talking to his colt.

Again Vititoe tried putting the rubber bit in Man o' War's mouth, but the big colt jerked his head back just when they thought he might take it.

"He's determined to have his own way," Feustel said.

"I don't want you to force him," Mr. Riddle told Vititoe. "We'd get no place if we did. He's smart enough to learn that we're too many and too strong for him."

"I hope so," Feustel said. "If he doesn't, we've got another Hastings on our hands."

"Don't let it get you down, Louis," Vititoe said. "We've got plenty of time and that's usually the answer."

Danny turned and looked at the ex-jockey. It was his job to break Man o' War and he should be more concerned than anybody else with the problems confronting them. Instead, he seemed the least perturbed.

"That's enough for today," Vititoe went on. "Tomorrow we'll make it."

But Harry Vititoe was mistaken. It was no better the next day nor on the one that followed. It seemed that Man o' War had no intention of ever taking the rubber bit. Each day was a nerve-racking experience for everybody concerned with the colt's breaking, and Danny took it harder than anybody else.

Far into the night he would talk to his colt, wondering what had gone wrong to make Man o' War so obstinate. "Perhaps," he said, "it's in you to fight the way your grandsire did. I thought you were smarter than that. How are you ever going to race without some control over you? Tell me that. And you want to race. Don't tell me you don't. Then be smart enough to give in a little. They're going to keep working on you until you do. It's just a question of time."

Finally the day came when Man o' War allowed Vititoe to slip the bit all the way into his mouth. Mr. Riddle and Louis Feustel stood by, watching. For a moment no one spoke, then Vititoe began attaching the checkpieces to the bit rings. "We don't want it too tight or too loose," he told Danny as Man o' War began champing on the rubber bit.

The bit was secure, and Man o' War stopped playing with it. He bolted forward with a giant leap, pulling the lead shank from Danny's hand and flying around the paddock all by himself! They could only watch, stepping out of his way and listening to his snorts of rage at the irritating piece of hard rubber in his mouth.

"Leave him alone," Vititoe told Danny as the boy started forward. "Let him get used to it. He can't hurt himself."

So along with everyone else Danny Ryan stood behind the paddock fence watching Man o' War. He continued fighting a long while but there was no way he could get rid of the bit.

Stop fighting, Red, Danny pleaded silently. *You can't beat these men. You're just making it hard on everybody, including yourself.*

Man o' War raced past them, the loose lead shank flying behind him. He stopped at the end of the paddock and reared and shook his head furiously, trying to spit out the bit again.

"He's a demon," Mr. Riddle said. "He'll fight us every step of the way. This is only the beginning."

"I know," Harry Vititoe agreed quietly. "But we'll never break him if we're rough on him. It'll just take more time than I expected."

Danny watched Man o' War twisting in the air, and his heart cried with the futility of it all. If only there was some way he could make Man o' War understand that he could submit to these men and still retain all his masculine pride and arrogance! "Use your brains, Red, please," he kept repeating over and over.

But as the morning wore on, Man o' War's constant fight with the bit continued. It was as if all he wanted was to be left alone, to go his own way, to live his life as he pleased. Yet Danny knew it was in this colt to race. It was only a question of time before Man o' War realized that he must submit to some control, even a rider on his broad back, if he was to run again as he had done in the pastures at home.

"You've got to be smart to race, Red," he said. "You've got to learn."

It was early in the afternoon when Man o' War quieted down and became interested in Danny's extended hand. Louis Feustel and Mr. Riddle had gone to do other work, and only Harry Vititoe was in the paddock with Danny.

"That's enough for today," the ex-jockey said. "Take him back to the stall, Danny. We've made some progress and tomorrow we'll make a little more. It won't be easy but we'll get there eventually."

During the days that followed, it often seemed to Danny that despite Vititoe's words of encouragement Man o' War would never be fully broken. He fought every inch of the way, and only Vititoe's infinite patience and experience offered any hope that one day Danny would see his colt on the racetrack.

"I never had one as tough as him," the ex-jockey said. "But he's not dumb. He knows what's going on. He's learning the hard way, one step at a time."

Danny learned, too. He came to value the virtue of patience as never before in his life. When he would have quit, Harry Vititoe went on. He watched the man wait quietly for the big colt's daily tantrums to cease and then gently school him in the use of the long reins that were now attached to the bridle. He persuaded Man o' War to walk forward a few yards, then back up. Slowly, ever so slowly, they were making progress just as he'd said days ago.

One morning there came another advanced step in the breaking of Man o' War. Danny had the bridle on him when Vititoe came into the stall and said, "We'll put the saddle pad and surcingle on him today. He's ready for it."

Man o' War displayed no objection to the pad when the man placed it gently on his withers. Danny patted his colt to calm him and let him know nothing terrible was happening to him. "He's used to my putting weight on his back," he said. "He shouldn't object to the saddle either."

Vititoe nodded and reached for the broad girth band dangling on the off side of Man o' War. "He might object to this," he said, tightening the band gradually about the colt's stomach. "We'll keep it a little loose. There, now."

"Easy, Red, easy," Danny said, comforting his colt. The surcingle was snug enough to keep the saddle pad from slipping but not tight enough to annoy Man o' War. Still the colt objected to it. He shifted uneasily about the stall, Danny moving with him. "Easy, fellow, easy," the boy kept repeating.

With a motion of his head Vititoe indicated that Danny was

to follow him out of the stall and leave Man o' War alone. "Nothing is going to be easy with this colt," the man said, watching from outside.

Man o' War shook his big body. There was no room to plunge and run in the stall.

"He can't hurt himself," Vititoe said. "He'll get used to it in a few minutes."

They continued watching, and finally Man o' War became more interested in Danny than in the band about his girth. He nuzzled the boy's hands, looking for carrots.

Danny said, "But it will be different when you get up on his back."

"I'm afraid it will," the ex-jockey said.

"Have you broken all the other colts?"

Vititoe nodded. "He's the only one left."

"When will you get up on him?"

"I'm not sure."

"It'll be quite a ride," Danny said, wondering at the absence of envy in his voice. Hadn't he always dreamed of riding Man o' War?

After a little while Vititoe said, "I'm going to turn him loose in the paddock now, Danny. He can't hurt himself there either, and we'll see what he does."

The big colt was all fire once Danny set him free to run in the paddock. He tried to spit out the irritating rubber bit in his mouth. He plunged to rid himself of the saddle pad and girth band. Once he got down and rolled, his legs pawing the air in his fury. But most of the time he raced from one end of the paddock to the other, his tail fanning the wind.

Vititoe saw only the beauty of Man o' War and said, "He'll make a runner, that one will. He'll be worth all the time we've spent on him. But like you said, Danny, it's going to be quite a ride." He was silent then, watching every moment of the plunging red colt.

For several days Vititoe did nothing more with Man o' War than add the weight of the light saddle to his back. There were no stirrups to jangle and upset the colt, so he showed no objection to it. It was never an easy job putting the tack on Man o' War, but he seemed to be getting used to it once it was on.

Watching him in the paddock, Vititoe said, "It's as if he's determined to fight discipline every step of the way ... but once he knows he can't get away with it, he's got brains enough to accept what's in store. He'll be hard to beat if his jockey is smarter than he is."

Then, finally, came the morning to ride Man o' War. Danny's stomach was in knots. He didn't think there would ever be another day in his life to equal this one. The time had come when the colt he had first seen standing on unsteady legs beside Mahubah would be asked to accept a rider. From this day on, Man o' War's racing career would be before him.

"Don't go trying anything funny," Danny told his colt while waiting for Harry Vititoe to mount. The ex-jockey was talking to Feustel and Mr. Riddle. They were all there, everybody concerned with the big stable ... all the other grooms, the stable manager, the exercise boys. They had come to see the colt who had been a demon to break. This was Man o' War with the hot blood of Fair Play and Hastings.

They were away from the barns where there'd be less chance of anyone's getting hurt when Man o' War jumped. Everyone took it for granted he'd do that once Vititoe was on his back. The colt wasn't going to do anything the easy way, ever. Danny leaned part of his weight on the saddle, hoping it would help make Vititoe's job easier. Man o' War shifted uneasily, but Danny thought his nervousness was due to the number of people around rather than to any objection to the extra weight.

Finally the ex-jockey came over to the boy and the colt. He patted Man o' War on the neck but his brow was furrowed and his voice anxious as he said, "I want you to have help this morning, Danny." He snapped a second lead shank to the halter beneath the bridle and handed it to another groom. "Both of you keep hold of him," he ordered. "A good hold."

Vititoe moved to the colt's side and leaned heavily on the saddle. Man o' War reared, his great body twisting and turning, while Danny and the other groom gave him all the lead shank he needed.

When he came down and was still again, Vititoe said, "He's going to dump me, all right. He's smart enough to do it, and big enough."

Once more the ex-jockey leaned his weight on the saddle. Man o' War went up again, bolting forward this time and almost pulling the lead shank out of Danny's hands.

"Take a better hold, Danny," Vititoe said when the colt was quiet. "I'm going up on him now. Keep him on the ground if you can. If I can manage to stay on him, most of our troubles may be over."

"We'll hold him," Danny said. But he wasn't certain they'd be able to keep Man o' War under control at all. He knew the signs, and his colt was determined to have nothing to do with a man on his back at this moment. "He's awfully hot," he warned Vititoe. "Maybe we should wait . . ."

The ex-jockey had his left leg bent so that Louis Feustel could boost him into the saddle. "I might stop with any other colt," he said, "but not this one. If I did there'd be no end to it."

Then Harry Vititoe was in the saddle, his legs drawn up, his body balanced. He had only a fraction of a second to wait before Man o' War squealed and bolted. The groom helping Danny jumped away to avoid getting hurt. Man o' War twisted in midair, and Danny's lead shank was torn from his hands. Man o' War made another lightning jump, coming down with both forefeet rigid. Harry Vititoe went flying from the saddle and crashed into Danny. Together they went down, rolling in the dirt.

When Danny got up, he saw Man o' War running loose, his mane and tail flying, and headed for the racetrack all by himself!

Harry Vititoe was getting to his feet, but it didn't occur to Danny to help him. Like everyone else, he ran after the runaway colt. Man o' War had already reached the racing strip, and everybody there was aware of his presence. A colt loose on the track at this time of year was not too unusual.

All work was stopped to prevent any accident and possible injury. The older horses stopped breezing and galloping. Yearlings being schooled were taken away so that they would not become excited by the horse running loose. The racetrack at Saratoga was very still except for the drum roll of Man o' War's galloping hoofs as he rounded the first turn.

Danny watched him go. *You couldn't wait*, he thought. *You just couldn't wait.*

Stablemen had stationed themselves at various points on the racetrack, waiting for the big colt to slow down. They were patient, having no wish to excite Mahubah's colt any further. It was just a question of time before one of them caught him. He had no place to go except around the racetrack.

Fifteen minutes later it was Danny who successfully got hold of one of the dragging lead shanks. Man o' War was tired from his long run; he went along willingly as if nothing at all had happened.

Harry Vititoe's eyes were sheepish when he joined the others at the barn. "The next time it'll be different," he said, not without confidence. "I don't like to be dumped so hard." He rubbed the seat of his pants.

The crowd laughed at Vititoe's expense, and one groom said, "You'd better stay on him next time, Harry, or maybe you'll end up walkin' hots like the rest of us."

Rider Up!

11

Harry Vititoe had no intention of losing his private battle with Man o' War. He went back to the barn with Danny and helped the boy strip down and wash the big colt. Later he gave Man o' War a carrot.

"I'll stick on him. You'll see," he told Danny.

The boy nodded in full agreement, but he wasn't sure of anything.

"He's the stronger," the ex-jockey continued, "but I'm smarter. At least I ought to be."

Danny nodded again.

"The trick is to kid a colt of this kind along," Vititoe said as if to get his own thoughts in hand rather than to convince Danny of his ability to ride Man o' War. "I'll outsmart him. I'll convince him that I'm stronger than he is."

Danny placed a blanket over Man o' War. "His dumping you today won't help any," he said quietly.

"No," Vititoe admitted, "it won't. But he's not a mean colt, just something of a rebel. He wants to make it plain that he prefers to be left alone to go his own way."

"You fight, and he'll fight back," Danny reminded Vititoe.

"I don't intend to fight him. There's a big difference between firmness and cruelty. But he must be made to do right."

"Maybe he doesn't know what *right* is," Danny suggested.

"I think he does. He's too smart not to know." Vititoe fed Man o' War another piece of carrot. "Tomorrow he'll learn I mean business . . . tomorrow and the day after that, and the one after that. It's only a question of time before he realizes we're in control, not he."

"I hope so," Danny said. "I sure hope so."

Harry Vititoe was back early the next morning and again he was thrown by Man o' War. But the colt didn't break loose this time, for Danny had all the help he needed in keeping hold of him.

Louis Feustel and Mr. Riddle were very much concerned. The big colt, it seemed, was not going to submit to being ridden. He fought from the moment the saddle was put on until he was worn down from twisting, rearing, and jumping. Only then would he allow Harry Vititoe to remain on his back. It was as if he knew everyone was too tired and breathless to go on with him.

Vititoe would sit quietly in the saddle, talking to Man o' War and rubbing his neck gently, letting him get used to the extra weight on his back. Unlike the others, Vititoe seemed confident that soon Man o' War would submit to full control.

After each back-breaking session, the ex-jockey would tell Danny, "He's coming along, getting a little better every day. Don't worry."

Danny couldn't see much progress being made but he never mentioned it. If Vititoe thought they were getting somewhere, he didn't want to be the one to discourage him. He felt most riders would have quit with Man o' War long ago.

"This colt will never in his life be saddled easy," Vititoe told Danny one day. "He'll always put up some kind of a token battle for his freedom whenever he's made ready. But like I've said many times, he's smart enough to know we're too many and too strong for him. He'll never forget these past few weeks, but he'll make a good racehorse. I'm sure of it."

Danny watched Man o' War take the carrot Vititoe offered him. Maybe the man knew what he was talking about. Maybe he did. One thing sure, he wasn't going to quit . . . and perhaps Man o' War knew that, too.

By the end of the week Man o' War's battles had become less furious and of shorter duration. He allowed Vititoe to remain on his back while Danny led him around the large walking ring beyond the barns. All the other spectators watched from a distance, so more than anyone else in the stable Danny was aware of the progress Harry Vititoe was finally making in the schooling of Man o' War.

He listened to the man's never-ending chatter as Vititoe talked to the colt, soothing him, comforting him. And when the rider wasn't talking, he was singing to Man o' War to get the colt used to his voice and to noise and commotion. Sometimes Vititoe would slap Man o' War gently on the neck and rump and brush his heels lightly against the flanks. At first the big colt reared with every touch of Vititoe's hand and heel, but eventually he became accustomed to them.

Then one morning Vititoe ordered Danny to move away from Man o' War and join the others who were watching. Standing next to Louis Feustel, Danny followed the big colt's movements as Vititoe guided him around the ring. The colt stopped from time to time and Danny thought there would surely be trouble. But Man o' War always moved forward again at Vititoe's firm but gentle urging.

"He's learning fast now," Louis Feustel told Mr. Riddle.

"Maybe we're going to have another racehorse after all."

"You had doubts, Louis?" Mr. Riddle asked.

"I sure did," the trainer answered.

"You'll have him for training before long," Mr. Riddle said. "Then the real work will start."

Danny shook his head. As if what Harry Vititoe was doing wasn't real work! It seemed to him that anything to come would be easy compared to this. Once they got Man o' War on the track, he would train himself!

Danny learned that Vititoe had no intention of hurrying the colt to the racetrack. Instead he kept Man o' War in the large walking ring, making him go from a jog to a trot, and often using an older horse in the lead.

"Gives him some company, Danny," Vititoe said. "And he's ready for it now. Helps to keep him calm."

There were times when Man o' War gave his rider trouble, but Vititoe stayed on him. Finally the ex-jockey had him changing direction about the ring, first in a trot, then in a canter. "But I never can relax on him," he confided to Danny one afternoon. "He knows what I'm doing every step of the way. If I make one mistake, he'll dump me."

"But he's not fighting you," Danny said.

"No, just ready to test my seat and hands, that's all. But usually I'm ready for him."

"He's bridlewise now."

"Easy for a smart colt to learn. He knows what the bridle is for, all right."

"Are you taking him on the track soon?" Danny asked, making no attempt to conceal his eagerness now that the time had almost come.

Vititoe rubbed Man o' War's head. "I think so, Danny," he answered quietly. "He's not apt to hurt anyone or himself now. We'll move out there tomorrow."

The following morning Man o' War went to the track for the first time under a rider. Harry Vititoe was balanced in the saddle and ready for almost anything. Danny was at the colt's head when they stopped at the gap in the fence. For a while they watched the other horses at work and gave Man o' War a chance to get used to all the noise and confusion.

"Just let him have a good look around," Vititoe said quietly.

"He didn't see much of this last time he was out here by himself," Danny answered.

Man o' War's eyes roamed. First he seemed to be looking at the huge grandstand as if expecting to find it filled rather than empty. Then he turned his gaze on the judges' pavilion before moving it on to the track itself. Maybe it was the sight of a set of yearlings coming down the stretch that had attracted his attention. He watched them gallop by, their action quick and nervous, with some moving from one side of the track to the other, and shying and bolting.

Danny held the lead shank short. "They're new at it, like you," he whispered to Man o' War. "But they'll settle down, too."

Another set of young horses came down the track, and their antics were even worse. Most of them bucked and kicked every few strides, and Danny wondered if any of them would ever make racehorses. At this stage of the game he almost doubted it. It was a trying time for everybody.

"Settle down, you big bum, settle down," Danny heard one rider call to his mount as they swept by. Danny noted that the tone of the rider's voice was not derisive but comforting and encouraging, and that the words had been spoken in rhythm to the beat of the young horse's hoofs. The chances were good that this rider loved his colt very much.

Danny rubbed Man o' War's head. "Don't be impatient. You'll be out there soon enough," he said.

Harry Vititoe kept Man o' War at the gap in the fence a long while before he finally signaled to Danny to turn him loose.

"Luck," Danny said, sweeping a hand down over the colt's neck. Then he leaned on the rail to watch. "Nice and easy, Red," he muttered to himself. "Nice and easy does it."

He saw at once that Harry Vititoe had his hands full keeping Man o' War from bolting down the track after the other horses. But the ex-jockey had no intention of letting the colt go, and he kept a snug hold on the reins. Finally Man o' War seemed to settle down, and Vititoe let him jog as they went around the track.

Danny saw Man o' War come to a stop on the far side. Vititoe let him sniff a wagon that was being pulled alongside the outer rail. Convinced that it was nothing to fear, Man o' War went on.

Danny turned his attention to a set of green yearlings coming down the track. Some of them evidently wanted to go back to the stable, for they were trying to make for the open gap in the fence. Their riders had a handful keeping them straight.

For a moment Danny studied not the skittish colts but their riders. Most of the exercise boys weren't "boys" at all, being closer to fifty than fifteen years of age. They were small, hardened men, many of them with wizened faces that looked as if they'd borne the brunt of a colt's heels at some time during their careers. But despite their rough appearance they were marvelously kind to their charges.

Danny listened to their voices, soft and patient, as they attempted to control the flighty mounts beneath them.

"This filly's a dilly," one called as he was almost thrown and taken through the gap in the fence. "She ain't afraid of nothin'! She's just lookin' for a chance to set me down in the dirt." His voice and hands were soft, and Danny could tell that the filly was listening to him because she had one ear cocked.

When they had passed, Danny knew he would have given anything to be small and wizened rather than the hulking figure he was. Raising his long arms, he snapped the end of the lead shank in the dirt. Maybe someday he'd be able to ride Man o' War in spite of his size. If that day came, he wouldn't change places with anyone in the world!

He watched his colt again as Harry Vititoe brought him around the far turn and into the homestretch. Vititoe rode with longer stirrups than the rest of the "boys." They helped him keep better balance, and he needed every aid he could get to stay on Man o' War. The colt shied across the track, but Vititoe stopped him at the rail and got him into a slow jog again.

They went past Danny, then Vititoe stopped Man o' War and came back. The big colt wheeled suddenly as if reluctant to leave the track. Harry Vititoe brought him under control again.

"Get the shank on him, Danny," he said. "We're calling it a morning."

Back at the barn Danny removed Man o' War's tack. "He did real well. Better than I thought he would."

Vititoe nodded, his eyes remaining on the colt. "Yes, everybody's happy with the way he went. Tomorrow I'll take him out with a couple of other yearlings so he'll have some company."

"Don't choose any flighty ones," Danny cautioned.

"No, they'd only make each other worse. I'll pick a couple smart yearlings. Red will learn from them."

During the days that followed, Man o' War went to the track with the more advanced yearlings in the Riddle stable.

Most of the time he worked willingly for Harry Vititoe. He learned to go in single file, both leading and following the other horses. Sometimes he was asked to go head and head with them, first on the inside of the group, then on the outside. Only then was he difficult to handle, wanting to extend himself while Vititoe fought to keep him in a slow gallop.

"He's not ready for breezing or any fast work," the ex-jockey told Danny. "My job is simply to get him legged-up and used to the presence of other horses. Feustel will take care of his real training."

"Then your work is almost done," Danny said. Man o' War was now being galloped twice around the track daily and he showed no signs of fatigue.

"Just about, Danny," Vititoe agreed. "He still gives us trouble when being saddled, but I don't think I'll be able to correct that, me or anyone else. He has a long memory. He won't easily forget the weeks we've spent breaking him."

It was almost the end of September and soon the stable would be shipped to Mr. Riddle's farm in Maryland. There, Danny knew, Man o' War would be asked to move along at a faster pace, as some of the other yearlings were already doing.

One morning he watched the small, compact colt that Mr. Jeffords had bought for the highest price in the sale. He was probably the most advanced of any yearling at the track and was breezing a furlong, from the eighth pole to the finish wire, in good time.

"He looks like he's worth every penny of the fifteen thousand six hundred dollars they paid for him," he told Vititoe, who was standing next to him.

The ex-jockey nodded in full agreement, his keen eyes following the rapid drive of the golden colt's short, powerful legs. "He flies along, all right," Vititoe said. "He's going to Maryland, too, you know. Mr. and Mrs. Jeffords have a farm next to the Riddles' so they'll probably be training their colts on the same track. It'll be something to see."

"You mean my colt might be working with this one?" Danny asked.

"They're bound to put them together somewhere along the line," Vititoe answered. "I'd like to be there to see it."

"I wish you were," Danny said. "Somehow I can't see anyone else up on him now."

The ex-jockey laughed and put an arm across Danny's shoulders. "You'll get used to it, Danny," he said. "Before you're done you'll see a lot of riders up on him." His eyes met the boy's and his voice softened. "You'll get used to it, Danny," he repeated. "Just give your colt all you've got. Who knows? Maybe the two of you will go a long way."

Vititoe's gaze returned to the Jeffords colt, which was easily pulling away from the other yearlings. "You might even make everyone forget what they paid for that one. You just might, at that."

A few days later the stable left Saratoga for the Riddle farm in Maryland, where training would be stepped up before winter arrived. During the weeks to come, Louis Feustel and Mr. Riddle would learn what they could expect from the yearlings they had bought.

Danny was confident that Man o' War would prove to be the best racehorse of the lot. But he knew that other caretakers felt the same way about their colts. Each expected his charge to be the one that would set the racing world afire with his blazing speed. Only time and fate held the answer.

Fall Breezes

12

When he arrived at Glen Riddle Farm near Berlin, Maryland, Danny found the countryside very flat compared to Saratoga and the rolling hills he had known in Kentucky. But the land was spreading and peaceful so it wasn't long before he felt at home. The farm itself included over a thousand acres, with stables for sixty horses. There was also a new mile track, which Mr. Riddle had built for the training of his own yearlings and those of Mr. and Mrs. Jeffords, who owned the adjoining farm.

The October days that followed were bright and sunny, and Danny was told by the stablemen that the climate on the eastern shore of Maryland was such that they'd probably be able to work the yearlings outside most of the winter.

Man o' War, too, settled down quickly in his new home. He was eating well, and when Danny turned him out in the paddock to get the kinks out of his travel legs he frolicked like the strong, healthy colt he was. But his play was soon to end, Danny knew. The purpose of Glen Riddle Farm was to prepare all the yearlings for the spring racing season, and the days to come would be a busy time for all.

There were more grooms at the farm than the Riddle stable had had at Saratoga, for taking care of racehorses in training required many skilled hands. At first Danny resented having anyone else help him with the care of Man o' War, but soon he realized how much had to be done to keep this colt sound and fit and, most important, how much he had to learn about the care of a racehorse and his equipment. Saddles and bridles, as well as all other tack, had to be properly cared for. A faulty bridle, rein, girth buckle, or stirrup could break and cause a bad accident. Blankets and coolers had to be kept clean, as did brushes, bandages, bits, and scrapers. To say nothing of a stall that had to be kept clean and fresh-smelling!

So Danny was happy for the help he received from the older groom who was assigned to Man o' War.

"Frank," he said early on the third morning after their arrival, "what do you think of him?"

The man was cleaning the colt's hind foot and he didn't look up. "He's the best there is, jus' like you say," he answered. "How else could we feel 'bout a colt we're rubbing?"

"Yeah, I sort of figured you'd put it that way," Danny said. "But just wait until you see him on the track, and then you'll know better what I mean."

Frank put down Man o' War's foot and straightened up. "He's still too thin for the size of him," he said critically.

"He eats plenty," Danny answered in stout defense of his colt. "It's only a question of time before he puts on more weight."

"I know he eats good," the man said. "But he gulps his feed down. A colt's got to *chew* his oats to do him any good. Feustel will slow him down. You'll see."

Danny didn't pursue the subject, knowing Frank might be

right. Man o' War *did* eat too fast for his own good.

A short while later Louis Feustel appeared at the stall door. With him were Mr. Riddle and a man whom Danny had never seen before.

"This is Clyde Gordon, Danny," Feustel said. "He's riding your colt this morning."

Danny snapped the lead shank on Man o' War's halter. The time had come for Man o' War to continue his work on the racetrack. Would he react differently under Gordon's hands than he had at Harry Vititoe's? Danny led him from the stall. He'd soon have the answer.

Man o' War drew back his head when Feustel slipped the bridle over his halter.

"Always the rebel," Feustel muttered, adjusting the bit. He told Danny, "Gordon is my top rider. He's used to handling difficult yearlings so he should get along with Red."

"I sure hope so," Danny answered, trying to keep Man o' War still.

The big colt shifted quickly, sending his hind legs flying when Feustel placed the saddle on his back. But the trainer had the girth band snug and the saddle was on to stay.

Clyde Gordon moved over to mount. He stepped back quickly as Man o' War swung his hindquarters around trying to get rid of the saddle.

Feustel called for more help, and additional lead shanks were snapped to Man o' War's halter. Then the trainer tightened the girth band another hole.

"He's holding his breath," Danny said.

They moved Man o' War around in a circle until the big chestnut exhaled and the girth was loose again. Feustel took it up another couple of holes, and Man o' War reared as the strap tightened.

Danny and the other grooms stepped back but held on tight to the ends of the lead shanks until Man o' War came down again and was still.

He'll always resent being saddled, Danny thought. *He'll always put up some kind of battle.*

Clyde Gordon was at the colt's side again, his leg raised, waiting for Feustel to boost him into the saddle. Then, before Man o' War knew what was happening, Gordon was on his back. He tried to rear but Danny and the others held him down. He shifted his hindquarters but Gordon stayed on him. So far so good.

Mr. Riddle spoke to Louis Feustel and then the trainer said to Danny, "We have a nice old hunter here that Mr. Riddle thinks will be good company for this colt. I want you to ride him out with Red."

Danny gulped a little. *He was going to ride beside Man o' War.* It was the next best thing to being on his colt's back!

A few minutes later one of the men came up with a tall, big-boned gelding. "This is Major Treat," Mr. Riddle told Danny. "He was a good hunter in his day, pretty fast and very wise. I think he'll have a quieting effect on this colt."

Feustel smiled at the intent expression on Danny's face. "Your being along should help, too," he told the boy. "Get up on him now."

Danny was boosted into the saddle and given one of the lead shanks attached to Man o' War's bridle. The other grooms removed their shanks, and Danny was on his own. Clyde Gordon looked at him a little anxiously but said nothing.

Major Treat was very quiet and Danny moved him closer to Man o' War. The big colt snorted at the gelding but didn't rear. Danny shortened the shank. "Come on, Red," he said quietly. "Let's go."

Man o' War moved willingly at Danny's bidding, and behind them Louis Feustel said, "This might be the answer to a lot of problems with this one."

Danny had never been happier in his life. Never had he been so close to *riding* Man o' War! He could even *feel* the colt's mounting excitement as they walked toward the training track. Man o' War was pushing hard against Major Treat but the old gelding kept moving along, his body rebuffing the big colt's jolts without giving an inch. Danny patted his mount. He was doing a good job.

Danny kept his eyes on Man o' War. How close he was to being actually up on him! He could see the track ahead between Big Red's pricked ears and even touch, if he wanted to, the arched crest of his powerful neck.

Nearing the gap in the track fence, Man o' War suddenly tossed his head and the silky foretop that crowned him dropped over his eyes. He came to a stop, surveying the track before him. Proud and long-limbed, he stood there, his great eyes bright and arrogant, missing nothing.

Danny held the lead shank tight and waited. Clyde Gordon, too, remained quiet in the saddle.

Never before had Danny been so aware of Man o' War's eagerness to run. He was standing absolutely still, but all his senses were keyed to the utmost. Suddenly he reared and came down, swerving sharply against Major Treat. The old gelding took the hard bump quietly but Danny almost lost his seat. For a few seconds there was bedlam in the big colt's movements as he tried to break free of the hands that held him. Then he quieted down as suddenly as he had erupted. All was peaceful again, and Danny touched him gently.

Gordon said, "I thought he was going to dump me for sure that time."

Feustel joined them at the track gate. "Jog him around once, and then come back," he said with some concern.

Danny moved out on the track, keeping Major Treat close beside Man o' War. There were other yearlings on the track and the big colt's eyes followed them. He wanted to run but Gordon and Danny were able to keep him at a slow jog.

Major Treat went stride for stride with Man o' War, and Danny patted him comfortingly. The old gelding seemed to be enjoying his work despite the buffeting he was getting. His heavy ears were pricked forward and he carried his head high, even tugging a bit on the reins. Perhaps Major Treat realized just how important his job was in keeping the young colt under control. It was good to be needed, Danny thought. He had a pretty good idea of how Major Treat felt.

Clyde Gordon was standing in his stirrup irons and had a snug hold on the reins. "This one seems to know all about speed right from the start," he said.

Danny nodded. "The big job with him is to hold him back so he won't overdo," he answered.

"Is he pretty well legged-up?"

"He's been walking, trotting, and cantering over two miles every day without strain," Danny answered.

"Then he's ready for something faster," Gordon said.

"He's ready, all right. Just wait until you see the length of his strides when he gets going."

"They should be long, all right," Gordon agreed. "He's got the height for it."

Man o' War tried to break into a run. "Easy, Red. Easy," Gordon said, slowing him down.

When the colt was quiet again Danny said, "He can beat any yearling in the barns."

"How do you know so much about his speed?" Gordon

asked, puzzled. "They haven't breezed him yet, have they?"

"I've seen him go in pasture," Danny said.

"We'll find out soon enough how fast he is," Gordon returned. "It's hard to tell what a colt will amount to until he starts breezing with others. Some of them fold up pretty easy."

"This one won't," Danny said. "He wants to *win*."

Gordon smiled at the boy's enthusiasm. "Don't get your hopes up too high, Danny. He's far from finished, powerful as he might seem to you. I know, for I've ridden an awful lot of colts."

Danny would like to have been able to say that in time. But he was almost certain that Feustel wouldn't even let him exercise his horses. Usually, the limit for any rider was one hundred and thirty pounds. Put any more weight than that on a yearling's back and you invite unsoundness, especially when you start asking a colt for fast work.

Man o' War shook his head as if he was becoming very impatient with the tight hold on his mouth. Danny took a better grasp on the lead shank and spoke to him. The colt pushed harder against Major Treat but didn't try to break into a run.

"I guess I'm too heavy to ever ride a racehorse," Danny said, "even as an exercise boy."

"You're not light," Gordon said, his eyes moving over Danny's body, "that's for sure."

"Maybe if I lost some weight . . ."

"Your bones are too big, Danny," Gordon said quietly. "Trainers look for kids with small bones before they take them on. They even make sure kids' parents are small, because then there's a good chance the kids will stay light long enough to be useful as exercise boys and possibly jockeys."

Danny turned to Man o' War. The colt's head was bowed down almost to his chest by Gordon's tight rein. It emphasized even more the arched crest of his neck, curving gracefully and flowing powerfully into his shoulders. There were lots of things you saw up here that weren't so evident from the ground. Well, he was coming this close anyway to riding Man o' War.

A set of three yearlings went by, breezing a fast furlong. In the lead was the golden chestnut colt owned by Mrs. Jeffords.

"I've never seen a classier looking colt than that one," Gordon commented. "No wonder he's the darling of the Jeffords stable. They've changed his name, you know."

"No, I didn't know," Danny said, still watching the lightning strides of the golden colt ahead of them. There was no doubt that the yearling had substance and speed as well as beauty. "What's his name now?" he asked.

"Golden Broom. I guess they figured it goes better with his coat, and they must expect him to sweep all his competition clean."

"Maybe," Danny said thoughtfully, "just maybe."

"It's a wonder Mr. Riddle didn't buy him," Gordon said.

"He wanted to. He liked him a lot, but he didn't want to bid against Mrs. Jeffords."

"Oh," Gordon said. "Well, that might prove to be carrying a family relationship too far. He could be the top colt around here."

"Maybe," Danny repeated.

Gordon smiled. "You're thinking we can beat him with this one?"

"That's what I think," Danny answered.

"We'll find out when the speed trials start," Gordon said. "You won't have too long to wait."

They were back at the gap in the track fence and Louis Feustel came over to them. Looking up at Clyde Gordon, he said, "Take one turn of the track at a gallop, then move him along at a slow breeze the last eighth of a mile." The trainer turned to Danny. "Keep Major Treat right alongside, Danny. All you have to do is help keep the colt running straight and true. No swerving or bolting."

Gordon turned Man o' War back on the track, Danny following. "Remember, kid," Gordon said, "a breeze is just a bit faster than a gallop. We go any faster than that and Feustel will have our heads. More speed and distance will come when he's sure the colt's fit."

"I'll remember," Danny said.

Man o' War tried to bolt forward as Clyde Gordon gave him a little more rein. Then he settled into the slow gallop his rider wanted, shaking his head in resentment but not fighting. Danny kept Major Treat close beside him, talking to him all the while.

"That's it," Gordon said, satisfied. "Keep him traveling in a straight line and I'll hold him back. That's all we have to do this morning."

They galloped a bit more rapidly as they swept around the track, the big colt's strides coming ever faster and longer. His head was bowed by the tight hold on his mouth, but he didn't seem to resent Gordon's hands.

The boy glanced at Gordon. "Maybe you'll be able to turn his speed on and off," he called hopefully.

The man grunted. "One thing for sure is that I couldn't gallop him with no twine string," he answered. "He sure takes hold."

Danny nodded, knowing full well that it wasn't easy holding Man o' War back. He wanted to go, yet in his own way he was responding to the reins. But he was a lot of colt to handle and his red coat was already breaking out in sweat, not from exertion but from his anxiety to run as he would have liked.

"Don't let him jump out from under you," Danny cautioned.

"You ride your horse an' I'll ride mine," Gordon answered, a little angry. He was having trouble keeping the colt in line. He shortened his hold on the reins still more.

Danny felt the hard bump as Man o' War swerved against Major Treat. The gelding withstood the blow, snorting a little and pushing back, as was his job. He kept Man o' War on the rail.

Again Danny glanced at Gordon's hands. He understood the difficult job the man was having, and he wanted to suggest, "*Ask* him for obedience. Don't *demand* it or you're in for trouble."

Man o' War's strides lengthened to a fast gallop, his long mane and tail whipping the air more wildly now. Major Treat lengthened out to keep up with him. The rail sped by and Danny began counting off the furlong poles. The last eighth of a mile was before them! Gordon was letting Man o' War go into the breeze that Feustel had ordered.

"Easy. Easy," Danny heard Gordon calling to the fast-moving colt. And he himself echoed the man's words as they swept down the stretch.

Man o' War *seemed* to be listening to them, for his ears were constantly flicking to the front, side, and back. But his eagerness to run was a powerful compulsion that sought release. Major Treat was trying to stay alongside, his body stretched out to its utmost, his ears cocked back and flat against his head.

"Easy . . . easy," Gordon kept repeating, and not once did he relinquish the tight hold he had on the big colt.

They swept past the finish line and the crowd that was there. Danny moved Major Treat still closer to Man o' War and, leaning over, grabbed the colt's bridle. He brought him to a stop just as they were going into the first turn again.

Only then was Gordon able to sit back in his saddle and catch his breath. "Like you said, he *wants* to run," he muttered. "Maybe we have got a good one, Danny."

Man o' War pranced and pushed hard against Major Treat, almost upsetting the gelding as they turned and went back.

"He's still full of run," Gordon said. "Hold him to a walk now. Nothing makes Feustel madder than to have you gallop a colt back to him."

When they reached the trainer he seemed pleased. "You did fine," he said. "We'll hold him to a gallop tomorrow and breeze him again three days from now."

Louis Feustel turned his attention to the other yearlings he had working on the track, and Danny was made to realize once again that Man o' War was just another colt in the big stable. It would take time before Feustel knew what he had in Man o' War.

During the weeks that followed, Danny tried to be as patient as everyone else in determining Man o' War's relative speed. The big colt was held to slow breezes every third day and walked and galloped on the mornings in between. By the second week he was breezing a quarter of a mile rather than an eighth. But Feustel never allowed Clyde Gordon to ease up on his tight hold of the reins.

Only on Sunday was Man o' War given a day off, and then Danny turned him loose in the large paddock with Major Treat. The grass had turned brown with the coming of fall but the sun was still warm. The first month at Glen Riddle Farm had been a succession of nothing but fine, golden days, made even more pleasant by the good news from Europe. The United States and its allies were winning the war, and on November 11 it ended, only a few short months after Man o' War and the other Nursery Stud yearlings had been sold. The war hadn't gone on a long, long time, as Major Belmont had thought. And now all his young horses would be racing for other owners throughout the country . . . to what destiny?

Louis Feustel joined Danny at the fence one Sunday morning and for a while watched Man o' War at play with Major Treat. The big colt had fire in his eyes and was running around the old gelding, trying to get him to run too. But Major Treat continued grazing and waited patiently for Man o' War to work off his excess energy.

"He needs this freedom," Feustel said. "If he stood in his stall on Sunday, he'd be so fresh Gordon would have his hands full staying on him."

"He's growing like a weed," Danny said. "He's getting stronger every week."

Feustel nodded in agreement. "But he's still too thin for his size. He eats too fast, like he does everything else. Give him his head and he'll overdo, in his feedbox or on the track. He needs restraint."

Danny watched Man o' War finally stop playing and settle down with Major Treat under a big tree. "The Major quiets him down a lot," he said. He felt jealousy of the old hunter surge within him and tried to quell it. He understood the reasons for it. Man o' War had become increasingly dependent upon Major Treat, who was now stabled next to him. The colt was impatient, even unhappy, when his friend wasn't around.

"Yes," Feustel agreed. "He's helped us a lot."

Suddenly Man o' War broke into a run, sending the earth flying behind him. They watched him awhile, then Feustel said, "He's fast approaching the point where he can be set down and really tried."

"Have you any idea what he can do?" Danny asked, glad of the opportunity to discuss Man o' War's speed compared to that of the other yearlings in the stable.

Feustel shrugged his shoulders. "It's difficult to tell, Danny, over the short distances we've been going. His reach is tremendous, I know. And I even suspect we might have something, but I'm not sure by any means. We'll know more as he goes along."

Once again Danny resigned himself to waiting and the days passed slowly for him. He rode Major Treat to the track every morning and, along with Man o' War, learned the first lessons of racing. Sometimes Louis Feustel had him take Major Treat in front of Man o' War so that the big colt would learn to get a little dirt in his face without ducking out or refusing to run when it hit him. At other times they ran close together, changing positions frequently from inside to outside. Gradually, distance and speed were increased until Man o' War was jumping away quickly from Major Treat, his fastest moves sandwiched in between slow breezes. Soon, Danny knew, it would be time for a speed trial, when his colt would be running against a horse much faster than Major Treat.

"Jeffords's Golden Broom is the colt Feustel will try him against," a groom said late one night when the air outside was crisp with the first frost.

Moving closer to the small coal stove, Danny answered, "We'll beat him."

"I wouldn't be so sure, Dan."

"Red's the fastest colt in the barns," Danny asserted confidently.

"Sure, so is mine," the other groom said. "Every colt we rub is the fastest."

"I'm serious," Danny said.

"So am I," replied the other.

"No yearling around here takes such big strides as mine," Danny went on. "Golden Broom won't even be near him."

"Maybe Golden Broom will be too far in front, that's why," the other groom said, laughing. Then more seriously he went on, "That Jeffords colt gets away faster than any I've ever seen. He's got trappy, lightning strokes."

"Red will catch him," Danny said.

"Maybe so," the other agreed. "I hope so, anyway. We don't want no Jeffords colt beatin' any of ours."

Another groom moved closer to the stove for warmth. "If mine was as quick on his feet as he is with his teeth, he'd dash 'em all to death," he said. "Never did see an ol' divil so fast in the mouth. He turns on yo' quick as the blink of an eyeball."

They laughed and the second groom said, "I like 'em with dash, any kind of dash. Sort of breaks up the peace an' quiet 'round here this time of year."

"The speed trials will wake yo' up."

"You, too!"

"Me, too," the other agreed. "An' everybody else around here, jus' everybody."

Early the next morning Louis Feustel told Danny, "We're pairing him off with Golden Broom today. Get him ready."

When the boy remained stone still, Feustel smiled and said, "C'mon, Danny, don't take this so seriously. The only reason for a speed trial is to give the colt some idea of what his job is."

"Then why is everybody taking this one so seriously?" Danny asked, going to Man o' War.

"Just natural rivalry between two stables," the trainer answered. "But the result won't be as important as they think. Some yearling colts that can't run a bit in the fall beat the tar out of the fast ones when the races come along. It's what a colt does in the spring that really counts."

Danny slipped the bridle over Man o' War's head. "Are the Jeffordses and the Riddles here?"

"Sure, they wouldn't miss this for the world," Feustel said.

Then it *was* important, Danny decided. Despite Louis Feustel's statement that the result of the speed trial was not important, everybody wanted to win. They'd all be picking their colts to win, and he was no different. Man o' War just had to beat Golden Broom!

The Trials

13

In the gray light of dawn Danny stood at Man o' War's head as Clyde Gordon mounted. The big colt had put up his usual battle over being saddled but now seemed to be resigned to control. He tugged on Danny's lead shank as if he were impatient to get to the training track, and paid no attention to the nickers of the stabled horses or the calls of their grooms.

Feustel nodded and said, "Okay, Danny, take him away."

There'd be no Major Treat alongside Man o' War this morning to keep him in line. Man o' War was on his own and ready to be tried against a colt as fast as, or maybe even faster than, himself.

Danny brought him to a stop at the gap in the track rail, waiting for Feustel and the others to join them. Golden Broom was already on the track; his trainer, Mike Daly, was talking to the exercise boy riding him. For a moment Danny studied the colt from whom so much was expected by the Jeffords stable.

There was no doubt that Golden Broom looked as if he'd be able to give his boy a ride that few jockeys were privileged to take at that hour of the day. The colt appeared small but actually wasn't. He had a lot more muscle than was noticeable at first glance. He was built to go a distance as well as for speed. But most people weren't aware of that. They'd been so carried away by his ability to get away fast, his white-stockinged feet churning the track like the wheels of a locomotive, that most of them hadn't looked him over closely enough.

Danny's hand moved down the deep, well-sloped shoulders of his own colt. "But you're faster than he is," he told Man o' War, "and you'll get him in the end." The smooth, short coat beneath his hand was as soft as glossy satin and just as smooth. There was not a smudge on Man o' War, not a hair out of place. He was as slick as Danny could make him and ready to go!

The boy glanced again at Golden Broom. The first rays of the morning sun shone on his light-chestnut coat. Here, too, was gold that glistened, Danny had to admit. The speed trial would be something to watch.

Feustel came up and placed a hand on Man o' War's strong, level back. "Remember this is just a trial," he cautioned Gordon. "Don't try to steal the best of the break. Let them come out together, keep them head and head, then ask them to race down to the wire."

"You'd better speak to Daly then," Gordon said, glancing at Golden Broom's trainer. "You know our colt's too awkward and long-legged to get away as fast as that other colt, Louis. You know it as well as I do."

A moment later Danny removed the lead shank from Man o' War and Clyde Gordon rode him onto the track. Danny moved over to the rail to watch. The Riddles and the Jeffordses were a short distance away from him, their eyes too on the colts. Everything was very chummy, Danny thought, with no one attaching any importance to the coming trial. But each and every one in the two stables, including the women, expected to see a sensational workout.

Danny watched the colts intently as they moved up the track together. Despite Feustel's instructions and, Danny supposed, Mike Daly's, neither rider would attempt to keep his colt head and head with the other. This was a race, regardless of what anyone said! They were out to beat each other. No one would have had it any other way. This was the first test of speed between the two top colts at the training track. What they showed here in action, training, and speed would give an indication of what lay ahead during the spring racing season.

For a few moments the two chestnut colts, one light gold, the other a fiery red, strode beside each other. Golden Broom was on the outside, his body short and close-coupled, every movement one of marvelous control. He made Man o' War appear bigger and more awkward than he actually was.

A groom from the Jeffords stable said to Danny, "Now all the yakking 'round here will stop. We'll *know* who's got the top colt. You ain't got a chance of beating us, kid."

Danny wanted no arguments now, but he couldn't help saying, "A good big one can beat a good small one any day."

The other groom laughed. "You're talkin' through your hat," he said. "Stick around the tracks long enough and you won't be so impressed by the height and heft of a horse."

Danny turned back to the track. The two colts were nearing the starting pole, which was only an eighth of a mile from the finish line. The trial would require nothing more from Man o' War and Golden Broom than a short burst of speed from a standing start. Hardly worth getting excited about, Danny decided, and yet he knew his heart was pumping as fast as anyone else's.

"You see, I figure it this way," the other groom went on, re-fusing to let the matter drop. "A good-muscled, medium-sized horse can beat a good big one because he ain't got so much of his own weight to carry around. An' it's been proved there ain't enough difference in lung capacity to matter."

Danny kept quiet. It wasn't just his colt's size he'd meant. Man o' War had a big heart that matched his big frame. He wanted to *win*. That was the most important thing of all.

Golden Broom swung around, showing his hind heels to Man o' War. The big colt jumped, and for a moment Clyde Gordon had his hands full. Then he had Man o' War under control but the colt was in a sweat. Gordon took up more rein.

Danny muttered anxiously, "Hold on to him, Clyde. Hold on to him."

More than anyone else Danny knew what was going on within Man o' War. His colt's every movement at the starting pole convinced him that he would extend himself as he never had done in pasture. He was trembling with eagerness to pull free of Gordon's tight hold on his mouth. His ears were pricked and his eyes were on Golden Broom standing next to him. It wasn't the first time he'd been worked with a horse alongside. But he knew this wasn't Major Treat, this was dif-ferent!

Danny watched Clyde Gordon lean forward and whisper something in the big colt's ear. There was no doubt that he was trying to calm Man o' War. Danny felt the growing uneasi-ness in his own stomach. "Easy now. Easy," he mumbled, wishing he could help.

Man o' War tossed his head and swerved, trying to unseat his rider. But Gordon stayed in the saddle, his hands and seat firm. He got the big colt straightened out again and facing down the track toward the finish line.

Golden Broom had become excited over Man o' War's antics. He sidestepped nervously, his rider standing in the stirrup irons and trying to calm him down. The rider's face was very grim and set. He liked his mount's eagerness but he didn't want him to go to pieces before the trial started. Worse still, he didn't want him hit by the big, awkward colt alongside.

The man who was to start them waited patiently for the two colts to straighten out and stand still. He had all the respect in the world for the little men in the saddles. It was not easy to control young racehorses; they were much too confident in their newly discovered strength and determined in most cases to have their own way. Moreover, flat-footed breaking wasn't easy for a colt to learn. It would be even more difficult next spring when an elastic barrier was stretched across the track before them. But he needn't think of that now, he decided. His job this morning was simply to do his best to get them off together.

Man o' War reared, twisting and turning, trying to unseat his rider again. He came down without hurting himself or Clyde Gordon. His red body was shining with sweat. For a few seconds he was still, his head up and straight. Golden Broom was still, too.

"Go!" called the starter. The speed trial was on!

Golden Broom broke fast, just as Danny had expected, his short, powerful legs driving into the soft dirt and sending him flying along. Never had Danny seen a colt whirl and get away from a standing start at such blazing speed. Man o' War was slow in getting away, more than a length behind before he seemed to untangle his long legs and start to move.

"C'mon, Red! C'mon," Danny shouted at the top of his lungs, not caring who heard him just so long as there was a chance of his words reaching his colt!

Both riders were sitting very still and well balanced in their saddles, allowing their mounts to settle into racing stride. Yet faster and faster moved Golden Broom, as if no force on earth could have stopped him! Man o' War was hard against the bit too, but he was losing ground to the other, whose short strides were coming with ever-amazing swiftness.

When they had raced no more than one hundred feet from the barrier, Golden Broom had opened two lengths of daylight between himself and Man o' War. The golden colt hugged the rail, his body low, his legs flying. Behind him Man o' War began to unwind his long legs and then he began sweeping over the track with enormous leaps.

"Now!" Danny shouted. *"Get him, Red!"* He saw Clyde Gordon begin to move his body in rhythm with the big colt's strides. The rider was pushing Man o' War. It was the race everyone had expected!

They came charging down the stretch. Golden Broom's strides never faltered; his speed never lessened. Now everyone around Danny was shouting, urging the colt of his choice to win this very special race. But their voices were lost in the sound of the onrushing hoofs.

Man o' War responded to Gordon's urging, slowly at first, then faster and faster. But it was plain to Danny that his colt would have to work for every inch he gained on Golden Broom. The smaller colt was surging toward the finish line relentlessly, his head up and small ears pricked forward, his tail billowing like a cloak. He was continuing to pull away from Man o' War!

Danny bit his lip until he tasted the blood in his mouth. The golden colt was being asked for more speed and was really turning it on! Danny held his breath as the two flying bodies whipped by him with Golden Broom a good three lengths in front at the finish and looking as if he could have made it more had the race been longer. The speed trial had ended almost before it began.

Danny watched the two riders pull up their colts gradually prior to galloping out another quarter of a mile before coming to a stop. Man o' War was giving Gordon a fight, but the colt couldn't beat the hard hold on his mouth. Slowly his strides shortened. Golden Broom was still in front, his light-chestnut body hugging the rail as he swept into the turn. Man o' War went wide, his large frame and long legs carrying him almost to the center of the track.

Danny continued watching until they came to a stop on the far side of the track. Then he left the rail and walked slowly toward the gap in the fence, the lead shank in his hand. The trial had proved nothing, he tried to convince himself. Nothing except that Golden Broom could get away from the barrier faster than any other horse on the grounds. Besides, Feustel had said these speed trials weren't very important.

He stood next to the trainer, waiting for Man o' War to return. He didn't look at Feustel, keeping his eyes on the colts coming back at a jog. Both of them were still full of run and under a tight hold.

Golden Broom arrived first. Danny was surprised at the bitterness he felt toward the colt. He watched Mike Daly and others in the Jeffords stable go forward to meet him. The colt was tossing his handsome head continually while his body shifted nervously from one side to the other.

Danny left off gazing at Golden Broom, but only a few seconds later he turned and looked at him again. Anyone would look twice at this colt, he decided, no matter how he felt about the results of the trial. Everything about Golden Broom was so finely balanced. Also, every movement was so elastic, and his manner so arrogant and proud. This colt would probably never admit defeat.

But he could be overeager, too, Danny told himself. *He could use up most of his energy in a race. If he does, we'll get him at the end.*

Man o' War was closer now, his great eyes sweeping the crowd, his body sleek with sweat. Danny hoped that Man o' War was looking for him.

Louis Feustel went forward accompanied by Mr. Riddle, and Danny heard the trainer say, "I'm not worrying. Did you see how our colt was going at the end? Give us a longer distance and we'll outrun Golden Broom."

"I believe you're right, Louis," Mr. Riddle answered. "At least we'll know a lot more when they move up a bit."

Danny followed them across the sun-baked track. Reaching Man o' War, he snapped the lead shank on him and said softly, "I'm proud of you, Red. You gave a good account of yourself. The next time you'll get him." There wasn't a scratch on the colt, only sweat and dirt that could be washed off easily.

Back at the barn Danny stripped Man o' War and washed him while listening to the comments of those most concerned with his training.

"I'm certain Golden Broom will fold early once we go any kind of a distance against him," George Conway, the stable manager, said.

"I don't think so at all," Louis Feustel disagreed quietly.

Surprised at his trainer's remark, Mr. Riddle said, "But you mentioned only a few moments ago that you were pleased with the way Man o' War was going at the end, that you felt we'd outrun Golden Broom over a longer distance."

"I meant every word of it," Feustel answered. "But George thinks Golden Broom will fold an' I don't. I believe it's going to be simply a matter of our colt running faster once he gets in high gear. The Jeffords colt has substance. He looks to me like he's far more than a sprinter and will be able to go a distance."

"You mean a *classic* colt?" Mrs. Riddle asked, her eyes on the trainer.

"Yes, ma'am," Feustel answered. "Golden Broom can turn on the speed and keep going, I think."

Man o' War tossed his head as the water from Danny's sponge reached his flared nostrils. The boy wiped them clean of sweat and dirt while the colt's tongue sought to catch the dripping water.

"Hold still," Danny said, more to comfort his colt than to reprimand him.

Man o' War stood quietly, his great eyes sweeping the group that had formed a ring around him. He was getting used to all the activity in the stable area, Danny decided, just as he was to the hustle and bustle of the racetrack. Man o' War was learning stable manners, which were as important as track manners. He was ignoring the throng just as he did the whinnies of the stabled mares and the calls of other young stallions.

"Well," Mr. Riddle said, "we can be *certain* of nothing at this stage of the game."

The group was breaking up, and Louis Feustel followed Mr. Riddle toward the barn. "No," he agreed, "but we can sure hope."

Danny finished washing Man o' War. It looked as though he alone was certain that when the distance of the speed trials was lengthened, his colt would show his heels to Golden Broom without any trouble at all.

However, a few days later Danny, too, was resigned to *hoping* they had the top colt on the grounds. Man o' War and Golden Broom raced a quarter of a mile, a furlong farther than the first trial, with the same result as before. At the end of the race there were several lengths of daylight between the two colts and Golden Broom could have gone on.

"We'll catch him when they race another furlong farther," he said convincingly.

But they didn't. The following week the two colts were raced over a still longer distance, three furlongs, and Golden Broom was again the winner. His margin of victory was narrower than in the two earlier speed trials, but there was no doubt in anyone's mind that he was the faster colt at this stage of training.

"Don't look so discouraged, Danny," Louis Feustel told the boy the next day. "I still think we have the better colt, and he'll prove it when it comes to racing next spring."

Danny said, "Sure." But at that moment he recalled too vividly the way Golden Broom had come billowing down the stretch in front of Man o' War to be certain of anything. Golden Broom had come into his own, and there'd be trouble ahead for everybody in the spring, including Man o' War at his very best.

Spotlight

14

Louis Feustel banged a boot heel against the tack trunk on which he sat. Then he stood up and went to the stall door to look inside at Man o' War.

"A colt doesn't usually mature as fast as he's doing," the trainer told Danny. "He fouled himself up in the trials. He's so big he got in his own way."

Danny remained seated on an overturned water pail. He scuffed his feet in the dirt and said, "He'll grow even more during the winter. Maybe he'll get too big for his own good."

"They don't come *that* big, Danny," Feustel answered without taking his eyes from the colt. "The bigger he is, the longer his stride will be."

"He's eating twelve quarts a day and looking for more," Danny said thoughtfully.

"But he's still bolting it down. Next time you feed him put a bit in his mouth. That'll slow him up."

Danny nodded. "He'll still be rattling his empty feed tub before any of the others."

Feustel started to leave. "If he loves to run like he loves to eat we're all right, Danny." He paused, turning back to the stall again. "His heart's got to be as big as the rest of him. That's more important than anything else. Nothing can make up for the lack of it, no world of speed, nothing. If he's got heart, we're in. If he hasn't, we've got just another fast horse."

Winter came to Glen Riddle Farm, and with the snow and cold all the yearlings were held to slow gallops. They continued going to the track every morning under saddle, for Louis Feustel believed that young horses grew and developed more rapidly under a program of regulated exercise.

"They're also apt to forget everything they've learned if we turn them out to run as they please," he told Danny. "Light work is best for them now."

Danny found that while the winter months were a time for his colt to rest, be cared for, and fattened, he himself was in some ways busier than ever. People were constantly coming to the stall to examine Man o' War. The big colt was tested for parasites and treated. His legs were checked thoroughly to make sure nothing had popped during his daily gallops through the mud and snow. His teeth were checked and sharp edges filed off; those that had to come out were pulled.

Danny didn't like to go to the dentist himself, and every time the man came around with the big file in his hand, he cringed.

"You're worse than your colt," the horse dentist said, waving the file in the boy's face. "A bad tooth can cause a horse a lot of discomfort. It can make him pull on one rein, fight the bit, and make for other trouble."

"Sure," Danny said agreeably but without enthusiasm. Proper care of the teeth was necessary, he knew. Just like everything else that was being done to make certain there would be no interruption later on when his colt would be subjected to more intensive training. "Go ahead," he added, turning away so that at least he wouldn't have to look at the rasping file.

He was learning lots about the care of horses these long winter months, he decided. His colt's stall was as clean as any other in the big stable. No one ever had to worry about where to step or put down a knee while examining Man o' War. Like everything else, there were certain tricks to mucking out a stall and saving clean straw. He had listened and learned a lot from Frank and the older grooms. The better he treated Man o' War, the faster his colt might run.

Take the matter of grooming Man o' War. There was a lot more to it than he had ever thought. First, he used a rub-rag, cleaning Red's head gently but not too rapidly. He went behind the ears and under the halter, then moved on to the neck, chest, and shoulders before whisking off the stall dust from the back. Then he went down the thighs to the legs, holding the hind leg a few inches above the hock in order to deflect the leg if the colt tried to kick him. As well as Man o' War knew him, there was always the possibility of being kicked, for every horse was apt to act on impulse.

The big colt objected more to the stiff brush that Danny used when he finished with the rub-rag. So the boy went very carefully over the head, cleaning the roots of the foretop well, and talking to the colt as he worked. He was extra careful when he brushed the legs and under the flanks and thighs. The skin about the heels was very tender so he took every precaution to avoid irritating it. When he was satisfied that he had his colt clean, he went over him again with a soft brush until Man o' War was shining as he wanted him to shine.

Only then would he use the comb, running it carefully

through the colt's mane and tail until he had the hair free and flowing. His greatest pride was that he could use a comb without pulling out a single hair!

There were days for play too. At least once a week Louis Feustel would order the colt to be turned loose in the big paddock with Major Treat. Danny would watch them from his seat on the fence, glorying in the length of his colt's strides as he played in the winter sun. Man o' War was so robust and full of fun that often he would rear and kick out at Major Treat. But the old gelding was far too wise to be caught napping by the frisky colt.

"It's a good thing he doesn't have shoes on," Danny said to another groom who had stopped to watch.

The other nodded in full agreement as Major Treat narrowly avoided being kicked. "He's fast with his hoofs. It's a good thing for all of us that Feustel keeps his colts unshod. We'd all be carrying hoofmarks the rest of our lives. My colt's as bad as this one."

"They're all pretty free with their feet," Danny admitted.

"Feustel will keep them barefoot as long as possible," the other groom went on. "Then when he sees their feet showing signs of wear, he usually shoes them only in front. With their hind feet bare they're not so apt to grab their front feet and cut up the coronary band pretty bad."

On January 1, 1919, all the yearlings in the big stable celebrated their second birthday. It didn't matter that all of them had some months to go before they were actually two years of age. Officially, in the eyes of the Thoroughbred Racing Association, they were two-year-olds, grown up and old enough to begin their racing careers the following spring.

The only festivities about the stable were extra carrots for the youngsters and a day of rest. Danny remained with his colt most of the day, thinking of another date, March 19, almost two years before, when he had seen Mahubah give birth to Man o' War. They had come a long way since then, but to him the most important thing of all was that he was still beside his colt.

He groomed Man o' War perhaps more lovingly than ever that morning. It was warm for the first day of the new year, so when he had finished with the soft brush, he dampened a sponge and went over the colt again. He cleaned out the flared nostrils and sponged around the eyes and in back of the ears. He went up and over the turn of the mane, and then over the rest of the big body.

When Danny had finished he stepped back, admiring his horse and his work. Man o' War would have been the envy of the big stable if anyone had been around to see him. But it didn't really matter that they were alone. He loved his horse so much that it was enough of a thrill just to see the rich sheen of color come out of his coat.

Man o' War was gaining in strength and size with every day that passed. He hadn't had a sick moment since the time of the flu and had never missed an oat. Danny had checked his feed tub after every meal to make sure, for when a colt backed off his feed it meant trouble.

He hadn't developed any bad stable habits, either, as some of the other youngsters had done. The worst were the cribbers, Danny decided, those who took hold of some part of their stall while inhaling and swallowing deep drafts of air with a grunting sound. He hadn't let his colt even *see* any of the cribbers, for that's how the habit seemed to get started—just from watching others!

Danny said to Man o' War, "Imagine, swallowing air just for the fun of it!" The colt stood quietly beside him. Man o'

War was the best-mannered colt on the grounds. It was only when he was taken outside his stall that he wanted to break loose and stretch out, his tail fanning the wind. *And then*, Danny thought, *it's all right. That's the way it should be.*

Man o' War's gallops were kept to a mile and a half during January and February. He went to the track every day except on those days when the track was frozen and dangerously slippery. Snow didn't keep him in his stall and he loved galloping in it, sending it flying in his wake.

Watching him, Feustel told Danny, "Snow is good for a horse's feet and legs. Even galloping in the mud is okay unless a cold rain is falling at the same time. Getting their bellies wet won't hurt them any. But getting their bellies *and* backs wet at the same time is liable to cause trouble."

By the first of March work started in earnest for all the two-year-olds. Danny, along with everyone else, crossed his fingers in anticipation of the spring races to come. He watched his colt's gallops lengthened to three miles, then the breezes came. First Louis Feustel had him run a quarter mile at a good clip, then the distance was extended to three furlongs until, finally, the big colt was going a half mile in long, wonderful strides.

Danny saw Feustel stop his watch at fifty-five seconds, good time for a two-year-old under a tight hold! *He's coming along*, Danny told himself hopefully. *He's coming along fast.*

But the boy knew that Man o' War still had much to learn about racing before he faced the starter. Like all the other colts, he was skittish and nervous on the track. If a piece of paper blew across his path he would shy quickly, almost unseating Gordon.

"He'll get over that soon," Feustel told him. "A couple of months from now he'll be running straight and true despite anything that happens."

"I hope so," Danny answered. "He's going to hear a lot of noise and excitement coming down the stretch."

So he waited patiently but with some concern as March passed and Man o' War's work was stepped up still more. His colt continued to rear skyward every time he was saddled and mounted. But everyone had come to expect this token battle from Man o' War. He'd always be something of a rebel, and it didn't matter very much so long as he didn't carry it too far.

The weather became warmer and Man o' War shed his winter hair. His coat was a fiery red bronze, becoming ever sleeker as the weeks passed. Danny noted that Louis Feustel was watching the big colt more carefully, too. Every lightning move Man o' War made was as dramatic as his glistening body. Those who had looked upon him as just another fast youngster, whose early speed was showing some promise, began to sit up and take greater notice.

"Maybe we've got a prize package in this colt," the trainer told Danny one night early in May. "We're moving the stable to Havre de Grace racetrack in a few days, but I don't plan to start him there. I'm going slowly with him, more slowly than with any of the others. I don't want to make any mistakes, just in case . . ."

Havre de Grace was only a short distance from the training farm, and the following week the Riddle and Jeffords stables moved there. The mere sight of the large number of horses preparing for the spring races sent quivers through Danny's body. He thought of what might be in store for his colt. He tried to quell his excitement, knowing that it would not have a good effect on Man o' War. But his horse was as excited as he.

"Take it easy," he told Man o' War, his words of caution meant for himself as much as for his colt. "We're not even going to race here."

Feustel ordered slow workouts, but Clyde Gordon had his hands full keeping down the colt's speed. Despite everything the trainer and rider could do, Man o' War was beginning to move into the spotlight.

"They still don't know what I've got in store for them," the trainer said one morning. "He's fairly hard and ready for more speed if I ask it of him. A few fast moves and he'll be ready to race. But I don't want to ask him for it too soon. First we've got to teach him to break from the barrier. He has to learn to get away faster."

"He'll learn, Boss," Danny said. "It may take a little time but he'll learn."

"We'll find out," Feustel said, "starting tomorrow morning."

The next day Danny had Man o' War rubbed and brushed until his coat gleamed like polished copper. He held the big colt while Gordon mounted. When the man was up and settled in his seat Feustel said, "Danny, take the Major out with him this morning. Go as far as the barrier. Leave him there."

Eagerly Danny saddled the old gelding and mounted, taking hold of the lead shank to Man o' War's bridle. He heard Feustel tell Gordon, "I'll have a pair of colts with you at the barrier. They're fast, so try to break him with them and come out together. He ought to remember his yearling trials and break straight."

They rode toward the track, the sun golden in the east, the mist rising from the river beyond the backstretch. Danny felt the enchantment of the early morning and the mounting excitement of the big colt beside him. Man o' War was fresh and eager to run.

"Take a good hold on him, Clyde," he said cautiously.

"I know. He's up against the bit even now, walking. No

one's ever goin' to have to drive this colt, Danny. He'll do everything with his whole heart, every single minute." The man took another wrap of the reins about his hands.

They kept to the outside rail going up the track. A short distance away was the elastic barrier with a set of four young horses behind it. Suddenly the barrier snapped up, sending the colts away. Danny recognized one of them as Golden Broom, whose pistonlike legs had driven him from the flat-footed start like a catapult. He watched as the golden colt flashed by, lengthening his lead more and more.

"We'll never get off like him," Danny told Gordon, "but we'll catch him in the end."

"Maybe," the rider shrugged, "if we don't run out of ground first." His gaze turned back to the barrier. "There's time enough for that later on."

The two colts that Feustel had sent with them were already at the barrier. Man o' War's body broke out in a sweat as he approached it, and Danny wondered if the elastic webbing would upset him. Except for that, the standing start would be no different from his fall speed trials.

Don't hurry him, he wanted to say to Gordon, but he kept his mouth shut. His advice wouldn't be welcome now. Gordon had enough to do. It took strong hands to control Man o' War.

Behind the barrier Danny removed the lead shank, and Gordon walked Man o' War up to the barrier beside the two other colts. Danny watched him anxiously. His colt was nervous and sniffing what to him must seem an awesome contraption. Suddenly Man o' War reared and twisted away from the barrier.

Clyde Gordon had a difficult time staying in the saddle. He grabbed everything he could in order to stay on as the big colt tried to unseat him. Finally the man regained his balance and his strong hands had Man o' War under control again. Once more he walked the colt up to the barrier.

"That's it," Danny mumbled to himself. "Let him get used to it. He's got brains. He'll learn what it's for."

The two other colts were quiet and in position. The starter stood just inside the rail watching Man o' War, waiting for him to settle down before snapping up the barrier.

Man o' War bolted, trying to break through the elastic webbing. Gordon pulled hard, turning him around. Again the colt reared, twisting and trying to unseat his rider.

"Easy, Red! Easy!" Danny called. He watched Gordon regain control again, turning Man o' War back. Danny knew how suspicious his colt was of the webbing. But he had to get used to it. What Man o' War learned now would affect his whole racing career. Those who were handling him had a big horse. They had to do it right.

Gordon had him right up at the barrier, his nose against it. For a few seconds he was quiet and ready. No more waiting was necessary. The elastic sprang up and the track was clear!

Danny watched the two other colts break ahead of Man o' War. He had expected them to get away first. It didn't matter, for his colt was now off and running!

Clyde Gordon sat low and forward, waiting for Man o' War to settle in stride and not urging him to catch the fast-breaking colts in front. Longer and longer came Man o' War's strides, and Danny could imagine the wind beginning to sing in Gordon's ears!

"Come on, Red!" he shouted at the top of his lungs. Major Treat, surprised by the shrillness of his call, almost jumped from beneath him.

This was no race, Danny reminded himself. There was no reason to get excited. His colt was simply learning to break from the barrier. He would go a short distance and be pulled up, perhaps to come back and break again if Feustel ordered it. But Danny's heart kept pounding as he watched Man o' War begin to catch up with the others.

The big colt had his legs untangled now, his strides no longer awkward. Suddenly, as though in one mighty leap, he had overtaken the others. He became nothing but a red, whirling blur in Danny's eyes. If he had been running before, he was flying now! Faster and faster he swept down the track, fighting for his head and pulling Gordon clear of the saddle. Never had Danny seen Man o' War run so fast before. Neither had anyone else! Only when Man o' War neared the first turn did he give in to Gordon's hold on his mouth. Slowly, ever so slowly, his strides shortened until in the far-distant backstretch he came to a stop.

As Danny rode Major Treat toward him, he knew that Feustel could no longer keep Man o' War's electrifying speed to himself. This morning everyone at Havre de Grace had been exposed to it, if only for a few blinding seconds. The word would pass from track to track until the whole turf world knew that the Riddle stable had a youngster to watch in the races to come.

Later, Danny walked Man o' War under his cooler. He stopped every once in a while to let the colt take a swallow of water. Only when Man o' War was thoroughly dry under the light sheet and ignored the water bucket did Danny take him to his stall. There he rubbed him down with a mild liniment.

Louis Feustel came into the stall and carefully inspected the colt's legs and feet. "He got away from Clyde this morning but, luckily, he didn't hurt himself," he said quietly.

"You've got him hardened, that's why," Danny said. He went back to work, Feustel watching every move he made. He

cleaned Man o' War's feet carefully, picking out all the dirt
and washing them inside and out.

"Golden Broom's got trouble," Feustel said.

Danny looked up. "Did he hurt himself this morning?"

"He's developed a quarter crack in his hoof," the trainer answered. "It might bother him all his running days. You can
never tell about an injury like that."

Putting down the colt's leg, Danny began stirring a bucket
of mud with a small wooden paddle. A horse's feet had to be
able to take hard training and racing. No feet, no horse, it was
said. And that might be true of the highly regarded Golden
Broom.

He added a little more water to the mud until he had a
smooth, doughy consistency. He wasn't going to let anything
happen to Man o' War's feet if he could help it. This mud clay
from Kentucky was playing an important part in his care.
When packed right, it kept the foot moist and soft enough to
withstand the hard, crushing impacts of the racetrack.

He spread the mud into the middle of the big colt's foot,
pressing downward toward the heel until the pack covered the
whole foot. Over it he put a small piece of paper that would
prevent the pack from coming out until it dried. He put down
the foot. Man o' War's weight would press the mud tightly
into the foot and frog. Then he went through the same proce-
dure with the next foot.

Louis Feustel said, "You've learned your trade well,
Danny."

"I've had good teachers," Danny said, not without pride.
"Frank, George, a lot of others." He noted the anxiety for Man
o' War in Feustel's eyes and understood. It took more than the
skill of a fine trainer to get a horse to the races.

Danny began wrapping Man o' War's legs with soft cotton

and gauze. He was almost done before Louis Feustel spoke again.

"You're sure that this is his water pail?" the trainer asked. He had the empty bucket in his hands and was examining it. "It doesn't look like ours," he added.

"It's his, all right," Danny said. "I'm sure of it."

"Influenza is catching up with a lot of horses on the grounds," Feustel said. "We've got to be careful it doesn't hit us."

"I'm watching him like a baby," Danny said. "I'm even scalding his feed box. He's not going to catch anything."

"I hope not."

"He's strong enough to throw off any flu germ," Danny went on. "He did it as a yearling. He could do it again, if he had to."

Feustel went to the stall door. "I hope he won't have to."

When Danny was finished with his work, he removed the colt's halter. "Everybody's happy with you," he whispered. "Just stay well and sound." He was not at all certain that his colt could withstand an influenza epidemic if it swept Havre de Grace. He was worried but thought it best not to brood about it.

During the days that followed, he continued to overlook nothing in the care and well-being of Man o' War. He tended to every minor and major chore, never getting out of seeing distance of the big colt's stall and making sure that his charge had plenty of rest during the afternoons, when the races were being run. He went so far as to close the stall door, making sure no noise from the stands would disturb the colt's nap. And when he took him out to graze and walk late in the day, he went where no other horses had eaten. Influenza germs could be left even on blades of grass.

He was really greatly relieved when the time came for the stable to move to Pimlico racetrack, a short distance from Havre de Grace. At that track the two-year-olds would continue their extensive training and some of them would make the first start of their young careers.

"But not Man o' War," Feustel told Danny as they were getting the colt settled in his new stall. "I think I'm going to wait until we reach Belmont Park before we start him. He'll be ready by then."

Danny wasn't worried about Man o' War's not being ready when Feustel sent him to the post. His only concern was that they might not have left the flu bug behind. Many of the older horses at Pimlico were sick and there was still a great danger of contamination.

"He didn't clean his feed tub this morning," he told the trainer, his eyes betraying his concern.

"Did you take his temperature?"

Danny nodded. "Normal," he said, "just 100."

"Keep taking it," the trainer ordered. "If it goes over 101 let me know."

During the week that followed, Man o' War resumed his workouts on the track, and every time he returned to his stall Danny took his temperature. After exercise it was always about 101 degrees but went no higher before dropping; there was no need for concern. By the second week at Pimlico several young horses in the Riddle stable had come down with the dreaded disease.

Danny watched Louis Feustel and the veterinarian go from one stall to another, attending the sick horses.

"You're strong enough to throw off any flu bugs," he kept telling Man o' War as the days passed and the disease swept the stable. But he knocked on wood for good luck each time he said it.

Late one evening Danny went into the stall and found Man o' War down in the straw. Dropping down beside him, he knew that the worst had happened. His colt was sick!

"Go get Feustel!" he shouted to a groom outside. "Red's down."

When the trainer arrived, Danny showed him the thermometer he held in his trembling hands. It had skyrocketed to 106 degrees.

Feustel said, "He can't have a fever like that very long without fatal results."

"Is the vet on his way?"

"I couldn't get hold of him. He's out on other calls."

Man o' War was burning up, his flesh hot beneath Danny's hands. "Can't we get another?"

"The only other veterinarians are in Baltimore. I've called them but they're out, too." Feustel said. "And now is the critical period." His eyes were as concerned as Danny's but there was no panic in his voice. He had seen too many sick colts that week. Turning to the other stableboys who had crowded close, he added quietly, "Get back."

"Give him some 'Dr. Green,' Boss," an old groom said. "I got some left."

"Dr. Green" was a piece of Kentucky sod. Many of the old grooms felt it could cure any sickness. Danny doubted its healing powers but eagerly awaited Feustel's reply.

The trainer said, "It wouldn't do him any good now, Tom." His eyes remained on the big colt. "Without the vet's help all we can do is wait. It's up to him to lick it by himself."

Danny watched helplessly. There was nothing anyone could do. Man o' War lay still, fighting the germs within him. Would the fire of Hastings and Fair Play outburn the disease?

Feustel broke the stillness of the stall. "The fever is only a symptom of the disease, and we have no medicine to kill the germs." He looked at the thermometer again. "It's up to 107 now," he said solemnly. "It can't go any higher."

Danny struggled to keep back the tears. He was too old to cry. The night dragged on with Feustel and others coming and going, kneeling beside Man o' War and waiting for the fever to break. When it did, Danny was still beside him. He listened to the chattering of the colt's teeth as a chill followed the long period of fever. He drew a light blanket over Man o' War, keeping him warm and saying comfortingly, "You're going to get well. I know you will." But he knew his words were more to reassure himself than Man o' War. His colt was fighting for his life all alone. No one could help him now, not even those who loved him very much.

Hour after hour went by with Man o' War's breathing becoming fast and irregular. This could be the most dangerous time of all, for pneumonia might quickly develop. Toward dawn the rasping breaths slowed down, and Danny took hope. Slower and more regular became the big colt's breathing. Finally Man o' War seemed to be in a sound sleep, and Danny closed his eyes, too.

He was awakened by the voices of Feustel and the veterinarian. They were kneeling beside Man o' War, and the stall was gray in the early light of morning.

The veterinarian was taking the colt's temperature. When he looked at it, he said, "It's normal. He's shaken off the bug himself. Let him sleep."

Once again Danny lay his head down beside that of his colt. This time he slept as soundly as Man o' War.

The Stirring Up

15

By midmorning Man o' War was up on his feet and demanding breakfast as loudly as on any other day. Danny, listening to his impatient whinnies, thought nothing had ever sounded so wonderful. The high fever had weakened Man o' War; so Danny, following Feustel's orders, kept him in his stall for a full twenty-four hours after his temperature had become normal. The trainer wanted to make sure that it wouldn't flare up again and that the disease was actually licked.

When the danger was past, Danny was allowed to walk the colt. He took him far from the barns to limber up his muscles and let him graze on the fresh young grass of early May. Man o' War loved the long walks as much as Danny did; he pulled hard on the shank, seeking his freedom. Danny held him tight. There would be time enough to run.

During the days that followed, Man o' War regained his strength fast. Nothing was too trivial for Danny to overlook in his care. He brushed and rubbed him until his coat had a burnished sheen to it, and there was never a night that Man o'

War did not sleep on the freshest of straw in the stables.

"He's eating good," Danny told Feustel at the end of the week. "He's not leaving anything in his box."

"He looks like he's ready, all right," Feustel agreed. "We can go on now. Some light exercise will be good for him."

Once again Danny relinquished Man o' War to Clyde Gordon's hands every morning. Sometimes he rode Major Treat alongside and, since Gordon was riding under orders to keep a tight hold on the big colt, Major Treat was never left behind. Danny gloried in the thrill of riding beside Man o' War, and there were mornings when he even allowed himself to dream of being up on his colt. But never in his wildest imagination did he actually believe such a day would ever come.

Danny was content watching Man o' War regain his full strength, moving up against the bit Gordon held firmly in his mouth. There was no doubt the big colt was more than willing to work faster than they were going. If Gordon hadn't been so careful, Man o' War would have slipped away from him.

Then the morning came when Feustel decided the colt was tight enough for faster works. Man o' War was sent trackward with other colts his own age. He broke from the barrier, slow as always, but caught up with the others quickly, his tremendous strides making a mockery of the workout.

Danny watched his colt surge down the backstretch, drawing farther and farther away from the others. He glanced at Feustel, standing beside him. The trainer had stopped his watch and his eyes were very bright when he said to no one in particular, "We've got a 'flyer.' "

Back in the stall, Danny rubbed Man o' War with the flat of his hand until the fine skin glistened more brilliantly than ever. He whispered softly, "I almost wish you wouldn't become too big a horse. If you do, I'll lose you for sure."

Man o' War whinnied as if he understood. It was a secret, Danny thought, that just the two of them would share.

The mornings that followed remained much the same, and only the afternoons changed. Not that it wasn't still very peaceful and quiet. But the day was fast approaching when Man o' War would go to the post, and the tension mounted. Everybody in the stable believed they had a prize package in Man o' War.

"We'll start him the first week in June, if all goes well," Feustel said.

Danny felt the undertone of expectancy rising within him as it must for Man o' War. He fought it, seeking to close his ears to the roar from the stands and the rush of hoofs every afternoon. He wanted these hours to pass peacefully, a little drowsily, as they had in the earlier weeks of training.

"It won't be here at Pimlico that you'll start, anyway," he told Man o' War. "We'll be in New York when you race. We've still got time to take it easy in the afternoons."

But his eyes, like those of his colt, were turned in the direction of the track. He could not deaden his ears to its sounds. How great would Man o' War become? he wondered. How far would he go? If he did everything expected of him, he would become a champion. A champion belonged to a lot of people and every move he made would be watched. Maybe, Danny thought, these were the best days he would ever have with his colt ... right now, standing alone with him in the big stall, unnoticed.

The next morning Louis Feustel showed up earlier than usual. He nodded to Danny and the other grooms, then said edgily, "Tack him up right this morning. No carelessness."

One of the older men had the stall door open but Feustel stopped him. "Not you, Frank. Let Danny do the saddling."

Danny went quickly into the stall, well aware that for a reason that Feustel chose to keep to himself, the morning would be different.

All eyes watched him as he slipped off the halter and buckled it around the colt's neck. That done, he had something to hold on to if Man o' War acted up.

"Easy, fellow," Danny said softly. But he knew that saddling Man o' War would never be an easy job no matter how often it was done. The moment the tack went on, Man o' War knew that the track was only minutes away.

Danny picked up the bridle from the straw at his feet and swung it carefully to the front, keeping his right hand on the colt's forehead to control and soothe him. He pressed the bit against the teeth but Man o' War wouldn't open his mouth until Danny slipped his left thumb into his mouth. No sooner was the bit in than he tried to spit it out. Danny kept tension on it, using both hands to get the headstall over the near ear.

"If I didn't know you, I'd think you didn't want to go out," he said, grunting. "Every day you have to put on this kind of an act." Man o' War jerked his head back, pulling the boy with him.

"Get it over the other ear," Feustel said gruffly. "You've got lots of room."

Danny nodded without pausing in his work. For the moment he was glad that he was tall, otherwise he never could have reached the top of the colt's head. He tilted the off ear forward and slipped the bridle over it. Now he had Man o' War under better control.

"Tacking up is no simple matter," Feustel was saying irritably, "even though there's little enough to put on. Maybe that's the trouble with some of you guys. It looks so simple that you figure anyone could do it. So maybe you forget to pay attention to little details."

Danny kept his mind on his work. He straightened out the colt's forelock and mane, which were caught under the headstall. He moved the reins back on the muscled neck and then fastened the throatlatch. He made certain that it was not too tight, for if so, it would bind the colt's throttle when he bowed his neck and pulled hard, as he was inclined to do. At the same time Danny didn't want it so loose that it swung in a loop below the jaw.

"That's good," Feustel said approvingly. "Now get the saddle on him."

Danny said, "Yes, sir," but he knew full well that saddling didn't begin with putting on the saddle. He picked up the saddlecloth and spread it across the colt's broad back. He pulled the front end well over the withers and made sure that the cloth hung evenly on both sides. He wanted it flat and unwrinkled. Satisfied, he placed the thick felt saddle pad across the back, making sure that the front part was well up on the withers but just a little to the rear of the forward edge of the cloth. He folded the cloth back over the pad, keeping it even on both sides. Then he took still another thick pad, oblong in shape, and centered it lengthwise on the saddle pad. Only then was he ready for the saddle. The big colt's back was well protected from chafing or rubbing.

Carefully he lifted the saddle, clearing Man o' War's back and setting the saddle firmly on the pads. He let the girth strap fall to the off side, thrusting a foot underneath the colt to catch it and prevent the buckle from striking a foreleg and upsetting Man o' War. Then he reached under the colt and threaded the girth strap through the buckle, drawing it up easily.

Man o' War didn't like the tightening girth. He half reared and tried to pull away. But Feustel and the others were at his head, holding him down. The stall was filled with their soft mutterings: "Easy. Easy, Red. Easy."

Once outside, the trainer went over all that Danny had done. He inspected the bridle, cloth, pads, and saddle, finally slipping his fingers under the girth. Straightening, he turned to Danny and smiled for the first time that morning. "Most boys get it too tight, and the horse only galls himself. You did a good job, Danny."

But Danny wasn't listening. Man o' War was ready for his morning work, but it wouldn't be Clyde Gordon riding him. Waiting for the colt was Johnny Loftus, the Riddle stable's contract rider and the leading jockey in America. It wasn't often that he appeared mornings to work horses. He was wearing black breeches as gleaming as his boots, a turtleneck sweater, and no hat. He was slick and well groomed, looking every bit the successful jockey he was.

Feustel had already turned to him. "I want you to get to know this colt, Johnny," he said. "I think you'll be going places together."

The jockey's eyes swept over the big colt and he seemed to like what he saw, for he nodded in full agreement. "I heard he's got plenty of speed. It goes with the rest of him."

"He's yours now," the trainer said. "Get acquainted with him."

The mid-May air was fresh and cool but Danny felt the heat of anger rising within him. He brushed the sweat from his forehead. He resented the fact that Johnny Loftus, more than anyone else, would be a part of all that was to come. It would be his hands that would guide Man o' War in the stirring battles of the racetrack.

Danny held Man o' War while Loftus mounted. *What'd you expect anyway?* Danny asked himself angrily. *Nothing is going to change for you, ever. It's enough that you're here when he gets back to the barn.*

Man o' War tried to break away, but Danny and the others were used to his antics and held on to him. Finally they walked him quietly toward the track gate.

Danny heard Johnny Loftus say, "I hear he's pretty sluggish at the start."

Feustel answered, "He doesn't like to wait, but he's too big to get away fast." Then, chuckling, he added, "He doesn't have any trouble catching the others."

"I'll stir him up," Loftus said. "Get him more on his toes. No sense in giving the others a handicap if we can help it."

"Don't get him too stirred up, Johnny," Feustel warned. "I believe he could be made to get away faster, but I'm not worried about that now."

"I'll take care of it," Loftus said.

Danny glanced up at the rider. Loftus would have to learn for himself that Man o' War could not be pushed around. To stir him up at the barrier would mean trouble. The big colt was excitable enough without any prodding.

Reaching the track, they stopped Man o' War while Feustel tightened the girth strap another hole. Just beyond, a black colt and a rider awaited them. Danny recognized the horse as Dream of the Valley, who had also been showing a lot of speed in his workouts. As Mr. Riddle had purchased him at the sales for only $3,500, he too looked like a real bargain. Man o' War had never worked with this colt before, so it would be something to watch.

Feustel was telling Loftus, "The black colt breaks fast, so he just might take your colt out with him. At least he'll show him how it should be done."

"I won't be left behind," Loftus said. "I don't like a sluggish colt at the barrier."

"Have them break together if you can," Feustel went on.

"Stay together for the first two furlongs, then let them race through the final quarter."

"Right," Loftus said, signaling to Danny and the others to release the big colt.

Man o' War plunged onto the track, eager to get to the business for which he had been bred and raised. There was no Major Treat alongside, no familiar hands on the reins . . . his racing days with Johnny Loftus had begun.

Danny remained with Louis Feustel as the trainer moved along the rail until he found a spot near the barrier. Other young horses were being schooled, and the shouts of the starting officials and riders filled the air.

Feustel nodded to one of the men lounging against the rail. " 'Morning, Mr. Parr," he said.

" 'Morning, Louis," the other answered, scarcely taking his eyes off the horses behind the barrier. "What's that chestnut colt you got there?"

"Man o' War," Feustel replied. "By Fair Play out of Mahubah."

"He's right big for a two-year-old. And the black?"

"That's Dream of the Valley. By Watervale out of Dream Girl," Feustel answered.

"Nice, too, if not as big as the chestnut," Mr. Parr said. "Mr. Garth and I," nodding to indicate the man next to him, "are betting a dollar apiece as to which of these schooling youngsters gets away on top. I've got a couple colts of my own here. Paul Jones is pretty clever at getting away fast. I like him."

"My black colt has a lot of foot, too," Feustel said, smiling. "Watch him."

"Oh, I will. And the chestnut? What about him?"

"Too big to get away fast," Feustel said. "But he should catch the black colt."

During the conversation their eyes had never left the two colts behind the elastic barrier.

"Your chestnut colt is eager to get away," Mr. Parr said. "He won't stand still."

"I know," Feustel said with some concern.

"My, there he goes up, fighting Johnny! He's an excitable youngster, all right."

"No, just *eager*, like you said before," Feustel corrected.

"There, he smashed into your black colt, Louis," the other said. "Johnny better be more careful. He's savage . . ."

"No, the colt's not vicious or mean," Feustel said. "He knows what's coming. He's on his toes more than I've ever seen him at the start. If Johnny can just get him straightened out now . . ."

Mr. Parr shook his head. "I'm afraid Johnny might succeed in stirring him up beyond his intentions. That colt's going to delay many a start by his behavior. There, Johnny's got him down and straight. They might be sent off now."

Danny had watched every move his colt and Johnny Loftus had made. Man o' War reared continuously, attempting to get rid of his rider. But Loftus knew his business and stayed in the saddle.

Suddenly the elastic barrier snapped skyward, leaving the track clear. Man o' War had never been more ready to go. All the excitement that Loftus had stirred up in his great body was unleashed with tremendous force. The fast black colt never had a chance to leave him behind. Man o' War's strides were longer than the other's, but coming as fast. Despite all Loftus could do to keep Man o' War even with the black colt for the first two furlongs, he began pulling away. And there was nothing more to the workout than a lone red horse sweeping around the track.

Danny heard Mr. Parr exclaim, "You've got a thunderbolt, Louis! You really have."

"Could be," Feustel said warily. "You can't be sure of anything with colts." But in his jaded eyes, too, could be seen the first glimmerings of a fire that was already burning at fever pitch in Danny Ryan's.

First Start

16

A week later the stable moved to Belmont Park just outside New York City. At first the big colt was extremely nervous in his new surroundings, so Danny took him for long walks about the spacious grounds. It was fitting, he thought, that Man o' War would be making his first start there, for the track was named after August Belmont, the founder of Nursery Stud. In a way it was a sort of homecoming.

The word had been passed along the "grapevine" that the Riddle stable had a two-year-old that would bear watching, so those already at Belmont Park provided their own manner of welcome. They turned out in force to watch Man o' War's first early-morning workout. The big colt did not disappoint them. Under Johnny Loftus he reeled off a half mile in the blazing time of forty-seven seconds!

In subsequent workouts he was clocked again and again in the same time until, finally, no horse his age or older was watched more closely. Man o' War took it all in easy stride, unruffled by the growing fuss being made over him. His only resentment was evident in his constant fight against the chok-

ing hold Loftus held on him to keep him from running his
heart out.

"We got a colt that's a real racehorse," the famed jockey
told Danny one morning when they returned to the stall.

The boy said nothing as he stripped the tack from Man o'
War. There was no doubt that Johnny Loftus had become very
fond of the colt. He'd continued showing up mornings even
when it wasn't necessary, and there were times when Danny
had caught him feeding Man o' War a carrot.

"Yes, Danny," the jockey went on. "I think we got a big one
here. There's something electric about him. I never felt anything like it before, and I've been on a lot of them."

Man o' War suddenly moved, reaching with his teeth.
Loftus jumped back, avoiding the bared mouth and slapping
the colt lightly on the muzzle.

"He's got a nice eye but he's quick with his teeth," the
jockey said.

"He's just hot," Danny said, apologizing for his colt. "He
wouldn't take hold."

"Maybe not," Loftus answered. "I don't mind. I like a horse
with a bit of dash. I like *him*. He does things to me. We're
going places together, him an' me."

"Sure," Danny said. "Sure you are." He paused, not quite
certain whether or not he should tell Loftus what he had in
mind. Finally he took the plunge. "I wish you'd stop stirring
him up so much at the start."

The smile left Johnny Loftus's face. "I don't like sluggish
horses, Danny," he said quietly.

"He's not sluggish. He's just big."

"I work him up an' he gets away with the others. It's as simple as that."

"Leave him alone and he'll catch them without fighting,"
Danny said.

It was several minutes before Danny was able to turn back to his work. He knew he should have kept quiet. It wasn't his job to tell Johnny Loftus what to do, when Feustel and everybody else was happy with the colt's progress. Instead, he should do everything possible to keep Man o' War calm in his stall and leave the "stirring up" to others.

But even the quiet of the big stall was disrupted as the day of the race approached. Louis Feustel realized now that never before had he had such a colt, and it was his responsibility to keep him safe and sound.

"I don't want him left alone for a minute, ever," he ordered. "And that includes night as well as day."

So other grooms joined Danny in the care of Man o' War to make certain that the prized colt would remain safe and secure. It was a lot of fuss to be making over a youngster who had not yet faced the starter. But the men in the Riddle stable knew the time had come to unfurl Man o' War in all his glory!

Man o' War knew before dawn, the morning of June 6, 1919, that things were different. He had had less hay than usual during the night and none at all in the morning. And he had not been given his full box of oats! He clamored for more feed, and when it was not forthcoming, he became anxious to leave his stall. But in this, too, he was frustrated.

There was a steady stream of visitors throughout the morning, but the door was always closed quickly behind them. Man o' War was rubbed over and over again with brush and rag until there was a burnished sheen to his copper coat. He listened to the soft murmurings of many voices, some familiar, others not. He sensed the anxiety and anticipation in the close air of the stall. Something *big* was going to happen. Yet he was not permitted to leave.

Danny had the colt's mane and tail clean and flowing. He glanced at the man who was kneeling in the straw, holding an oval-shaped foot in his hand. "He knows what's coming, all right," he said quietly to Frank, the other groom.

"Yeah, he's ripe and ready to race."

"It's going to be a long day," Danny added. "The waiting, I mean."

The man grunted. They were both aware that Man o' War was watching them with a calm and knowing eye.

At noon Danny gave Man o' War a light feeding of oats and remained in the stall with him. His own nervousness and tension were mounting even if the colt's weren't. It wouldn't get any easier during the afternoon. They had to wait until the very last race on the program, the 8th, a race solely for two-year-olds, most of them making their first starts like Man o' War.

Somehow the hours passed. The area outside the stall became even more crowded with visitors. The colt's excitement mounted and lather showed between his legs.

Louis Feustel watched him closely. "He's tight," he said, "but not nervous. He's in top shape."

Mr. Riddle was there, looking very confident but as nervous as anyone else. He said quietly, "You used good judgment in holding him back until now, Louis."

"He picked his own time," Feustel answered. "He furnished his own spark like all good horses do."

"I suppose so," Mr. Riddle said. "If he wasn't ready to go we'd know it."

The trainer stepped back from the stall. "Physically he's fit and, just as important, he's in the proper mental condition to race." He smiled encouragingly at Mr. Riddle. He enjoyed working for this man. They made a good team, as an owner and trainer should. He believed he knew Sam Riddle as well as he did every horse in the big stable. He realized how much money it cost to race and how much was at stake.

Mr. Riddle turned to meet Feustel's smile, his own face lightening. "Then we might have a good one, Louis," he said. His eyes said more.

"A *great* one, sir."

"We'll know before long," the owner answered, refusing to allow himself to be too optimistic. He enjoyed watching his horses race whether they won or lost, for Louis Feustel never annoyed him with every little irritating detail that came up in a stable as large as his. Feustel took care of the details without running to him. He did his level best to get winners, and that was all any owner could ask.

It was two o'clock. "Take the water pail out of his stall, Danny," Feustel ordered. "Give him a few more swallows just before he leaves for the paddock."

He turned again to Mr. Riddle and they walked away, their heads together. Each understood the other. Each had learned to give and take. They were about to embark on a new venture, probably the biggest of all although neither would have admitted it. Each expected great things of Man o' War, but they were prepared to take defeat if necessary.

Back in the stall Man o' War was not touched again. The last few hours of waiting had begun. But for Danny they were, perhaps, the longest hours of all. He listened to the roar from the stands with each successive race on the day's program. He watched the other horses in the stable area come and go, their caretakers busy and joking. He remained silent and tense, conscious only of the colt in the stall behind him and the ever-lengthening shadows.

Finally Frank came up to him. "It's time, kid."

They went into the stall and went over Man o' War with a damp sponge for the last time. Neither said a word as they cleaned head and nostrils, then went over the turn of the

mane, back to the tail, to the root and under, and finally down
the long, sleek legs. A few swallows of fresh water and they
were done.

The short walk to the paddock was made quickly, quietly.
Man o' War tugged on his lead shank as if he knew his time
had come. And now he wore a cooler that was all black with
yellow around the edges, the racing colors of the Riddle stable.
He looked very beautiful, very worthy of these colors.

Feustel was waiting for them just within the fenced paddock. The trainer glanced at Major Treat and was glad that he
had decided to have the old gelding come along, for he was
definitely having a quieting effect on Man o' War. Just the
same, Feustel decided to take no chances of the colt's acting
up in the strange surroundings. As they approached the saddling shed he said, "Have him face the back of it until we get
him saddled. We'll have less trouble if he's looking at the partition."

There were few people in the paddock compared to earlier
in the afternoon. The shadows cast by the wide-spreading
chestnut and oak trees were long and empty. The late air was
cool. A small crowd hung over the paddock fence, watching
last-minute preparations for the last race of the day.

Mr. Riddle stood with some of the other owners a short distance away from Man o' War. He saw Johnny Loftus come
into the paddock, carrying his light racing saddle. For a moment the owner's eyes studied Johnny's slight figure, the white
breeches, and especially the black-and-yellow silk blouse.

All was as it should be, Mr. Riddle decided. He had the best
jockey in America and Man o' War was ready to run.

Louis Feustel took the saddle from Loftus and placed it
carefully on the colt's back. Man o' War half reared, taking the

boys at his head off their feet. They managed to hang on and brought him down, their mutterings filling the stall.

When Feustel tightened the girth strap, the colt half reared again, banging his handlers against the sides of the stall. They were more afraid Man o' War would hurt himself than of any injury to themselves. But the saddle was on and the big colt quieted down as if he knew it was of no use to protest any longer. Feustel noticed the dark spots of sweat beginning to show on the red coat. Man o' War was becoming very impatient. He had been waiting a long, long time.

Feustel turned to Loftus. "You've got yourself the hottest horse in the race," he said. "They've made him the favorite."

Loftus thought the trainer sounded a little uneasy. "That's to be expected," he said lightly. "None of the others have worked as fast as he has."

"Still, all six are high-class youngsters. Don't get overconfident."

Loftus smiled. "I'm not," he said. "I just happen to think he'll make the others look like pretty cheap horses."

"We can't be sure of anything," Feustel warned. "Most important, see that he doesn't get hurt. Make certain he has plenty of racing room. Anything can happen in a race for two-year-olds. There'll be a lot of swerving and bumping. Keep him clear of it. We know he's not wanting in speed, but he may not have racing luck. And he's had no experience. Don't be too disappointed if things don't go your way and you lose. Just get him back sound."

Loftus nodded.

Louis Feustel ordered Man o' War taken out of the paddock stall and turned around so he faced the ring. Now the big colt was all eyes and ears. He began sweating again.

"*Danny*," Feustel ordered, "get Major Treat over here where he can see him. *Clyde*, you get up on the Major and ride to the post with him. *Frank*, get a better hold on his bridle. *Johnny*, you ready?"

All was in order. The other horses were already in the walking ring. The time had come.

"Riders mount, please," the paddock judge called.

Johnny Loftus sat easily in the saddle, listening to Feustel's final instructions and nodding as he should.

"I'm more afraid of an accident at the barrier than anywhere else," the trainer was saying. "So don't try to break him like he was a quarter horse. You understand?"

"Yes, Boss."

"Hurry back, then."

Loftus took up the reins, wrapping them about his hands. Gordon and the old gelding would be with him a little longer, but soon they would be gone. He dropped Man o' War into line behind the red-coated marshall taking them to the post. There were seven two-year-olds, all accompanied by old, well-mannered stable ponies to keep them out of trouble.

Man o' War was on his toes, but he ignored the other youngsters as if they weren't there at all. Loftus enjoyed the attention he was getting from the paddock crowd. There was no doubt that his colt was the one to watch. He touched Man o' War's neck. There was a tenseness about it that made him think of a tightly drawn bow.

Loftus glanced at the other colts. He decided that Gladiator was the only one they'd have to beat. The race itself was unimportant to the crowd, a program "filler" with a winner's purse of only five hundred dollars. But to those directly connected with the colts, it would provide an inkling of what was to come during the hard campaign ahead. They had to start someplace, and this race made as good a beginning as any.

Man o' War pranced uneasily as they moved toward the track. Loftus knew his mount was becoming more and more excited by the track sounds and the tightly packed crowd on either side of them as they made for the gap in the fence.

He was easily the biggest, the best-looking colt in the field. He held his head high, his large eyes protruding and bright. He was excited but unafraid and very, very eager. His body moved quickly, confidently. He was the picture of smoothness and grace, a big colt who could handle himself. Loftus felt very proud of his mount.

Just before they stepped onto the track, the jockey glanced back, nodding at Feustel and grinning. He also caught a glimpse of young Danny, who was holding the black-and-yellow cooler tightly to his chest. The kid looked scared to death.

The marshall turned up the track, leading the field past the stands. Every neck and flank was a little dark with sweat; every eye showed a bit of white. Man o' War wanted to dance, but old Major Treat kept him steady by taking the bumps without fighting back. Although the big colt was the last in the post parade, almost everybody's eyes were on him. Not only did his great, glistening body stand out among all the others, but his brilliant workouts had also made him the colt to watch.

It was five o'clock when Johnny Loftus took Man o' War behind the barrier. The jockey waved Gordon and Major Treat away. Now it was the way he wanted it ... just the two of them with a race to be run. Between the colt's ears he could see the sun dropping behind the city skyscrapers to the west. "Easy, Red," he said softly. "Easy." His answer was a quick flicking of alert ears.

One of the starter's assistants took hold of Man o' War's bridle, seeking to walk him up to the elastic barrier. The colt swept around in a fast circle, dragging the man with him.

Loftus wasn't disturbed by his mount's antics, which he had expected. All the other two-year-olds were acting up, too. They were giving the assistant starters and their riders a hard time. It would take a little while to get the field standing straight and balanced behind the barrier.

He remembered Feustel's instructions. There must be no accident or interference at the start. He must not prod Man o' War today. The fast breaks would have to wait until later races, when they would be more needed and there was less chance of an accident. The colts in this field were too inexperienced for him to take any chances.

Loftus continued speaking softly to Man o' War but yelled and showed his whip to all the other horses and their riders. He tried every trick he knew to keep them away from Man o' War.

The keen eyes of the newsmen high up in the press box were on Johnny Loftus and his mount. Through their binoculars they watched America's leading jockey use all his skill to keep the big colt from throwing him. Man o' War wouldn't stand straight or still. He fought to get to the barrier before the others and yanked one of the assistant starters off his feet.

They followed every movement he made, for he was the reason they had not left the press box. Usually they paid little attention to the last race on the day's program. It was a time to relax, to take it easy and get ready to get out before the big crowd. But today they stayed in their seats, as did most of the people in the stands. Everybody, it seemed, had been drawn by the appearance of the Riddle colt in the post parade. They sensed something unusual in the way he handled himself. And to the newsmen it was something that might mean a story for their papers.

They checked their programs again. His name was Man o'

War, a chestnut son of Fair Play out of Mahubah by Rock Sand. He was bred to be a racehorse, all right. They checked his morning workouts. His time was brilliant—forty-seven seconds for a half mile—and this race was just one furlong farther. No wonder he had been made the favorite. But could he live up to his sensational morning works? Afternoons were often different for a fast-working colt. Now the chips were down.

They continued watching him through their glasses and felt the electricity he generated. He was something to see. There was nothing sluggish about him even behind the barrier. Johnny Loftus had his hands full.

The jockey was tired, dead tired. His arms and shoulders ached from trying to hold Man o' War back from the barrier. All the other two-year-olds were standing straight and still. Lady Brighton was on the rail, American Boy alongside, and then Devildog, Gladiator, Neddam, and Retrieve, in that order. For a few seconds Loftus thought Man o' War might have used up too much energy fighting the barrier. He recalled that the kid Danny had worried about just that point. Maybe he *had* overdone the schooling lessons a bit. But it was too late now.

Again the assistant starter reached for the colt's bridle. "Easy, Red. Easy," Loftus coaxed. "Let's go this time."

Man o' War began moving toward the barrier and the jockey got ready to go. He took up another wrap in his reins, glancing at the other horses and riders waiting quietly. He'd let them get away first, just as Feustel had ordered. He knew how much horse he had under him. He'd catch them even at so short a distance as five furlongs. The most important thing was that nothing should happen to this chestnut son of Fair Play in his first start.

The elastic barrier swept up, and no longer were there any

strands of webbing between the colts and the track beyond. The yellow flag fell. The race was on!

Johnny Loftus leaned forward but unlike the other riders he sat still, not using heels or whip. Instead he took a tight hold on his colt's mouth, holding him back, watching the traffic jam in front as the youngsters bumped into each other and swerved from one path to another. He heard the cries of their riders shouting for more racing room. He was content to wait until the track was clear before making his move.

For almost an eighth of a mile Johnny Loftus held his tight hold on Man o' War's mouth. Then, seeing the way becoming clear, he let him out a notch. He felt the great muscles heave with a power and suddenness that took him—even after all his morning rides—by surprise. He felt as if he had been released from a catapult! But the catapult was still under him and its surging power became ever greater!

With tremendous ground-eating strides the big colt caught the pack as if they had ceased running. Only the leader, Retrieve, was beside him at the furlong pole, giving every ounce of speed he had. Then he too fell back, done in. Johnny Loftus turned Man o' War loose another notch and there was nothing more to this race than a running sheet of red flame!

Loftus knew then that he and all the others concerned with Man o' War's training had, with all their enthusiasm, underestimated this colt. Here was *greatness*. Here was something that only the whipping wind could have foretold. And Man o' War continued fighting for his head, fighting to be turned loose completely so he could run still faster!

They approached the hushed and strangely quiet stands, for the spectators too seemed to know what Johnny Loftus was riding. They saw him turn in his saddle to look back as if he still couldn't believe Man o' War had left the others so far behind.

Then he straightened again, his strong arms trying to hold back a whirlwind with a flowing tail. The crowd came to life. Thousands of voices exploded in an ever-mounting roar as people jumped to their feet, watching the blazing spectacle of this running colt.

Loftus knew his mount was responding to the crowd's applause, for Man o' War pulled harder, dragging him forward in his saddle until he was standing in the stirrups. The jockey used all his muscle power to hold him back, and finally Man o' War responded to the choking pull, slowing almost to a canter as he passed beneath the finish wire.

Danny Ryan watched Man o' War turn and come back. The black-and-yellow cooler he had been holding was at his feet. Stooping, he bent down and picked it up, brushing it unashamedly across eyes that were moist. His colt was everything he'd known he would be. He had heart and a will to win, both as important as great speed.

There was too big a crowd for Danny to get near Man o' War in the winner's circle. Everybody seemed to be on the track, all cramming to get close to touch Man o' War. The roar from the stands was still rolling down to the track, where the colt stood in all his glory. To Danny it looked as if his colt knew what the pandemonium was all about. He stood there quivering and magnificent, his wet satin coat gleaming like bright copper. There was a flicking of his ears, too, as if he wanted to catch the sweet music of the swelling applause and the voices of the admirers on all sides of him.

The Riddles were there, standing beside Feustel, who held Man o' War's head. Loftus was still in the saddle, trying to keep the colt in position and at the proper angle for a good picture. Never was there a more beautiful colt. The eyes of all who looked upon him glowed. They were reluctant to let him go, to bring this moment to an end. They seemed to sense they were watching the beginning of something that happened just once in a lifetime.

But soon, Danny thought, the ceremony would be over. Then he would be able to put the black-and-yellow cooler on Man o' War and take him back to the barn. Soon the colt would be his alone again. Or would he, now that he was on his way to greatness?

Rising Star

17

Danny found that he didn't have Man o' War to himself back at the barn. Louis Feustel hovered around the colt like a mother hen, keeping outsiders away from Man o' War and telling all the stableboys what to do in short, terse commands.

"We've got ourselves a champ," he said. "See that you take care of him right. Where's the warm water? Danny, get a move on. Don't just stand there gawking. And Frank, you got the water too hot. Cool it down some. Mike, get his halter. Quick."

Feustel removed the colt's bridle and slipped on the halter. "There . . . that's better. Give him a sip of water now, Danny. Just a swallow. Whoa, that's enough. Careful now. Here . . . hold him, Danny. I'll do the washing myself. Set that warm water down, Frank. Step back, Mike, take off that cover first. Strip him down, that's it. Now give me the sponge."

Feustel filled the sponge with water, held it between the colt's ears, and squeezed gently. The water ran down over the head and face, carrying much of the sweat with it. Man o' War tried to catch the water with his tongue, then he shook his head and reared.

They all stepped back until he came down. "Better put the chain through his mouth, Danny," the trainer said. "He's still full of beans."

Feustel continued his washing, sweeping the sponge carefully over the colt's face, eyes, muzzle, and nostrils. He squeezed some of the water into the colt's mouth to carry out the saliva. Then, carrying the pail of water, he began moving faster, dipping the sponge often and sweeping the glistening body in long strokes along the neck, back, sides, and rump.

Everybody else stood clear, not caring if the water was splashing over them or not. Danny's gaze left Man o' War a moment to take in Mr. Riddle and a group of friends who were standing a short distance away. He heard one of the men say to Mr. Riddle, "You rung in a four-year-old on us, Sam. No two-year-old could be as big as he is. And not as fast!"

Mr. Riddle laughed with his friend. His eyes didn't leave his colt as he said, "Yes, he's going to be hard to beat, if he doesn't go wrong."

"Don't you worry about that," Louis Feustel said, stopping his work. "He won't go wrong, sir, not this colt. He'll thrive on all the work we give him. He's big through and through."

"He's got the will to win and that's certainly one of the greatest attributes a horse can have," Mr. Riddle answered.

"He's got class, this colt has," Feustel agreed. "You know, they say that a horse with real class sometimes *does* have a heart that's larger than normal for his body. I'll bet his is big, real big. When he caught those other colts, they just pulled themselves up like a man putting brakes on his car. Yes, sir, he's got as much class as any horse I ever saw."

Danny held the lead shank tight as Feustel moved to the

front again and began washing the colt's chest. Then the swift, sure strokes of the trainer's hand swept the forelegs and belly clean. He changed water often, barking orders when the pails weren't ready fast enough for him. He cleaned the hind legs. He was thorough but careful to avoid getting kicked or stepped on, for Man o' War was fussing in his excitement. He washed the long tail, also under it, putting the tail into the bucket and sloshing it around in the water. Then he lifted the tail and whisked out most of the water. He stepped back to observe his work, then started again on the lower legs.

As Danny's eyes swept over the crowd, he knew that his days alone with Man o' War were a thing of the past. Major Treat was in his stall, waiting for his evening feed. The stable dogs were barking and the smell of mash being cooked was in the air. But the men from the other stables weren't going to dinner as usual. They were all here, just standing around Man o' War, gawking as if they had never seen a racehorse before.

"Yep, we've got ourselves a champ," he heard Feustel mutter to himself again as he picked up the curved scraper and began removing most of the water from Man o' War's dripping body. Danny watched the sure, sweeping swipes of the scraper. Even the head trainer wanted to take care of this horse. Man o' War belonged to everybody.

Having finished with the scraper, Feustel used a clean sponge, squeezing it as dry as he could. Then he went all over the big colt again, squeezing water out of the sponge as it collected. When he had the colt as dry as possible, he called for a heavy cooler and covered Man o' War carefully.

"There," he said finally, satisfied that the blanket was even all around and snug enough not to slip back. His keen eyes turned to Danny, and for the first time that afternoon his face seemed to lose its grimness. He even smiled as he said, "You walk him, Dànny. Cool him out carefully, now. Just a few swallows of water slowly, and warm it up some . . . don't want it cold. Off with him, now."

Danny, too, was grinning as the crowd opened up for him and his colt. He held Man o' War close. He hadn't lost him yet. "Come on, Red," he said. "We're going for a nice long walk, just you and me."

For the next two days Man o' War rested and loafed. Louis Feustel had him walked each day and held to a jog on the track. The big colt's racing campaign was off to a flying start and everybody wanted to keep it that way. They all knew what they had in the burly colt, as did everyone who read the newspapers.

The headlines proclaimed: "Man o' War a Whirlwind." And sportswriters reported in detail the impression left in the minds of all those who had seen him easily win his first race. They prophesied great things for him among the juveniles, for he had made "six high-class youngsters look like $200 horses." They were all certain he would be a hard colt to beat in the rich stakes to come.

"He'll be hard to beat, all right," Danny said, reading the lengthy accounts about his colt. "Nothing will even come close enough to touch him."

And on the third day after his first start, Man o' War was bridled and taken again to the paddock at Belmont Park. The event was the Keene Memorial, his first stakes race for a winner's purse of $4,200. His opposition consisted of five colts, all more highly regarded than those he had beaten in his first race. Three were being especially watched: On Watch, Ralco, and Hoodwink. Most of the crowd's interest was on the meeting of Man o' War and On Watch because they were sons of Fair Play and Colin, and those sires had been intense rivals in their

racing days. Colin had emerged the champion. Would Man o'
War avenge his father's defeat? Both colts were carrying the
same weight of 115 pounds. Both were highly regarded. The
spectators made up their minds as the horses went to the post.
They recalled Man o' War's impressive victory three days earlier. Again they made him the favorite to win.

Danny watched as his colt went postward, prancing closely
beside Major Treat. He felt Man o' War wouldn't let any of
his followers down. The track was sloppy from an earlier rain
but that wouldn't bother him. He'd be able to handle himself
without trouble. He might do even better than he'd done in his
first race. He hadn't been so nervous in the paddock and
seemed to be getting used to all the noise and hullabaloo. He
was almost keeping in time to the music from the track band,
his heels dancing in the mud. He was as eager as ever. He knew
where he was going.

Danny hugged Man o' War's cooler. "C'mon, Red, show
them again," he muttered to himself. Oh, he'd like to have
been up on him, all right. But the big colt was the thing.
Nothing else mattered much, so long as Man o' War raced the
way he could. "C'mon, Red. C'mon," he repeated loudly.

He knew Johnny Loftus again had orders to break Man o'
War from the barrier slowly and to go only fast enough to win.
Everybody, including Feustel and Mr. Riddle, didn't want to
overdo Man o' War. He had too much racing ahead of him.

"Keep a good hold of him once you're out in front," Feustel
had instructed Loftus.

Danny watched the field line up behind the barrier. Man o'
War was quiet for a change, and the others were steady too.
There was no delay. The barrier went up and the yellow flag
fell. The Keene Memorial was on!

Ralco came out of the pack first. Danny searched the surg-

ing mass of horses for the black-and-yellow colors of Man o'
War. He found them well back in the middle. Another horse
moved up beside Ralco to the front. Johnny Loftus had Man o'
War three lengths behind, but the big colt was steady and out
of trouble.

"Now, Red. Now!" Danny shouted.

Man o' War came forward with great, ground-eating strides
as if he had actually heard Danny's call! For a few seconds another colt stayed alongside and Danny recognized On Watch.
But the other couldn't stay with Man o' War as he swept down
upon the two colts leading the field. He bounded past them as
if they had come to a dead stop. On Watch swept by the two
spent leaders too, but he was no match for the big red colt.
Man o' War moved easily away, and when he passed under the
finish wire Johnny Loftus was again standing in his stirrup
irons in an attempt to slow him down. Once more Man o' War
had won in classic style, making his competition look like
"cheap" horses rather than the high-class stock they were.

Danny watched his colt come back. Like everyone else, he
was beginning to wonder how fast Man o' War could really go.
There was no doubt that he could race much faster than he
was being allowed to. But how fast was that?

Now Feustel was convinced more than ever that he had the
best two-year-old of the season. He nodded in complete agreement and understanding when Mr. Riddle said, "Don't overdo
him early, Louis. I want him at the top of his form for Saratoga, still over a month off. His possibilities are immense."

"I know," the trainer answered, "but after today's race it
won't be so easy. They got a better line on him now. He'll
never go to the post so light again. They'll start throwing the
weight on him to slow him down."

"It can't be helped," Mr. Riddle said.

"I know," the trainer said.

The meeting at Belmont Park closed, but racing resumed the next day at the Jamaica course just a few miles away. There it was planned to start Man o' War again although the stable remained at Belmont. To get him used to the Jamaica track and crowd, Feustel received permission from the officials to work him one afternoon between races.

Danny watched his colt closely. Perhaps the public workout would show how fast Man o' War could really run. Loftus took him five furlongs under a snug hold, but the big colt acted as if he were in a race. He took the bit and fought for his head every stride of the way. His eagerness to run electrified all who watched, and when he flashed under the wire, his time equaled the track record!

Man o' War, the newspapers reported that evening, was the equal of any of the older horses in training. But Danny knew that, powerful as the colt seemed to the public and the press, he still had a lot of growing to do. Only fate knew the full potential of Man o' War. Only time held the answer.

Man o' War raced on, meeting only youngsters his own age. And, as Feustel had predicted, to make the races fair the track handicappers added more weight to his back. Lead plates were inserted in the colt's saddlebag with each successive race.

But the leaden weights failed to keep him from winning. He carried 120 pounds in the Youthful Stakes and won in an easy gallop. Two days later Feustel sent him postward in the Hudson Stakes, and on his broad back was the heaviest impost of his young life, 130 pounds! Still he won easily. It seemed that no matter how much weight the track handicappers assigned him, there was no slowing him down.

Feustel told the press, "The only problem we got with him is to keep him from wolfing down his feed. He tries to eat like he races. I put a bit in his mouth to slow him down some."

Danny didn't consider the colt's habit of eating too hastily their only problem. What bothered him more than anything else was that Man o' War was using up more energy behind the barrier than ever before. And with the heavier weights the handicappers were assigning him, it was only a question of time before it would tell on him.

No two-year-old in history had carried so much weight so early in the season. Everyone knew it, including the other jockeys, who were doing everything possible to increase Man o' War's restlessness behind the barrier, hoping the heavy weight would wear him down.

Danny also wished Feustel would stop racing Man o' War so often with so little rest in between. Of course, he was a big colt and could take hard racing as well as work. But he was still only a two-year-old. His next race was just as few days off and in it he'd be meeting for the first time the top two-year-old filly of the year, Bonnie Mary.

Danny let his hand slide over Man o' War's neck. He supposed he shouldn't question Feustel's program when the big colt seemed to be thriving on his frequent races. He was gaining weight and growing like a weed. He was full of spirit and he was sound. What more could anyone want from a young colt? There was no reason to worry about anything.

But the following day Danny, as well as the others in the stable, had cause for concern. Man o' War became uneasy in his stall. He got down, rolled, and got up again. He began sweating profusely and bit his flanks. He was in pain, and the signs pointed to a colic attack.

Louis Feustel sent for the veterinarian. "It's from wolfing down his feed," he said anxiously. "I knew it would come sooner or later. Get the colic medicine, Danny."

Watching his colt paw away at the straw bedding, Danny hoped Feustel was right. Man o' War might just have a stomach ache from eating too fast. But he knew, too, that colic could be the outward sign of something far more serious than indigestion. The abdominal pain could be caused by twisted intestines or something even worse. The veterinarian would know.

Danny found it hard waiting for the doctor to come. He recalled the hard races this growing colt had run and his fractious antics at the barrier. Had Man o' War hurt himself without their knowing it? He knew that he was worrying needlessly, that there was no reason for so much concern. The colt was big and strong. He had thrown off influenza earlier in the year. He could lick this, too. Colic attacks were nothing new or unusual around a stable.

The veterinarian arrived and, after examining the big colt, confirmed Feustel's diagnosis. "It's indigestion, all right."

Everyone in the stable relaxed and the veterinarian added, "The pain is leaving him already. He'll be himself soon enough and clamoring for feed. Go light on him for a few days, Louis."

"Sure, we'll drop him out of the Great American and wait for the Tremont Stakes the following week."

So Man o' War stayed in his stall while Bonnie Mary won the Great American carrying 127 pounds, only three pounds less than Man o' War would have carried had he gone to the post. What was even more impressive, Bonnie Mary lowered the race record a full second by doing the five furlongs in 58 ⅖ seconds, faster than any of Man o' War's races over the same distance!

A week later, on July 5, Man o' War emerged again to reclaim his share of two-year-old honors. Fully recovered from his attack of colic, he went postward in the Tremont Stakes.

Despite the fact that Bonnie Mary was not in the race, the great stands were overflowing with people who wanted to compare this colt to the brilliant filly. Only two other stables would send their charges against Man o' War, and the spectators quickly made him the favorite, even though he was carrying the heavy impost of 130 pounds. His very presence on the track excited them and they watched his quick movements with wonder. Here was a horse that was all Thoroughbred . . . and something else. They had no doubt about the outcome of the race and yet they awaited the start breathlessly.

Man o' War did not let them down. He put on his usual performance behind the barrier, almost unseating Johnny Loftus. But once the barrier whipped up, he broke on top and ran the six furlongs under a strangling pull to win. His time was unimpressive, a slow 1:13. But it did not matter to the crowd. He could have gone much faster if he had been let out the way he'd wanted to be. Here, they knew, was a champion.

It was only then that Man o' War was given the rest from racing that Danny thought he needed. The stable moved to Saratoga immediately after the running of the Tremont. Everyone knew that Mr. Riddle liked this track best of all and would cherish every victory his horses won there. The Hopeful Stakes would be his prime objective, just as it was for every other horse owner in the country, for the winner of the Hopeful usually ended the season as the champion of the two-year-olds.

But the Hopeful and the races that preceded it were still a long while off. The Saratoga meeting would not open until August 1, so for the rest of July, Man o' War loafed.

Danny relaxed with his colt. He loved Saratoga for its quiet, natural beauty. The air from the Adirondack Mountains was cool and exhilarating, and yet the pace was slow and serene. He thrived on it, the same as everyone else. No wonder stable owners liked to come here with their horses, he decided. Nowhere was the grass more luxuriant, the water more sparkling, the weather more pleasant.

Often at night, when Man o' War was bedded down, Danny would walk the quiet streets of the town, passing the large hotels with their long porches where people sat even now, weeks before the races started. Saratoga was a health resort as well as the site of the oldest track in America.

He passed, too, the brightly lit white-painted houses set well back from the streets, their lawns level and green. In one rambling villa on Union Avenue the Riddles lived. He would watch guests enter and, with no trouble at all, visualize Mr. Riddle extolling the great speed of Man o' War to them, the same as he did at the stables. The guests would listen attentively and nod their heads in complete agreement.

It was easy to say nice things about such a colt, especially with old friends who shared one's interest in the goal common to all horse owners, the winning of the Hopeful. They would know, of course, that the best two-year-olds in America were beginning to arrive at the track. Jim Rowe was already there with Upset and Wildair, both ready to race. He had another youngster also, John P. Grier, who, according to stable talk, was not quite ready to go but was supposed to be the best of the lot. Mike Daly, too, was due in with Golden Broom, who had fully recovered from the quarter crack he had developed in the spring.

Danny moved away from the house. He recalled Golden Broom's speed very well, but he didn't think the Jeffords colt would give Man o' War any trouble. Neither would any of the others. His colt was fully rested. He looked more like a four-year-old than he had at Belmont, standing over sixteen hands in his plates and with the weight to match. He was now close to 1,000 pounds, which was big weight for a two-year-old. And there was not a pimple on him.

Early the next morning Danny walked Man o' War through the pine woods that surrounded the track. Soon these golden, easy days would be over and his colt's real work would begin again. Man o' War was ready for it. He was destined to be a greater horse than his sire, Fair Play, ever was, Danny decided. And for a moment he recalled again his days at Nursery Stud with its stallions and mares and foals.

Man o' War was much leggier than Fair Play. Bigger in body, too, and broader across the loins. All in all, this colt was much better balanced than his sire.

Danny watched as Man o' War decided to get down and roll. Carefully he lowered his great body and then, turning on his back, thrashed the air with his legs. Finally he stood up, shaking himself.

Would any of the top two-year-olds he'd meet at Saratoga really make him run? Danny wondered. If Man o' War was ever extended it would be something to see. Even so, five and six furlongs were much too short for him. He needed more distance to stretch out. But that would have to wait until the following year.

Suddenly Man o' War snorted. Danny followed his altered gaze and saw another horse being walked a short distance away. He recognized Bonnie Mary, the brilliant filly who had won the Great American at Belmont when Man o' War had been confined to his stall. She was scheduled to go to the post against Man o' War in his first race at Saratoga. Would she be the one to make him extend himself?

The big colt tugged at the lead shank, trying to move toward her. Danny shook his head at Man o' War's eagerness. "A *filly*," he muttered. "Wouldn't you know?"

Golden Broom Again

18

On August 2, 1919, Man o' War went postward for his first start at Saratoga. It was the thirty-sixth running of the historic United States Hotel Stakes at three-quarters of a mile and worth $7,600 to the winner. Danny stood at the gap in the fence through which the horses had passed. It was the largest and best field his colt had faced, but he had no doubt Man o' War would win. Neither, it seemed, did the spectators have any doubt, for they had once more made him the heavy favorite even though he was carrying 130 pounds and giving weight to all his opponents.

Danny studied the field of ten horses, his eyes finding Bonnie Mary. She was the only one carrying close to high weight, 127 pounds. The crowd had made her second choice. Could she carry her heavy impost against such a colt as Man o' War? A few minutes more and Danny, along with everyone else, would have his answer.

The others in the field were lightly weighted even though they came out of some of the best stables in the country and were being ridden by outstanding jockeys. Upset was the third choice of the crowd, but he had been beaten by Bonnie Mary in the Great American. He carried the same weight as he had in that race, 115 pounds, but today's distance was six furlongs, an eighth of a mile farther. Would the extra furlong and weight advantage mean that he could catch Bonnie Mary?

Man o' War was the idol of the overflowing stands, and Danny's skin tingled as he heard the applause for him. Would his colt's name be added to the names of the famous winners of the United States Hotel Stakes . . . Hanover, Old Rosebud, St. James, Pompey, Scapa Flow, and Jamestown? Danny had read about them all.

He watched the field round the far turn and go up the backstretch, where the barrier awaited them. Racing around a turn didn't bother Man o' War any more than a straight course. He had proved that in his last three races.

Danny was more fearful of the other jockeys than of their mounts. Eddie Ambrose was up on Upset; Buddy Ensor on Bonnie Mary. McAtee was riding David Harum, while Fator, who could rate a horse better than any other jockey in the country, was up on Carmandale. Those were the fellows to watch, he decided, for they were out to put an end to Man o' War's victories.

"Just get him clear, Johnny," Danny muttered to himself. "Get him clear and running." But he knew Johnny Loftus would have a difficult time. He had drawn eighth position, and there was a good chance the others would jam him at the start.

The field had reached the barrier and Man o' War was already giving the starter a lot of trouble. He was eager to get off and Loftus was shaking him up still more. Twice he broke through the barrier, taking several colts with him.

Danny's eyes never left them. There was no doubt that

Johnny Loftus wasn't going to wait until the others got off today. He meant to take Man o' War to the front right away, afraid perhaps of the traffic jam that might develop ahead of him if he broke too slowly. But he was having his hands full restraining the big colt, and as he broke through the barrier once more Danny wondered how much the heavy weight was telling on his colt.

It was all of six minutes after post time when Mars Cassidy, the official starter, had the field lined up the way he wanted it. Only then did he press the lever, making the barrier spring upward. The race was on!

Danny saw Man o' War plunge forward. He was out in front and running! The deep breath Danny had been holding was expelled in a great sigh of relief. The way was clear for Man o' War. There would be nothing to stop him, nothing more to this big stake race but *his* colt.

Everyone else at the track knew it, too. They all sat back and watched in silent awe as Man o' War drew easily away from the rest of the field until Loftus started pulling him back. From then on it was only a case of watching the red colt fight for his head and a chance to run the way he would have liked. At the end of the race Loftus, smiling in his moment of triumph, was looking back at the others strung out far behind him. Upset was the horse nearest to him, followed by Homely and then by the filly Bonnie Mary. The winning time was a good 1:12 ⅖, made under the strongest kind of restraint.

The crowd went wild over Man o' War's spectacular and easy victory. Horsemen and fans alike followed him back to the open stable area, and Danny along with the other grooms tried to keep order by splashing water all about while washing the big colt. They did this despite the fact that Mr. Riddle and his prominent guests were there. They kept the newsmen and photographers back, too. No one could get close enough to touch Man o' War. It didn't matter that they were getting soaking wet themselves. They were dressed to tend horses, but these others, these tourists (they were all tourists now, even Mr. Riddle), had to keep back because of their fancy clothes. Not only that. After the race he had run, Man o' War needed all the room and air he could get.

Danny washed the colt's forelegs, muttering, "They'd make fools of themselves over far lesser horses than this one. Stand still, Red."

Mr. Riddle had stepped back from the spraying water along with the other visitors and newsmen. He understood the grooms' actions as well as the next man. But his pulse quickened as he looked over the long, powerful lines of his statuesque chestnut colt. He was very proud of Man o' War, more so than of any horse he had ever owned. He smiled patiently as drops of water fell on him from the broad sweeping motions made by men with dripping sponges in their hands. And he listened to the glowing comments of the men around him.

"He is the greatest two-year-old I've ever seen since I came home from France," one friend said. "Nor did I see one in all Europe that I would class with him."

Mr. Riddle nodded. He knew Thomas Welsh was usually very sparse in his praise of racehorses. It was a good sign.

Andrew Joyner, another friend, said, "I have to admit that he's as good as his daddy was at two. I think he might even make as great a distance-running three-year-old as Fair Play."

Mr. Riddle nodded, satisfied again with this critic's opinion, even though he thought it had been given a little reluctantly. Andrew Joyner had trained Fair Play, so it wasn't easy to admit that Man o' War might be as great as his sire. Mr. Riddle smiled. "He'll be greater than Fair Play, Andrew," he said confidently, "much greater. You'll see."

Behind him someone said, "I'm sure he can shoulder as much weight as any two-year-old of the last twenty-five years and still win."

A newsman seemed to agree, for he exclaimed loudly, "He can carry all the weight they put on his back, all right. Did you notice how Loftus was just looking around at the scenery in the last stage of the race? There never was a more glorious two-year-old, and I'm including Colin and St. Simon, even Spendthrift and Eclipse and Herod."

"Whoa," Mr. Riddle said, turning to the reporter. "Don't go too far, son. He's a great colt, but still a colt, not a legend."

"I never saw anything like the way he raced," the newsman went on enthusiastically. "He was living flame. He was all fire. He could have won by a hundred lengths over any distance, at any weight."

Mr. Riddle raised his cane, not brandishing it angrily but to command attention. "Don't make a fool of yourself," he said in a clear, ringing voice. "As good as this colt is, he's still a horse. Don't drool over him. He's blood and bone. His interest is in oats and clean hay, not idolatry. And right now he needs most what we're not giving him room to have . . . proper cooling out and a comfortable stall. Let us leave."

Then Mr. Riddle, his face set in stubborn lines, left the area, giving the others no choice but to follow him.

Danny watched them go. Mr. Riddle was prouder of Man o' War than most people are of their children, but he didn't let it go to his head. He could be a gracious host and a good companion, but this was not the moment. He realized Man o' War needed to be alone despite his clamoring audience. And Mr. Riddle usually got his way.

With the Saratoga race meeting well under way, the mornings were no longer quiet. People crowded into the clubhouse stands to watch the sets of horses move through the clear, bright days. At times they saw a better show than what went on during the afternoons. When the morning workouts were over, they would roam through the open stable area, sharing the smell of woodsmoke from fires over which water and mash were being heated.

Often they would watch Man o' War standing in his stall. Even motionless he attracted more attention than any other horse in the area. Most of the time he stood with his head over the half-door, his ears pricked and eyes bulging with interest at all that went on about him. He was the picture of controlled energy and fire. Yet he looked, too, as if he would explode at any given moment. So visitors watched, waiting eagerly for the fury to be unleashed.

Danny was ordered to stand by the stall door when Man o' War was inside. It was a job he loved more than any other, for he felt closer to his colt then than at any other time. He kept the visitors back, listening to their remarks and often answering their questions.

"I heard he takes a full twenty-eight-foot stride," one man said. "Could that be possible?"

"That's what they measured in his last race," Danny replied.

"Someone said they're going to work him one of these mornings with Golden Broom. Is that right?"

"I don't know," Danny answered. "Feustel's the trainer."

"I heard that Mike Daly has Golden Broom at his best," the man went on. "He had a quarter crack, you know. It kept him back."

"Yes, I know," Danny said.

"He's come along nicely. I watched him work the other morning. He's regained all he lost by being idle."

"I heard that, too," Danny admitted.

"He might even steal the show from your colt."

Danny didn't answer.

"It helps the sport all around," the man went on, "having this sort of rivalry. I'm looking forward to their being tried together. . . . You know how it came about, don't you?" he asked when Danny remained silent. "Well, this is the way I heard it. Mike Daly suggested to Feustel that they alternate the big stakes instead of racing their colts against each other. He thought he was doing Feustel a favor, I think. Feustel got mad and wanted to settle the matter once and for all as to which was the better colt, so he agreed to this private match at three furlongs."

"That's too short for Man o' War," another visitor said. "Golden Broom breaks like a meteor."

"Yeah," the first agreed, his eyes still on Man o' War, "he gets away fast, all right. But there's only one horse for me, even at three furlongs."

The next morning, with the sun bright on the lofty elms and the dust shimmering over the track, Johnny Loftus rode Man o' War out for his work. There to meet him at the barrier was his old training comrade, Golden Broom, looking every bit the picture horse he was. To Danny he seemed more finished than ever. His superb head with its white blaze was beautiful to see, and there was fine perfection to the symmetrical lines of his golden body. Golden Broom was lithe and powerful and very fast.

Danny had looked forward to the private match as much as anyone else. He hadn't forgotten the defeats his colt had taken from Golden Broom as a yearling. The intense but friendly rivalry between the Jeffords and the Riddle stables had resumed. Glancing back at the clubhouse veranda, he saw that there were many early-morning risers who had forsaken sleep to watch this workout. Mr. Riddle was sitting next to Mrs. Jeffords.

At the barrier Man o' War was eager to be off, as usual, but Loftus had him in position. He was no awkward yearling now, who would have to untangle his long legs in order to get away. It would not be the same as it had been in last fall's speed trials, even at so short a distance as three furlongs.

The barrier swept skyward and Danny saw the timer's yellow flag descend as the colts were off. Golden Broom broke as fast as Danny remembered, his powerful short legs driving his white-stockinged feet into the soft track and sending the dirt flying. But he was not alone. Alongside was Man o' War, making up for his rival's flowing action with ground-eating strides! He refused to be swept behind by Golden Broom's blinding speed. He raced much higher off the ground than his rival, but he dug into the dirt as if the wrath of the heavens were following him; the track seemed to heave beneath the lash of his power.

Watching him, Danny was silent. While his stomach churned in rhythm with the sounds on the track, he knew in those few seconds that there never had been, never would be, a horse like Man o' War. He saw him pull in front of Golden Broom at the end of the first furlong and lengthen his lead in the second and third furlongs. The timers caught him in 33 seconds, faster than any horse, regardless of age, had ever raced before! And to make the record-shattering time even more fantastic, all who watched were convinced that Man o' War was not going all-out!

Golden Broom, despite his defeat, had given a good account of himself, and there were many in the crowd who believed that since he had not had any races to date, he needed the trial to bring himself to top speed for his stake engagements. A few even thought that Golden Broom had shown enough in the trial to be the colt that would beat Man o' War when they met under racing conditions.

Those who backed Golden Broom in the golden colt's first race a few days later on August 9 were not disappointed. While Man o' War remained in his stall, Golden Broom won the Saratoga Special, beating the good colt Wildair easily. His smashing victory heightened interest in the forthcoming Sanford Memorial four days off, when he would meet Man o' War in a race for the first time.

Danny told Feustel the next morning, "Golden Broom needed that race but I still don't think he'll give our colt any trouble on Saturday."

The trainer nodded his head. "He needed that race to get him in feather-edge, but I feel Mrs. Jeffords should have kept him in his stall if she expected him to stay with our colt. Winning the Special means the handicapper will put more weight up on him in the Sanford. If he hadn't raced, he would have got in light, maybe as much as fifteen pounds lighter than our colt."

Feustel was right about the weights, for the day of the Sanford Memorial, Golden Broom was assigned 130 pounds to carry, the same as Man o' War.

It was August 13, but for Danny thirteen was a lucky number and he had no qualms about Man o' War. Besides, it was the seventh running of the Sanford and this was his unbeaten colt's seventh start. A good omen. He watched Man o' War standing in the shade of an elm tree in the paddock. For a moment his colt was motionless, which was most unusual for him before a race. His ears were pricked forward and his eyes were focused on something in the distance. Danny turned too, trying to find out what it was. But he could see nothing unusual beyond the paddock area, only the track. Whatever it was that held Man o' War's attention was for his eyes alone.

Mr. Riddle stood nearby, alongside Louis Feustel. "He looks good, Louis," he said.

The trainer nodded. "He's as tight as a coiled spring. He shouldn't have any trouble today."

Danny turned to the men. There had been talk that Mr. Riddle had offered to withdraw Man o' War from the race in order to give Mrs. Jeffords a better chance of winning with her colt. But Mrs. Jeffords had refused. She believed Golden Broom could beat Man o' War despite her colt's heavy impost of 130 pounds. He was fit and ready to go. Let the better colt win!

The afternoon was very warm, and Man o' War's chestnut coat was already wet and glistening when he stepped from the shade out into the sunshine. He was bridled and saddled. All that remained was for Johnny Loftus to mount. The jockey stood next to Feustel, getting his last-minute instructions. But there was little the trainer had to tell him that he didn't already know. He knew what sort of horse he was racing. Get Man o' War away clear of the field and the Sanford Memorial too would be his.

Upset

19

The bugler's call came and the paddock judge said, "Riders, mount your horses, please." There was a shimmering of colorful silks in the sun as the jockeys mounted, their horses sliding quickly, impatiently beneath them, tugging on lead shanks and impatient to be away. The pageant was on; the parade to the post had begun!

Danny walked beside Man o' War and Major Treat, reluctant to leave his charge. As always before a race, his stomach churned. "You won't have any trouble, not a bit, Red," he whispered. His colt had eyes and ears only for the track beyond, and Danny knew that he spoke just for his own benefit and solace.

They were sixth in line going to the gap in the fence. Up ahead was Golden Broom, looking more beautiful than ever and holding the eyes of the crowd. Despite the 130 pounds he carried and the public knowledge of his defeat by Man o' War in their morning workout, the crowd had made him a close favorite to Man o' War.

Upset was the third favored horse in the field, carrying only 115 pounds. None of the other four colts was expected to give the big three any trouble.

The stands were overflowing with spectators, all wrought to a high pitch of excitement over the coming race. Danny listened to their screams while watching Man o' War attempt to throw Loftus the moment he set foot on the track. It turned his stomach inside out and he held the black-and-yellow cooler close to his chest for comfort. He'd never make a rider, he thought, not even a good groom, if he couldn't learn to watch a race more easily than this. His stomach rumbled on.

He found a place on the rail, finally. He would have liked to have a pair of binoculars, as some of the others standing nearby had; then he would be able to see what happened at the barrier, far across the track.

Johnny Loftus tried to keep Man o' War still and alongside Major Treat, but the big colt was as full of fight as he'd ever known him to be. Johnny's eyes moved to Upset just ahead of him. He feared that colt more than Golden Broom, for Upset was going very light at 115 pounds and he had Willy Knapp in the saddle. Willy had been riding for seventeen years. He had been up on Exterminator the year before, when he won the Kentucky Derby. Willy knew what he was doing every minute, behind the barrier and in the race. He was one to watch.

Eddie Ambrose was up on Golden Broom. He'd bear watching, too. Just get clear of those two, Loftus decided, and the race was his.

They neared the webbing stretched across the track. Man o' War was eager to reach it. He reared when Major Treat was ridden away, and lunged toward the barrier. Johnny managed to stop him before he broke through it; he backed him up, only to have the big colt fight for his head and lunge forward again. One of the starter's assistants caught hold of the bridle and was abruptly pulled off his feet. He held on grimly, his legs dangling until Man o' War came down.

Loftus started backing up Man o' War from the barrier again, only to be banged hard by another colt from inside. Man o' War, jostled by the impact, plunged forward again, almost breaking through the barrier before he was brought under control.

Once more Loftus backed him up while trying to keep clear of the other horses and riders. He sought the help of the official starter, shouting to him that he ought to keep the field more under control.

The old man in the starter's stand didn't like his job at all. For thirty years and more it had been his whole life, but he had retired from such work months before. He was much too old for it now. His regular job was that of presiding judge, and he had been pressed into service today because Mars Cassidy, the official starter, was sick.

He watched the crowding and interference going on behind the barrier and called for attention. But his words were futile, falling upon deaf ears. It took a younger man to control these riders, intent as they were upon wearing each other down even before the race began. If he'd been in top form, he might have been able to do it. They were paying little if any attention to him. A starter's job in America lacked authority, let alone dignity, he decided. In England it would have been different; there they had respect for the official starter.

"Take that colt back again," he shouted to Loftus. "And Ambrose, keep your colt clear of him. Knapp, keep yours steady!"

He might as well have been talking to the people in the stands for all the good it did. He watched the confusion of horses and riders with anxious eyes, the time ticking away, the crowd anxious for the race to begin. He bit his lower lip, recalling with great uneasiness an important race twenty-six years before when he'd had to keep the horses at the barrier one hour and forty-five minutes before he could get them away. It was unprecedented, before or since, and he didn't want anything like that ever to happen again to mar his record. So he watched anxiously, waiting for the horses to reach the barrier in any kind of line so he could send them off. The horses and riders continued to jostle each other, Man o' War plunging constantly at the barrier. Meanwhile, the minutes were ticking away. The old man wanted to spring up the webbing and get his job done. He wanted very much to have it over with.

Johnny Loftus was very anxious to get off, too. Once the barrier was lifted the big colt would be away in a flash. He had sixth position, next to the outside, an excellent one for keeping clear of the kind of bumping he was taking back of the barrier. Loftus's anxiety increased as the webbing stayed down and the moments ticked away. His face was already wet with sweat as he glanced at the starter. Why didn't the old man send them off? Man o' War plunged forward once more, almost pulling his arms from their sockets. He managed to stop him at the barrier. He started backing him up. The big colt half reared, twisting as he came down. The jolt almost unseated Loftus and he rested a second, his mount turned almost the wrong way on the track.

The barrier swept up! Johnny Loftus, despite all his anxiety to be off, had been caught napping . . . and Man o' War, the unbeaten colt, was left at the post!

Furious with himself and the starter, Loftus whirled the big colt around. He'd made a mistake but there was still plenty of time to correct it. He leaned into Man o' War, straightening him out and urging him on. The big colt bounded forward, only to be pulled up again as Loftus saw that they weren't the only ones left at the post in the straggling start. The Swimmer and Capt. Alcock were off slow, and to make matters worse they had swerved in front of him! He pulled harder, trying to hold Man o' War back from the heaving hindquarters of the two colts directly ahead. Man o' War was determined to break through. He ran into the colts and almost over them before Loftus could pull him back. More furious than ever, the jockey got Man o' War clear and on the outside. He had lost many more lengths to the leaders. But there was still time to catch them.

Golden Broom was far in front, his short, pistonlike strides taking him toward the turn like a whirlwind. Hard after him was the light-weighted Upset with Willy Knapp in the saddle; he seemed to be biding his time, content to wait for the home-stretch before making his bid to catch the leader. Some distance behind them were Armistice and Donnacona, running close together. Still farther back were the three stragglers, Capt. Alcock, The Swimmer, and last of all Man o' War.

Loftus turned the big chestnut loose, and they swept past Capt. Alcock and The Swimmer in devouring strides. Approaching the turn, the jockey took his mount over to the rail, determined to make up even more ground by passing Donnacona and Armistice on the inside. Six furlongs wasn't a long race and they'd already gone half of it. But before he could get through, the hole on the rail closed and Man o' War was shut off again.

The big colt fought back as Loftus once more took hold of his mouth and jerked hard. Reluctantly he slowed his strides going into the turn. He was pulled to the outside, then the hard hold on his mouth loosened and he was permitted to run.

He swept around Donnacona and Armistice. Again his long strides devoured the track as he came off the turn and into the homestretch in third position.

Loftus knew he should have kept Man o' War clear of Armistice and Donnacona. He had made still another mistake and Golden Broom was setting a dizzy pace, with Upset right alongside the leader and challenging him. Had he still the time and distance to catch the two of them?

There was only a furlong to go, and the crowd was on its feet, screaming to the heavens. Man o' War was catching the leaders fast, outrunning them with every magnificent stride! Danny was silent, too scared to move let alone shout. His colt was only a length and a half from Golden Broom and Upset when he saw Johnny Loftus take him over toward the rail again!

The breath came from Danny in a loud groan. "*No!*"

Golden Broom was beginning to tire and Danny knew that Loftus, figuring the colt would weaken enough to leave an opening, was going to try to get through between him and Upset! It was a mistake, Danny thought, a big mistake, not to go around both colts. Man o' War had the speed to do it.

As Golden Broom tired, Willy Knapp kept Upset back, too. He glanced at Man o' War trying to come between them. He didn't move his colt past Golden Broom as he could have done. He had Johnny Loftus and the unbeaten favorite in a pocket and there they'd stay, if he could keep them there!

Danny knew that Loftus hadn't figured on Knapp's racing strategy. He had made another mistake, his third of the race. He couldn't take Man o' War past the leaders without pulling back now and coming around outside. And there was hardly time for it!

The sixteenth pole flashed by, with only one hundred and

ten yards to go to the finish. Man o' War's strides shortened as Loftus slowed and started to swing him around the two leaders. It was then that Willy Knapp moved Upset past Golden Broom in a final all-out drive to the wire!

"Get him, Red!" Danny shouted.

He watched Man o' War leap forward, gaining steadily. But he knew, too, that his colt was running out of ground. Upset, with a fifteen-pound weight advantage and having had an unmolested race, was lasting to the wire despite Man o' War's final charge. The big colt was alongside at the finish but Upset still had his nose in front, winning the race and living up to his name. He had defeated Man o' War!

Revenge

20

The Grand Union Hotel surrounded three sides of a large square and was one of the most impressive buildings in Saratoga. The night of the Sanford Memorial it was crowded with people discussing Upset's victory over Man o' War. They spoke of it in the cool and leafy darkness of the garden, in dining rooms, and in the lobby. But the most serious conversations of all took place on the hotel porch. There in the deep and comfortable veranda armchairs famous trainers gave their expert and varying opinions of the race.

Joking, and happier than anyone else in the celebrated gathering, was Jim Rowe, trainer of Upset. "I've been listening to you fellows for two weeks tell me Man o' War couldn't be beaten," he needled the others.

"It wasn't a truly run race," another answered. "You know that as well as we do."

Jim Rowe grinned. "We still got the winner's share of the purse and took home the trophy."

"But not the glory," the other said quietly. "Never was Man

o' War so great as he was today in his first defeat. The crowd knew it. They gave him a bigger hand than they did Upset."

Jim Rowe shifted in his chair. "They've been reading too much about him, that's why. He's a good colt but not as brilliant as they say. We beat him once. We'll beat him again."

A newspaperman rose to his feet. "You're trying to be hard-boiled about this colt, Jimmy, and you know it. Never before did Man o' War have to prove his courage as he did today. He was never put to a test before. And let me tell you he was not found wanting!"

"You're sure right," a second trainer agreed. "Loftus made three *big* mistakes, and still Man o' War came on. If Willy Knapp had moved over just an eyelash an' let him out of that pocket the last eighth, the big colt would have won from here to the sidewalk. Willy says so himself."

"The point is," Jim Rowe said, "that he *didn't*, an' good racing calls for good riding."

"Some say Mr. Riddle will take him off the colt."

"I doubt it," the newspaperman said. "He knows Loftus is one of the most able riders we've ever had. Anyone can have a bad day. Bad racing luck, you might call it. Mr. Riddle will keep Loftus on Man o' War. Mark my words."

"I hear Golden Broom pulled up lame," another guest remarked, more to change the subject than anything else.

"Yeah," Rowe said. "His quarter gave away again. He's done."

"He finished third. He had heart."

"But Man o' War is the colt with class, real class," a trainer in the back said. "He needs no excuses for his defeat."

"We'll see," Jim Rowe said, needling the other trainers once more. "We'll go after him again ten days from now. Beaten once, he can be beaten again." He sat back in the cool night breeze, enjoying his moment of triumph.

The trainer sitting beside him smiled. "Enjoy it while you can, Jimmy," he said. "It won't last long. You might as well admit you and your big Harry Payne Whitney Stable have got to move over for a new outfit. Riddle and his colt are going to bring home the prizes for a change. You've got nothing that can outrun Man o' War an' you know it."

"There are other ways to win a race," Rowe said wisely. "Who knows? Man o' War might get more bad starts. Or maybe Loftus is losing what he had for so long. He might go rail-happy again. If he does we'll lick him every time."

During the days that followed it was made plain to all that despite the great criticism of Johnny Loftus, Mr. Riddle's confidence in him was unwavering. The owner told Louis Feustel that Loftus would ride Man o' War in the coming Grand Union Hotel Stakes, when once again he would meet Upset.

Danny watched Loftus mount Man o' War for the next big race and felt Mr. Riddle was right in keeping him in the saddle. The severe criticism of his riding in the Sanford had cut Loftus as the lash of his whip never could have done. He had been punished enough, and Danny was certain he would make no mistakes that day. Loftus would seek revenge and so would the big colt. Together nothing could stop them, not Upset or any of the other nine colts going to the post.

It was a big field, made big because Man o' War had been beaten. And what had happened once might well happen again. The opposition stables had taken heart. The distance for the Grand Union Hotel Stakes was six furlongs, and the big colt was carrying his now-standard burden of 130 pounds. Upset had been assigned 125 pounds because of his victory. Danny believed Upset had no chance of defeating Man o' War at that weight. He noted that the crowd agreed with him, for

Man o' War once more had been made the favorite.

Danny walked beside his horse to the track, shading his eyes against the bright sun as the field went postward. With the exception of Upset none of the others had raced in the Sanford. It was a good field, with all the trainers and owners taking heart after Man o' War's defeat; he was not invincible after all.

Blazes, Gladiator, and The Trout had won previous races. Rouleau was there too; he had grown up with Man o' War at Nursery Stud and had been bought for $13,000 at the Yearling Sales. It was their first meeting on the track.

Danny's gaze returned to Man o' War, and he swelled with pride at the roar that greeted his colt. He was second in the parade, a good post position providing he got away fast, bad if he didn't. Danny wasn't worried about Man o' War's being left at the post today. Mars Cassidy, the official starter, was back and he'd be able to keep the jockeys and horses in line. And Loftus would be ready this time. He would make no mistakes. He was out to redeem himself.

It was 3:55 when they reached the post. Man o' War was full of fire, trying to break from Johnny Loftus's strong hands. But the jockey was not to be denied today. Man o' War was held under control and Mars Cassidy quickly lined up the others. The colts were still. It would be a clean start, a truly run race.

The barrier went up, the yellow flag fell, and the Grand Union Hotel Stakes had begun! Yet it was over almost at once. Man o' War surged to the front, passing Upset and all the others in great bounds and opening up a gap of many lengths. He continued drawing away until Johnny Loftus succeeded in shortening his great strides. Finally the jockey was standing in his stirrups as he turned to look back at the field straggling far behind. He pulled with all his might in the run to the finish wire, and yet when the time of the big colt was posted, it was two-fifths of a second faster than the race record!

The crowd thundered its ovation when Man o' War returned to the winner's circle. All knew that what they had witnessed was not really a race but an exhibition of extreme speed. There was no telling how fast this fiery chestnut colt could run. Surely he was king of the two-year-olds. He had only to win the forthcoming Hopeful Stakes and the Belmont Futurity to clinch the coveted title. There were few in the packed stands of over 35,000 people who doubted his ability to be victorious in both.

During the days that followed, Danny watched his colt closely. He fought for his right to be with him every moment but gave way beneath the weight of all those who now felt they had seen the greatness in Man o' War long before anyone else.

On August 30 Man o' War went postward again to run in the Hopeful Stakes, his chestnut body already wet with sweat from his restlessness and the blistering heat of the day. Even the air was heavy, as if sharing the suspense of this, his final race at Saratoga. The sweltering sun and ominous black sky to the west had not kept an enormous crowd from the track.

The fiery colt was third in the post parade of eight two-year-olds. He was the heavy favorite, and his being there had led owners to withhold numerous colts and fillies that ordinarily would have been sent to the post for a share of the $30,000 purse. He carried high weight of 130 pounds for the sixth consecutive time.

Danny's gaze left the horses for the threatening sky. If the heavy black clouds let go, the torrents of rain would turn the track into a sea of mud. Could his colt carry high weight on such a track, particularly with the other jockeys doing everything possible to interfere? It would be a decisive test.

It was four o'clock when Danny watched the horses round

the far turn on the way to the barrier. He felt the first drops of rain, and the people nearby began moving under the grandstand. The rain came down harder and he was barely able to see the horses. He knew the race was going to be decided at the barrier and he wasn't going to stay there where he would miss it. Quickly, he ran across the wet track and entered the infield. Lightning flashed through the sky as he raced into the sheets of rain. He thought of what the electricity in the air and the loud thunderclaps were doing to his colt. Man o' War would be more fractious than ever, and so would the other horses.

Nearing the barrier, he could see the horses milling about in back of the webbing. The darkness was shattered by their frenzied movements and the hushed stillness broken by the cries of their riders for more room. He went close to the starter's stand, peering through the half-light while the rain poured down his face.

He saw Upset skitter nervously across the track and bang into Man o' War. Then Constancy hit him from the other side. The big colt plunged forward, almost breaking away from his handler and going through the barrier.

Starter Cassidy was trying to bring the horses and riders under control but the blinding rain only added to his burden. It was evident to Danny that the jockeys were making every possible effort to prevent Man o' War from getting off well. Each time Cassidy had them close to being lined up, the start was spoiled by the willful maneuvering of horses to either side of Man o' War.

Man o' War lashed out with his hoofs when any of the others got close to him. He hit the filly Ethel Gray, who should have been four positions away from him. He lunged at Upset when Willy Knapp brought his colt across the track. Then he reared and tried to break through the barrier.

Mars Cassidy was almost losing control, Danny knew. It

seemed every rider was trying to wear down Man o' War under his high weight. The minutes ticked on, with the rain turning the racing track into deep mud. Could Man o' War still win under such a handicap?

Danny glanced at his watch. Nine minutes had already gone by. The flagman had his yellow flag raised. He would drop it when the barrier was sprung and the horses moved down the track. But when would the moment come?

The rain was streaming down Man o' War's flanks. Loftus finally had him straight and in position. Dr. Clark was steady and on the rail. So was Constancy. The others were lining up too. Danny turned to the starter. *Now?* The barrier went up!

Constancy broke first with Dr. Clark right beside her. Capt. Alcock was next and then came Man o' War.

Danny let out a yell of relief, now that his colt was clear of interference. He watched him move past Capt. Alcock and go after the two leaders. Man o' War was moving in an easy gallop, and Danny knew he'd be able to catch them any time Loftus chose to have him do so. Already Man o' War was fighting to be turned loose. Danny could just make out the horses' flying bodies in the half-light as they rounded the far turn. He saw Man o' War sweep by Dr. Clark in three mighty strides, then he had caught Constancy, flashing by her as if she had been standing still.

There was no more to the race, and Danny knew he had seen the most exciting part at the barrier. Man o' War was all by himself when he passed the stands, the mud flying behind him. The other high-class colts were strung out far to his rear, lost in the blur of his extreme speed.

Even Danny had not expected Man o' War to rise to such lofty heights as he did after winning the Hopeful Stakes. Photographers and newsmen never let him alone, and pictures and stories of Man o' War began appearing with ever increasing frequency in the daily press and turf journals, including publications that had never before paid any attention to a racehorse.

He heard Montford Jones, who had bought Rouleau at the Yearling Sales, offer Mr. Riddle $100,000 for Man o' War.

Danny held his breath awaiting Mr. Riddle's answer.

It came with a laugh and a shake of his head.

"Then $125,000," Mr. Jones said.

"No, I think not."

"What about $150,000?"

Danny felt tenser than ever.

Again Mr. Riddle laughed and shook his head. "I can't be tempted," he said. "I have no intention of parting with Man o' War."

The meeting at Saratoga was over, and after a few days' rest the Riddle stable moved back to Belmont Park on Long Island. Within the next two weeks Man o' War was scheduled to run his final race of the year, this time the Belmont Futurity, the richest and most coveted race for two-year-olds in the country.

"Nothing can beat him," Feustel told Danny one morning while the boy was grooming the big colt. "But it makes me uneasy just to think of it. No matter how brilliant his other wins have been, they mean nothing if he doesn't cop the Futurity. That's how it's always been. Win the Futurity and you're the head of your division. Lose it, no matter what the excuse, and you're done."

"He's rested and ready for it," Danny said confidently. "He won't lose."

"It'll be a straightaway for him this time," the trainer said. "Right down the middle for six furlongs."

"His strides are meant for straight courses," Danny said. "It will be easier than ever for him."

Feustel picked up the colt's left forefoot and examined it

closely. "They'll still jam him if they can," he said. "The field
will be a big one. It always is. Sometimes as many as twenty
horses go to the post."

"But not this time," Danny said. "He's beaten too many of
them. They won't show up at the post."

"Don't be too sure," Feustel answered. "Large shares of the
purse go to the second, third, and fourth horses in the Futurity. They'll go after them, if nothing else."

Danny said, "I hear Jim Rowe is going with three horses to
try and beat us."

Feustel nodded and put down the colt's foot. "Yes, he's got
John P. Grier ready. He claims he's a far better colt than
Upset. If so, he might make a race of it."

"Any way you look at it they'll be out to beat us," Danny
said.

"They sure will," the trainer agreed. "And that's what
makes me so uneasy. Like everybody else Mr. Riddle wants
this one bad, maybe even more than we do. This is his first try
at the Futurity and here he is with the favorite. Most of the
other stables have spent years tryin' for a winner with no luck.
They'll do everything they can to beat us."

"Sam Hildreth is a wily one," Danny said. "We'll have to
watch his Dominique."

"All of them," Feustel muttered. "We've got to watch every
last one of 'em. The thirteenth might not be such a lucky day
for us."

"The thirteenth? Is that the date of the Futurity?" Danny
asked, his hand coming to a stop on the colt's neck.

"Yes, and it was the thirteenth of last month that Upset
beat us."

Danny said nothing more, for now he too was uneasy. And
for the first time that he could remember, he welcomed the in-

vasion of photographers who arrived at the stall wanting to take pictures of Man o' War. He posed the big colt for them, listening to the clicks of their shutters but thinking only of the important race that would be run on—of all days—the 13th of September. Not that he was superstitious. Not at all. He would just rather have had the Futurity fall on some other day!

The field that went postward the following Saturday was not as big as Louis Feustel had predicted. Still, there were nine colts and fillies whose stables had the courage to race Man o' War. Danny walked beside his colt well onto the track, for Man o' War was more restless than he'd ever been. He lunged hard, plunging against Major Treat and dragging Danny with him. Two men ran out to help, and the big colt took all three of them into the air, this time plunging away from Major Treat.

"I don't know what's gotten into him," Danny said as he tried to bring Man o' War down. "Unless it's because he hasn't raced in two weeks. He'll raise the devil at the barrier."

The crowd watched Man o' War, but it seemed no one was worried over the possibility of his post parade antics taking anything out of him. They had made him the favorite at the shortest odds, with one exception, ever quoted in the long history of the Futurity.

He was carrying the highest weight in the field, this time 127 pounds, and conceding from five to ten pounds to all the other horses. The track was fast and, the fans believed, much to Man o' War's liking. A stiff wind was blowing up the track, but other than that nothing should impede this brilliant red colt in his final race of the season. It was possible that John P. Grier and Dominique might make a race of it, but Man o' War had beaten most of the others entered in the race and no one expected the decision to be reversed today.

Danny watched Man o' War prance up the track. He was acting better, now that he knew the business of racing was at hand. He slid hard against Major Treat, who took the shock of the plunging tornado quietly, as he was resigned to do by now. Together they continued past the stands, eighth in the field of ten. Only John P. Grier and On Watch were behind him. Dominique was in second post position while Upset, trying again to repeat his victory of just a month ago, was sixth in line.

The barrier awaited them at the start of the long three-quarters of a mile "chute." As Danny had guessed, Man o' War was dynamite behind the barrier. Even from where the boy stood, he could see his colt fighting to break through. The other jockeys weren't helping to soothe him down, either. They were the top riders in America and all experts at getting the best of the start. They were doing everything possible to bother the favorite, and Loftus had his hands full with them as well as with his own mount.

The minutes ticked away with Mars Cassidy trying to control the field and bring the horses into proper position. Five minutes passed by, then six, then seven . . . and at the eighth minute they were suddenly in line. The barrier was sprung and the yellow flag fell, waving them on.

They came out in a bunch and Danny looked for the yellow-and-black silks. He thought Man o' War, being so excited, would come out first and make every post a winning one. But out of the pack emerged Dominique, while John P. Grier flashed across the track from far outside and raced head and head with the leader!

Danny looked back and found his colt, a stride in front of the rest of the pack, nicely placed, and running well within himself. It was easier now to see the compactly bunched field, and the crowd roared as Man o' War began to move up. In front, Dominique seemed to feel the effects of the stiff headwind and gave way to John P. Grier.

It was at that second that Johnny Loftus must have spoken to Man o' War, for the big red colt moved with electrifying swiftness. He hurtled past Dominique and then John P. Grier as if in play. Faster and faster he went until Loftus began pulling him back. Even then he was galloping faster than the other horses raced! By the last quarter of a mile, Loftus was once more standing in his stirrups and looking back at those who would challenge Man o' War.

It was another romp for the champion, and the overflowing crowd rose to its feet applauding him. When he came back to the winner's circle, the cheers rose to still greater heights, for the time on the board was 1:11 ⅗, the fastest Futurity ever run! Man o' War had won as he pleased. What might have happened if this great colt had been extended? the spectators asked themselves. Already they were looking forward to the following year when Man o' War would reappear and their answer might be forthcoming.

Danny waited outside the winner's circle. He watched the photographers take pictures of Mr. and Mrs. Riddle standing beside Man o' War. He had never seen them any happier. A short distance away he recognized Major August Belmont, owner of Nursery Stud. He, too, was smiling and Danny believed that he must be the happiest of all, for it was he who had decided that Mahubah should be bred to Fair Play. Major Belmont had sent from Nursery Stud the best colt bred there, perhaps the best in the world. What a pity he hadn't kept him for himself!

The Unwinding

21

"But will he go on?" a newspaper reporter asked Louis Feustel the morning after the Futurity. "He's never raced more than three-quarters of a mile. Our readers will want to know if you think he'll still be sensational when the distances are stretched out next year."

Feustel smiled, a little patiently, Danny thought. "You know," he replied, "you're the first reporter I've talked to who's asked me that question. None of the others have been so skeptical. They seem to know that we have a top-class horse, one who has *stamina* as well as speed."

The reporter did not smile back. "*The New York Sun* editorial policy is more *conservative* than other newspapers," he said seriously. "We have seen other horses receive the acclaim your colt has, only to fade badly in later performances. We believe our readers prefer to sit back calmly and await results rather than to place a young two-year-old in equine history before he's actually had a chance to prove himself."

Feustel shook his head. "Horsemen feel differently about

226

Man o' War," he said solemnly. "Regardless of the fact that he's still a colt we know he's among the greatest we've ever seen, and we include older horses as well. We rank him among the best of the best, and I would say this even if he was not in my stable."

The *Sun* reporter smiled for the first time at Feustel's serious but glowing praise. "I'm afraid our paper thinks you and others are being carried away by Man o' War's triumph in the Futurity," he said. "We prefer to think of him as a brilliant colt who has done everything a colt should do. But he is only on the threshold of his racing career. As to his being the greatest ever, we'll have to wait and see."

The reporter paused, his gaze turning to Man o' War. "All we would like to know just now is this: In your opinion, will he be able to carry his speed over longer distances?"

Feustel shrugged his shoulders resignedly. "He will go on," he said simply.

"Has Mr. Riddle decided *not* to race him again this year?" the reporter asked. "He needs to win only $20,000 more to set a new record for his age. And as you so eloquently pointed out, he dominates his division. It would be easy for him to . . ."

"He's not racing any more this year," Feustel interrupted. "Mr. Riddle and I have decided he's done enough; he needs the rest. We're not out to break any purse records."

"But it's very tempting, isn't it?" the reporter persisted.

"No, frankly, it isn't," Feustel said. "We have bigger things in view."

The following week Man o' War was taken to the track only for light exercise. He began the "unwinding" that would take him back to the pastures of the Glen Riddle Farm in Maryland for the winter. Even though he was galloped slowly in the mornings, he attracted more attention than any other horse at the track. The acclaim of all turfdom still lingered in the air, for despite the fact that he was only a two-year-old there was no question but that Man o' War was the "horse of the year." It was the highest honor that exacting horsemen could bestow upon him. He towered above all other stars on the track. He had raced 10 times, with 9 firsts and 1 second, for $83,325 in purse winnings. That he would go on to become even greater as a three-year-old, few horsemen doubted.

With the approach of cool weather, the Riddle stable moved to Maryland. Danny was glad to get away from the race-track for a while. It was nice to relax, to rest. And for Man o' War it was a time to play. Danny enjoyed his colt to the ut-most, taking care of him all by himself. Once more they were the close friends of Nursery Stud days, for as big and famous as Man o' War had become, he still had many coltish ways about him.

Danny watched him roam the lush pastures of Glen Riddle Farm, his curious eyes finding familiar sights, his ears and nose catching sounds and scents he had known before. He played like a colt, romping and kicking from one end of the pasture to the other. But he ran as no other colt had ever run! He dug into the earth, cutting it with flaying hoofs and sending great chunks of sod behind him in a mad, whirlwind dash along the fence. Here he ran as he wanted to race . . . with no bit, no hands to hold him back! Perhaps that was the reason Man o' War never ran as other colts did in pasture, well within them-selves. Only here was he free from all restraint. And most of the time it was only Danny who observed this blazing speed. More than ever he was humbled by it. There was no horse in the world like Man o' War. There never had been. There never would be again.

Fall passed into winter, and Man o' War became a three-year-old. He had grown like a weed. By spring he stood well over sixteen hands and his red chestnut coat was rich and glowing with good health and vitality. His body had thickened to keep up with his rapid growth. Weighing 1,100 pounds, he had a remarkable girth of seventy-two inches.

Never had a three-year-old looked as magnificent as Man o' War, Danny thought. His powerful forehand and quarters were matched by a barrel that was almost a perfect cylinder. His forearms and shoulders had developed enormously, keeping pace with the weight and thickness of his long, round barrel. His flanks were deep and well skirted and his loins broad and powerful. His stifle joints were wide and flaring so that when he ran through the pasture they swung free and clear of his barrel.

Feustel watched him one morning with Danny and said, "He's matured better than any colt I've ever seen. He's filled and rounded-out to perfection."

Danny's eyes glowed as Man o' War came whipping around the fence toward them. "He looks more like a stallion than ever," he said. "See how his neck dips in front of the withers. And how it rises to a crest. No horse could look more masculine."

Feustel nodded. "You notice a lot about this colt, Danny. You seldom miss anything."

"We've been together a long time," Danny answered quietly.

"A long time," Feustel repeated. His eyes left the horse to study the boy. He noted how much taller and broader Danny had grown since he'd been with the stable. The kid was maturing along with the colt. In a way they were a good deal alike. Danny had lost a lot of his awkwardness, too, moving with a deftness now that belied his big frame.

The trainer turned back to Man o' War. It was too bad in a way that Danny had been born big-boned. The kid wanted to do more than rub Man o' War. He'd have given anything to be a jockey and he probably would have made a good one. But there were other jobs for him besides rubbing horses. Danny was bound to do something big someday. Not that rubbing Man o' War wasn't pretty important in itself.

They watched the colt run from one end of the pasture to the other. Feustel said, "You're both a lot alike."

Danny said, "I wish I could go so fast." He hadn't meant it as a joke and didn't smile. How much he would have given to be up on Man o' War's back!

Feustel leaned against the fence. "Being with him is what counts, Danny," he said understandingly. "That's more important than anything else. And you've been closer to him than the rest of us. You saw him foaled."

Danny nodded but said nothing more. Later, when he put Man o' War back in his stall, he stroked the colt's head. *Feustel is right*, he thought. *Just being here is what counts . . . that's all that matters.*

He continued rubbing Man o' War's broad forehead, then followed the line of the tapered nose down to the fine, delicate muzzle. He knew every inch of Man o' War, maybe better than anyone else, just as Feustel had said. How many other people had noticed that the colt's jowls had widened this winter and the muscle over them had thickened?

He pushed Man o' War's head gently away. "If looks mean anything, nothing will stop you ever," he said quietly.

When he closed him up for the night, he called, "Good night, Red." From within the stall came a muffled snort.

The Preakness

22

The other stables had not yet given up hope of beating the big red colt who had swept everything before him the preceding year. They knew from long experience that many sensational juveniles reached their peak at two years, never to improve. Many of the trainers believed that their own colts had been slow in developing and would show their real class at three years of age when the race distances were lengthened.

Few turfmen had any idea what was taking place at Glen Riddle Farm. If they had seen Man o' War in the spring, they would not have held such high hopes of defeating him.

"Going in the Kentucky Derby with him?" Feustel asked Mr. Riddle one morning.

The owner shook his head without taking his eyes from the chestnut colt. "No, the first of May is much too early to ask a three-year-old to go a mile and a quarter."

"Even him?" Feustel studied the good bone structure of Man o' War, the flat cannons and feet so large and healthy. The Kentucky Derby's distance wouldn't break down this colt.

"Even him," Mr. Riddle answered.

"There'll be a lot of pressure put on you to run him," Feustel went on. "It'll take much of the public interest away from the Derby if he doesn't go."

"We'll still wait," Mr. Riddle said adamantly.

Louis Feustel nodded. "Okay," he said. He would have liked to see Man o' War in the Kentucky Derby, but there'd be no changing the boss's mind. Mr. Riddle could be an extremely stubborn man.

"No horse of mine will go to Churchill Downs so early in the year," the owner went on. "Let the others knock themselves out. We'll wait."

Feustel said, "He's in top physical shape. We'll step up his works now."

"The middle of May will be early enough to race him," Mr. Riddle decided. "We'll go in the Preakness, right here in Maryland."

Feustel's brow furrowed. "But I thought your plan called for us to move back to Belmont Park."

"It does. I haven't changed it. We'll move the stable to Belmont the first of May and prepare there for the Preakness. It will be quiet with no racing there, and the facilities are better. We'll ship him down to Pimlico a couple of days before the race and return to Belmont immediately after."

Feustel shrugged his shoulders. "It might not be the wisest thing to do, shipping just before the race, but I think he can handle it."

"I think so too," Mr. Riddle said. "There's always a lot of confusion at Pimlico around Preakness time. The later we arrive the better."

"The public will maul him anyway," Feustel said. "Racing is in the blood of all Marylanders, and he'll heat them up still more."

Mr. Riddle smiled at his trainer's words but said thoughtfully, "Maryland is his home. It's only right that he makes his first start in the Preakness."

"What about Johnny Loftus?" Feustel asked. He and everyone else in the business knew that the jockey was having a difficult time getting a license to ride that year. Too many trainers and owners had complained about his not following their riding instructions.

"I appealed to the Jockey Club to reinstate him," Mr. Riddle said, "but it didn't do any good. I doubt that he'll get his license."

"Whom do you have in mind?" Feustel persisted. "It'll take a lot of jockey to handle him, and we don't want to make any mistakes in his first start."

"I'm not sure who it will be," Mr. Riddle said, closing the subject.

By the first of May they were at Belmont Park, and Man o' War continued his preparation for the Preakness on the 18th. His very presence at the New York track aroused the curiosity of fans and trainers alike, and they watched every move he made with Clyde Gordon in the saddle. Every day that he was given anything approaching a fast trial, the stopwatches in the hands of clockers clicked. The morning gallery grew as the big colt was galloped longer and faster. Slowly they became convinced that this colt was not just a sprinter who had come to hand early to top his division. In the past they had seen many three-year-olds "pay the price" for their earlier, brilliant victories.

Man o' War would go on, they decided. He overshadowed everything else at the track. Each stride was effortless and he went about his business with a determination they had seen only in much older champions. He was eager to run and had a will of his own that delighted them. They knew that here was a courageous colt who wouldn't quit. And from the looks of him he wouldn't break down.

On Saturday, May 8, 1920, Paul Jones won the Kentucky Derby at Churchill Downs in Louisville, Kentucky, with Upset finishing second. The results of the historic race didn't worry anyone in the Riddle stable. Paul Jones wasn't eligible for the Preakness and they didn't expect any trouble from Upset. A week later they moved to Pimlico, eager for their colt to begin his campaign for the three-year-old championship.

Marylanders welcomed Man o' War as their native son, flocking to the stable to see him. Danny enjoyed their neighborliness compared to the metropolitan sophistication of the "backside" guests at Belmont. The air at Pimlico was that of a cozy picnic ground rather than a famous racecourse.

He had only one concern as the day of the Preakness dawned. Mr. Riddle had taken his time about deciding on the jockey to pilot Man o' War, and only the night before had named Clarence Kummer. It wasn't that Danny didn't think Kummer was a good choice, for he was a young, successful rider. But it was too bad that Mr. Riddle had not named Kummer early enough for the jockey to get to know the big colt as he should. It might mean the difference between victory and defeat.

The day grew very hot, and Danny found himself sweating so much that his shirt stuck to his back. Man o' War, too, was spotted with dark wet splotches that no amount of grooming could conceal. Danny watched him closely, knowing that more than the heat was causing Man o' War to perspire. The big colt was aware that he was going postward. Perhaps he sensed it from the tremendous crowd that he could see in the distance or in the number of people who passed in and out of his stall as the day wore on. At any rate, Man o' War was uneasy. He would give Kummer a hard time, and the new jockey had better be on his toes.

Danny groomed him again. He had the golden coat shining like a copper kettle. Man o' War looked good, and yet Danny's gnawing doubts persisted. His colt had been away from the races a long time. Maybe he wasn't at his best despite his fast workouts. Most horses weren't, their first time out. And Man o' War had a new rider.

Clarence Kummer watched Man o' War enter the saddling paddock, the track police clearing the way before him. The jockey noted the big colt's uneasiness as he skittered to one side, scattering the crowd. Some people moved quickly back to Man o' War, trying to reach out and touch him.

It looked to Kummer as though Man o' War was ready to explode, and that he was probably in for the ride of his life. But he felt that he could handle the big colt. Hadn't he ridden Sir Barton, Omar Khayyam, Exterminator, and many other top horses? And yet. . . . He watched the fiery colt go skyward again, trying to break away from the boy who held him. His hindquarters swung far around, grazing the men behind. Man o' War was as edgy as a cat, and just as quick.

The young jockey turned to Louis Feustel and Mr. Riddle, who were standing alongside him. "Is he always this way?" he asked.

"He's not usually quite so worked up as this," the trainer said. "But you'll know you've got a horse under you."

Mr. Riddle was concerned. "Maybe we'd better have Clyde and Major Treat accompany you to the post," he suggested.

"No," the jockey said. "I'd like to handle him myself. I can do it all right."

Mr. Riddle and Feustel exchanged glances, and then the owner said, "All right, Clarence. If you're to be his pilot, it's best for you to find out for yourself what he's like. Just remember, he's a powerful colt. Don't let him get away from you."

"I won't," the jockey said, flecking some dust from his boot.

Feustel watched his new rider closely. "I'd much rather have you confident than leery of him," he said quietly. Then he went forward to saddle Man o' War.

A few minutes later the call came. "Riders, mount your horses, please."

Clarence Kummer felt the tenseness of the colt's muscles beneath his legs. He knew Man o' War might explode any minute but he was ready for him. He took another wrap in the reins as the colt swept hard against the old gelding alongside. Clyde Gordon held Major Treat steady, and the two riders exchanged glances. Kummer patted his mount's neck. He and Man o' War would have company only to the gap in the track fence. It was the way he wanted it. He'd learn quickly what he had under him.

The red-coated marshal was directly in front of them. Their post position was number 7, but the track officials had decided Man o' War should lead the post parade for the Preakness. There were a lot of people in the stands and infield who would be getting their first look at the two-year-old champion, now going into his first race as a three-year-old. Kummer also knew that every horseman in the East was there.

They reached the track, and the jockey signaled to Clyde Gordon to turn them loose. Danny still had hold of the colt's bridle. "Okay, kid," Kummer said, "let go."

The track band had begun to play the immortal Preakness hymn, "Maryland, My Maryland." Kummer tied a knot in the reins, making them still shorter. The huge crowd was on its feet, listening and singing to the first strains of the music while watching the horses step onto the track.

Man o' War bolted. Kummer pulled hard, trying to restrain him. The music continued but the fans were no longer listening. Their roar drowned out the Preakness hymn as Man o' War swept up the track, his head thrust forward and tail streaming behind him. He ran faster and faster, with Kummer standing in his stirrup irons. There seemed to be no holding him. Then, suddenly, he slowed down, as if of his own accord. He turned in the direction of the packed stands, his ears pricked and alert, his eyes blazing yet curious, too. It seemed that he had pulled himself up to find out what all the commotion was about. Before he had a chance to move again, the red-coated marshal caught hold of his bridle.

A roar of applause and laughter came from the crowd as once again the band played the Preakness hymn and the field caught up to Man o' War. But everyone wondered, too, how much the run up the stretch had taken out of the fiery colt.

Clarence Kummer had been humbled by Man o' War but not beaten. He had more respect for the colt's quickness, but still felt confident that he could handle him. In the future, however, he'd let Clyde Gordon and Major Treat accompany them to the post. It was better to save the running until later.

The eight other three-year-olds were lined up at the barrier, six inside, two on the outside of him. Kummer wasn't worried about any of them. He'd ridden against most of the field before, including Man o' War. It was good to be sitting on the top horse for a change, he decided. He expected to go a long way with him, maybe becoming as famous as Johnny Loftus. Man o' War could do it for him, but one thing was certain: he had no intention of stirring up the colt. It wasn't necessary, for Man o' War had enough run in him to catch the others without prodding, especially now that the distances were longer. Today a whole mile and an eighth stretched before them.

On the rail St. Allan and On Watch were fractious and raising the devil. Upset, alongside Man o' War, was just as bad.
Kummer spoke to him, trying to keep his mount quiet. He was
eager to get away himself, but he must not be overanxious in
the saddle. It would only stir up Man o' War still more.

Kummer glanced at Blazes in the fifth position. That colt
was a great sprinter. He'd be away first, but he wouldn't last.
King Thrush, with Earl Sande up, would be out fast too, trying
to run them into the ground. The strategy of the other stables,
Kummer decided, was to set a furious pace and hope to wear
down Man o' War while Upset, Wildair, and On Watch
caught the big colt in the homestretch.

The strategy wouldn't work. He had too much horse under
him to be caught.

For six more minutes the horses and riders milled behind
the barrier, all bent on wearing down Man o' War one way or
another. It was a tough first outing for a three-year-old. Kummer kept his mount back. Feustel's instructions were simply to
keep Man o' War out of trouble, and that's what he intended
to do. The big colt responded to his quiet commands. He was
anxious to be off, but was not rebellious. He had brains, Kummer decided. He had proved it in his dash up the track earlier.
Any other colt would have kept running and had nothing left
for the race.

The starter had them all in line and straight. Kummer
leaned forward for the first time, waiting for the barrier to go
up. The elastic webbing flew skyward, the yellow flag came
down, and the famed Preakness had begun!

Man o' War plunged forward, his head up and eyes blazing.
Kummer gave him full rein, surprised that the big colt was so
quick on his feet and went into stride so easily. He was near
the front and showing amazing speed at this early stage of the

race. Kummer gave him his head, and only King Thrush stayed alongside as Man o' War's strides lengthened. Earl Sande, up on King Thrush, was using his whip but Kummer had no need to urge his mount on. Man o' War was running for the sheer love and excitement of it. He seemed to glory in his freedom and the thrill of racing.

Before they had reached the first turn, Man o' War was in front. He swept around the turn going faster and faster, and when Kummer saw that they had killed off King Thrush, he began taking hold of the eager colt.

At first the jockey felt Man o' War's resentment. The big colt fought him, trying to get his head down and to run as he pleased. Then, slowly, there was a response to his hands and the long strides shortened. They passed the half-mile pole with Man o' War running easily and well within himself. He was still eager to show his best, but Kummer found that he was able to control him while in full stride. There was no need to saw on the reins.

The backstretch was deep and rough, giving way under Man o' War's flying hoofs. Kummer glanced back at the straggling field from five to thirty-six lengths behind them. Upset was the closest to them, but not near enough to be any threat. They sped around the final turn.

Entering the homestretch, Upset made his bid to catch them, but Kummer didn't turn Man o' War loose. He knew Upset was being driven under the hardest kind of punishment and wouldn't last.

Man o' War moved easily past the stands, receiving ever-increasing applause as if it was his just due. His tail streaming out behind him, he drew still farther away from Upset and the cream of the season's three-year-olds. He seemed to be enjoying himself and was barely taking a long breath. He swept beneath the finish wire not extended, not tired.

The cheers continued as he was turned around and came back to the winner's circle. The crowd pressed hard against the enclosure to get close to this colt who had made a mockery of the historic Preakness. The ovation rose to its greatest heights when the horseshoe of black-eyed Susans was placed about his neck. He stood quietly, his head held high, his gleaming flanks scarcely damp. He looked every bit the noble champion he was.

Far back in the crowd Danny waited, his eyes leaving Man o' War to glance impatiently into the dusk of the eastern sky. Only with the coming night would Man o' War be his alone again. Then he would be able to tell him what a great three-year-old he was.

The Way of a Champion

23

It was early evening when Danny finished "cooling out" Man o' War. The crowd in the stable area had lingered, feasting their eyes on the chestnut colt, unable even then to let him go.

Danny offered him a drink of water but the colt refused it. Man o' War pulled on the lead shank as if he were still feeling fresh and wanted no part of the closed stall. Danny let him have his way, walking rapidly just to keep up with him. They passed beneath the trees, and the gazes of all who remained in the area followed them.

The throng nodded in full appreciation of what it saw, for Man o' War held his beautiful head high and the long star on his nose stood out dramatically in the night. His long, sinewy neck curved like that of a war horse. He seemed to know very well that people were watching him, and yet there was aloofness, perhaps even disdain, in his brilliant eyes.

"He certainly looks as if he hadn't raced at all," a newspaperman said.

Louis Feustel nodded. "He's in fine physical shape," the

trainer agreed, "but he wasn't nearly at his best today. He needed the race under his belt. He'll improve fast now. You'll see."

"We saw plenty already," the newsman said.

Feustel went on, "Unless I miss my guess, he'll show the American public something very unusual in speed and stamina before the season ends."

The trainer's eyes left the colt, turning to Mr. Riddle. "Don't you agree, sir?"

"Yes, Louis, I do," Mr. Riddle said. "I expect him to improve considerably over today's race."

The newspaperman took another tack, turning also to Mr. Riddle. "Is it true you've been offered $500,000 for him by a syndicate?"

Man o' War's owner smiled. "I've been flattered by many offers," he replied. "But I've never taken any of them seriously. I have my own plans for him."

"Do you plan to race him in the big handicaps?"

"Just in the ones for his age only," Mr. Riddle said. "My object is to give him the best possible opportunity to show the public how great a horse he is. But I don't want to see him carrying any more weight than the handicappers have already put on his back. It's enough to ask of any three-year-old, even Man o' War."

Mr. Riddle turned back to his friends, but the newspaperman was persistent. "But would you race him against older horses, if he didn't have to carry any more weight than the 126 pounds for his age?"

Mr. Riddle smiled. "There'll be exceptions, of course. We're not afraid of Sir Barton, Exterminator, or any of the other older horses, providing we don't have to give them weight, too."

"I'm sure the public would like to see such a race," the reporter said.

Mr. Riddle nodded. "Man o' War belongs to the public as much as he does to me," he said quietly. "He's the greatest horse that ever set foot on a racetrack."

Danny walked Man o' War through darkness lit only by a moon in its first quarter. "Don't let all this talk go to your head, Red," he whispered.

The boy knew that by the next day the world would echo Mr. Riddle's praise of Man o' War. His easy win in the Preakness had demonstrated that he was a stayer. Nothing his age could hold a candle to him!

The following morning Man o' War was shipped back to Belmont Park. Those who went with him, including Danny, felt as only people can who are in the entourage of a great champion. This was their hour as well as Man o' War's. He belonged to everybody in the Riddle stable. Victory was theirs. History was theirs. They would make no mistakes this year. There would be no flukes, no races not truly run in which their colt would be defeated. Nothing would stop Man o' War. Not Paul Jones who had won the Kentucky Derby. Not Sir Barton, Exterminator, or any of the older horses. Their colt was king, and they stood proudly beside him, sharing his glory.

Danny moved over to make room for all those who now claimed Man o' War as their own, too, and watched the colt carefully. Feustel had been right in saying that Man o' War had needed the Preakness under his belt and would improve still more. Daily at Belmont, the colt seemed to grow in stature. There was not a pound of surplus flesh on him anywhere, and his form on the track matched the heroic proportions of his glistening body.

He worked six furlongs in the blazing time of 1:11, and the

morning before his next race he was blown out a furlong in 10 ⅕ seconds, both under the strongest kind of pull and fighting for his head.

Danny washed him off while Mr. Riddle and Louis Feustel stood quietly by. He swept the wet sponge over the colt's powerful quarters, and through the perspiration he could see the black spots Man o' War had inherited from the maternal line of Fair Play. Danny was certain his colt was destined for greater glory than his sire or any of his noble ancestors. Man o' War would stand alone at the top of the world before his racing career ended.

Louis Feustel said, "I don't like all this hero worship he's getting, Mr. Riddle. It's gotten out of hand. But I guess it can't be helped."

Mr. Riddle nodded, then smiled. "Well, if it'll make you any happier there's one dissenter. Jim Rowe is out to stop our colt."

Feustel shrugged his shoulders. "He did it once with Upset. But everyone knows that race was a fluke. It couldn't happen again."

"But he's a fine trainer," Mr. Riddle said.

"The best, I guess," Feustel admitted. "That's why everyone listens to him. For some fifty years he'd been enjoying the best of everything the track has to offer, and that includes working with the finest stock and the top breeders and owners. He's had a world of experience, so people pay attention to what he says. But this time he's dead wrong. He's not going to stop our colt, and he knows it. It's hard for him to take."

"Especially since I'm a *new* owner," Mr. Riddle said quietly.

"That's part of it," Feustel admitted. "Jim has been training for Harry Payne Whitney for the last twenty years now. Their big goal has always been to win the principal two- and three-year-old races. They don't care much about the races for older horses. It's the juveniles they want to win. So they come out each year with a whole team of high-class colts and fillies. They race on a grand scale with all the resources of the Whitney breeding farms behind them. Any one of their youngsters might prove to be a champion. So that's why the rest of us have always felt a certain amount of terror in racing against them."

"But not this year," Mr. Riddle said, enjoying the success of Man o' War.

"Yeah, we come along with a wonder colt that takes the Hopeful and the Futurity. We upset all their plans. And here they were this season with three colts they thought the world of—Upset, Wildair, and John P. Grier—all of Ben Brush's male line crossed with mares carrying the blood of Domino, which have produced the most brilliant early-speed and stakes-winning juveniles of the day. I guess they got a right to be a little bitter."

"Perhaps so," Mr. Riddle answered, "but that's racing."

"Sure, but that's why Jim Rowe won't admit defeat yet, either. He's got skill and energy, and he'll use them both to advantage. Maybe he figures we've got Upset beaten, but now he'll push harder with the other two colts. Wildair finished third to us in the Preakness, then he won the Metropolitan the other day. So now I'm sure that Rowe figures he's ready for the Withers tomorrow. I don't know why he's holding John P. Grier in reserve. Some of the fellows say he's the best colt in the Whitney stable."

"We'll find out soon enough," Mr. Riddle said. "One colt at a time, Louis, and tomorrow Man o' War will finish off Wildair."

The next afternoon Man o' War went postward on a New York track for the first time as a three-year-old. It was a far different crowd from the one that had watched him at Pimlico. There they had been ready to accept Man o' War as a champion and their very own, belonging to the state of Maryland, home of Glen Riddle Farm. At Belmont Park it was a more hardened, show-me crowd, one ready to accept Man o' War as the champion of his division *only* if he proved it to them.

There were horsemen in the stands who were known equally as well in Europe as in the United States, but the bulk of the spectators were working people from the city who had managed to get the afternoon off. They had come to see Man o' War in action. They wanted to decide for themselves if he was still the wonder colt they had seen as a two-year-old. They even discounted his brilliant win in the classic Preakness the week before. Man o' War must prove his greatness to *them*. The weather had cooperated. It was a sunny May 29, warm but not hot, and the track was lightning fast.

Danny inched his way through the crowd to get a good view of the course. He pushed as hard as everyone else to get near the rail. He wanted to miss nothing, for Clarence Kummer had been told by Feustel to go to the front and stay there. This might be the day Man o' War would show all his matchless speed!

He watched Man o' War and his heart swelled with pride at the very sight of him. Major Treat was accompanying the big colt to the post with Feustel himself up on the gelding. The trainer wasn't taking any chances on Man o' War's breaking away from Kummer, as he had done in the Preakness post parade. Kummer had had no objection to being taken to the barrier. It seemed that he had learned his lesson.

There were only two other colts out there with Man o' War. Jim Rowe had saddled Wildair in hopes of stopping Man o'

War, just as he had said he would. The third colt was David Harum, who was running solely for the third-place money. All the other trainers and owners had declined to send their horses postward in the Withers, knowing they faced certain defeat. Only Jim Rowe stubbornly refused to accept Man o' War's supremacy.

The Withers Stakes was raced over a mile at level weights, each horse required to carry 118 pounds. That in itself had been enough to scare away all other entries. It was the first time since his earliest starts that Man o' War would race with such a light impost and give no weight allowances to other horses. Danny knew this would be the big colt's day. It would be an exhibition of his great speed and not a race at all. Wildair couldn't stay with him, no matter what Jim Rowe thought with all his years of experience!

The trio reached the post and for a moment the crowd was silent, awaiting the break. Man o' War was in number 2 post position. He straightened out with the others and faced the barrier. There would be no trouble today with just the three horses. The crowd held its breath. The start would come fast and soon.

In less than a minute the barrier sprang up and the three colts came out in a perfect line. For five strides they moved together, then the yellow track was shattered by the hurtling red body of Man o' War! Long and smooth his strides came as he bounded to the front, opening up a large gap between him and the others.

The crowd watched him sweep into the first turn with Kummer sitting very still on his broad back. He pulled farther and farther away from Wildair, who was running hard, trying to keep up with him. He passed the quarter pole and entered the long backstretch all by himself.

"He's loafing," said a man next to Danny. "And Kummer's

got such a snug hold on him his head is back to his chest. Look at it."

Danny knew that Kummer had a tight hold on Man o' War, but his colt wasn't loafing. His strides were so long and smooth that he just didn't seem to be moving fast. But he was! All one had to do to realize that was to look back at Wildair and see how hard that colt was working.

As if to lend added emphasis to Danny's thoughts, a trainer with a stopwatch called the first quarter mile in the blazing time of 24 seconds flat. Man o' War might be under a snug hold, but he wasn't loafing at all!

Down the long backstretch and around the far turn Kummer sat coolly on Man o' War, his hands low on the colt's withers and keeping a steady pull on the reins. The crowd roared for him to turn the colt loose when Man o' War began fighting for his head. But Kummer kept the bow in the big colt's neck, holding him to what seemed to be an easy gallop. Behind him Wildair was attaining his utmost speed in a futile attempt to catch up.

In awed silence the spectators watched Man o' War sweep under the finish wire. But as Kummer sought to bring him to a stop by taking a still shorter hold of the reins, the crowd roared. Man o' War had broken away from Kummer and was speeding down the track! He was still fresh and full of run! He had fought his way into the turn before Kummer managed to bring him under control again.

Man o' War came back to the winner's circle to the wildest ovation Danny had ever heard. It mounted to still greater heights when it was announced that his time had set a new American record of 1:35 ⅘ for the mile! What might he have done had he been let out? The ease with which he had won the Withers impressed the crowd more than his record-shattering time. Here was a colt without equal, perhaps the best Thoroughbred ever seen on the American turf. The ovation continued for a long, long time, and Danny knew that New York too had now accepted his colt for the great champion he was.

It had been a big day, but it was just the beginning. It was the height of the season and now his colt would get little chance to rest between races. As great as Man o' War was, the way would not be easy, for the public would accept no excuse for a poor showing. He had been placed on the pinnacle of racehorse fame, and he had to live up to the great expectations of the fans, regardless of his competition or the distance of the race or the weight put on his back or, simply, the way he felt. Man o' War had found his rightful place in the sun.

Two weeks later Man o' War won the historic Belmont Stakes with the same ease as in his previous victories. What made the race more spectacular than the others was the distance. For the first time Man o' War went a mile and three-eighths. He won by twenty lengths over Donnacona, the only horse sent against him. And once again it was not a contest but an exhibition of extreme speed. With Kummer holding him back as much as possible without too choking a pull, Man o' War set a new track record of 2:14 ⅕!

Ten days after winning the Belmont he was in the winner's circle again, adding the Stuyvesant Handicap to his growing list of victories. He had carried 135 pounds, more weight than had ever before been placed on his back, and he had cantered home in front of the only other entry, Yellow Hand under 103 pounds, to win as he pleased.

Danny took Man o' War back to the barn with the cheers of the crowd still ringing in the colt's ears. He seemed to know that the applause was for him, and he took it as his just due. He danced rather than walked, his chestnut coat barely wet and glowing in the sunshine. And his bright eyes did not denote defiance but rather a final acceptance of the cheers and adulation.

"You're a ham, that's what you are," Danny told him. "They clap for you and your eyes light up like a Christmas tree." Or, he wondered, was Man o' War laughing at everybody?

The photographers and newsmen were waiting for them at the barn; there was a constant click of camera shutters as Danny posed the colt for them. It didn't take much doing, for Man o' War seemed to have full knowledge of what was going on and he almost posed himself.

"Why do you keep this colt under wraps?" a reporter asked Louis Feustel. "Why not let him run as he'd like to go?"

"He's winning, isn't he?" the trainer growled in answer. "What more do you want? Keep him under wraps and he'll last longer. He won't go breaking down like most of them."

"One of these days he just might break the strangle hold Kummer has on him, and pour it on all by himself," the reporter said.

"You'll have to wait until that day then," Feustel answered.

Another newsman said, "Perhaps you and Mr. Riddle feel it's not wise to humiliate the other stables by beating their colts too many lengths. Is that it?"

"No one likes to see high-class colts made to look like cheap racehorses," Feustel admitted.

"You're scaring them off," the reporter went on. "If you keep up this way, Mr. Riddle will have no choice but to retire him. There'll be nothing left to race."

Feustel shrugged his shoulders. "That's up to Mr. Riddle," he said quietly.

"I heard he was offered a million dollars for him," the reporter said. "Will he take it?"

Feustel laughed. "Mr. Riddle doesn't need a million dollars," he said. "He's got a million dollars; lots of people have. But there's only *one* Man o' War."

"Jim Rowe hasn't given up hope of beating you yet," the reporter went on. "He's got John P. Grier ready to go in the Dwyer next week. The talk's going around that Grier's the fastest colt Rowe has ever clocked at a mile."

Feustel smiled. "Then he'll make a race of it," he said.

"Just the two of them, Man o' War and John P. Grier," the reporter said thoughtfully. "It should be something to see."

"It should," agreed Feustel.

John P. Grier

24

Before the horses stepped onto the track for the running of the Dwyer Stakes, Jim Rowe had pulled one of his tricks. Somehow he had succeeded in convincing the track handicapper that John P. Grier should carry only 108 pounds while Man o' War was given 126. At once the stable talk began. *"The Whitney colt is getting an 18-pound pull in the weights. If he's as good as everyone thinks, he might beat Man o' War!"*

More than 25,000 people jammed the stands at Aqueduct racecourse to see what might turn out to be one of the most famous races in American turf history. There were only the two starters, John P. Grier and Man o' War. It hadn't been set up as a match race but that was what it was turning out to be. All the other stables whose horses had been eligible to race in the Dwyer had been scared off by Man o' War's great record. Jim Rowe had brought his colt along carefully with this race in view. Under the weight arrangement he had a chance of beating Man o' War.

The crowd swarmed to the saddling paddock to watch the

two colts. They pressed against the rail, trying to touch the horses and overhear the words of anyone who might give them a clue as to the outcome of the race.

Danny held Man o' War while Louis Feustel tightened the saddle girth. His gaze shifted momentarily to John P. Grier, standing quietly a few stalls away. Jim Rowe's colt was ready to go, Danny decided. He was on his toes and looked fresh and full of run. He was put together much differently from Man o' War, being small and compact, and looked every bit the sprinter he was. He could go a mile without a doubt. But could he hold his speed for still another furlong, the full distance of a mile and an eighth?

Danny turned back to his colt, holding him still as Feustel tightened the girth strap. He recalled Man o' War's easy win over this same colt in the Belmont Futurity, the last race of his two-year-old season. He had beaten John P. Grier then over a much shorter distance than today's race. The homestretch here at Aqueduct was a very long one. It would take a colt with great staying qualities to match strides with Man o' War in the run for the wire. Danny didn't believe John P. Grier could do it.

Major Treat was led over to Man o' War, and the big colt snorted when he saw him. Feustel would be riding the gelding to the post, accompanying Man o' War. They were going to make sure nothing happened on the way to the barrier.

Feustel finished his saddling and stepped over to talk to Mr. Riddle and some friends. Danny heard the trainer say, "He's a little too nervous, a bit on edge."

Mr. Riddle smiled confidently. "You've been listening to Jim Rowe too much, Louis," he said. "You're a bit too uneasy yourself. He's never looked better to me."

Feustel shrugged his shoulders but the concern remained in

his eyes. "I'm not worried over Rowe's challenge. Our colt's in top physical condition, as you say. But he's had too much going on the past few weeks, too many people around. He could do with a few days of peace and quiet."

"We'll give it to him," Mr. Riddle said, "after the race."

Danny's gaze shifted back to his colt. He didn't think Feustel had anything to worry about. Man o' War had held up well in his workouts despite all the clamor and attention he had received. He even seemed to thrive on the adulation. Maybe he was a bit on edge, Danny admitted to himself, but that was only natural. Man o' War knew what was to come and his eyes were bright and eager, his ears pricked.

Clarence Kummer came across the paddock, stopping for a moment to pat Man o' War's head.

Danny glanced at the jockey. "You're not worried, are you, Clarence?" he asked. "You've ridden John P. Grier twice this year and won with him both times. But you know you've got the winner under you today, don't you?"

"I know it, Danny," the jockey said. "Grier's a fast colt, one of the fastest I've ever ridden. But nothing alive can beat Man o' War, nothing." He gave the big colt a final pat and went over to Feustel and Mr. Riddle.

Danny felt better. It didn't even bother him to overhear Jim Rowe telling some friends close by, *"We'll trim Man o' War today!"*

Kummer mounted and Danny listened to Feustel's riding instructions. "I'm a little worried about him, Clarence," the trainer said quietly. "He's not as tight as he might be, a little on the edgy side. So watch him. I don't want him pushed too hard today and hurt for the races to come. Lay along with Grier all the way, and if you find you can win, don't try to ride him out but just be satisfied with a length or two."

Man o' War shifted, moving with lightning ease and swiftness. He swept around Major Treat but Danny managed to keep hold of the bridle, bringing him to a stop. The moment of the race had come. The crowd around the paddock was shouting, and there were many who were flocking back to the stands for a place to watch the drama unfold.

Feustel mounted Major Treat and reached for Man o' War's bridle. His eyes, still concerned, met Danny's, then shifted to Jim Rowe, who was still holding court beside John P. Grier. For a few seconds he listened to the other trainer's defiant, confident words while waiting for the band music to signal the start of the parade to the post.

Danny felt the intense excitement being held in check and Louis Feustel's anxiety as well. Would John P. Grier really prove a worthy challenger to Man o' War? Was this the day their colt would be tried to his utmost, driven to the wire, matched stride for stride? Was this the day the crowd had been waiting for?

The bugle sounded, calling the horses to the post, and as its notes ended the band began playing. Feustel moved Major Treat forward and Man o' War stepped quickly alongside. Danny followed. A few minutes from now it would be over. Everyone would have the answer to his questions.

John P. Grier was the first out on the track, and the applause mounted when the crowd saw the small, compact horse ridden by Eddie Ambrose. A top colt, lightly weighted, and a top jockey ... this was the combination to challenge the great Man o' War!

The champion skittered onto the track, trying to break away from his more dignified stablemate. But Major Treat would not be pulled very far and Louis Feustel held firmly onto Man o' War's bridle. They paraded before the stands, and the eyes of all closely examined the two colts.

Many in the great stands had come to the course only to see

Man o' War. But as they watched John P. Grier move smoothly, confidently postward their interest heightened, and they too were caught in the flurry of excitement over the prospects of his matching strides with the champion. Was this to be a *real* race, as Jim Rowe had proclaimed in all the newspapers? They recalled he had beaten Man o' War with Upset last season. Might he not do it again with John P. Grier? There was always a moment of weakness even in the greatest of champions. Who knew? Perhaps this race might be the finest ever run on American turf. And some of the spectators, loving a challenger in any sport, cried, "*Get him, Grier! Get him!*"

The two colts finished their parade past the stands and went around the first turn to the other side of the track, where a long chute entered the backstretch. The barrier awaited them at the far end of it.

They would race down the chute for a furlong before entering the track's backstretch, then continue down the long straightaway to the only turn they would have to negotiate. After rounding the turn they would have the long, grueling homestretch ahead of them to the finish wire.

Danny liked this inverted U-shaped course for his colt. Man o' War's huge, ground-eating strides were meant for the two long straightaways he would have to run. The only trouble he might have would be in rounding the sharp turn. He would be going awfully fast by the time he reached it, and his momentum might carry him wide. But he wouldn't lose enough lengths for John P. Grier to beat him, Danny decided. His colt would be far in front and Kummer, as in all the races past, would be standing in his stirrup irons and looking back at the end.

From where he stood it was difficult to see the colts as they went down the chute to the barrier. But he felt certain that with only two colts to handle, Mars Cassidy wouldn't have any trouble getting them away.

As the minutes ticked away he saw Man o' War rear and plunge forward repeatedly. Then John P. Grier began acting up, too. Finally the moment came when both colts seemed to be still behind the barrier. Man o' War was number 1, on the rail, and Danny kept his eyes glued to the massive body, which hid John P. Grier from view.

His colt lurched forward and for a second Danny thought he had broken through the barrier. But no, the tape was up and the race was on! Danny saw his colt surge down the chute, running alone, and he shouted at the top of his lungs, "Run, Red!"

His eyes swept back for a fleeting second, seeking John P. Grier. But the small colt wasn't to be seen. He was nowhere, nowhere at all! And then Danny had a sinking feeling. Grier must still be on the other side of Man o' War, his small body hidden by the champion's great bulk!

Out of the chute onto the main track, Man o' War thundered. But now Danny and all those who watched could see John P. Grier matching strides with Man o' War. They were locked together, moving as one down the long backstretch! This was no romp for Man o' War. *This was a race!* Here his courage as well as his speed would be tested!

They remained locked together, moving as a team down the long backstretch. Man o' War began inching ahead as they approached the turn, but he could not shake off John P. Grier! The excitement became more intense. At long last a horse was pushing the big red champion. How fast would Man o' War have to go to win and, even more important, would he have the courage to face the challenge of the fighting colt at his side?

The two colts flashed by the half-mile pole, and a clocker standing beside Danny glanced at his stopwatch and said, "Forty-six flat, *a track record!*" At five furlongs, he said, "Fifty-seven two, *a track record.*" At the three-quarters, "One oh nine three, *a track record.*"

Danny listened. The colts were traveling faster than the speediest sprinters had ever raced . . . and there were still three furlongs to go! He thought, too, how many more strides the small colt must be taking to stay beside Man o' War. And yet John P. Grier came on!

Around the sharp turn and into the homestretch they came together, and as Danny had foreseen, Man o' War lost ground in making the turn. No longer was his colt a nose in front of John P. Grier. The small challenger, fighting Man o' War as no horse had ever done before, came on head to head with the champion!

Danny couldn't join in the tremendous roar that rose from the stands. He did not hear the clocker beside him say, "Mile in one thirty-six flat, *a track record.*" His throat was constricted; his jaws seemed to be glued together. His eyes never left the bobbing heads coming toward him. John P. Grier had to crack under the terrific pace. He couldn't last. He couldn't keep pushing Man o' War. Or could he?

John P. Grier kept coming on doggedly, never missing a beat of the smooth strides that had kept him alongside Man o' War throughout the race. And Danny knew, as everyone else did, that never before had Man o' War been brought to such a grueling, punishing drive to the wire—and perhaps he never would be again!

"Come on, Red, come on!" Danny managed to shout at last.

But it was John P. Grier who moved, his jockey asking for

everything he had. The small colt responded, pushing his black muzzle in front of Man o' War, and for the first time forging to the lead!

"Grier wins!" the cry went up from the stands. *"Grier wins!"*

Danny jumped up against the man in front of him in an effort to see the finish. He unclenched his fists and grabbed the rail. His voice joined the great roar of the crowd. This was racing! Man o' War had met a colt worthy of his best!

Danny saw Kummer swing his whip. Never before had Man o' War been touched with it. What would happen? The whip came down hard against the colt's haunches.

In an electrifying second Man o' War became a thunderbolt! He moved with the swiftness of living flame, catching John P. Grier with one magnificent stride. Then he swept on, running as no horse had ever run before, thundering to racing glory and leaving behind him a gallant but beaten colt!

The greatest ovation in his life greeted Man o' War as he was turned and brought back to the winner's circle. His courage had been brought to a supreme test and had not been found wanting. He was still the champion and his luster was brighter than ever. The crowd did not forget John P. Grier in its applause. The small colt had been ahead of Man o' War, if only for a fleeting second. Next to the champion he was the best colt in America!

Danny listened to the wave upon wave of cheers that greeted his colt as Kummer rode him into the winner's circle. He stood nearby, waiting for the moment to come when he could take Man o' War back to the barn. The pandemonium reached even greater heights when the time of the race was posted for all to read. Man o' War had broken still another American record, running the mile and an eighth in 1:49 1/5!

Danny knew that his colt's record-shattering performance was secondary to the race itself. Never would he, or perhaps anyone else, ever see another like it. The true test of greatness in any horse was to meet a driving challenge, furlong after furlong, as Man o' War had done in defeating John P. Grier. His colt had fought back every step of the way. There was no question now of his gameness and courage. Man o' War was truly great, and Danny knew that never again would there be exactly this moment for him and his horse.

He studied Man o' War in the winner's circle. There was no doubt that the big colt had been extended to his utmost; his body was dark with great splotches of sweat and in places flecked with foam. His head too was wet, but he managed to keep it high, looking over the crowd that pressed close to him. Tired as he was, he seemed to be enjoying every minute of it.

Danny became more impatient than ever to get Man o' War back to the stable and sponged off. Never had his colt looked more tired to him. He would need a complete rest.

Finally the ceremonies ended and Louis Feustel called him to take Man o' War away. He hurried forward. The Dwyer was officially over and would go down in the books as one of the most exciting races in all turf history.

Again, Saratoga

25

That night Danny tossed restlessly on his tack room cot. He could not sleep. Maybe it was the mutterings of the grooms outside. Or it might be the deep breathing of the two men in the cots alongside his own. He didn't know what it might be ... except that it wasn't like him not to be able to drop off to sleep the moment his head struck the pillow.

The pitch-darkness of late night was familiar enough. The smells were those he loved, the odors of hay and leather, of horses and liniment. So what was it that was keeping him awake?

He closed his eyes, only to open them again quickly and stare into the darkness, searching for ... *what?* The reasons for his restlessness? Finally he got up, switching on the small overhead light that wouldn't bother the sleeping men. He leaned against the black tack trunks with the yellow trim and bold lettering, GLEN RIDDLE, and his eyes found everything in order. The pails, brooms, and rakes were all hanging where they should be, all freshly painted.

The muffled voices of other grooms had hushed completely; the stable area was deathly still. He bit his full lower lip while listening for any movement in the adjacent stall. But Man o' War must be sleeping too, exhausted after the hard race against John P. Grier.

Still, Danny wanted to go to him . . . not to disturb him, but just to be alone with him for a few minutes. Maybe then he, too, would be able to go to sleep.

Danny left the tack room and quietly opened the stall door. He looked inside. The dim outside light penetrated the darkness and he could make out Man o' War. The colt was down in the straw, his big body sprawled to its fullest extent, his eyes closed.

Danny moved closer, ankle-deep in the straw bedding. Reaching Man o' War, he bent down, touching the colt's velvet-soft neck without awakening him. Moments passed and then Man o' War's breathing was broken by a snore. The noise was quiet at first, but became louder with each successive breath. After a while the colt moved his legs in his sleep and there was a whisk of his long tail.

Danny smiled to himself. His colt dreamed at night after almost every race, as if he were running it all over again.

The long legs moved a little faster as the snorting became louder. Man o' War was in full flight now, perhaps with John P. Grier right alongside him.

"Beat him, Red," Danny whispered. "Beat him."

Still asleep, Man o' War snorted; then suddenly the legs stopped moving and the snoring hushed. The stall was quiet again. The race was over. Man o' War had won.

Danny got to his feet and went to the feed box. It was empty. His colt had cleaned it out, so nothing was wrong with him. And the hay had been eaten, too, all the good timothy with a little clover thrown in for dessert. Man o' War was a terrific eater, and good feed was important in a hard racing campaign.

The colt snorted again, breaking the quiet of the night. Danny turned to him, only to find him still asleep. He started to leave the stall but stopped, not wanting to go, really. His face looked old for his years, and there were deep white creases in his tanned skin. What must it have been like to be Kummer today, riding Man o' War in such a race? He could only guess. He would never know.

Danny left the stall, closing the door securely behind him. Jim Rowe would be back again with John P. Grier. The Dwyer had by no means discouraged Rowe, for his colt had given a very good account of himself, and, who knew, perhaps racing luck would be in their favor the next time. Danny stretched out in his cot and went to sleep listening to Man o' War's snores.

The next few days were easy ones for Man o' War. He did nothing but loaf in his stall and go for long walks about the stable area. Everywhere Danny took him people followed ... other grooms and trainers, owners and their guests, photographers and reporters.

Man o' War's favorite spot was beneath a towering shade tree. While the colt grazed, Danny listened to the comments of the men gathered around them.

"He's the greatest horse we've ever had," an aged newspaper columnist said. "He's even greater than Hindoo, Salvator, Sysonby, and Colin!"

The trainers and owners were silent after the man's hero-worshiping outburst. Danny knew that while they might agree with the columnist, their quiet homage was more revealing than the other's lofty claims.

The shutters of the photographers' cameras clicked and the old newsman went on, "Maybe you couldn't say he was the *greatest* before the Dwyer. He had things pretty much his own way until that race. But when Grier stayed with him for over a full mile, even heading him in the stretch run, he had to *prove* his gameness. He just had to. And that he did, despite the fact that he was giving Grier eighteen pounds in the weights. Any other champion, if he was only a front runner, would have quit right then. So that's why I'm telling my readers that Man o' War is the greatest of all time."

The columnist turned to the professional horsemen in the group, awaiting their reaction to his heated, enthusiastic comments. But the eyes of the trainers never left Man o' War, and they remained silent.

"*Everybody* who saw the race feels the same way," the old man added. "*Everybody.*"

Danny chewed thoughtfully on a blade of grass. If this man thought he was going to get the trainers to give any statements as to Man o' War's supremacy, he was mistaken. Their comments would best be noted in what horses they sent to the post *against* Man o' War in forthcoming races. If they refused to race their colts against him, that would be their answer.

"Maybe you fellows don't think he's met horses of real class?" the newsman asked. "Well, let me tell you that I've been covering races for over twenty-five years and it's Man o' War's supreme speed that has made the others seem weak. John P. Grier would have been a champion three-year-old any year but this one. Upset, On Watch, Wildair, Paul Jones, and Blazes are all top-class horses and stakes winners once they get away from Man o' War. Make no mistake about that. It's true as anything could be, and you all know it as well as I do!"

Finally one of the trainers turned to the columnist. "All right, John," he said quietly, "you've made your point."

The days went quickly by, one very much like the other, while Man o' War rested and loafed. Mr. Riddle decided not to enter him in any further races in New York and toward the last of June shipped his stable to Saratoga. There the big colt began his workouts again, this time for the Miller Stakes on August 7, 1920.

For the first time Danny felt uneasy. Nothing had changed at the historic track. The course was as beautiful and spacious as ever, and the air as pine-scented. It was hotter than usual, or at least as he remembered it. He perspired a little more as did the horses after their works. And the flies were worse. The nights were cool but they didn't make up for the uncomfortable days. He hoped all this wasn't a bad omen.

Man o' War was working well, so Danny wasn't worried about his ability to run. There *was* a problem in that Clarence Kummer had taken a spill in a race at Belmont and had broken his collarbone. Now it was up to Mr. Riddle to decide on another jockey to ride Man o' War at Saratoga. Danny felt it might be better not to race the colt at all until Kummer recovered. If Man o' War didn't like the man on his back, there was no telling *what* might happen. But Danny couldn't say anything. He'd just have to wait until Mr. Riddle made up his mind. It wasn't easy to wait, either. The heat didn't help at all.

The Saratoga meeting opened August 1, and on that day Danny watched a race that almost equaled the Dwyer in excitement. It was the Saratoga Handicap in which the outstanding older horses met. He saw Sir Barton give four pounds to Exterminator and outrace him, setting a new track record for the mile and a quarter of 2:01 ⅕! As he listened to the clamor of the huge crowd, Danny knew the public would insist that a match race be held between Sir Barton and Man o' War. The big three-year-old had yet to race a mile and a quarter, but coming up soon would be the Travers Stakes at that distance.

Then the fans would have a comparison in time to make. Meanwhile, the clamor to race the two champions would continue, and only Mr. Riddle could make the decision to start Man o' War in such a special event.

Back at the stables Danny heard Mr. Riddle tell reporters, "It's far too early to consider such a match with Sir Barton. We have a hard campaign ahead of us as it is. When it's completed I'll decide whether to send Man o' War against Sir Barton."

It was that day, too, that Mr. Riddle made a decision of more urgent concern to all. Turning to Louis Feustel, he said, "I'm going to let Earl Sande ride Man o' War in the Miller Stakes."

Feustel nodded but said nothing. It was good copy for the newspapers, for Earl Sande was a young, brilliant jockey. Even more newsworthy was the fact that Sande had just ridden Sir Barton to victory in the Saratoga Handicap. After the forthcoming race his opinion of the two champions would be particularly significant to readers. The Miller Stakes was just seven days off.

August 7 came and as Danny watched Man o' War go postward he knew he had been right about one thing, anyway. The trainers who had remained silent concerning Man o' War's invincibility after the Dwyer Stakes had now spoken, not in words but in something stronger still. They kept their horses in the barns, only two of them willing even to try for second money. Donnacona, whom Man o' War had beaten several times before, was one, and a newcomer named King Albert was the other. Man o' War carried 131 pounds, giving twelve pounds to Donnacona and seventeen to King Albert. Danny, as well as the crowd, knew that Man o' War would have the track to himself.

The boy's eyes remained on Man o' War as Earl Sande took

him postward. The big colt was full of run after his long rest but well under control. Sande wasn't having any trouble with him. Either Man o' War liked Sande, Danny decided, or he was becoming a racing machine, responsive to the hands of any competent jockey.

The horses were at the post barely a minute when the barrier sprang up. Danny watched Man o' War come out fast and in stride. Donnacona and King Albert were already trailing and beaten. Sande had a strong pull on Man o' War but the big colt continued to draw away from the others. Rounding the far turn, Sande took a still stouter hold on Man o' War, and he came into the homestretch galloping easily and unextended. He crossed the finish line far ahead of Donnacona, with King Albert still farther to the rear and totally outclassed.

The applause of the crowd swelled as he came back, even though it had been more of an exhibition than a race. Danny's eyes shifted to the time being posted on the board, and he along with the crowd stopped cheering. Even under the strongest kind of restraint Man o' War had raced the mile and three-sixteenths only three-fifths of a second off the track record!

The crowd's silent homage was shattered by a new burst of applause as Man o' War was taken into the winner's circle. There was scarcely a mark on him and he was breathing easily. It was then that the reporters asked Earl Sande for a comparison of Man o' War and Sir Barton, since he had now ridden both horses.

The young jockey grinned. "I'm a lot more tired than he is," he said. "It was like tryin' to pull up a runaway locomotive. I've never had one like that under me before. He's the best horse I've ever ridden."

"Are you including older horses like Sir Barton?" the reporters persisted, anxiously.

Sande reached down to pat Man o' War's bulging neck. He

was under contract to Commander Ross, owner of Sir Barton, and there would be other races astride the older champion. In addition, Sir Barton had set a new record for a mile and a quarter just a few days before.

As he hesitated, the reporters said, "Maybe Sir Barton isn't as spectacular as Man o' War, but do you think he's faster?"

Sande dismounted without answering, and the newsmen could get nothing more out of him.

Danny stood quietly, waiting for the photographers to finish taking their pictures. "Watch out!" he yelled suddenly to one of them. "He kicks to the off side."

The man jumped back just in time to avoid a well-aimed hoof. "Thanks," the photographer said. "Seems like you know this colt pretty well."

Danny nodded.

"He hasn't a mark on him," the photographer said. "Man, he's big. He must put away a lot of feed."

"He does," Danny answered. "Three meals a day. Six quarts of oats, four whole and two crushed. Maybe thirty pounds of hay, too, special from the farm, timothy and a little clover thrown in for dessert. Sometimes I give him salad for good measure. That's lettuce with a little endive, romaine, and leaves of the chicory plant."

The man's eyes were now on Danny rather than Man o' War. "I'll bet you enjoy feeding him."

"I sure do," Danny said quietly.

The ceremony in the winner's circle ended and Feustel called for Man o' War's blanket. Danny ran forward with it, giving it to the trainer, who placed it carefully over the colt's hindquarters. Then he led Man o' War back to the barn through the murky veil of heat.

Racing His Shadow

26

Mr. Riddle decided to start Man o' War only once more at Saratoga. Two weeks later the big colt went postward in the Travers Stakes at a long mile and a quarter. Again the stands were crowded with those who had come to watch him in action. They even had hopes that the Travers would be more than a parade performance by the champion, for Jim Rowe was again furnishing the competition against Man o' War. He alone of all the trainers had not given up hope of toppling the colt from his pedestal. His grudge against the Riddle stable was deep-seated and he would fight it out to the very end.

Danny watched Upset and John P. Grier follow Man o' War in the post parade. Two against one! He knew, as did everyone else, what Jim Rowe's strategy would be. Eddie Ambrose, who was riding John P. Grier, had been instructed to set the blazing pace he had run in the grueling Dwyer back in early June. The small, courageous colt had not raced since then; he was rested, fresh, and full of run. He would go as far and as fast as he could, trying to take everything possible out of Man o' War;

269

then Upset, who had not raced since June either, would come on in the homestretch, hoping to finish the job and beat the champion.

It was fine race strategy, one that might even work, Danny decided fearfully. He had watched Upset and John P. Grier in their morning works and their performance had been brilliant. They might be more than a match for Man o' War if the race was run according to Rowe's strategy.

Danny's gaze shifted from Man o' War to his rider. There was someone new on Man o' War's back and this, too, was a cause for anxiety. Earl Sande had had commitments at another track. Clarence Kummer's shoulder had mended but was not yet strong enough for the jockey to control Man o' War. Mr. Riddle had chosen Andy Schuttinger to ride in the Travers.

Schuttinger was a good judge of pace, which would help today with John P. Grier due to go out in front. Still, it would be a difficult task for a new rider.

He won't have any more trouble, Danny thought, *than Sande did. Man o' War will go for anyone now, anyone who will just sit there and not interfere too much with the way he likes to run.*

The horses were moving up to the barrier. Danny watched closely, wondering if the other riders would again try to wear down Man o' War at the post. His colt was carrying 129 pounds to Upset's 123 and John P. Grier's 115. Danny never quite understood the track handicapper's allotments of weight. After the Dwyer, Grier should be carrying more poundage, he thought. With only 115 pounds on his back the small colt would fly!

The horses pushed their noses up to the elastic tape and were straight and still. The huge crowd was quiet. A mile and a quarter of empty track faced the colts, the same distance over which the older champion, Sir Barton, had set a new track record on opening day. The spectators would have a comparison to make between Man o' War and the older champion. Now they remained silent, the seconds ticking away.

"THEY'RE OFF!"

The horses had been behind the barrier less than a minute. Danny saw his colt spring forward, going to the front immediately, his great body concealing John P. Grier as in their last race. But this time Man o' War moved a stride in front, then two! Danny felt a sudden heaviness come to his chest. He saw immediately that there was no holding Man o' War today! No judgment of pace was necessary to guide him. John P. Grier's early speed and Jim Rowe's race strategy were swept aside in the long sweep of his legs. He ran in front and he kept going! Nothing would slow him down, neither the pull on his mouth, the weight on his back, nor the distance of the race. He was running as he wanted to run!

Along with the thousands of others, Danny watched Man o' War in complete silence. His speed was blistering; they had only to look back at John P. Grier, already under the whip and losing ground every step of the way, to know that. Still farther behind, Upset was under the whipping drive as well.

There was no catching Man o' War. He passed one quarter pole after another in the fastest time ever recorded at Saratoga. When he entered the homestretch, Andy Schuttinger was standing in the stirrup irons in an attempt to slow him down. Gradually the colt's strides shortened, as if he had decided to give in to the urgent pull on his mouth. He passed the stands and swept under the finish wire, easy, flowing, and still going strong.

Only then did the great crowd come to life, giving him an ovation that reached its height when the time of the race was announced. Slowed down throughout the stretch as he had been, Man o' War had equaled Sir Barton's track record!

Danny tried to reach his colt but was thrown back by the milling throng. Everybody, it seemed, wanted to lay a hand on Man o' War. He watched the ceremonies from several tiers back while Mr. Riddle received the trophy and Feustel held the champion.

It was at this very same track, Danny recalled, that Man o' War had stood in the sales ring, a gangling, underweight yearling. No one had any idea then of the potentialities of this colt, regardless of what they might say now. The bidding for him had been slow, wary, and almost reluctant before Man o' War had been sold. And at the time Mr. Riddle had said, *"If he can't run, we'll make a hunter of him."*

That was a far cry from what was going on in the winner's circle now, Danny noted. He was close enough to hear Mr. Riddle tell one of the track officials, "No, I can't run him here again in the Saratoga Cup. It's too close to his race in the Lawrence Realization at Belmont, which I consider more important."

"But Sir Barton is eligible for the Cup race," the official prodded. "With Man o' War racing too, it would be the event which the public and press want very badly."

"To race Man o' War in both the Saratoga Cup and the Lawrence Realization with only three days in between, including a railroad trip to New York, would be too much to ask of him," Mr. Riddle said quietly. "I'm not going to do it."

A reporter sidled up to him. "It wouldn't be that you don't want your colt to meet Sir Barton, would it?" he asked.

Mr. Riddle didn't bother to answer. He turned away, concluding the interview.

Later, when Danny led Man o' War back to the barns, he

decided that Mr. Riddle was right in having resisted the temptation to race his colt in the Saratoga Cup against Sir Barton. Ahead of them was the longest race yet for Man o' War, for the Lawrence Realization was at a mile and *five* furlongs. A week after that event would come the Jockey Club Stakes, another long race. The fall classics were at hand! It made sense for them to beat the rush of horses that would soon be leaving Saratoga for Belmont Park.

Within a week they were back at the Long Island track, and in some ways Danny found it worse than ever so far as he was concerned. There was no doubt that Man o' War belonged to the public now; every move he made was watched, and Danny could no longer call even the nights his own. Two and sometimes three grooms were stationed at the colt's stable door. Mr. Riddle was worried that someone might harm him. What couldn't be done on a racetrack might be accomplished in the stable area.

Danny became more and more resigned to seeing people follow Man o' War everywhere, especially on chilly mornings when he went to the track. There they would hang on the rails, watching the big colt work, and never quite believing the stopwatches they held in their hands. Man o' War took such giant strides that when he ran alone one was never aware of his great speed.

During his final workout a few days before the Lawrence Realization, he broke the world record for a mile and a half. Back at the stable Feustel said, "That time's going to scare the others off. He might be racing all by himself on Saturday."

The Realization was what its name implied, the end result of all the high hopes that horsemen had for promising colts in their stables. But as Feustel had forecast, Man o' War's blistering workout blasted the hopes of all other trainers and owners. None wanted to see the big colt make a sorry spectacle of their entries. It looked as though Man o' War would go to the post alone until Mrs. Jeffords decided to start Hoodwink and give the Realization the semblance of a race.

In the saddling paddock Danny heard a track official tell Mr. Riddle, "It's probably the biggest crowd we've ever had at Belmont. Since it won't be a contest against Hoodwink, won't you let him extend himself? It's what almost everybody has come to see."

"Perhaps we'll let him run home the last quarter at top speed," Mr. Riddle replied warily. He glanced at Clarence Kummer, who would be back in the saddle again. There was nothing to worry about today.

The Belmont track official was shrugging his shoulders, still dissatisfied with Mr. Riddle's answer. The public wanted a lot more than a final drive from Man o' War.

Mrs. Riddle turned to her husband. "Why not let him run *all* the way, Sam?" she asked. "It's what the crowd wants, and I must say that I'd like to know myself if he can set a new record." She turned to Louis Feustel. "Isn't he in shape for it?" she asked.

Feustel smiled at the woman's persistence. It sounded as though she, too, was tired of seeing Man o' War's head bowed under a tight hold. "He's never been more ready than he is now," the trainer answered. He shifted his glance to Mr. Riddle. "And for a change," he added, "he's carrying 126 pounds, the weight for his age."

Mr. Riddle met Feustel's eyes, then turned uneasily to his wife and back again to the trainer. Finally he nodded. "Let him run then," he said quietly.

The bugle sounded and Feustel boosted Clarence Kummer

into the saddle. "You heard the boss," Feustel said. "We're letting him run. But that doesn't mean," he cautioned, "that you let him have his head all the way. No horse can go top speed the full distance, as you know even better than I. You've got a clock for a head. Use it today. Race him like you can."

The track was fast, the day perfect for racing. Danny watched Man o' War approach the barrier. The Lawrence Realization would be one to remember. It would be no contest but an exhibition of Man o' War's speed and a test of Kummer's judgment of pace over a long, grueling distance. Danny glanced at Hoodwink, now going up to the tape with Man o' War. If he had been Mrs. Jeffords, he decided, he never would have let Hoodwink out of the barn. But she hadn't known what Mr. Riddle's final instructions would be.

Clarence Kummer patted Man o' War's bulging neck. "Easy, big fellow, easy," he said quietly. With only Hoodwink beside him, they'd be sent away from the barrier without any waiting. It felt good to be up on Man o' War again; the last time had been the Dwyer, over two months ago, a race he'd never forget. His broken bones had knit well and he felt confident that he could control the big colt. "Steady, fellow," he said. "Steady."

The barrier swept up in front of them. Hoodwink broke first, a stride in the lead. Another stride and Man o' War had caught him. Kummer gave the colt his head. He was full of run, and a blistering first quarter would burn some of the fire out of him, making him more responsive to the reins.

At the quarter pole Kummer glanced back at Hoodwink, some twenty lengths behind. He began taking hold of Man o' War. It was not that he was sorry for the Jeffords colt; it made no difference to him whether Hoodwink was beaten by twenty

lengths or a hundred. But Man o' War still had a mile and furlong to go and it wasn't possible for any horse to maintain the
speed he had set the first quarter.

Kummer steadied the colt and felt the stiff resistance to his
tightening hands. He wasn't going to pull Man o' War's head
into his chest, but he wasn't going to let him run himself into
the ground either. Feustel had said to pace him carefully so as
to get the most out of Man o' War over the whole distance,
and that was what he intended to do.

There was some response to his bidding and the colt's
strides slowed. They swept through another half-mile, Man o'
War tugging for his head. He was running easily and main-
taining a speed that would certainly create a new record *if he
kept going.* And there was no indication that he wouldn't!

For another half-mile Kummer kept Man o' War under
wraps, fighting the colt's anxiety to be turned loose and his
own temptation to give in. But the clock in Kummer's head
kept time with Man o' War's strides and he restrained himself
as well as his mount. A new record could be set only by accu-
rately spacing the champion's speed to the unreeling quarters.
They had gone a mile and a quarter, but there were still three
long furlongs to go!

Coming off the far turn and into the homestretch, Kummer
heard the roar of the crowd. For a second he thought Hoodwink might be coming on! Turning in his saddle, he saw the
Jeffords colt plodding along some fifty lengths to the rear. Man
o' War was racing only his shadow and the cheers were for
him.

Kummer gave him his head and Man o' War began flying,
as if he were just beginning to race! They whipped by another
pole, and Kummer had no doubt Man o' War had covered the
mile and a half faster than any colt in history! Still a furlong to

go, an eighth of a mile, and the colt's swiftness increased with gigantic strides. Kummer sat still in his saddle. There was no need to urge Man o' War along. At the end of the long race he was running with the breathtaking speed of a sprinter. He flashed under the wire more than one hundred lengths in front of Hoodwink!

Later, Man o' War came back with his tail in the air and barely taking a long breath. His time was announced as 2:40 ⅕, faster than any horse in the world had ever gone before and, perhaps, never to be equaled! The huge mass of people moved upon him, leaving no room for Danny Ryan to reach his horse.

The Campaign Ends

27

It was several hours before the stable area grew quiet and Danny was able to give Man o' War his evening feed. The big colt had cooled out well from the race and was hungry. He whiffed the oats in his box and occasionally lifted his head to snort at Danny or kicked out a hoof without meaning any harm. He just felt good. He was enjoying himself, even now after the exhausting distance of the Lawrence Realization.

Danny remained in the stall, while outside the night mutterings of other grooms filled the air. He knew Man o' War didn't mind his staying there. The big colt liked attention; that was why he did so well despite the clamor from thousands upon thousands of fans every race day. He would be most unhappy, Danny decided, without it. He belonged to the public and the public belonged to him, just as Feustel had said.

Finishing his feed, Man o' War moved over to Danny, the straw rustling beneath his hoofs. He took hold of the boy's sweater.

"Let go," Danny said. "It's the only one I've got." There

was no anger in his words, and his hand moved up and down the colt's nose.

In the adjacent stall Major Treat whinnied, and Man o' War went quickly to the door. He peered into the night, his ears pricked, his eyes bright and inquisitive. His chest, like his neck, was most impressive. Man o' War had become all stallion. He was perfection itself.

"You don't want to miss anything," Danny said, looking into the darkness with him, "nothing at all. You'd think that after today's race you'd want to quit for a while and just rest. But not you. You want to be on the go all the time. You won't have long to wait, that's for sure. A few more days and you'll be racing again."

On September 11 Man o' War went to the post in the Jockey Club Stakes. The distance was a mile and a half, and only one colt was sent out to oppose him, Damask from the Harry Payne Whitney stable. This was done only out of a sense of sportsmanship by Mr. Whitney. No other owner or trainer would attempt to beat Man o' War after his record-shattering performance in the Lawrence Realization!

The great stands were packed again, this time with spectators who had come to watch a race they knew would be virtually a "walkover" for Man o' War. Earlier in the week they had hoped that Sir Barton would run in the Jockey Club Stakes, since it was a race for three-year-olds *and upward,* and the older champion was on the grounds. The track management had added its voice to the possibility of such a contest by increasing the value of the purse if the two champions went postward. But Commander Ross, owner of Sir Barton, declined. The Jockey Club Stakes was a race in which horses would have to carry weight for their age, and he wouldn't allow

Sir Barton to go postward carrying four pounds more than
Man o' War.

So the fans watched Man o' War stride toward the barrier,
their sole interest being the speed in which it would be run.
Danny's gaze, too, followed Man o' War to the post. He knew
what they expected, and anticipated their disappointment
when the champion was held under the tight hold that Feustel
had ordered.

"Rate him evenly, Clarence," the trainer had said to Kummer. *"Win by a comfortable margin, but no more. I don't
want him extended today."*

Man o' War had been given a good rest since his last race,
and he acted it. He was more fractious than usual on the way
to the barrier, and Danny knew Kummer would have his hands
full following Feustel's instructions. He supposed the trainer
was becoming more careful than ever that Man o' War should
finish the season unhurt and sound. One more race after this
one, and his three-year-old campaign would be over. Danny
had heard Mr. Riddle say that he was thinking seriously of retiring Man o' War at the end of the season. If that happened,
Man o' War would never see the tracks as a four-year-old.

The big colt had become too much of a responsibility for almost any owner, Danny decided. He had to be watched every
moment, and even the difficulties in properly taking care of
him were mounting with every day that passed. There was also
the fact that he dominated racing so much that he was making
a mockery of any contest in which he entered. Even the owner
of Sir Barton had refused to race against him! A truly great
horse like Man o' War was a problem to the management of
every track at which he raced. Celebrated races became nothing more than "walkovers" for him, costing the management

money and leaving the customers nothing to watch but a one-horse exhibition, usually at a slow gallop. Like today, Danny mused.

Or would Man o' War put on another exhibition of extreme speed, contrary to Feustel's orders? Watching the big colt's eagerness to run, Danny knew it just might happen.

Man o' War reared behind the barrier, taking an assistant starter off his feet. The crowed roared its approval of the champion's restiveness. There seemed to be no holding him today.

Danny watched and thought, *The only way they'll ever stop him will be by weight. If he raced next season the track handicappers would put the heaviest weight on him ever carried by a Thoroughbred. Mr. Riddle wouldn't stand for it. It would break Man o' War down. He's sure to be retired. And where he goes, I go.*

The barrier swept up! Man o' War went to the front in a mighty leap and began drawing away. Kummer had a good hold on him but the gap between him and Damask continued to widen. All eyes remained on the red colt as he fought for more rein while lengthening his lead. Kummer was unrelenting and Man o' War's head was pulled in to his chest.

Sweeping into the far turn at the end of a mile, he was a dozen lengths in front of Damask and still fighting for his freedom. He pounded into the homestretch and, while the crowd roared, broke from Kummer's strangle hold. For a short distance he was all-out, silencing the stands with his dizzying speed. Then Kummer had him under control again, shortening Man o' War's strides so that he finished the race in an easy gallop. So easy, in fact, that no one in the huge crowd believed the time on the board. For his 2:28 ⅕ was a new American record! Man o' War had again beaten the clock, just as he had beaten Louis Feustel, who would have had him win slowly, comfortably.

Later, the trainer said, "He ran faster than you should have let him go, Clarence."

The jockey rubbed his shoulders. "Try holding him back yourself sometime," he said irritably.

The new record went into the books as the fifth consecutive one established by Man o' War. But everyone, including the press, again wondered what it might have been had he been allowed to run all-out. How fast could this horse really run? Were they ever to know? He broke records, of course, but always under a hold that never allowed a true indication of his top speed. Perhaps next time. The Potomac Handicap was just a week off.

The Riddle stable moved to Havre de Grace, Maryland, and as the day of Man o' War's final engagement approached, Danny was concerned about one thing only. The track handicapper had given Man o' War 138 pounds to carry, more weight than any three-year-old had ever been asked to assume. What Danny feared most of all, his colt's breaking down, might become a reality before he even had a chance to retire!

Bitterly, he said to Louis Feustel, "I thought Marylanders regarded him as their own."

"I guess they do. Why?"

"A fine way they have of showing it," Danny muttered, "assigning him *that* weight."

Feustel smiled grimly at the boy's concern. "It's not *Marylanders*, Danny," he said. "It's the track handicapper. He thinks it's the only way to make an even race of it."

The trainer picked up Man o' War's right forefoot, examining it closely. *But why,* Feustel wondered, *had the handicapper given Paul Jones, winner of the Kentucky Derby, only 114 pounds? And how come Jim Rowe's crack colt Wildair got in the race with just 108 pounds? And a brilliant sprinter like Blazes with a light 104 ½?*

Feustel put down the colt's foot. "Sometimes it doesn't make sense," he admitted to Danny. "It's almost too severe a test for any horse, even Man o' War."

"Why doesn't Mr. Riddle scratch him then?" Danny asked. "He could keep him in the barn."

"He'd disappoint too many people. Besides, it won't happen again. This is the last time Man o' War will go against a field."

"*Against a field,*" Danny repeated. "You mean he might race Sir Barton alone? A *match* race?"

Feustel nodded. "Mr. Riddle has decided in favor of it," he said quietly.

Saturday afternoon Danny led Man o' War into the saddling paddock. His colt was no ordinary colt, so he wouldn't be carrying ordinary weight. If it was good handicapping, as some people thought, the horses should come down to the wire together. But he didn't think it would happen that way. It wouldn't be the first time the scales were against Man o' War. Besides, his colt was in top shape. There wasn't a mark on him; he was raring to go!

Danny's optimism faded as he held Man o' War still and Feustel saddled him. The trainer and Mr. Riddle were concerned over the condition of the track, something that Danny had not taken into account. It had rained the night before and the heavy loam footing was loose and "cuppy," making it dangerous for any horse that took a stride as long as that of Man o' War.

"Maybe we should have scratched him," Danny heard Feustel say to Mr. Riddle. "With the tremendous burden he's carrying . . ."

"Too late now, Louis. He'll manage."

Clarence Kummer was boosted into the saddle. The track might be "off," the jockey thought, but the day was perfect, just right for riding. And nothing seemed to be bothering Man o' War.

Kummer patted his mount's neck. "Easy, Red. Easy," he said quietly as they moved to the track. The stands as Havre de Grace were more packed than Kummer had ever seen them; the infield too, had been opened to the crowd, and people hung over the inner rail from one end of the stretch to the other. Across the track they were lined up on the backstretch as well.

Feustel took one look at the immense crowd and said, "Danny, you lead him to the post."

The barrier was stretched across the track directly in front of the packed stands. Danny walked toward it, his feet sinking deep into the loose soil. The eyes of everyone were on Man o' War, and the colt seemed to know it. He started putting on a show, sliding his hindquarters in a circle and cleaving the air with his hoofs.

Danny tried every trick he knew to keep him in position, fourth behind the others. He slipped and almost went down as Man o' War whirled. Regaining his feet, he felt the mud oozing around his ankles. The hoofprints of the horses before him were deep, but Man o' War's were deeper. He realized more than ever the dangers of such a track. With every tremendous stride in the race to come, Man o' War would have to pull his hoofs out of several inches of heavy, sucking dirt. The weight and drive behind his strides would give him little chance of re-

THE CAMPAIGN ENDS   285

covery and put great strain on his tendons.

They reached the barrier, and Danny's job was done. Carefully he turned Man o' War over to one of the assistant starters
and moved to the inner rail.

He watched Man o' War rear and wheel, trying to break
from Kummer's hold and slip past the elastic webbing. If he'd
only been up on him instead of Kummer, he would have said,
*"Easy, Red. It's no time to be putting on a show for the home-
folks. Stand still and come out slow until you find your stride.
I'll let you run."*

He would have felt the heavy strips of lead beneath his
knees, but he wouldn't have worried about them. They were
forward on the withers, where they should be. The pad was
buckled down tight. It would not slip forward or backward or
from side to side. It would stay put while Man o' War was in
full stride. Even 138 pounds would not stop him today.

Kummer had Man o' War in position, but the colt's body
was quivering with eagerness. The crowd hushed, expecting
the break from the barrier any second and wondering if weight
and loose footing would finally stop this colt.

Danny's eyes never left Kummer. He would have said at this
moment, *"Don't move, Red. Don't move. You're on the outside with nothing to bother you. Wildair is quiet. He's the one
to watch. And Paul Jones is ready. Blazes is fussing over on the
rail but he'll settle down. He'll get off fast with only 104
pounds on his back. But he won't last. You've got this race,
Red. You've got nothing to worry about."*

Kummer moved forward in his saddle but said nothing to
Man o' War. He had his own weight where the lead was, over
the colt's withers. He sat very still and crouched low, waiting
with Man o' War.

The barrier swept up and Kummer brought his mount out

even with the others. For one stride, two strides, they raced together, then Man o' War bounded forward and only the
sprinter Blazes stayed alongside. The run to the first turn was
short and Kummer didn't attempt to get clear of Blazes and
cut over to the inner rail. Instead, he kept Man o' War under a
snug hold, trying to find out how he was taking to the track.

They swept around the first turn and there was a sudden
lurch to the hurtling body beneath him as Man o' War's speed
increased and he had to fight to get his flying hoofs out of the
deep, hollow cups. Kummer felt him recover, then surge to the
front once more. He gave him his head momentarily and daylight opened between them and Blazes. Going down the backstretch, he saw that the sprinter was no longer a threat and
again took up on his mount, fearing the track more than those
following in his wake. Wildair had taken up where Blazes had
left off, but the others were already out of the race.

Sweeping past the three-quarter of a mile pole and rounding
the far turn, Kummer continued the strong pull on Man o'
War's mouth. Wildair was still running steadily behind them,
but Kummer wasn't worried about the Jim Rowe colt. His only
problem was the condition of the track. Yet, he thought uneasily, it was the first time Man o' War wasn't fighting for his
head every stride of the way. The big colt seemed to be content
to be rated, running only as fast as his rider wanted him to go.
Kummer's expression became grim. Had Man o' War hurt
himself in that early surge around the first turn? A sudden
strain could do it in such footing. Or was Man o' War smart
enough to know it was better to run eased up on this kind of
track? Kummer knew he'd soon have to find out which it was.

Wildair was hanging on as they pounded into the homestretch. It was time to move if they were to stay ahead. Kummer gave Man o' War more rein and awaited the big colt's re-

sponse. Wildair was almost alongside and under a whipping drive.

Man o' War met the challenge with a rush of his own. He took the free rein Kummer gave him and began drawing away from Wildair. When the jockey knew they had the race to themselves again, he eased off Man o' War. He kept him going fast enough to win without putting any strain on his tendons. They swept under the wire to the great ovation of the crowd, a roar that lasted long after Man o' War had been turned and brought back to the winner's circle. For once again the board showed that he had set a new track record; this time under the greatest of handicaps!

There remained only one question: would he now be retired or would he race Sir Barton?

Mr. Riddle answered it in the winner's circle.

"Commander Ross and I have agreed to the terms of a match race," he said happily. "Since it's what the public wants, we feel we should comply."

Danny wasn't listening to Mr. Riddle's plans for the future. Instead, he was watching Louis Feustel, who was bent over the colt's right foreleg. Had Man o' War hurt himself? Only when they got back to the barns would they really know.

Match of the Ages

28

Feustel led Man o' War back to the stable area, and that in itself was indicative to Danny that something had gone wrong in the running of the race. He followed them, trying to catch a glimpse of his colt in the middle of the large throng. If Man o' War had hurt himself, would it prove to be serious enough to keep him out of the match race with Sir Barton? Neither Mr. Riddle nor Mr. Feustel would take any chances with the colt, regardless of how much the public looked forward to the match.

Danny walked along shed row with its orderly tack trunks and hanging pails, brooms, and rakes. He paid no attention to the stabled horses that stretched their heads over stall doors, nickering to him and expecting him to pat them. That he ignored them so completely was most unusual.

George Conway, the stable manager, had dropped back, too, before the onslaught of the crowd accompanying Man o' War to the barns.

"Did he hurt himself?" Danny asked anxiously, walking beside the man.

"Feustel says so. He struck himself in front."

"Is it serious?"

The stable manager shrugged his shoulders. "Any trouble, no matter how slight, is something to worry about now."

"Any injury to the tendon?"

"Feustel doesn't know yet. If it fills, the colt's done for sure."

Danny nodded gravely. No horse could race successfully after bowing a tendon. If that had happened, Man o' War's career had ended with this race. There would be no other place for him to go but to stud.

In front of the stall Danny pushed his way through the crowd until he had reached his colt. Frank had him by the bridle and Feustel was once again bent over, examining the right foreleg. Danny's eyes followed the trainer's hands as they felt the tendon. No one spoke. Fearfully he awaited the trainer's decision. His gaze moved to the sleek and shining colt. There was no pain showing in Man o' War's eyes despite the fact that he had placed full weight on his leg coming off the track. The injury might only be a slight one.

Feustel took his hands away from the leg, and Man o' War swung around on the lead shank, his strides free and powerful. Everyone nodded with relief. There seemed to be nothing wrong.

Feustel said, "The tendon started to bow, all right, but it's not as serious as it might be. We'll give him a rest and see what happens. If it fills, he's done."

"Does that mean there'll be no match race?" a reporter asked anxiously.

"I think he'll be all right," Feustel answered. "But as I said, we'll have to wait and see."

"A few days? Or longer than that?" the reporter persisted.

"We should know in a few days' time," Feustel said quietly.

For another week they remained at Havre de Grace while Man o' War was rested and Feustel worked on the injured leg. He rubbed the tendon gently and very patiently, well knowing the seriousness of such an injury if the tendon didn't heal. But it responded to treatment and Man o' War became more and more restless in his confinement. Feustel decided that it was time to ship the big colt back to Belmont Park and resume workouts. He advised the press that Man o' War would race Sir Barton as planned.

The first day back at the metropolitan track Feustel let Kummer gallop Man o' War and the leg held up without strain. In fact, the colt never looked better. The week's rest had done him a lot of good. He could be asked for more speed any time now, any time at all.

The next day Feustel had Kummer move him a mile in 1:45; then two days later he had him go a mile and a quarter in 2:09. The track was sloppy but Man o' War was fighting for his head all the way. Feustel knew then that Man o' War was in perfect condition and ready for any kind of test against Sir Barton.

In many ways, Feustel decided, he would be glad when it was all over. He was weary of reporters following his every move and of having to answer their persistent questions. They were calling the coming race "The Match of the Ages." Well, the trainer mused, it was what the public had wanted for a long while, beginning back at Saratoga, when both Man o' War and Sir Barton had set their records. There had been no avoiding the insistent clamor for such a match, and the only question had been where and when. Churchill Downs had offered a purse of $25,000 if the two horses met there. Then Laurel had bid for the attraction, increasing the purse to $30,000. Finally, Kenilworth Park in Canada had got it, with a fantastic bid of $75,000 to the winner! It was the largest single purse ever offered and if Man o' War won it, he would go to the head of the list of America's leading money winners.

Feustel would have preferred seeing the race take place in New York rather than away up in Canada. He couldn't understand why none of the metropolitan tracks had bid for the contest that would decide the kingship of the American turf. The demand for the race had been loudest here, and the crowd would have been larger than anywhere else. But Commander Ross, owner of Sir Barton, was a Canadian and that, together with the large purse offered, had won Kenilworth the match race. It was just across the river from Detroit, so Americans would have easy access to it. It wouldn't be too bad, but it wasn't perfect.

Two days before shipping Man o' War to Canada, Feustel sent him the race distance of a mile and a quarter with Kummer up and carrying full weight of 120 pounds. He watched the colt run easily, seemingly without extending himself, and clocked him in 2:02 flat. He wouldn't have believed his watch if others hadn't caught him in about the same time, with one "clocker" still faster. He turned away from the reporters who pursued him and Man o' War, seeking the quiet that could be found only behind the closed doors of the stall.

Soon it would be over, he thought with relief. No longer would his every movement be watched, his casual remark repeated and published for the world to read. No longer would he be the subject of intense criticism as well as envy. It was not easy to be the trainer of a wonder horse. It took more endurance, more stamina, than most people realized. The fans didn't seem to know that even a great horse could be beaten by a misstep on the track, a stable accident, a bad slip, even a slight cold or an off day. A severe public would tolerate no excuse, even the thousand or more trivial ones that could defeat Man o' War.

Yes, I will be glad when he's retired, Feustel thought wearily. *Maybe there'll never be another like him, as they say, but if there is I don't want him in my stable.*

He didn't like match races, and he would have preferred unwinding Man o' War now, in preparation for his retirement, to the contest at Kenilworth Park. A match race was a *spectacle* more than a part of the great sport he loved. It was a big show, and big business, too, with a purse of $75,000 going to the winner. He didn't even think it was in the best interest of racing. But he was only a trainer and, it seemed, a lot of other people thought differently. It was his job to get the big colt ready to race and to keep him sound. He had accomplished both. Man o' War was ready to do something greater than ever before, if necessary. And he was sound. His injured leg had cleaned right up and was cool and hard. The track at Kenilworth was as loose as the one at Havre de Grace, but it wouldn't bother him. Man o' War was a real champion.

The Riddle stable arrived at Kenilworth Park on October 7, and Danny's most important job was to see that no one who was not directly connected with the stable touched Man o' War. Not that he didn't have plenty of help. With the race only a few days off, Mr. Riddle had ordered all his employees to take every precaution to assure the champion's safety. So night and day Man o' War was guarded, and the hundreds of strangers who visited the stable area were kept well away from him.

At first Danny thought Mr. Riddle was being overconcerned. Then his apprehensions, too, became greater as the pressure mounted and crowds began pouring into Kenilworth from all over the United States, Canada, and even Europe. Newsmen and photographers were everywhere, never giving the Riddle stable any peace, and their stories and pictures appeared in all the newspapers and magazines.

Never in his wildest dreams had Danny anticipated such tremendous interest on the part of the public in the match race. People who had never seen a horse race or never before been interested in one were being made aware of the contest. For descending upon Kenilworth were the most eminent dignitaries of the world, and this in itself focused attention on the race to come. Everybody who was anybody was there.

Danny watched the temporary stands being constructed to accommodate the thousands upon thousands who demanded seats. The infield would be thrown open too on race day, and special trains were already running between American and Canadian cities.

He would be very glad when this last race was over, he decided. It was time to go home, to call an end to the growing legend that had begun at Nursery Stud. He wanted the peace and quiet of a farm, *any* farm, just so long as Man o' War was there, too. He had expected his colt to be a champion because he had loved him, but never one of such overwhelming magnitude as this! The only escape for them was *home*.

The weather was perfect on race day, the sun hot but the air cool and bracing. In the stall, Man o' War jerked his head away from Danny's hands. He was ready to go. He seemed to know the time had come.

Samuel Riddle, glad too that this was the very last race for Man o' War, watched his colt come into the saddling paddock. He had taken just about all he could from the public, from newsmen, even from other horsemen. Ordinarily he was not a nervous man, but the ordeal of racing such a horse as Man o' War had been almost too much of a strain for him. One went into the sport of racing horses for the enjoyment of it. This had developed into something far more than that. Oh, it was true that Man o' War had provided thrills for him never to be equaled again. But at the same time, never had life been more nerve-racking.

A motion picture company was filming the race, and its director asked him to go forward to greet Man o' War. He refused adamantly. He had too much at stake today to be agreeable. A great mob was surging into the paddock, and he wondered why the track police weren't more efficient about keeping the people back. Didn't they realize Man o' War could be injured seriously?

"Is it true you're going to exhibit him at the Chicago World's Fair?" a reporter asked, pulling on his coat sleeve.

"No!" he almost shouted in answer. His eyes remained on Man o' War, and a great sense of pride suddenly swept over him. Despite all his problems, no feeling in the world could compare with this moment.

"He'll run Sir Barton into the ground!" a friend said.

"I hope so," another interjected. "Sir Barton hasn't been working well, but he never was a workhorse. He waits for the races. He's ready to go in this one, I hear. We've got to watch out."

Mr. Riddle sighed wearily. He wasn't listening to his friends anymore in their predictions, whether in favor of or against Man o' War. He felt like an old hand at this game in which he was comparatively new. With a horse like Man o' War you learned fast.

He glanced at Sir Barton a short distance away, well aware

of the tremendous pride the Canadians had in their champion. He seemed to be fit and eager to go. They'd find out more about him in a few minutes' time.

Clarence Kummer came into the paddock, carrying his racing saddle. Feustel took it from him, examining the girth and stirrup leather carefully before placing the light saddle on Man o' War's back. Kummer smiled patiently at the trainer's close inspection of his tack. It was in perfect shape, but no one was taking any chances today.

In a way he was glad it was to be his last ride on the big colt. So far he'd been able to pilot him without making a mistake. He didn't want to make any wrong moves. If he ever lost with the eyes of the world on Man o' War, public criticism would be so severe he'd never be able to rise above it.

Feustel boosted him into the saddle. Picking up the reins, Kummer spoke softly to his mount. He noted the black and yellow ribbons Danny Ryan had braided in the mane. Pretty, very pretty. The kid cared about his job and his horse.

They started around the walking ring and Kummer's gaze shifted to Feustel. "Any instructions?" he asked.

"Don't let this race get you excited," the trainer said. "Ride it as you would any race. Go to the front as soon as you can and that will be it."

The crowd pressed close, wanting to touch Man o' War. Kummer tried to move away, but it took the track police to clear a path for them. He glanced at Sir Barton just beyond.

The short, compact horse might give them trouble, he decided. Sir Barton looked eager to run, his strides even now showing restlessness. He wore blinkers and was up against the bit; he didn't seem to be bothered by the crowd.

Sir Barton looked more like a sprinter than the stayer he was. He had won many long races including the Kentucky

Derby, the Preakness, and the Belmont at a mile and one half. He had the speed with the inner courage to go on. Kummer knew that his rider, Frank Keogh, would try to go to the front with him, setting the pace, so the first quarter of a mile should be a horse race anyway.

Kummer's eyes remained on the rival jockey. Only a few hours ago, around noon, Earl Sande had been taken down from Sir Barton and this fellow had gone up in his place. That, too, was part of riding Thoroughbreds ... make one wrong move and you found yourself on the ground without a mount.

The "backside" talk was that Sande had made his wrong move months ago, when he had ridden Man o' War for the first and only time in the Miller Stakes. After winning it, he had remarked to the press that Man o' War was the best horse he had ever ridden. Commander Ross hadn't liked having his contract jockey make such statements in favor of another horse. So Sande, after two years of riding Sir Barton, found himself on the ground today. If the story was true, Kummer decided, Commander Ross had chosen a spectacular time for switching riders.

Kummer dropped Man o' War behind Sir Barton as they left the walking ring for the track. He didn't blame Sande at all for turning in his contract with Ross and announcing publicly that he'd never ride another horse for that stable. It was humiliating to be taken down in such a way, and Kummer decided he would have done the same thing.

But right now he had his own problems. The trainers of both horses had said their entries were ready to race, and there would be no excuses in case of defeat. Kummer knew *he* wouldn't be allowed any excuses, either. He had to make this a good ride, his *last* ride on Man o' War.

There was a lot of applause when they rode onto the track,

and Kummer thought most of it was for Man o' War. He watched Sir Barton a few strides ahead of them; the older champion was still restive and straining to be turned loose. On the other hand, Man o' War was more quiet than ever before.

Kummer wondered if he should shake up his mount a bit. It wasn't like Man o' War to walk so placidly past the milling thousands who were applauding him. He decided to do nothing to stir up the colt and let matters stand as they were. Man o' War was smart enough to know what it was all about. Maybe he missed the band music, for there was none at Kenilworth today. It could be something as simple as that. At any rate, he wasn't going to worry about it.

From his saddle he seemed to tower above the jockey just ahead of him, for Man o' War was at least a hand taller than Sir Barton. The older champion was chunky and robust compared to his mount's great bulk. But he mustn't underestimate Sir Barton, Kummer decided; it would be fatal if he did. The older horse had the habit of smothering his competition in the early stages of a race and "winning all the way," just as Man o' War did.

The barrier was waiting for them at the top of the homestretch. Since the Kenilworth track was a mile oval, they would come down the full stretch, passing the stands and going around the course to finish in front of the crowd again. It would make an easy race for the spectators to watch.

Kummer took Man o' War behind the barrier, aware that even now his mount was much quieter than usual. He hoped he wouldn't have to stir him up to get away, and yet he didn't want to be left behind either. Sir Barton was on the rail, and Kummer had no doubt that Keogh would try to make every pole a winning one. It would be a duel of speed, stamina, and heart from the very beginning. Neither horse could run all-out over the full distance of the race, but *one* would carry his speed longer than the other. Kummer was convinced it would be his colt who would accomplish this feat.

Man o' War went forward, his eyes becoming suddenly alert when he saw the webbing in front of him. Kummer kept him in position, all the while glancing at Keogh up on the smaller horse. He mustn't underestimate this rider. Keogh would be out to win every way he could. Being up on Sir Barton was his big chance, and he wouldn't miss a trick.

Man o' War tried to bolt through the barrier, but an assistant starter held on to his bridle. For a moment Man o' War was still, and so was Sir Barton. Kummer knew the break would come any second.

The barrier went up, and there was nothing but empty track before them! The roar from the stands momentarily drowned out the pounding of their hoofs. The Match of the Ages had begun!

Kummer felt the great lurch as Man o' War bounded out from behind the barrier. He glanced at Sir Barton, who was head for head with Man o' War. The strides of both horses came faster. Sir Barton had a choppy way of going, but he didn't drop back as Kummer had hoped. Keogh was hurling his mount forward.

Kummer sat down to ride. The furious battle the crowd had expected was under way!

Man o' War dug into the loose dirt of the track, his strides devouring it in great leaps. Suddenly he surged to the front and began drawing away from Sir Barton! Kummer hadn't expected the dizzy burst of speed so soon. He took advantage of it by moving his colt over to the rail before passing the furlong pole. They swept by the stands for the first time with open daylight between Man o' War and Sir Barton. Was this race over, too, before it had hardly begun? Kummer wondered, along with everybody else.

He steadied Man o' War as they went into the first turn and, glancing back, saw that Sir Barton was already under Keogh's whip! They were trying to come on and collar Man o' War in the backstretch. But entering the long straightaway, Kummer glanced back again to find Sir Barton falling still farther behind! It looked as though the older champion could not stand the pressure of Man o' War's blinding pace.

Kummer took up the reins another notch, trying to ease up his mount still more. Man o' War was making a mockery of the race that had been billed the greatest of all time! It was just another horse race to this colt, and he was winning as he always did!

Kummer's only duel now was with Man o' War. His colt was full of run and fighting for his head. The jockey didn't want him to get hurt by running himself out over the loose footing or by fighting for more rein. So Kummer gave way a little. Man o' War took the extra rein greedily, increasing his speed as they swept into the final turn. Kummer took him wide, careful to see to it that he did not slip or pull his flying feet out of the deep track too quickly.

Entering the homestretch, he glanced back once more. Sir Barton was vanquished but still trying hard. Kummer wrapped the reins around his hands for a better hold and slowed down Man o' War. They were seven lengths ahead of Sir Barton, far enough to win this final race without disgracing the game horse any further. The crowd cheered them all the way through the stretch and under the wire. The match race and Man o' War's turf campaign were over.

Kummer slowed Man o' War and, rising in his stirrups, took him into the first turn again. Suddenly the right stirrup gave

way and dropped to the track! Luckily Kummer had Man o'
War almost to a walk and had no trouble stopping him. Lifting
his leg, he saw where the stirrup leather had parted.

If Man o' War had given him any trouble at the barrier,
Kummer thought . . . *if it had been a hard race, calling for
quick movements in the saddle . . . if the stirrup had given way
any other time but now, he would have been on the ground
and, perhaps, under flying hoofs.*

Turning Man o' War around, Kummer rode slowly back toward the winner's circle, where a jammed throng was awaiting
them. He saw Sir Barton, exhausted and staggering, leave the
track. Someone shouted that Man o' War had run the race in
2:03 flat, lowering the track record by six full seconds! He
couldn't have been less interested. How fast might Man o'
War have run had he let him? The police kept the huge crowd
back. Everybody in the Riddle stable was going to be very
happy tonight, Kummer thought. Everybody . . . including
himself. He was very happy just to be getting back alive.

Ruling Monarch

29

Man o' War returned to Belmont Park in a special railway car, and everywhere the train stopped, crowds gathered to look at him. They peered into the car, bug-eyed at the sight of the famous horse. He appeared every bit of what he was, the ruling monarch of the turf.

Danny was very proud to be part of the champion's entourage. There was no harm in letting the crowds look at Man o' War during his triumphal journey home, but Danny and the other grooms kept them from entering the car.

Although Man o' War was a super horse, there was no haughtiness in his manner. He accepted the adulation of all who gazed upon him in a friendly, good-natured way. It was as if he knew he had attained his speed and greatness through the careful, thoughtful planning of others. He could have acted no other way, any more than he could have ignored the power in his smoothly functioning body. Man o' War had taken his rightful place in the world of racing, and about his gleaming bronze body was an aura of greatness perhaps never to be seen again.

302   MAN O' WAR

The train rumbled on, carrying him ever closer to Belmont
Park, where he would carefully be taken out of training. Soon
it would be over for keeps. The crowds would leave. The newsmen and photographers would be a thing of the past. The last
race had ended and was recorded in the books. Only silent
homage, if anything, would be paid to the great champion.
Man o' War, only three years old, had become history, his
track career finished.

Danny kneeled in the freshly made and clean-smelling straw
bedding. He ran a hand down the colt's right foreleg, which
had been injured at Havre de Grace. There was no filling from
yesterday's match race. But with further racing the tendon
might easily bow. That was another reason for Mr. Riddle's
deciding to retire Man o' War. There was no sense in taking
the risk of hurting so valuable a stud prospect.

Danny got up from the straw and sat on a low, flat tack
trunk. *It doesn't mean that it's the end for him or me,* he
thought. *I can get a job with Mr. Riddle at the stud farm. In
time there'll be his colts and fillies to watch, all just as spindle-
legged and starry-eyed as he was.*

Man o' War had his head raised and turned toward Danny.
His eyes were large and lustrous, burning with a fiery energy
none of his races had ever diminished. His silky foretop hung
low between his eyes, and his nostrils were dilated as he
breathed in the cool air of the coming night. He was on his
way to complete retirement and yet he was still far from having
reached his full growth or greatness.

"Try to think of it as the beginning of something else for
him and for you," Danny told himself, half aloud. "Try it that
way." Maybe they had *both* reached a turning point in their
lives. Maybe they had.

From the far end of the car, the other grooms looked up

from their card game to glance in Danny's direction. One aged black man called, "What you all mutterin' to yo'self about, Danny-boy?"

"Nothing," Danny answered. "Nothing at all."

He listened to the click of the iron wheels on iron rails and was grateful for the coming darkness that would soon envelop him and his horse. Man o' War was taking the long trip in stride, just as he did everything else.

How many horses of his temperament would ship as quietly as this? Danny wondered. You asked him to load and he loaded without fuss. It always came as a surprise to those who only knew him on the track. But then it was different. Every horse needed to be on his toes at race time.

Man o' War knew when it was time to rest, and perhaps that was one of the reasons he had become so great. He saved all his nervous energy for the racetrack. He was a true campaigner, not a man-eater, as some reporters had led their readers to believe. But the long trail was fast coming to an end. Man o' War stood quietly in his stall while the train clanked along the tracks at ever-increasing speed.

The voices of the other grooms reached Danny.

"First comes Man o' War, then all the other horses we've ever known," Frank said.

"You're sho right, man," Buck answered.

Danny glanced up at the old groom, who had known more great horses than any of them.

A wide grin was on Buck's toothless mouth as he went on, "I know'd Domino, Sysonby, Sweep, Ben Brush, an' a few others like 'em. But like you say, this Man o' War comes first."

"We'll never know how fast he could really run," Frank said. "Feustel was always afraid to let him out. I guess he thought he'd go so fast he might hurt himself."

"He sho might have, at that."

Frank shifted his weight on the overturned bale of hay. "What do you think, Danny?" he called loudly. "You ain't said hardly a word."

"I think he could have gone lots faster, all right," Danny said. "But he did everything that was asked of him and that's what counts. He sprinted when they asked him to sprint, and went a distance when they asked for that. He carried as much weight as they could put on his back, and it didn't stop him one bit. He ran on all kinds of tracks, slow and deep and muddy, or fast and hard-packed that were torture to any hoofs not as perfect as his. He did everything, Frank, and it's hardly right to think of how much faster he might have run. What he did was enough."

For a moment the others were silent after Danny's long response. Then Frank asked, "You mean you don't think we should even *discuss* it?"

"Have it any way you like," Danny answered.

"Well, he taught me something, that horse did," Frank went on. "You see, I always thought a horse traveled fastest by moving close to the ground, covering a lot of track without wasting too much motion. But he didn't run that way. He ran long and *up*. I never seen a horse bound along like he did."

"He sho did," Buck agreed, nodding his gray close-cropped head. "But fo' all his racin', man, he'll be know'd as the hoss that beat the clock, not his rivals."

"Except for John P. Grier," Frank reminded him. "Don't ever forget the Dwyer race, Buck."

"Jus' that one little ol' brush," and the old man grinned. "He was extended, sho, but still not enough to make him go all-out. No, suh, man."

"And don't think for a minute he didn't have horses of real

class to beat," Frank persisted. "Many of them would have been tops in any year but his. He made them look like cart horses, all of them, even Sir Barton."

"He sho did, man."

Danny couldn't sit still any longer, so he went to Man o' War again, pulling the black and yellow blanket up on the colt's neck. The night was getting chilly.

How could such a horse as this ever take to settling down on a stud farm? he wondered. The confined paddocks could never take the place of the racetrack; the whinnies of mares and foals could never replace the roar from the stands. Or could they? In time Man o' War might forget all the excitement he had left behind.

Danny stroked the colt's head. Was it himself that he was really wondering about? Would it be enough for him to stand around and watch and wait?

The others must have been watching him, for suddenly Frank called, "You'll miss him, won't you, Danny-boy?"

"Miss him?" Danny turned to them, his lips open in a half-smile. "I'm not going to leave him, Frank. I'm going along."

Frank studied the boy's face a moment, then he turned to Buck and said solemnly, "You hear that, Buck? Danny's going to retire too."

The old groom grinned. "He sho is mighty young to be turned out to pasture, man. He sho is."

Danny laughed at the men's reference to his age. "I've got a lot of years on this fellow," he said jokingly. "If he's ready for retirement so am I."

They laughed, too. But there was no levity in Frank's voice when he said, "There's a difference you're forgettin', Danny, a *big* difference. Man o' War has broken all the records, and broken down all his competition. There's nothin' left for him to do *but* retire. You now . . ." He hesitated, studying the boy's face again before going on. "Well, you're a handy fellow with a horse and I guess you know this one as well as any man . . . but you still ain't made no mark yet in life. I suspect you got a long way to go yet before you think of quitting."

Danny's face flamed with his mounting anger. "I'm not quitting, Frank, or retiring either. I'm going with him, that's all. I'm going to work."

Frank turned to Buck, and the two men exchanged knowing glances.

"Son," the old man said, "you ain't goin' to make no stud groom for this heah hoss. Frank knows that, an' so do I. No, suh."

"But I . . ."

"Hold on, Danny," Frank said quietly. "It's not that maybe you *couldn't* be his stud groom someday, if that's what you really want to do. But look at it this way for a minute."

He rose from the tack trunk and went over to stand beside the boy. "Things are goin' to be pretty quiet for a while, maybe a long while. Mr. Riddle's never bred racehorses before, so he has to start at the beginning. First, he's got to buy a good band of broodmares. That ain't going to be easy, even with all his money. Most people who have well-bred mares would rather keep them than sell 'em. I hear that he's thinkin' of buying some in Europe. But he can't do it by himself. He's got to look around and get someone who knows more about breeding stock than he does to help him. That'll take time, and buying the mares and gettin' them over here will take still longer. So what are you goin' to do, just sit around and wait?"

"I'll be with *him*," Danny said adamantly.

"Maybe you will, and maybe not," Frank answered patiently. "Mr. Riddle likes you for sure, but when his breeding operation does begin, I suspect it'll be in Kentucky under the management of someone with a lot more experience than he has. Mr. Riddle may own the greatest racehorse in the world but that doesn't mean Man o' War can do without the best mares and the best *supervision*. Whoever handles Man o' War will have his own stud groom, his own staff, believe me."

"There'll be a place for me," Danny said, but a note of anxiety had crept into his eyes and voice. "I'll get a job taking care of his colts and fillies."

Frank smiled sympathetically. "You'll have to wait well over a year more for that," he said patiently. "Buck and I will be waiting for his colts and fillies, too, but meanwhile we'll be handling horses that will be running after the records he's set for them. It'll be interesting, even exciting . . ."

"After him it could never be the same," Danny said. "Not for me, anyway."

Frank shrugged his shoulders resignedly. "You're older than I thought, Danny. Maybe you're even older than Buck an' me here. Maybe you oughta' retire at that."

Buck grinned. "Yeah, man, put him out to pasture . . . that's what we oughta' do."

The railway car became silent and only the clicking of the wheels could be heard. Danny didn't feel very well at all, and he took solace and comfort in the nearness of Man o' War.

The days that followed at Belmont Park were easy ones for Man o' War, if not for those who took care of him. The big colt's workouts were shortened and slowed, and his afternoon walks became longer. Throwing him suddenly out of training would have caused serious damage and no one was taking any chances, even now. But Danny's duties were the same, for the stable routine was no different from what it would have been had Man o' War's campaign continued.

Danny knew his colt was suspicious of the long gallops rather than the bursts of speed he had been asked for before. He was anxious to run, for his leg had healed completely and there wasn't a blemish on him. Never had Danny seen him look better. He had reached his full height of 16.2 hands and weighed a heavy 1,200 pounds. He *looked* like the great horse he was. Most people who saw him thought it a pity that he would race no more.

Danny didn't let his thoughts wander far from the business at hand, which was the unwinding of Man o' War. That the big colt could have gone on to still greater glory in the United States and Europe was beside the point. Man o' War was a great champion who had needed no excuses during his campaign, and his day of full retirement was drawing near.

The crowds still came to see him at the stables, and he was truly worthy of their admiration. He had no imperfections. He was the perfect horse. He had everything a great horse should have, including heart. What he might have done, had Mr. Riddle decided to go on with him, no one would ever know.

Late one afternoon Louis Feustel came up to Danny as he was letting Man o' War graze at the end of a long shank.

The trainer's gaze swept over the horse, and then he said, "He's ready for the farm, Danny. I don't think the quiet life will bother him so much now. He's adjusted well to the light training we've given him."

"He'd still like to run," Danny said.

"He always will," Feustel answered. "But he would have been a lot worse if we'd taken him directly to the farm from his last race. Most horses don't like the quick change in tempo. They lose flesh and are very nervous. The time we've spent here letting up on him has been well spent."

"Then it's definite that he's going to Glen Riddle?" Danny asked.

"For a short while," Feustel answered. "He'll go to Kentucky as soon as Mr. Riddle gets a broodmare band together. He has people buying some mares for him in Europe now."

"Where will he go in Kentucky?"

"Mr. Riddle hasn't as yet found a suitable farm to buy, so he'll send him and the mares to Hinata Stock Farm. You know the place?"

Danny nodded. "Just six miles outside of Lexington," he said, "at the junction of Russell Cave and Iron Works Pikes."

"I guess so," Feustel said, turning back to Man o' War. "You know that country better than I do."

Danny could have told him more about Hinata Stock Farm, for it was only a short distance from Nursery Stud, where Man o' War had been foaled. It was close, too, to his own home, and there was a big elm tree with his initials cut in its trunk just outside the main gate. Hinata was managed by Miss Elizabeth Daingerfield, who, despite the fact that she was a woman competing in what a lot of people thought was a man's game, had a long, distinguished record as a stock-farm manager. And John Buckner was her stud groom. He, too, was one of the best. The farm and its staff were worthy to handle a horse such as Man o' War.

For the first time since he had left it, Danny thought of going back home. He didn't hold much hope of getting a job at Hinata, but at home he'd be near enough to watch Man o' War and see everything that happened.

Feustel turned to him again. "I hope he makes a great sire, Danny."

"He will. He'll get good colts, maybe not as great as himself but they'll be winners."

The trainer smiled at the boy's enthusiasm.

"I hope you're right. But even the best sires get more failures than winners, Danny. The mares bred to him will have as

much influence on the colts as he will, maybe more, for they're
the ones who will raise and nurse the foals. A lot depends too
on the kind of soil his youngsters graze on, the feed they eat,
and the training that follows. Getting winners is always a long
gamble, Danny."

"He'll still get them," Danny persisted. "He'll stamp them
all with his great qualities. It couldn't be any other way, not
with him."

Feustel placed a hand on the boy's shoulders. "Okay,
Danny," he said. "I'll listen to you. I haven't forgotten how
much you saw in Man o' War as a yearling."

The trainer turned his gaze toward the nearby barns. "Now
that he's going I'm giving you another colt to tend. I think we
have some good ones this year, and they're all ready for their
first lessons."

Danny shook his head. "I don't want another horse, Mr.
Feustel," he said. "I'm going home, too."

The trainer was still for a moment, then he said quietly, "I
guess I knew you might say that. But think it over a little more,
Danny. Give me your decision tomorrow."

The Big Gamble

30

That night Danny lay in the darkness of the tack room without trying to sleep. He listened to the night noises and the deep breathing of the men in the other cots. He listened to the quiet movement of Man o' War in the adjacent stall.

It was all decided. He was going home. He did not need to think it over, as Feustel had suggested. If he couldn't get a job at Hinata Stock Farm during the months to come, he would still be near Man o' War.

He turned over on his cot, still not wanting to sleep even though he had made up his mind. Somehow he kept recalling Frank's words on the train:

"Man o' War has broken all the records, and broken down all his competition. There's nothin' left for him to do but retire. You now . . . you still ain't made no mark yet in life . . . you got a long way to go yet before you think of quitting."

And old Buck had said, *"He sho is mighty young to be turned out to pasture, man. He sho is."*

Danny turned back on his other side. Just as he'd told them, he wasn't quitting. He just didn't want any part of the race-track anymore with Man o' War gone. It could never be the same without him. So, instead, he'd watch Man o' War become a famous sire.

"You'll have to wait well over a year more for his colts and fillies to come along," Frank had pointed out.

Danny shifted his weight again and the cot creaked beneath him. He tried to shut out their words of friendly advice. He'd be busy. There'd be lots of things to do besides watching other people handle Man o' War and just waiting around for the foals to come. Maybe . . . sure, maybe he'd even go back to school. It would be hard finishing after the two years he'd been away. He'd be kept busy, *real* busy.

Danny closed his eyes. That idea appealed to him more than anything else. He'd be studying hard and yet be close enough to Man o' War to watch what went on. He'd sure feel funny back in school, two years older than all the others in his class and bigger, lots bigger. He must weigh about 150 pounds now and was growing some every day, it seemed. There was no telling how big he'd get to be.

He opened his eyes. If he weighed about 150 pounds, that was just twelve pounds more than Man o' War had carried in winning the Potomac Handicap. He closed his eyes quickly, startled by the thought he had let enter his mind.

Minutes passed, and his throat became so tight he couldn't swallow. He must be crazy even to think of it. His heart kept pounding until, finally, he had to swing his long legs from the cot and sit up. He couldn't be seriously considering it. Yet he was. Why not? What had he to lose? He had waited a long, long time. But Man o' War, what about him? He might get hurt. Not if he kept him at a slow gallop, he decided. All he wanted was to ride him, just once.

He pulled on his coveralls without awakening the others, then stole across the room where the bridle usually hung. Even though he couldn't see anything in the darkness, his hands had no trouble finding it or the saddle. Carrying both, he quietly opened the door and went outside.

The night was pitch-dark with a heavy overcast that blotted out the stars. He had only to be careful about the stable's night watchman seeing him. Everyone else was asleep. He tiptoed to the door of the next stall. The watchman would be in his office at the far end of the row and might even be asleep. Strict vigilance of Man o' War had ended with the match race.

Danny opened the stall door and Man o' War whinnied. "Shh," Danny said quietly as he slipped inside.

Quickly he put the bridle on his colt, drawing the forelock beneath the black and yellow browband. The light saddle went on next, and Danny was ready for the lightning shift of the big body when he tightened the girth. But, actually, he had less trouble than when Feustel saddled Man o' War.

Man o' War snorted. Danny hushed him again, speaking quietly with his hands, the language both of them knew best of all. He knew he was breaking every rule in the book. If anyone saw him, he would be fired immediately. But it didn't matter now.

Outside, he looked each way, up and down the shed row. Again the big colt snorted, his eyes bright and ears pricked. The night wind swelled his nostrils and fanned his mane and tail.

Danny walked beside him, keeping one hand on the bridle, the other on the colt's neck. "Shh," he kept repeating.

He led Man o' War into the wind, heading for the open gap in the big track. He wasn't going to take any chances of hurting his colt. He wouldn't ride more than a mile at a slow gallop, just enough to remember forever that he had ridden Man o' War!

The stands loomed in the distance, a hovering bulk of steel and concrete and emptiness. Beneath his hands he felt Man o' War begin to quiver. Even without the tumult of a crowd or the music of a band, he was becoming excited. It seemed to Danny that Man o' War sensed the quickening of his heart as he stepped on the track rail and mounted him.

"Easy, Red, easy," Danny kept repeating, but there was no easiness in his body as he let his weight come to rest in the saddle.

Man o' War shifted beneath him, his movement lightning swift and carrying him onto the track. Danny was ready for him. He had carefully watched other riders move with Man o' War in this very same situation.

"Easy, Red, easy," he said again, and although he tried to keep the anxiety from his voice, he knew it was there for the colt to hear. He took up on the reins. *Not too tight*, he reminded himself. *Don't fight him or you're lost. But take hold or he'll get away from you. There, that's better.*

He was riding Man o' War! He was moving him down the track, feeling the Herculean strength beneath him and wondering, oh wondering, if he could control it. The world had never looked so beautiful. No other night had ever held such suspense.

"Slow, Red . . . that's it. No hurry now. Just a gallop. No hurry. Slow . . . slow." His hands, too, pleaded with Man o' War. But with every stride the surging power mounted.

He was standing in the stirrup irons as they went past the long, dark stands, and the wind was cold, stinging his face.

"Easy now, Red." He let his weight fall back in the saddle, knowing that if he kept standing in the irons he wouldn't be able to stay on Man o' War. He felt the mighty leap the second his pants touched the leather. It was comparable to nothing he had ever known before. Almost before Man o' War's hoofs struck the packed dirt of the track he leaped again, throwing Danny forward onto his neck.

Danny was scared now, not so much for himself as for Man o' War. It was important that he shouldn't let the colt go all-out. He shortened rein, taking a snug hold on Man o' War's mouth as he had seen the others do. Man o' War was finished with fast workouts. He was being let down. He mustn't extend himself.

"Slower, Red," Danny called, and he shortened the reins still more.

Man o' War didn't like the tight hold that pulled his head against his chest. But he was responding to Danny's commands, for his strides shortened going into the first turn.

Even then they were flying, and Danny's excitement grew along with his ever-mounting confidence that he could control Man o' War. He gloried in the tremendous leaps that carried his colt far above the ground with all four legs almost drawn together! And yet with all of Man o' War's speed and strength, he was no wild-eyed monster, grabbing the bit and rushing headlong around the track. He was intelligent enough to respond to his rider's will, and that was one of the traits that had made him so great.

Danny felt the tremendous pull of Man o' War at the end of the reins; his arms were already beginning to ache from holding him back. That Man o' War would respond to his rider's wishes did not mean that he wasn't constantly asking to be turned loose! It took strong and experienced hands and arms to keep the reins snug and to let Man o' War know what was wanted of him.

To relieve the strain on his arms, Danny finally had to loosen his hold. There was sudden movement beneath him as Man o' War immediately lengthened stride. The track rail became only a blur and Danny's eyes were dimmed by the rush of the wind. All he could see now was the heavy red mane sweeping against his face, stinging his flesh.

Going into the long backstretch, he took up rein again, wondering if his strength would last so he could continue to control this powerful horse. His snug hold became a tight one. Pain stabbed muscles that never had been used for such a task before. Then a growing numbness came to his arms and Danny knew this would be followed by a general weakening.

"Easy . . . easy, Red," he said, his voice, too, weakening beneath the mounting strain.

Man o' War's ears flicked back just once, as if perhaps he was listening to him. But the reins slipped still more in Danny's hands and the big colt thundered on!

The iron bit was hard against the bars on his mouth, and Danny no longer had the strength to hold him back. The furlong poles whipped by, and Danny realized that Man o' War was now running as he had always wanted to run. His incredible speed mounted as he began digging into the track still more.

Danny kept the hold he had on him, but lowered his own head, pressing it close to Man o' War's neck. This was not the way he had wanted it to be, but there was nothing he could do. The mistake he had made was in taking Man o' War out on the track at all. All he could hope for now was that his colt was strong enough and sound enough to run all-out without injury.

Faster and faster went Man o' War, running for the sheer love of running. Danny couldn't see, couldn't feel anything but the pumping of giant muscles beneath him and the thumping of his own heart. Whatever might come, he would never in his life forget this ride! He had no trouble keeping his balance. There were no other horses, no crowding, no slamming of riders and their mounts, as there would have been in a race. Just himself and Man o' War, and suddenly they were not even of this world!

His hold on the reins slackened still more. There was no rail, no stands, no track . . . nothing but a flying horse whose hoofs barely touched the ground before coming up again. He knew, by the leaning of Man o' War's body to the left, that they were going around the far turn, and he bent in the same direction with his mount.

Straightening out into the homestretch, Danny found his hands being pulled forward still more. He didn't know if they had lost their strength completely or if he had done it willingly. All he realized was that his hold on Man o' War wasn't strong enough to make the big colt shake his head. Man o' War was running free!

There was no roar from the stands to greet him as he came down the stretch like scorching flame. Only the emptiness of the stands and track welcomed the rapid beat of his hoofs. It made no difference to him or to the boy on his back. He streaked through the night, went past the finish pole, and swept toward the first turn again.

Only then did Danny slip back in his saddle and try to take hold of Man o' War. Ignoring the shooting pains in his arms, he pulled back and prayed that his strength would last until he stopped the colt. For a few seconds his only response was a vigorous shaking of Man o' War's head. But the colt, too, was tiring and Danny succeeded in shortening the reins still more. He eased him over closer to the rail to slow him down, and by the time they had completed the turn he had him in a gallop.

Somewhere in the backstretch he brought him to a stop and straightened in the saddle. He looked around. All was still except for his own heavy breathing. Quickly he slipped from the saddle to walk Man o' War and watch every step he made. There was no lameness, no misstep. It would take several hours before he could be certain there was no injury. But the outlook was good, and he had the rest of the night before him . . . and all his life to remember.

Together they walked around the track, lost in darkness.

The Summing Up

31

The big man stirred on the couch, turning to look at the portrait of Man o' War hanging over the entrance to the racetrack restaurant. No, the colt hadn't hurt himself that night, some thirty-nine years ago. In fact, Man o' War had lived to a ripe old age for a horse, being thirty years old when he died. That was comparable to a spry old gentleman in his late eighties.

The man roused himself as a cumbersome bear might have done after a long winter's rest. At fifty-seven he didn't feel exactly young himself these days. Perhaps it hadn't been such a good idea to recall those years so long ago. He leaned back, his giant frame slumped in the luxurious couch like a bulging sack of grain. Usually he wasn't one to go back, reliving the memories of his youth. It never worked. A man had to look ahead always, regardless of his age, and he wasn't yet ready to be turned out to pasture.

He leaned forward, preparing to get up. His hands dwarfed the arm of the couch, his long fingers, blunt and square at the tips, curled over the edge. Pulling himself upright, he stood still a moment, his gaze on the portrait on the wall.

He had never set the world on fire as Man o' War had done. But Man o' War had had a great influence on him. He had given him a goal and taught him the value of courage and heart. To learn that in one's youth was pretty important.

Music from the track band reached him through the open doors, and for a moment he listened to the medley of Irish airs being played. When the music came to an end, he realized that the applause from the crowd was not as hearty as it should have been. That meant the day's races were well under way, for the fans' enthusiasm for band music always diminished as the afternoon wore on. He must have been sitting here a long, long time.

Turning on his heels, he looked back into the luxurious restaurant. It was jammed with diners, so he decided there was still a while before the feature race. That was good, because he didn't like to hurry at his age.

From far across the restaurant a man sitting alone at a table beckoned to him. He waved back and strode toward the velvet rope that "protected" the diners of the exclusive Man o' War Room.

The headwaiter quickly unfastened the rope. "Would you like a table, Mr. Ryan?"

"No thanks, George," he answered. "There's an old friend over there I want to see." He paused. "What race is it, anyway? I seem to have lost track."

"The fifth is coming up," the headwaiter replied, smiling. "Then comes the Man o' War Handicap." His eyes searched the other's. "You saw *him* race, didn't you?"

"Yeah, I saw him," Danny Ryan said, moving on.

The waiters, splendid in new uniforms that matched the brilliant decor of the Man o' War Room, nodded to him as he made his way around the tables and came to a stop before one by the window.

Louis Feustel was very gray now and carried a lot more weight than he had in the old days. But his eyes were as keen and alert as ever.

"Sit down, Danny," Feustel said. "It's good seeing you again. It's been a couple of years now. Santa Anita was the last time, wasn't it?"

Danny Ryan nodded, easing his heavy frame into the fragile dining chair. "You still in California, Louis?"

"Yes. Just came east for the race. Aqueduct is picking up the tab. Sort of a promotion deal for the first Man o' War Handicap. Ex-trainer stuff. You know how it goes."

Danny said, "Yeah, I know." His eyes were on the other's full plate. "You're eating well," he added, smiling.

"Why not? There's nothing like broiled shrimp in wine for an appetizer. I could eat it every day. And this Dover sole amandine is great for the waistline." Feustel hit his stomach with the flat of his hand. "I think I'll even have fresh strawberries for dessert."

"Fine," Danny said. "You've earned all of it."

The other's eyes sobered. "So have you, Danny," he said quietly.

"Yeah, I've got it pretty good at that, Louis. I can't complain."

"You're a big man, Danny."

"*Big* is right." Danny Ryan laughed loudly, and other diners turned in his direction. "I never would have made a race rider even as a kid. You know that, Louis."

"No, you wouldn't have," Feustel agreed. "But you used what you knew about him in your career, and that's what is important now."

"I guess so," Danny said softly. "I wouldn't be here otherwise, that's for sure."

"Nor me," Feustel said. "That's for sure, too." He paused

to glance at the television sets around the room. It was possible to watch the day's races without ever leaving the restaurant, if one liked. "Things have changed a lot since the old days. Right, Danny?"

"Right," Danny repeated, his eyes too on a television screen that showed the field going to the post for the fifth race of the afternoon.

"Can you imagine what it would have been like if we'd had television in *his* day?" Feustel asked. "Can't you just see Man o' War moving into living rooms across the nation?"

Danny Ryan nodded. "It would have been something," he said, looking out the windows to the west. The sun was trying to come out from behind the clouds, so maybe it would be a golden autumn day after all. He could see the panorama of the New York skyline twelve miles away. He noted, too, that the huge parking area near the entrance to the track was jammed and closed. It was a big day, a very big day.

His gaze moved on. Just below, almost in the center of the colorful gardens and landscaped grounds, was a tall green and white pole with a round ball on top. On its sides was painted the figure ⅛.

"Some of the old Aqueduct is still here," he said quietly. "They call it *his* pole now, the Man o' War Pole, for all to see and few to remember."

"That's where he caught John P. Grier in the Dwyer," Feustel said thoughtfully, "an eighth of a mile from the finish. Right at that pole he broke Grier's heart. Maybe it was his greatest race, Danny. Maybe it was."

Both men continued looking at the pole, both remembering. Finally Danny Ryan said, "I've got work to do."

Feustel nodded. "Yeah, it won't be long now before the feature. I'll be there, Danny. I'm not watching it on any TV screen." His eyes turned back to his plate with the Dover sole amandine still on it. "But it won't be the same," he added quietly, pushing the food away. "It could never be the same again."

Danny Ryan didn't hurry across the large room. There were other diners who greeted him, and he stopped often to shake hands agreeably. He found himself enjoying this day even more than he had expected. Somehow, the very breathtaking vastness of this new track provided an air of unreality that seemed to go with Man o' War. He cautioned himself that he must not let his imagination soar with his high spirits. He must remember Man o' War as he really was. His record needed no embellishment.

He saw two women beckoning to him as he was about to leave the room. Reluctantly he moved toward their table. Their faces were familiar but he could not remember their names.

"Was Man o' War *really* a super horse," the younger of the two asked immediately, "or is it just that, as the years go on, he's become . . . well, you know, sort of a legend?"

She awaited his answer in open-mouthed wonder, and Danny quickly decided that she was the daughter of one of the track directors. "Man o' War was truly the kind from which dreams are made, miss," he answered.

"Oh, *that* kind!" she exclaimed.

He looked at her puzzledly until the elderly woman with her said, "And, Cynthia, here's something else you may not know. It was a *woman*, a Miss Daingerfield, I believe"—her eyes shifted to Danny Ryan for confirmation, and he nodded— "who managed Man o' War when he was retired," she went on glowingly. "And *she* made him as famous a sire as he had been as a racehorse. It took a woman, one of *us*, didn't it, Mr. Ryan?"

He studied her without answering right away. Maybe she

was the wife of one of the other directors. Her clothes were as smart and fashionable as the room's decor; her face as smooth and cared for as the rest of her; and her hair as delicately tinted as any shade of pastel at colorful New Aqueduct. She was far different from the woman he had known at Hinata Stock Farm ... the one who had spent her life with horses, who had known Domino, Spendthrift, Kingston, Sysonby, and Colin, to name only a few, before handling Man o' War. A woman who had grown up with great horses and knew how to breed them as well as train them, and whose management of them had been her life. No tinted hair, no smart clothes, but familiar with the most fashionable bloodlines the world had ever known.

Finally he said, "Yes, it took a woman, ma'am. Miss Daingerfield handled Man o' War for ten years, first at her place, Hinata Stock Farm, then at Mr. Riddle's Faraway Farm close by."

The younger woman had been watching him closely. "Were you with Man o' War then? I mean, when he left the race-track?"

"Yes, I was." He turned to her, wondering how much she saw.

"Did you cry? You must have been very young."

He was caught unprepared by her question, and his gaze shifted uneasily back to the older woman. At his age, he didn't like to talk about crying ... that was for kids.

"Did you?" the young woman persisted.

"I ... I guess everybody did, a little. We'd shared his triumphs on the track. It was only natural to feel bad that it had come to an end." He shifted his feet. What was he doing here anyway? He'd better get along.

But the older woman held on to him, and not by voice

alone, for her hand was on his arm. "So you see, Cynthia," she said, "it must not be too difficult a profession for a woman."

"You have to grow into it naturally, as Miss Daingerfield did," he said quickly, a little coldly.

"I suppose so. But another thing, Mr. Ryan, wasn't it she, too, who selected the broodmares that made his sire career such a great success?"

He nodded again. "With the help of a *man*," he said, surprised at the sudden defiance in his voice. "An Englishman named William Allison. He was a writer."

"A *writer?*" the older woman repeated puzzledly.

"Who knew the pedigrees of horses as well as anyone in the world," he finished.

"Oh," she said quietly, as if a little frightened by the defiance in his voice. "Well, anyway, it took a woman."

He smiled. "It always does," he said. This was no day to be angered by anyone's questions, foolish though they might be. Besides, these women were interested in Man o' War as a *sire* and not simply as a legendary racehorse. In a way, it was refreshing.

"Even Man o' War couldn't have done it alone," he went on. "He needed Lady Comfey, Colette, Star Fancy, The Nurse, Christmas Star, Understudy, Thrasher, Batanoea, Shady, Florence Webber, Blue Grass, Earine, Fairy Wand, Escuina, and Uncle's Lassie . . . to name just a few. They were the mares who helped make his first five years at stud the dramatic success they were."

His voice had risen and the two women were listening intently, nodding their heads as if in full agreement with everything he had to say.

"He sired twenty-six stakes winners during those years," Danny concluded. "Four were $100,000 winners and one of them, Clyde Van Dusen, copped the Kentucky Derby, the only big race that Man o' War missed."

For a few seconds more the two women were thoughtfully silent. Then the older one said, "So you see, Cynthia, I was right. The distaff side *is* most important."

"Of course," he said, shrugging his shoulders and taking a step away from the table. "Isn't it always?"

The younger woman was still watching him closely. "Did you work for Miss Daingerfield?" she asked. "You seem to know so much . . ."

"No, I went back to school," he said, "then, later, I got a job on a Lexington horse journal as sort of a copy boy. That way it was easy for me to keep track of what went on at the farms."

It was very easy, he thought. Just as it was easy now to recall everything that had happened.

The fifteen mares had romped across the winter fields at Hinata with everybody watching them. Six had come from England, the rest from America. Some had never seen a race-track. All were of the best of bloodlines and of the finest type to make good broodmares. Upon them depended the success of Man o' War as a sire, and only time would tell what strains combined best with his own. Luck would play an important part in the matings, of course, but skill and knowledge, too, had taken a hand in the careful selection of these mares.

The new stallion barn had been ready for Man o' War when he arrived in late January. He was a hundred pounds heavier than when Danny had last seen him. He stood in the cold of that winter day looking every inch the emperor he was. Man o' War had come home to Kentucky, and Danny was one of those who had lined the long fences at Hinata, calling out his name and waving to him.

"He must have been bored," the young woman said, interrupting his reverie, "really bored after all the excitement of the racecourse." She paused, smiling. "I mean, even with his big harem it must have been pretty dull compared to the clamor and the glamor of the life he had known while racing."

Danny Ryan smiled back. "No, I don't really think he was bored," he answered. "Red . . . I mean Man o' War . . . had more brains than most horses. He adjusted quickly to the new life set out for him. Of course, he was restive at first, as any fine stallion would be. But soon he took it all in stride."

Nothing ever seemed to be hurried in those days, he recalled. *Man o' War had seemed to know he was back in Kentucky. Maybe he even recognized some of the hills and barns and fences of that countryside. He'd been cantered each day, going down the back roads and lanes around Lexington. First Clyde Gordon had ridden him, then John Buckner, Miss Daingerfield's stud groom. Danny had seen them often on the wintry roads.*

"No," he said aloud, turning back to the young woman. "They never gave him a chance to be bored that first year. They made everything interesting for him. He never got lazy and fat. He'd run like a colt when they turned him loose in the paddocks, and I think he looked forward to seeing his foals as much as anyone else."

"Did you see them, the first foals, I mean?" she asked.

"I saw them," he answered.

In the very first crop had been American Flag and By Hisself, Gun Boat and First Mate, Florence Nightingale and Maid at Arms, Flagship and Lightship, Flotilla and . . . heavens, he couldn't remember the other names anymore. His memory wasn't what it used to be. He was getting old. But there had been thirteen foals, nine of them chestnuts like Man o' War. He remembered their colors because he'd been one of

328 MAN O' WAR

those looking at the muzzle hairs to determine true color. Masquerade's filly had died soon after birth, so that had made a total of twelve in the first crop, and all had been given names as dramatic as their sire's.

"Were they like him?" the young woman asked, interrupting his thoughts again.

"How do you mean? Speed?"

"Well, yes," she said.

"Some were very fast and became champions," he said. "But none were as fast as he was. Not any of them or any in all of his other great crops that followed. There never was *another* Man o' War."

His eyes shifted to the older woman, and he found her listening intently, too. Strange, he thought, that these two women so far removed from the track as he knew it should be so keenly interested in the breeding of racehorses. Maybe beneath all this modern sophistication and concern for one's appearance and self . . .

"Another thing," he went on. "While Man o' War was a very successful sire, he never got colts with the early speed he'd shown himself. They didn't do too much as two-year-olds, but matured slowly. They raced best at three or later. American Flag was the best of his first crop, then came Crusader and Mars and Edith Cavell the next year. Scapa Flow and Genie and Bateau and Clyde Van Dusen followed. Those were his outstanding runners but he had other colts winning, too, lots of them, all from his first five crops."

"And after that?" the young woman asked. "Did he continue being so successful?"

He studied her face a long while, his own eyes clouding. "Not quite," he admitted. "War Hero and Boatswain came along in the 1929 crop and War Glory in 1930, all pretty good horses. But we had to wait until 1934 before he struck it rich again with the champion War Admiral and the excellent filly Wand. And after them came War Relic . . ."

"But what caused his decline after such a brilliant beginning during those first five years?" the young woman persisted.

Danny Ryan glanced at his watch. It was almost time for the big race. "I have to go," he said abruptly, his gaze shifting to the television screen a short distance from the table. "This is no place to watch the running of the first Man o' War Handicap."

He hurried across the room, rousing himself from the past as he went along. Leaving the restaurant, he entered the vast, open level of the third floor. There were thousands of people milling about but no one was being mobbed or trampled. New Aqueduct was so spacious in every respect that everyone had room to breathe. He wasn't certain at all that he liked so much comfort.

Despite all the room, a man with his head down bumped into him. "Sorry," the jostler said.

"Quite all right," Danny Ryan answered politely. The collision had made him feel better. Some things at a track would never change.

As he neared the escalator someone else bumped into him. This man, too, had his head down, reading his program. There was no apology and the man beat him to the moving stairs.

Reaching the lower lobby, he noted that the track police were everywhere, not so much to keep order as to direct people to proper gates and answer questions. New Aqueduct was still a little confusing to New Yorkers not used to such lavishness.

He moved slowly through the throng, almost feeling his way toward the one special gate he was aiming for. It made him think, somehow, that he was at the bottom of a vast, spectacular monument, and he became very eager to reach the top. He tried to move faster, his general mood of gaiety darkening despite the lobby's bright panels of orange, yellow, green, and red.

Reaching his gate, he nodded to a track policeman, showed his pass, and stepped through the double doors. Once within the structure's vast confines, he breathed easier and walked more freely down a long corridor. On either side of him were many rooms and offices. He passed them quickly. Only those who "belonged" were allowed in this section. It was quiet, almost peaceful compared to what was going on in the four tiers of stands overhead. But it was still like groping one's way through the catacombs of another world.

A man standing at the door of an office marked PLACING AND PATROL JUDGES waved and said, "Hello, Danny. You're late today."

"Not late. Just been looking around," he answered, almost defensively.

"Tell me, Danny, was he as really, truly great as they say he was?"

"He broke all the records. He broke down all the horses that ran against him. What more do you want?" Once again, Danny was surprised at the defiance in his voice. What was wrong with him today? People were just interested in Man o' War and wanted to know more about him, that was all. It was natural, today of all days.

He turned around and went back to the man at the door. "Maybe you'd understand better if I reminded you he was the odds-on favorite in every race he ever started, all twenty-one of them. You ever heard anything like that before . . . or since?"

"No, I never have, Danny. As you say, I understand better when you put it that way . . . in facts and figures, I mean, not legends or saga. They're for the people up in the stands."

Danny was glowering in the other's face. "And after he was retired he had at least one offspring win a race each year from 1924 through 1953. That's a span of thirty years, Clem. Ever hear of any other sire matching it?"

"No, Danny, I never did," the man said, backing off. "Like you say . . ."

Danny Ryan didn't wait to hear any more. He continued down the corridor of concrete, wanting very much to be alone, if only for a moment.

"Speed an' mo' speed, dat's what makes a good hoss," he had heard a groom say in a slow, quiet drawl long ago. But there had been lots more to Man o' War than sheer speed. He had stamina, courage, and heart. And, fortunately, he'd been able to pass much of it on to his colts and fillies. His record as a sire was a great one, but it might have been still greater if Mr. Riddle had not been so adamant about restricting most of Man o' War's services to his own collection of broodmares. No one person, even a very wealthy man, could maintain the quality of mares so necessary for a great sire.

As he had told that young woman back in the restaurant, those first five crops by Man o' War were his banner years. After that . . . well, as she so quickly observed his reluctance to discuss it, there was a decline in Man o' War's record as a sire. Not that he didn't get race winners and a few great ones like War Hero and Boatswain, War Admiral and Wand. But never again was the proportion of exceptional horses the same as it had been during those first five years.

Danny scuffed his way along the corridor. He knew from having been there that it hadn't been due to the decline of Man o' War himself, for he had remained a vigorous, healthy stallion. Instead it had been the lack of distinguished mares with which the farm had been restocked after Miss Daingerfield's retirement in 1930. The mares that had been purchased by Mr. Riddle after that had, for the most part, been inferior to those in the first band. And, of course, Mr. Riddle would allow very few mares not his own to be bred to Man o' War.

Had that been a selfish decision? Danny shrugged his big shoulders. Who was he to judge Mr. Riddle's actions? Hadn't he been as selfish as anyone else in his hunger to call Man o' War *his very own?* Didn't he, even now—some forty years later—still feel a certain resentment when anyone questioned the record and legend of *his* colt? What Man o' War might have done had he been retired to an established, successful stud farm with many *proven* mares was not for him to say.

Men waved to Danny as he passed the Film Patrol Room and the Barber Shop, but, lost in thought, he ignored them all and plodded deeper into the confines under the stands.

"There goes Danny," one of them said. "It must be getting time for the feature."

"You'd never know it to look at him," another answered. "He looks lost."

"No, he ain't lost. He's thinkin'. Danny's a walkin' record book."

Danny Ryan came to a sudden stop before one of the rooms and peered inside. It was such a huge room that it made the little men occupying it seem smaller than they actually were.

"Hi, Bill," he said to a jockey sitting close to the door. "You've got a good horse going for you in the feature."

The young jockey smiled. "We're goin' light, if that's what you mean, Danny. Just 108 pounds."

"That's light," Danny agreed, and for a moment he shifted uneasily on his big feet. "You ought to make it real tough for Bald Eagle."

"That's for sure," the jockey said.

Danny Ryan glanced around the room, noting the water basins, low and just the right height for the little men. At the far end was a recreation lounge, where some of the boys were playing Ping-Pong and pool while awaiting the call for their races. There were bunks and dressing rooms and showers and steam rooms . . . everything to make the jockeys comfortable and, like everything else, a far cry from the old days.

He walked on. *How much he wished he'd been born small . . . even now, after all these years.*

There was a large crowd waiting for the elevator and he joined them, nodding and smiling.

"It turned out to be a fine day after all, Ed," he said to an old friend.

"Yes, I was afraid the sun wouldn't make it," the other answered. "Can't take the cold like I used to."

Danny said, "Me, too." Ed was about his own age. Ed had seen Man o' War. "It *had* to shine today," he added in a low voice. He didn't want the others to overhear. They wouldn't have understood.

"I suppose so. But it never mattered to *him* what kind of a day it was, Danny. He always ran the same way, hot, cold, muddy, or dry. He was a big horse, all right."

"He sure was. They don't come like him anymore. They never did. They never will. Everything about him was *big*."

"Omaha and Sun Beau were bigger in size," the other reminded him.

"Taller, you mean, and not so muscled in chest and shoulders."

"But Roseben was."

"Yeah, but Roseben didn't have his large and powerful quarters," Danny answered.

"Whopper did."

"But not his stride. No other horse ever covered twenty-nine feet in one leap."

"No, and I guess they never will," the other admitted. "He

had the best of everything and in perfect proportion. It'll be a long time . . ."

"It'll be never," Danny said louder than he'd meant to.

A young reporter standing behind them said, "You old-timers sure all sound alike today. But just *what* did Man o' War ever beat?" he needled.

Danny didn't turn around. "Golden Broom, Upset, Blazes, John P. Grier, Wildair, Paul Jones, On Watch, and Donnacona," he answered, ". . . all top horses that would have been champions any year but his."

"But he was never thoroughly tried," the young man persisted. "He never raced after three, so he never proved himself as a handicap horse."

Danny felt the hot blood flushing his face, but still he didn't turn and face the young man behind him. "Man o' War didn't have to prove himself any further," he answered evenly. "He carried more weight at two than most horses carry at three, and at three he carried higher weights than any older horse has ever been asked to race with. Don't you ever read the record books?"

There was complete silence behind him. He had known such arguments before, often from sportswriters who, even though young in years, should have known better. He was resigned to it, realizing that such comparisons of today's "super horses" with Man o' War would never end. If they had only *seen* him!

The elevator doors opened and Danny went inside the car with the others. A few jockeys came running up, too, crowding into the large cage. Quietly, the elevator left the ground floor and began rising.

"Upsy-daisy," one of the jockeys said, his small body lost in the center of the packed throng. "We're leavin' the gate."

"Then don't lose your whip like you usually do," a photographer said. "You'll need it to get out."

"Imagine," the jockey went on, "a track providin' us with a rooftop penthouse to watch the races from. That's class, brother."

"Maybe they expect you guys to learn somethin'," the other answered.

"Wise guy," the little man muttered.

They rose to the topmost tier of the great stands, the height of a ten-story building, before the doors opened. Danny didn't push his way out. He was in no mood to hurry. There was still plenty of time before the horses came onto the track for the running of the first Man o' War Handicap.

He found he was not alone; the young reporter had waited, too, for the others to leave. "Another thing, Danny," the fellow said eagerly. "I know I haven't been around as long as you and maybe I'm stepping on your toes, but Man o' War seems like something Hollywood dreamed up. He couldn't have been as good as you old-timers say."

"He was no Hollywood horse," Danny said patiently. "Come to think of it, what he did was not in the Hollywood tradition of an exciting racehorse at all. He had things too much his own way. He made every race look easy at any weight, any odds. He was exciting only if you *saw* him do it."

Danny waited for the younger man to leave the elevator, then followed him down the corridor. Together they entered a door marked PRESS. There was nothing within to obstruct the view, and for a moment Danny's eyes swept over the vastness of open space that stretched before him.

The mile and one-eighth track with its dun-colored surface was directly below. Inside the main oval was the mile turf strip, and inside that was the seven-furlong steeplechase course. *All*

kinds of courses for all kind of horses, that was New Aqueduct,
Danny mused. And, as if that wasn't enough for the spectators,
two blue-water ponds decorated the infield.

His eyes traveled beyond the sprawling track to the stable
area with its modernistic barns and dormitories for the grooms.
That, too, was a far cry from the old Aqueduct he and Man o'
War had known so well.

He watched a jet airliner take off from Idlewild Airport a few
miles in the distance, following its flight until it disappeared
over the jagged New York skyline. Only then did his gaze return to the track below, and he muttered aloud, "It's the same
old clay base, anyway."

The young reporter was still standing nearby, and he said,
"You mean they put a new surface on the track without
changing the base?"

"Yeah, it's the same old base all right," Danny said. "Just as
Man o' War's hoofs knew it, and those of Equipoise, Exterminator, and Domino, going all the way back to 1894."

"That's interesting," the young man said, making a note of
it on a piece of paper.

"It's a fast track, they say," the young man went on.

"Naturally," Danny said, his eyes following the takeoff of
still another jet airliner from the huge airport. "Like everything
else these days," he added. He wondered if the arrival and de-
parture of so many planes bothered the horses and decided it
did not. They, too, had adjusted to the new era.

Then he saw the familiar deep blue of Rockaway Inlet flowing in from the Atlantic Ocean, while above it fluttered hundreds of seagulls. There were some things that would never
change. Mother Nature was here to stay.

"They've got a three-inch cushion of dirt and sand out
there, sifted and filtered so it's fast without being abrasive to

horses' hoofs," the young man said, as if eager to impress.

"I know," Danny said. "The surface is as fast as they could make it." What would Man o' War have done on a track like that? he wondered. What records would he have set with such an opportunity? All track surfaces were now almost two seconds faster to the mile than in the days his hoofs had known them. And yet most of his records still hung high, *records he had made without even being allowed to extend himself!*

Danny turned to the younger man beside him. How could this fellow, how could *anybody* talk about their Whirlaways and Citations, their Nashuas and Native Dancers, being a "second Man o' War"?

Never would there be another like him! Never, until a champion came along who could outsprint the sprinters, outstay the stayers, carry the highest weight ever put on a horse's back, and win on every kind of track! And while doing it, such a champion must break record after record. After that he must sire champion colts and fillies and broodmares that would produce still more champions. Only then could a horse be called "a second Man o' War"!

Danny moved on through the crowded room on top of the stands, nodding to many. But his thoughts were far afield. Someone bumped into him, and he heard a quick apology, "Sorry, Danny. But I can't seem to find a pencil sharpener anyplace. Imagine a $33,000,000 joint like this with no pencil sharpener!"

Danny smiled. "Yeah, how about that," he said, relieved to have found something missing at this fantastic racing plant. "It'll never make it."

He looked far below and saw that the horses were ready to step onto the track. George Seuffert's band had stopped playing. The flags on the infield pole were barely moving, so the wind had died. The sun was out. All was as it should be for the first Man o' War Handicap.

A red-coated bugler, wearing shiny black boots and a black hunting cap, stood in the middle of the track. He placed a four-foot-long coach horn to his lips and for a few seconds held it there without blowing. The sun glistened on the golden horn and finally the music came forth, sounding the call to the post.

Danny shivered. The call would never change. It meant the same now as it always had, and he reacted to it the same way. He watched the horses leave the paddock. There were a couple of flighty ones trying to throw their riders. Everybody was tense. Everybody was waiting. New Aqueduct might be a racing Utopia, but only fine-blooded horses could make it a success. No modern facilities, no glistening pomp, could change things from the way it had to be. The grueling test of speed and stamina was all that really mattered to the eighty thousand people this new track could hold.

Danny's heart beat faster as he watched the horses parade. Was there among them just one who might have stayed within the shadow of Man o' War? No, none of these, he decided. Not today or tomorrow or any of the days to come. Not for him.

His eyes grew dim as he moved past clicking typewriters and teletype machines. Few men paid any attention to him, for they were watching the post parade and listening to the introductions coming over the public address system.

He sat down in a chair and drew his own typewriter toward him. The man next to him said, "Pity we still have to pound out our own stuff, Danny. You'd think that with all the modern machines they've got around here . . ."

Danny wasn't listening. He saw only a fiery phantom and heard the roar of a multitudinous throng of another day. The years that had passed were many and other champions had come and gone. But Man o' War was the one they should always remember.

The shadows of the stands lengthened across the track, and the breeze blowing off the ocean became colder. Danny put a sheet of paper in his typewriter and stared at it. He never expected to see another Man o' War in his time. But the very young, might they not one day see *his* return? They had more time to wait and hope and dream. Perhaps if he helped them a little by telling them of the colt he had known so long ago. . . . Perhaps . . . yes, just perhaps, history might repeat itself.

Danny Ryan began typing, not for his newspaper, but for all boys and girls who might read his story of Man o' War.

ABOUT THE AUTHOR

Walter Farley's love for horses began when he was a small boy living in Syracuse, New York, and continued as he grew up in New York City, where his family moved. Unlike most city children, he was able to fulfill this love through an uncle who was a professional horseman. Young Walter spent much of his time with this uncle, learning about the different kinds of horse training and the people associated with each.

Walter Farley began to write his first book, *The Black Stallion*, while he was a student at Brooklyn's Erasmus Hall High School and Mercersburg Academy in Pennsylvania. He finished it and had it published in 1941 while he was still an undergraduate at Columbia University.

The appearance of *The Black Stallion* brought such an enthusiastic response from young readers that Mr. Farley went on to create more stories about the Black, and about other horses as well. In his life he wrote a total of thirty-four books, including *Man O'War*, the story of America's greatest Thoroughbred, and two photographic storybooks based on the two Black Stallion movies. His books have been enormously popular in the United States and have been published in twenty-one foreign countries.

Mr. Farley and his wife, Rosemary, had four children, whom they raised on a farm in Pennsylvania and in a beach house in Florida. Horses, dogs, and cats were always a part of the household.

In 1989 Mr. Farley was honored by his hometown library in Venice, Florida, which established the Walter Farley Literary Landmark in its children's wing. Mr. Farley died in October 1989, shortly before the publication of *The Young Black Stallion*, the twenty-first book in the Black Stallion series.